I0719163

EARTH

THE ELEMENTALS BOOK 4

L.B. GILBERT

Earth © 2020 L.B. Gilbert

All rights reserved under the International and Pan-American Copyright Conventions. No part of this book may be reproduced or transmitted in any form or by any means, electronic or mechanical, including photocopying, recording, or by any information storage and retrieval system, without permission in writing from the publisher.

This is a work of fiction. Names, places, characters, and incidents are either the product of the author's imagination or are used fictitiously, and any resemblance to any actual persons, living or dead, organizations, events or locales is entirely coincidental.

Warning: the unauthorized reproduction or distribution of this copyrighted work is illegal. Criminal copyright infringement, including infringement without monetary gain, is investigated by the FBI and is punishable by up to 5 years in prison and a fine of $250,000.

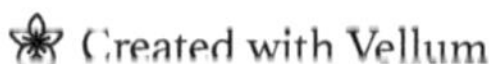

DEDICATION AND CREDITS

In loving memory of Francisco R. Gilbert

Cover Design: Siren Book Covers
https://www.facebook.com/groups/338807490129354/

Logo Design: Juan Fernando Garcia
http://www.elblackbat.com/

Editor: Cynthia Shepp
http://www.cynthiashepp.com/

TITLES BY L.B. GILBERT

Discordia, A Free Elementals Prequel Short,
Available Now
Fire: The Elementals Book One
Available Now
Air: The Elementals Book Two
Available Now
Water: The Elementals Book Three
Available Now
Earth: The Elementals Book Four
Coming April 20, 2020

Kin Selection, Shifter's Claim, Book One
Available now
Eat You Up*, A Shifter's Claim, Book Two
Available now
Tooth and Nail, A Shifter's Claim, Book Three
Coming Soon

Writing As Lucy Leroux

Making Her His, A Singular Obsession, Book One
Available Now
Confiscating Charlie, A Free Singular Obsession Novelette
Available Now
Calen's Captive, A Singular Obsession, Book Two
Available Now
Take Me, A Singular Obsession Prequel Novella
Available Now
Stolen Angel, A Singular Obsession, Book Three
Available Now
The Roman's Woman, A Singular Obsession, Book Four
Available Now
Save Me, A Singular Obsession Novella, Book 4.5
Available Now
Trick's Trap, A Singular Obsession, Book Five
Available Now
Peyton's Price, A Singular Obsession, Book Six
Available Now

The Hex, A Free Spellbound Regency Short
Available Now
Cursed, A Spellbound Regency Novel
Available Now
Black Widow, A Spellbound Regency Novel, Book Two
Available Now
Haunted, A Spellbound Regency Novel, Book Three
Coming Soon

Codename Romeo, Rogues and Rescuers, Book One
Available Now
The Mercenary Next Door, Rogues and Rescuers, Book Two
Coming Soon

*As Lucy Leroux

PROLOGUE
THE PAST

The music stoked his blood like a drug. Mammon sat in the VIP booth of the club like the king surveying his kingdom. The packed dance floor seethed and swelled with human bodies—so much young ripe flesh.

Mammon leaned back in his private VIP booth, savoring the burn of the fine whiskey as it went down. He had to hand it to the humans. This was better than anything they had in Sheol, the hell dimension he called home. And the humans themselves. They were spectacular. In just a few hundred years—a blink of an eye for him—they'd gone from sackcloth and preaching Puritans to *this*. Debauchery and vice as a culture. There were entire cities devoted to it.

Las Vegas was his favorite. The young people congregated in the clubs, their only purpose to drink, dance, and fornicate. People gambled away their entire fortunes in the casinos or dropped a wad of sweaty cash for the privilege of seeing naked females or even nude muscular males.

Speaking of which...what was he in the mood for tonight? That tasty buck over in the corner had been eyeing him for several minutes. So many bulging muscles. It would be criminal to let that one go. However, the cluster of girls wearing matching outfits near the stage had multiple choice specimens as well... The one wearing the flimsy veil was the most attractive, but the entire group was downright delectable. So juicy.

Many leaned back and watched as the bride-to-be was helped to the stage by her friends. The beauty put her arms up, swaying to the beat. Her curvaceous body was a temptation, but the buck was so bronzed and toned. A prize that fit had been difficult to find the last time Mammon visited. Now all he had to do to find one was to walk into any gymnasium.

How could he decide? This place was a veritable smorgasbord, and he'd been hungry for so long...

Mammon had been patting himself on the back all week. He'd been on this plane of existence for a few weeks now, and he had only killed and consumed two—no, *three*—people. Normally, a demon came out of his hell dimension and wreaked bloody havoc. Inevitably, the carnage attracted the attention of some do-gooding witch. Nine times out of ten, the demon's ass would get booted back to the pit.

Of course, those had mostly been minor demons. Mammon was royalty, one of the seven princes of hell. His strength of will rivaled Lucifer himself, but that remarkable restraint was paying dividends now. Mammon had made it all the way to Sin City, then had set himself up in a very sweet situation at one of the strip's monstrous hotels—the one with the fountains. The servants there had treated him very well, particularly after he'd hinted he was a very successful Hollywood producer. Mammon didn't know precisely what a producer did, but he knew humans bent over backward trying to impress them.

He even had staff. Jessica, his lovely birdlike assistant, made calls, scheduling endless 'interviews' for him. Gina, the female guard the agency had sent over, stood behind his left shoulder, her presence signaling his stature.

Oh, that's right—his body count was technically four, but he didn't think Sam, his first bodyguard, should count toward his tally. That one had been killed for his insolence. True, Mammon had eaten his heart afterward, but, in his mind, a successful producer was like a king. A ruler needed to put down dissent in the ranks as soon as it appeared. Anything else was irresponsible.

Mammon's remarkable restraint and foresight was going to pay dividends now. He was in a huge metropolis with a transient population that shifted and turned over nightly. If a person went missing here or there, no one would blink an eye. A group of a half-a-dozen women? Sure, the human authorities would take note, but as long as he didn't indulge like this too often...

He straightened the jacket of his bespoke suit before signaling Gina.

"Invite the ladies to my suite at the Bellagio. Make sure they know I'm interested in casting a couple for a movie." He handed over his card for her to present. For some reason, humans loved those little squares of cardboard. They accepted anything they read on them as gospel.

With flawless obedience, Gina nodded, sliding through the crowd to approach the group. A minute later, the giggling gaggle hurried toward him.

Excellent. They had taken the bait. Satisfied, he waved over a waiter and ordered a few bottles of champagne for the table.

It wouldn't do to show his eagerness. He'd have them all to himself soon enough. And, tonight, he would feast.

MAMMON AIMED CAREFULLY. He popped the cork on the champagne, making it hit the roof of his limousine at such an angle that it rebounded, landing in the cleavage of the bustiest bridesmaid.

"I get a hundred points," he yelled. Cheers and hoots of laughter followed.

Anastasia, the bride to be, grabbed the bottle of champagne—their sixth—out of his hand, then began to chug it.

The situation couldn't have gone better if he'd planned it. The ladies had responded to his overtures predictably. A few bottles of the best bubbly later, they'd been piling into his limousine with Gina behind the wheel.

Mammon was so taken with his delicious dinner he didn't look out the window until they were well away from the gridlock of the Strip. By the time he noticed they weren't near the hotel, the lights of the city were a distant memory.

"Where the hell is that woman taking us?" he muttered.

There was a beat of silence before one of the girls tittered a bit nervously. "We told Gina to take us to the desert. There's a big bonfire later—some girls we know are organizing it."

Mammon frowned. "Are they there now?"

He didn't like to eat in public. And depending on the size, a crowd would hamper his plans for the evening.

"No," Anastasia said, clutching the bottle's neck. "But we have enough booze to last us until they arrive. Hope that's all right…"

Mammon sniffed. He didn't like to eat and run, but if he got to work quickly, then he didn't have to alter his dinner plans. The girls resumed chattering, playing a pop tune from one of their little portable telephones. They handed the bottle back and forth, taking sips with lush pink lips. The two across from him began to kiss each other.

Mollified, Mammon took the bottle, relaxing in his seat. "I suppose it's fine," he murmured, his eyes fixed on the show. *You used to have to force humans to get them to do this.* Damn, he loved this century.

In fact, he didn't mind the bonfire excursion. It was a fortuitous turn of events. By doing his business in the desert, he wouldn't have to expend any energy on soundproofing or illusion spells for the suite. They were simple rituals, but he didn't like wasting time. And then he wouldn't have to barter with that annoying group of gremlins to come in and clean up the mess.

As a prince of hell, Mammon would eventually have staff on hand for that sort of thing. But for the moment, he was still keeping a low profile. The gremlins still thought he was a regular demon. For now, he was willing to let them think that. He didn't want to expose his new identity in the city just yet. Otherwise, he would have just left the mess in his room and moved on to another set somewhere else. They just kept building new luxury hotels out here anyway. The humans were practically asking for it.

Yes, a trip to the desert was a much better idea. After he killed and ate these sweet young things all up, he could just throw them in the limo and drive them deeper into the desert where they would be harder to find. He might not even have to bury them. Mammon could leave their bones to bleach in the sun, a little decorative touch to remind him of home. No muss, no fuss.

Reaching for one of the champagne bottles, he let one of the glittering beauties rub up against him. Hmm...Well, there was no rule saying he couldn't have a little bit of fun before his meal. He didn't normally play with his food. Mammon wasn't a carnal being. He normally got his thrills the old-fashioned way—through decapitation and dismemberment. But he was going to have to make an exception for these girls. They were all so succulent and sparkly.

He pressed his lips to the woman's neck, only to have her slide to the floor of the limousine in a sinuous movement. A flare of annoyance had him reaching down to strangle her, but then she reached for his zipper.

Her timing was abysmal. Just then, the vehicle stopped, and his driver came around to open the door. Like a gentleman, Mammon waited until every lady had stepped, or, in some cases, stumbled out of the vehicle before following.

Once outside, the girls ran from the limousine to where Gina stood waiting.

"Where's the fire, ladies?" he asked, reaching inside for a bottle.

Anastasia shivered, wrapping her bare arms around her middle. "A demon, Gia, really? He's so—ugh. I'm going to stink of brimstone for a week."

Confused, he dropped a touch of his glamour. He still looked human, but far less harmless than before.

"What the fuck is this?" he asked. How did they know what he was? This pack of airheads couldn't find their way out of a paper bag.

Mammon froze in his tracks as his driver and bodyguard removed her glasses. A wave of power rolled over him. It was compelling enough to make him stagger back in surprise. A witch—stronger than any he'd ever encountered before. Fuck, how had he missed it? He should have been able to detect that kind of talent, regardless of whatever spell she'd used to mask it.

"Sorry, Tasha, but it had to be done," the woman masquerading as his bodyguard said.

Like nervous chicks, the gaggle of women huddled behind her. She flicked her fingers, sending a ripple along the ground.

Roaring with rage, Mammon dropped the bottle, hurling toward the group.

GIA HAD SHIFTED the desert floor, drawing the circular demon-trap runes with her talent before she even stopped the car. When Mammon flew across the ground toward the group of nymphs, she tightened the circumference to leave the limo outside of the circle.

The demon hit an unseen barrier, rebounding violently. He landed on his ass, hitting the back of his head against the ground with a loud thunk. She knew he didn't feel pain, but it was still a satisfying sound.

"Do you want to take the car back to town?" she asked the nymphs, keeping a watchful eye on the demon.

"Ugh, no thanks," Tasha said, shuddering as the other girls huddled around her. "His scent is all over that thing. It's probably soaked into the upholstery."

Another girl—Gia thought her name was Saffron—peeked around the others. "Can't you just do your mojo thingy to send us back?" she asked, wiggling her fingers.

"Back to the strip, or somewhere else?" Gia asked. She could send them anywhere on the continent. The only question was timing. She didn't want too many eyes on the spot where they rose from. Luckily, in the desert, she could send a little borrowed wind to go with them, just enough to kick up the sand. It would ensure no one was looking right at the spot they emerged.

"Let's go to Malibu," Saffron enthused.

"I want to go back to the strip," another chimed in.

The demon roared, getting their attention.

"Um, I think I'm going to vote for the strip, too," Tasha said, clutching the sleeve of Gia's bodyguard disguise. "That would be the fastest, right?"

"Yes," she confirmed, patting Tasha's hand. "Thanks for helping tonight."

There wasn't a male alive who could resist a group of nymphs in all their glory. Sure, there had been a lot of ways to trap this particular demon, but Gia was on something of a time constraint.

"Happy to help," Tasha lied, her head pulling back as the demon continued to roar, banging on the invisible barrier of the circle. "We owed you," she added, a bit more honestly.

Gia waved her hands, adding more symbols to her pentagram. The howls of the demon died abruptly.

Tasha cleared her throat. "By the way, are we square now?"

She and the other nymphs were paying off a longstanding family debt. Humans were mowing down forests at unprecedented rates. Gia and the other Elementals did their best to stop the incursions, but it had grown damn near impossible in recent years.

But Gia wasn't the Earth Elemental for nothing. She'd found a solution...of sorts. When she'd been unable to find a way to stop a particularly aggressive group of deforesters, Gia found a more expedient solution—calling on the Mother for a reward. When the gold and gemstones had materialized from the ground, she'd taken them and bought the land, signing it over to Tasha's grandparents so it would be protected for future generations.

It wasn't a perfect solution, but until humans relearned to respect nature and the benefits of clean air and water, it would have to do.

"Of course," she said, touching Tasha's back lightly and gesturing for the girls to gather in a tighter circle. "I'll send you back now."

She was about to call on her magic when Tasha grabbed her hand.

"I shouldn't have asked that—I know the debt we owe is much greater than this. Whenever you need help again, please let us know. Just...you know...if it's maybe not a demon next time, that would be great."

"We love helping! And if it's at a club again, count us in," another girl said, shimmying to music Gia couldn't hear. "But yeah, those demons reek—I thought I was going to hurl in the car."

A third nymph nodded sagely. "It's as if a thousand yak butts were collected, doused with gasoline, and thrown into a barrel... and we found the barrel a hundred years later."

The others agreed. "I can't understand why the humans don't run screaming. The stench alone is reason enough."

"Nymph noses are much more sensitive than humans. I apologize and understand—no more demons, I promise," Gia said. Although, truthfully, there was little reason to worry. Most of the time, she didn't need beautiful bait. The events that had led to Mammon's release from hell weren't likely to be repeated again anytime soon.

The demon continued to inaudibly wail and punch the barrier, but when Gia opened the earth and the girls disappeared, he quieted down, prowling inside the tight circle like a lion trapped in a cage.

Once they were alone, Gia removed the silencing spell.

"You know, I've seen the man you're wearing in real life before," she informed him, crossing her arms. The glamour was a good one, but not perfect. "I don't think you got the hair right, but then your true form doesn't have hair...more like feathers? Or is the word I'm looking for spikes?"

Technically, they were something in between.

Mammon had taken the form of a young and wealthy man, a hotel owner who lived in Boston, one of the three or four people inadvertently responsible for the demon's release from hell.

"You have no idea who you're dealing with, you stupid witch," the demon spat.

"Mammon, High Prince of Greed and Avarice, purveyor of false dreams and breaker of oaths and promises." Gia shrugged. "And I'm not a witch."

The demon sneered, but Gia could see the uncertainty in his borrowed eyes. "Oh, I keep my promises, *witch*, so believe me when I say I'm going to enjoy ripping your throat out. Then I'm going to pull that pretty head right off and fuck your dead mouth."

"As appealing as that sounds, we're going to have to table that because you have to go back to hell now."

The demon smirked. "You think *you* can do that, little witch?"

Refusing to let him goad her, Gia kept working. "The spell *is* rather involved... I won't lie—there are many other things I'd rather be doing on a Saturday night."

True, she didn't love clubs like her younger sister Logan, or diving for lost undersea treasures like her sister, Serin, but Gia still knew how to find plenty of amusements. Chasing down trespassing demons wasn't one, but, hey, who loved their job a hundred percent of the time?

Technically, Gia had never rid the world of a demon prince, but she'd seen it done. Her mentor—Tarni—had done it twice in her career. The second time, Gia had been there as backup in case things went wrong.

Most lower demons were easy enough to banish. Their bodies didn't have the strength to leave their plane, so they left them behind, becoming shades. To get around on Earth, they possessed human bodies—or sometimes even animals.

Dealing with lesser demons was straightforward. They had to be bound—both silver and gold restraints worked well. Then one threw a little holy water on them, chanted, and *bam*—the demon was getting a one-way trip back to their nether region of origin.

A prince of hell, however, was going to take a bit more effort. Unlike lesser demons, they were strong enough to drag their bodies across the barrier between dimensions. A physical door was necessary to get that body back because they were damn hard to kill on this plane.

Calling for her supplies, Gia stood back as a table appeared, one fully laid out with the items she needed. Planning was the key to efficiency. She got to work, mixing ingredients and crushing them in the mortars with her marble pestle. All the while, the demon alternated between hissing and screaming obscenities.

After one particularly colorful epithet, she laughed aloud.

"What is so funny, you fucking witch? The way I'm going to suck the marrow from your bones, or how I'll use your skull as a toilet?"

"It was the toilet actually," she said. "Although I can't say I haven't heard that one before."

The demon appeared confused. "*What*?"

Gia looked up from her nearly finished mixture. "You'd be surprised at how often someone threatens to rip my head off and defecate in it."

"So, you make this sort of thing a habit?" The demon was still confused.

Gia added the last drop of mercury to her mix. "Clearly, princes of hell need to get out more. Otherwise, you would have heard of my sisters and me. There isn't a Supernatural on Earth who doesn't know what I am, but then you're a tourist...and it's about time for you to go home."

She tossed her spell mix onto the ground, then murmured the words to open a portal to hell.

"It won't work," Mammon yelled. "You can't just open a doorway to my world. No one in their right mind would."

He had a point. Not only was opening a portal to any dimension incredibly difficult, but doing so to one of the hell dimensions also had an added risk. She had to craft a complicated multilevel spell capable of punching a hole in the universe *and* close it, making sure there wasn't a chink or a crack left when she was done. Even a scar would be a disaster. The barrier had to be seamless, as if it had never been opened in the first place, else it was a weak spot, one that could be exploited by others of Mammon's kind.

And then there's the time when it's open. It was like throwing the barn door open to find a pack of starving wolves on the other side, and, for some reason, she was wearing a suit made of dinner bells.

But this wasn't Gia's first time at the demonic rodeo. There was one way to make a door damn difficult to enter from the other side.

Raising her hands, she pulled the soil around the opening into a funnel with a ring of dirt that revolved from top to bottom, a fast-moving current that would be impossible to scale without wings.

Well, some of the denizens of hell do, so you better get your butt in gear.

"What the—" the demon sputtered as Gia held up one hand, then pulled the earth out from under his feet. With the other, she reached around the door. Taking care to maintain the perfect circularity of the door, she slowly pushed them together.

"*Stop,*" the demon screamed. "I can give you anything you want! Wealth beyond your wildest dreams. Or *power*. With my help, you can rule this country."

This time, she let a smirk escape. "Only the completely selfless or the very corrupt want that job. I am neither."

He was almost there. The circles had overlapped. Half the diameter of the pentagram had disintegrated, falling through the pit to hell.

"Wait! I can do get you anything you want. You don't know what it's like in Sheol."

Gia edged closer to the pit. She stopped short at the edge, safely on the other side of the barrier. Nevertheless, she felt it, a wave of despair and bitter hatred—the collective turmoil of hundreds of thousands of beings, perhaps millions.

Blinking, she swayed and stepped back. She hadn't felt that the first time. But then, she hadn't been the one to banish the last demon prince. Her mentor had closed the circle. It hadn't been necessary to get this close to the door.

Catching herself, she stepped away just as Mammon fell through the pit, cursing her at the top of his lungs as he went.

Hands up, she focused on closing the circle, taking every precaution to reknit the fabric of reality back together. When she was done, the barrier was flawless, as if nothing had happened. And she was exhausted.

Despite her weariness, she knelt on the ground. She began to pray to the Mother, thanking Her for the abilities She'd given her and for safeguarding their world.

Gia didn't have to imagine a world without Her. She'd just witnessed one firsthand.

1

Salvador Delavordo knelt in front of the dirt altar that had magically appeared in the antechamber of his clinic.

The woman lying on top hadn't moved during his startled cursory inspection. Edging closer, he searched for signs she was breathing, but he couldn't see if her chest moved under the brown leather jacket she wore.

Salvador went to pull it off her, but he thought better of it. He couldn't risk damaging his patient. Every inch of the woman's exposed skin was covered in thick black strands, signs of some terrible contaminant in her system. He'd already foolishly touched one without gloves, but his magically honed diagnostic senses hadn't picked up any signs of illness. It was probably a toxin and not a contagion, but he needed to confirm that.

Salvador dug through his supplies, fishing out a hand mirror. He held it to the woman's lips, relaxing when he saw the surface fog up.

He heaved a sigh of relief. At least she wasn't dead. And whatever had happened to her didn't appear to be progressing further, at least to the naked eye.

I need samples. Hurrying to his exam room, he gathered supplies in a woven basket. The petri dishes, vials, scalpel, and syringes rattled as he knelt to grab his largest pair of scissors.

Setting the basket next to the woman's hip, he lifted the scissors, preparing to cut away the leather jacket.

A hand shot out, grabbing his wrist with an unyielding grip. Rearing back, he yelped, dropping the scissors when the hand suddenly heated, burning him.

"What the—" He gasped, turning wide frightened eyes on the woman who held him. She had red hair, her eyes filled with flame.

Another much-colder hand pried the first from his wrist. "Diana, calm down."

"I'll calm down when this *brujo* tells me what the hell he's planning to do with those scissors."

Witch? Guess they knew who he was.

"I, uh..." Salvador's mind blanked as he glanced around. The room was full now. In the space between blinks, six other people had appeared.

The two men opposite him were tall and built, their muscles straining their shirts. Both were menacing, but one more so than the other. He was a *Were* with a scowl dark enough to make Salvador want to back away—and he was used to defending himself. The other read as human. For some reason, it didn't make the man seem any less dangerous.

As intimidating as the men were, it was nothing compared to the women at their sides.

Salvador flinched as his senses were overwhelmed. The sheer power radiating from the females was awesome—in the most terrifying sense of the word. Twisting, he studied the woman holding him again. Her touch had cooled, but she hadn't let go. Those flames in her eyes hadn't been his imagination.

Aw, shit. He was surrounded by Elementals.

"Salvador, we need your help."

It took him a moment before he could manage to tear his gaze away from the woman to focus on the man who spoke. When he did, Salvador recognized the man instantly.

"Alec," he unsteadily said. Alec Broussard was one of the few vampires Salvador did business with. A wealthy scholar, Alec was a useful friend to have. However, Salvador used that term loosely...

The vampire nodded reassuringly. After prying the woman's hand off Salvador, Alec urged her back a step.

"As I said, we need some help. I'd like you to meet Diana, my mate. The ones over there are Serin and Logan. Daniel and Connell are their partners," Alec said, pointing at each woman in turn.

So, the rumors were true. Alec had landed an Elemental as a mate. Salvador was going to have to ask him how the hell that had happened—but some night far in the future, once Salvador had recovered from the shock.

Good manners eventually overrode his fear. Nodding with a small bow, he tried to mask his feelings, but his upper lip had broken out with telltale beads of sweat.

He cleared his throat, turning to the one called Diana. "I was going to cut her jacket off to examine the black veining more closely."

Diana's head pulled back. She looked him up and down, her scrutiny more unnerving than the nuns at his childhood parochial school. She—the Fire Elemental presumably—took a slow and audible breath. "Our sister has been poisoned. Can you help her?"

"I...do you know who I am?" There was no way an Elemental would ask him for help. Not if they knew who he was, who his *parents* were.

"Alec told us that he worked with you before. You're a Delavordo. He also said you've been disowned."

That came from another Elementals, the dark-skinned one with the afro. Her voice was lyrical, almost Caribbean in its cadence. It was nearly as beautiful as she was, but all these women possessed more than their fair share of attractiveness.

The better to capture their prey with...

He had to remind himself that they could crush him with one hand tied behind their back. "And you're willing to let me touch her despite my family history?"

That part was still difficult to believe.

"If you don't help, we'll kill you," the *Were* spat.

Crossing his arms, Salvador glared at the shifter. He'd listen to threats from an Elemental, but he wasn't about to take any lip from a werewolf.

The small Asian girl put her hand on the *Were's* arm. "Don't, babe. He's our best shot."

"Logan, you can't trust him," the *Were* began, but the Caribbean Elemental forestalled him.

"Connell and Daniel, can you wait outside?" she interrupted.

"But—"

"She's *our* sister. Wait outside."

Salvador suppressed a shiver. The steel in that voice was ice cold.

The *Were* and the human man shuffled outside without another word, but not before the former gave Salvador a killing glance. Alec stayed, but Salvador knew better than to expect much help from that quarter. Not against three Elementals.

He put his arms at his sides, determined to appear as nonthreatening as possible. "I can't help you."

"Can't or won't?" Diana asked.

"*Can't*. I don't know what's going on here." He waved his hands over the woman on the altar. "I've never seen whatever that is."

"Neither have we, which is why we need you. Alec says you study black magic and curses. You're also reputed to be well versed in poisons."

He inhaled. "They are something of a family hobby," he said, then wondered why he'd bothered. These women knew all about that.

The Delavordos were a powerful witch clan. But with all that power came temptation. And, at least for his family, abuse of their abilities. Salvador had seen his relatives do terrible things. He had been taught to believe if they had the ability, then they had the right.

It was difficult to pinpoint exactly when he had realized most everything he had been taught was wrong. All he knew was he'd never felt *right*. Not until he'd broken ties with his family once and for all.

He stared down at the Earth Elemental. "Is she the one who killed my uncle Thiago?" he asked.

"No, that was me," Serin said. Her stunning face was unreadable. "Is that going to be a problem?"

Nightmare images rose in his mind. He pushed away the memories, but it took some effort. Blinking, he met her fathomless blue eyes. "No...and thank you," he whispered before turning away.

Salvador wanted to rub his face, but he was wearing gloves. Choked up, he reached behind himself, taking the basket so he could at least pretend to sort his supplies.

This is more emotion than I wanted to feel today. In fact, it was more than he'd wanted to feel ever again.

He cleared his throat. When he spoke, though, it still sounded as if he'd swallowed gravel. "I don't know if I can help her. What happens if I fail?"

Diana moved until she stood in front of him with her hands behind her back. "Don't fail."

It sounded like a threat, but the words were weighted with so much emotion it didn't feel like one. No, it was a plea.

She's scared, too. It was there in her eyes, which were red and shining with unshed tears. A quick glance confirmed all the women wore similar expressions. But they were too disciplined to cry.

"I will do my best. But this malady is completely unfamiliar. Nor have I come across a similar reaction in my studies. Do you know what happened?"

Logan, the smaller Asian woman, approached the altar, taking the unconscious woman's hand. "We found her like this."

Nodding, he picked the scissors back up, cutting what had been a spectacular leather jacket. "Was there food or drink nearby? Did she ingest the poison?"

"No, she was covered in the stuff," Logan said.

Salvador's eyes flared, locking onto their joined hands. "Let her go," he urged.

"It's okay. Serin washed it away."

"All of it?" He glanced up, brow creased. "Because a sample would be extremely helpful."

The girls glanced at each other, dismay clear on their faces.

"The sea took it. It's too diluted for me to get it back," Serin said, her tone betraying her regret.

Salvador winced, then returned to his task, using a scalpel to gently scrape the surface of a black thread. His first impression stood. This vein thing was hard as a rock.

"Did the threading stop growing or thickening when you washed it away?" he asked, continuing to probe the different strands. Even the smaller ones had that same rigid quality, but they were slightly more pliable.

Serin shook her head. "I believe they stopped thickening, but it's difficult to say. I was...upset, and I didn't pay attention."

"That... and the goo made them hard to see until you washed it off," Logan added.

Interesting. So, did the threading stop because the poison was washed off or because the patient's blood had already hit the saturation point?

"Should we dig up the basement where she was attacked?" Logan asked.

Diana frowned. "Is that even possible without Gia?"

"If it's not, maybe I can slip in through a crack or something," Logan said. "I could try to blow some of the poison to the surface."

"I guess it's worth a shot," Serin began when one of the men poked his head through the window next to the front door.

"What about the gloves?" he asked.

Salvador blinked at the strange sight of the large head sticking through the small window. Daniel, the human, had been eavesdropping.

"What?" Serin asked.

"My rubber gloves," he continued, disappearing only to walk through the door a second later. Like Salvador, Daniel had to duck to avoid hitting the frame, but the *Were* following him was in too much of a hurry. Connell's head smacked the frame with a satisfying thump.

Serves him right. Salvador knew a lot of shifters. They shared similar aggressive attitudes, but they usually knew better than to act that way with him. He may have made his name as a healer, but that didn't mean he was a pacifist.

"I touched the toxin with rubber gloves," the human continued.

"But the earth reclaimed those," Logan said. "The Mother was probably trying to protect us from the poison."

Serin nodded sadly. "I think they're gone, Daniel."

The human shrugged. "Can't you ask for them back?"

"I don't understand," Diana said.

Neither did Salvador.

"The ground did that melting thing, and it did it without Gia's intervention. It reacted to all of you." He paused, letting that sink in. "If it did it then, it's possible it will do it again now. Why don't you try asking for the gloves back?"

Serin frowned. Seeming a bit exasperated, Daniel shrugged and knelt on the ground himself. He banged on the ground as if he were knocking on a door. "Hey there, dirt. Can you give me those gloves back?" he called.

The *Were* snickered aloud. Salvador bit his lip to keep from joining him.

"Um, Daniel dear, I think..." Serin trailed off as the ground rippled. A blink later, a mound formed. On top was a pair of purple latex gloves, the tips stained with a greenish-yellow tint.

"Huh," Serin murmured. "That's...new."

Salvador raised his brows, but then shrugged. That was hardly the weirdest thing to happen today. No, that he was standing in his clinic with Elementals and he was still breathing definitely took top prize on weirdest.

"These should do," he said, reaching for the gloves.

He would have to cut them up, soak the pieces in different solvents, and run some tests. "I should be able to identify the major components from the residue. If we can identify what was in the poison, I'll have a much better chance of crafting an antidote."

That last was a stretch, but Salvador had been in the healing business for a long time. He knew what his patient's families needed to hear.

"Connell, our friend here, has identified some of the components. He can write them down for you," Alec said with a nod to the *Were*.

Paper materialized in the *Were's* hand, and he grudgingly began to write.

"Your setup here is a little rudimentary," Alec said. He was intimately familiar with the clinic from his previous visits. "Is there anything I can get you that might help? Maybe an HPLC machine or a mass spec?"

Salvador glanced up, noting confusion on more than one face. "Those are machines humans use to identify chemical compounds," he explained to the assemblage of superwomen. To Alec, he said, "And no thanks. I can do something similar with a few spells."

It was a technique he was still perfecting, but a lot of his work was reversing hexes and spells. The majority of the time, they were delivered via potion, usually slipped into the victim's food or drink. Breaking down the components was difficult, but not impossible. It would be faster than the human way.

"Are you sure there's nothing I can get you?" Alec asked, examining the woman on the earthen bed with genuine concern. The Fire Elemental may have been his mate, but the vampire was clearly fond of them all.

An added layer of responsibility came to rest on Salvador's shoulders. "I'm waiting on some local herbs, but until I identify the components of this mix, I won't have an accurate idea of what I'll need. If I hit a wall, I'll let you know."

"All right." Alec shifted toward Diana, rubbing her lower back comfortingly. She rested her head against his broad shoulder.

The intimacy of the gesture was startling under the circumstances. How in the world had a vampire ended up with a Fire Elemental?

"Are you all going to stay?" Salvador asked, holding his breath.

Please say no.

"I'm staying," Alec said. "But the ladies have some hunting to do. I assume they'll be taking the other two along with them."

"Logan's not going anywhere without me," Connell stated.

Logan nudged Serin. "He won't slow me down. But what about..."

The petite woman nodded in the direction of the human man.

"Daniel will be fine as long as he's with me," Serin said.

At the same time, the man interjected, muttering he could take care of himself.

"Well, if John could take out the strongest of us, does it matter if he's human?" Diana asked.

"Who knows? It might even be an advantage," Daniel pointed out. "That poison is made for Supernaturals, but we don't know what effect it has on humans—maybe none. If I were this John character, I'd try to make something that didn't kill humans in case of accidental exposure."

"Do you think that's even possible? To target Supes but not humans?" Logan asked.

Daniel shrugged. "It doesn't matter one way or another. That asshole is not getting anywhere close enough to Serin to douse her with his poison."

To illustrate his meaning, he patted a sidearm on his side Salvador hadn't even noticed.

Logan appeared skeptical, but Serin nodded. "At this point, we should be ready and willing to try everything to stop him."

Coming from anyone else, those words might sound desperate, but Salvador almost shivered. Whoever this John was, the fucker was in for a world of hurt.

2

John spread the map in front of him, tracking the line of his proposed route. It would take some time to drive to Yellowstone. Flying would have been more expedient, but there was no way he could have transported his lab in a few suitcases, which was why he had gone mobile.

His luxurious RV had been earmarked for a rock star, but he'd manipulated the salesman into handing over the keys to him instead. All it had taken was some sleight of hand and a touch of mesmerism.

Technically, he could have paid for it. John had more than enough funds to cover the expense. A being didn't get to be as old as he was without having an excellent financial portfolio. But what fun was there in paying for things like a good citizen?

John had spent the better part of a century acting the part of the benevolent and wise uncle. It had been the longest undercover con in history. Although there had been some days when he'd genuinely enjoyed himself learning all he could in T'Kaieri, the cradle of magic, he was grateful his time there was at an end. Now he could shed that cloak of benign goodness and please himself in ways he'd been unable to indulge in for far too long.

Stealing the RV was just the start. It had been completely

outfitted to suit his needs. The vehicle was spacious enough for most of his gear. True, he'd had to forsake his bulkier pieces of laboratory equipment, but that was fine. He no longer needed them. The RV even had a mobile garage with an expedient getaway car underneath the main cabin.

Ah, technology... It had grown so wondrously decadent in the last few decades. As far as he was concerned, the little doohickeys and giant monster trucks were proof of human superiority. He was going to make sure every creature on Earth knew it, too.

It had taken decades, but John had finally perfected his formula. He'd crafted a poison that could kill any Supernatural being on Earth. It would work on shifters, vampires—even those damn tricky Fae. He'd been testing his formula long enough to prove that. The evidence of his successes floated in dissection jars in the cabinet over his head.

The most staggering part was how common the ingredients were. True, a few had been hard to get, but that was to be expected. Certain botanicals were thin on the ground these days, but John wasn't a self-described genius for nothing.

It hadn't been an easy road. Time and time again, John had met with failure. He'd almost given up his venture when he'd discovered a couple of the plants he needed were extinct, or rare enough to seem so. But then, he'd had an epiphany. As long as he knew the chemical structure of the compound he needed, he could have the ingredients synthesized.

John had managed to find a gifted and severely underpaid chemist to do the synthesis. It had taken the man some time, but he'd come through. Now John could simply add what he needed with a dropper.

The advancements in the field of chemistry and physics in the last century were staggering. He could only imagine what the next hundred years would bring.

What did this world need with Supernatural creatures in the face of human innovation? Witches and their ilk were evolutionary throwbacks, beings who belonged to the primitive ages of the past.

John was going to show the world it didn't need magic—at least not the kind one had to be born with. He'd come into the world without it, but he had learned to work around that small liability. Other humans would learn as well. Once the Supernaturals were gone, he planned to teach his secrets to a select few students. Only those worthy. He already had candidates in mind. A few good men and a couple of likeminded females.

He sniffed at a sudden memory. Gia had been dead wrong. He didn't dislike women or resent they had been given so much power. Yes, he believed the Mother creature had been misguided to entrust her greatest gifts solely to females, but that was plain common sense. Putting all of Her eggs in one basket was foolish.

Soon, it wouldn't matter. His last test had proved it. There was no witch on Earth who could stand against his poison. Not even the most powerful subspecies—the Elementals. The trial run on the Earth Elemental had gone better than his most optimistic projections.

The mightiest had fallen. Well, *almost* the mightiest. But so, too, would She succumb. All he had to do was physically get to Her, but he wasn't worried. His agile mind had just figured out how...

3

Salvador twisted the stopper on the distiller, letting a few drops fall into the collection vial.

The liquid was clear with a purple tint. He frowned, making a note in his experimental log. Salvador couldn't say for certain, but his instinct told him it needed to be colorless—clearer than spring water. His previous two attempts had failed, getting no reaction, but three times was supposed to be the charm, right?

"I think adding a few more evaporation cycles will achieve the effect you're searching for."

Blinking, he glanced up, startled to see someone else in the room. Alec Broussard stood a few feet away, leaning against the wall. A corner of his mouth tilted up. "You forgot I was here, didn't you?"

"I did. Sorry." Salvador rose, stretching his stiff limbs. His neck ached from staying in one position for so long.

"Don't apologize," Alec replied. "I'm exactly the same way. The last time I was so engrossed in a Sumerian text, I nearly got fried."

Salvador raised a brow, and Alec shrugged. "When Diana put her hand on my shoulder, I leapt on her, fangs out, ready to defend myself..."

Salvador didn't bother to ask if the Fire Elemental had been hurt. "Did she set you on fire?"

Alec laughed. "No. Fortunately for me, Diana has excellent reflexes and good impulse control. She just brushed me off, kind of like you would a gnat. Of course, if she *had* lit me up, I wouldn't have burned."

Salvador waved his arm in a silent "go on" gesture.

The vampire's expression was simultaneously smug and abashed. "Mating has its privileges."

Salvador snorted. "I guess so. How the hell did you two happen to be anyway?"

Alec glanced behind him at the complicated distillation apparatus. "I'll tell you the story after I get you some food. You're going to need fuel to keep going."

Salvador put down his logbook, then went to wash his hands. "Is this why they left you behind? To crack the whip?" he asked.

"And to make sure you don't intentionally kill Gia."

Salvador frowned at the vampire. Alec shrugged. "I know you're not going to do that, but the ladies aren't prepared to risk leaving their sister without some form of protection. They know your family too well."

Salvador didn't need to be told that. He'd been hearing about Elementals from the cradle—mostly warnings not to attract their attention.

Of course, if his father or mother ever learned he'd had one under his care, completely at his mercy, and he *hadn't* tried to kill her...he'd probably be disowned all over again.

He glanced at the door leading to the antechamber. "What do you know about my patient?"

Alec cocked his head. "She's Earth. Gia is the oldest of Diana's sisters. Which means—out of all—she's probably tangled up with the Delavordos the most. And from what I heard, she's not a big fan."

"She's hardly alone in that." In fact, Salvador strongly shared her opinion. Not that it would matter to this Gia woman—provided she recovered enough to learn his identity. He stared at the wall, lost in thought.

"Have you heard from them lately?" Alec asked softly.

"Just my mother, but you know about her hit and runs," he said, bending over his logbook.

Alec knew he wasn't referring to Lucia Delavordo's skill behind the wheel of a car. Salvador doubted his mother had ever been in a vehicle without a chauffeur in her life. No, his mother specialized in another type of collision—her out-of-the-blue messages—vitriolic blasts about duty and family loyalty.

It didn't matter how many times he changed his number or how many filters he added to his email—his mother's magic always managed to find a way through. One time while hiking in the Andes, he'd even received a missive via giant raven.

It was his mother's considered opinion that Salvador needed to get over his foolish desire to help others. Selflessness was for the weak. Only the strong survived. His crusade to atone for the past sins of his family was stupid and self-serving.

"You owe it to your family to let go of this foolish charade," she had said on more than one occasion. "You are a Delavordo. *Act* like one."

Sometimes, he thought his mother was right. Not about being more like his family, but about his calling. Salvador had taken on an impossible task. He had foolishly thought to atone for the evil his family had done. But the Delavordos were the wickedest witching family in all of history. It was like trying to empty the water from Lake Michigan with a child's sand bucket.

"Fulgencio hasn't contacted you?"

Salvador almost laughed. "My father hasn't spoken to me since he threw me out of the house for healing that *Were* cub."

"That's right. One of your cousins was responsible..."

He nodded. "Analia. She got away with it, too. She claimed she had no idea her little hex on the mother would concentrate in her fetus. Once I reversed the damage, the wolves dropped the matter."

"But you *did* undo the curse—it was a remarkable feat. One that put you on the map as a healer."

And it got Salvador kicked out of his family, despite the fact the hexing had been against the treaties his family had signed with the shifter pack. His father had claimed he hadn't sanctioned the act, but Salvador had known Fulgencio been impressed by his cousin's accomplishment—targeting the unborn, but leaving the mother untouched... It was a hellish innovation in the world of magic, and yet another weapon in his family's arsenal—if they ever used it again.

A knock sounded at the door.

"That'll be the food."

Salvador blinked. Alec hadn't left the room. "Does mating with an Elemental give you access to their way of communicating?" he asked, slightly awed.

Some witches could transmit messages along the aether, but it was a rare talent. All the Elementals could do it, of course. They were even able to move along it, accessing it with their dominant power, the element they controlled.

"Not exactly," Alec hedged. "I mean, Diana would know if I were in trouble, so I have some tie to it, but I can't use it the way she does."

Alec held up a sleek cell phone. "I ordered the food with an app. Do you still like *posole*?"

"How in the world did you convince a delivery person to come all the way out here?"

Alec rocked on his heels. "I tip *very* well."

Snorting, Salvador nodded. Alec went outside to get the food, closing the door behind himself, presumably so the delivery person didn't get a look at Salvador's patient. Meanwhile, he set up the first steps of the new distillation again, the ones that took the longest and didn't need to be monitored first-hand, before following Alec outside.

They sat at the rough picnic table he'd been given as payment by a wood nymph he'd helped once. The light evening breeze did much to refresh Salvador's senses. Some of the chemicals he used in the distillation process were disproportionally pungent. He'd set up a decent-enough ventilation system and boosted it with air-clearing spells, but certain odors still managed to seep into his clothing.

Alec told him about meeting Diana over the meal. Halfway through, Salvador paused, the spoon he held next to his mouth forgotten—the story was that compelling.

"*Damn*. So that's where the whole thing started? With an illegitimate Burgess witch?"

Alec passed him a beer. "Your family hasn't cornered the market on black witches. Not completely."

"And the villain the ladies are chasing down helped this woman?"

"Yes, along with a few others. John must have been tinkering with dark magic for a long time—and right under their noses. He excelled at setting others up to do his dirty work."

"But he must have continued doing his own, right? Otherwise, he'd never have succeeded in creating that poison."

Contemplatively, the vampire narrowed his eyes. "Personally, I don't believe that's as much an achievement as we're making it out to be. Destruction is always easier than creation, than healing. You, of all people, should know that."

"Very true," Salvador conceded. "Still, it's hard to believe we're dealing with an old-school alchemist in this day and age."

Self-styled alchemists—humans who dabbled in magical experimentation and the occult—used to be common, at least until the last century. But they had died out with the Industrial Revolution, or so he thought.

No wonder the Elementals were pissed. According to Alec, the alchemist had infiltrated the cloistered T'Kaierian community years ago. The Water Elemental had considered him a part of her family. They'd all trusted him. Salvador knew something about betrayal...

Alec sniffed one of the containers, taking a cautious bite. He didn't eat a lot, but Salvador knew Alec still enjoyed the mechanics. "I sent word to the Elemental archives, asking for whatever texts they have on poisons capable of affecting Supernaturals. The archivist told me that they would arrive later today."

Salvador stilled. "They're sending that stuff *here*?"

"Yes. Noomi, the head archivists, said she's pulling anything and everything she thinks might help. Although, it's probably pointless now you've identified the components of the poison."

"Don't discount your precious books yet. We don't know if my antidote will work. It may take several attempts. Or they may not work at all..."

Alec nodded. "I know. Nevertheless, a little optimism never hurt anyone."

Salvador grabbed a tortilla from one of the heat-conserving foam containers. "I can't believe they gave you access to their archives."

The T'Kaierian community hoarded knowledge the way dragons did gold. The fact they would let an outsider have access was unbelievable, even if he was mated to an Elemental.

"Grudgingly, but yes...eventually." Alec hesitated as if he wanted to say something else, but he stopped, simply adding, "Sometimes, I have a hard time believing it myself."

"What's it like?"

The Elemental archives were the stuff of legend, but no one Salvador knew had ever been inside.

Alec's eyes went glassy and distant, but his expression was one of pure bliss.

"If I believed that my kind had a heaven, I believe it would look like the Elemental archives." He laughed. "Well, scratch that. It's probably only heaven to me."

Salvador had known Alec long enough to assume that meant a ton of books and crumbling scrolls, but it was the *Elemental* archive, so there were probably all sorts of weapons and magical artifacts, too. Salvador's grandfather had often groused about the various antiques the Elementals had confiscated from his great-grandmother. The fact they were cursed objects responsible for hundreds, possibly thousands, of deaths was never really acknowledged.

Wrapping up dinner, Salvador got back to work. Alec had been right. Extra distillation rounds did the trick. When the resulting potion was crystal clear, he took it into the antechamber and set it next to the altar.

Normally, Salvador would be concerned with dosing, but since the poison had been introduced topically, he was going to apply the antidote the same way. He would have to trust the Elemental's body would only take up as much as it needed.

"Do you need either of these?" Alec held a syringe in one hand and a dropper in the other.

Salvador shook his head, then unstopped the vial. Tipping his hand, he dropped it all onto the Elemental's chest.

Nothing happened. He waited, but didn't see a reaction.

"How long do you think it will take?"

"I don't kn—"

Without warning, the liquid disappeared. The woman's body had absorbed it all.

Salvador held up a ruler to one of the thick black veins on her chest. It was difficult to see, but he eventually confirmed a change. A small retraction in the length of one of the strands.

"It shrank, right?" Alec asked. "That wasn't just a trick of the light."

Exhaling in relief, Salvador nodded. "We're going to have to make more. A lot more. Judging from these results, I don't have anything close to enough raw ingredients."

Alec was already on his phone. "Don't worry. I'll get you whatever you need."

4

Salvador lifted the bucket, pouring their antidote into the tub.

"Are we sure we need to immerse her?" Alec asked, handing Salvador another full bucket of the liquid.

"It can't hurt," he muttered. "We need to purge the toxin as quickly as possible."

Thanks to Alec's resources, Salvador had been able to synthesize enough of the antidote to fill a kiddie pool. However, that wouldn't have covered her completely, so Salvador had asked for a cast-iron tub, the kind with clawed feet.

At least I can keep the tub afterward. A bath would be a novelty. He hadn't had one in years. His bathroom only had a shower—an inadequate one at that. It was too short for his six-foot-two frame.

Salvador poured in the last bucket, then grabbed the snorkel he used when diving from the beach down the road. He handed it to Alec, watching as he fit it over the patient's head and mouth. "Diana said Gia could borrow her other sisters' abilities to some extent," Alec pointed out as he nudged the mouthpiece between the woman's lips. "I'm almost certain she can breathe underwater."

Salvador paused to meet the vampire's eyes. "I'm not sure she can with all this crap in her system. Do you want to risk it?"

Alec conceded with a shake of his head. "Let me lift her. All the Elementals are warriors, and Gia has been serving the longest. If she suddenly wakes up, she might come out of it swinging. It will hurt, but I can take it. And at least she knows my face."

There was also the fact Sal's friend was a vampire. Alec was stronger and faster, despite the physical similarity of their builds. If the Earth Elemental decked Alec without thinking, he would recover more quickly than Sal would.

Alec picked up the woman with surprising gentleness. Taking care to keep the open end of the snorkel above the surface, he set her in the tub.

Enough liquid was displaced to spill over onto the earthen floor, but the muddy mess would have to wait.

Salvador hovered at the woman's feet with his magnifying glass. Eventually, the black threads began to shrink, but the process was excruciatingly slow.

"I wish there were a more efficient way to deliver the liquid," he muttered.

"We can take out the snorkel," Alec suggested before he zipped in front of Sal.

Salvador blinked as the vampire appeared, his enthusiastic grin just inches away.

"Never mind, I have a better idea," Alec said.

"What is it?" Salvador asked, drawing back slightly. They had known each other for years, but seeing a vampire excited was always a touch unnerving.

Alec didn't answer. Instead, he knelt, grabbing a fistful of wet dirt. Lifting the women's hand, he smeared it with mud.

Salvador glanced down. There was now a big gouge in his dirt floor. "I hope you don't need much more of that." He didn't want to spend all night packing the floor back down.

"Actually, we will," Alec said triumphantly. "Look!"

Salvador leaned closer. The skin under the wet dirt appeared smooth. He rubbed the mud off, exposing the now-pristine skin.

"They're *gone*. How did you..." He trailed off, scratching his head. "How the hell did that work?"

Alec waved the woman's hand around. "Well, she's Earth, isn't she? Stands to reason that actual soil would help conduct the healing properties."

"It does?" Introducing dirt into the equation went against everything Sal had ever learned about hygiene in healing and spellcraft, but he supposed he should have known. Why would normal rules apply in this case?

He put his hands on the edge of the tub, staring at the woman. The tendrils around her face weren't disappearing any faster than the rest, but the fraction revealed was enough for him to get a good look at her for the first time. The lines of her face were so pure...almost ascetic. Their combination of strength and delicacy was arresting.

She's really quite beautiful. But even in sleep, Gia was intimidating.

"Well, I guess we have to turn this into a mud bath."

"I'm on it."

Salvador reached out to stay his hand. "Do you think we could use the soil from outside?"

The altar had disappeared the moment they brought the tub inside, so there was no longer an extra pile of dirt in the waiting room. And the last thing he needed was a giant hole in his floor.

Alec's lip quirked up. "*Oh.* Of course."

In a flash, he headed outside, taking the empty buckets with him.

Salvador looked back down at the woman. "If this works, try not to wake up swinging," he whispered.

A few hours later, the tendrils were nearly gone. Everywhere he and Alec scraped the dirt off, her skin was clear. But the woman still hadn't woken.

Elementals were renowned for their ability to withstand almost any trauma, so her body recovered faster than Salvador would have guessed. Gia breathed on her own, and her heartbeat was strong. Physically, she was fine. He and Alec were at a loss for her continued coma.

It took Salvador a long time to figure out the cause—several days, in fact. Then, one morning at sunrise, it hit him.

Gia's problem wasn't physical. It was spiritual. Her body had healed, but her soul wasn't there.

It was gone.

5

———————

Salvador prepped yet another healing ritual. It was probably pointless—the last two hadn't done any good. But he had to keep trying. According to Alec and the remaining Elementals, the fate of the world might depend on it.

"What do you do when the soul is gone?" Alec asked, gazing at Gia. She was lying on Salvador's bed now, dressed in a simple pair of shorts and a tank top. "Where does the soul go?"

"You know I don't have those answers," his mate answered, pacing in front of the bed.

Diana had returned from her hunt a few hours ago. Alec had sent for her the moment Salvador had diagnosed the reason for Gia's continued coma. The others were still out scouring the globe for their perpetrator, but from the Fire Elemental's sour expression, he gathered it wasn't going well.

This John character must have serious mojo, he thought as he ground the herbs he needed. If the man could successfully hide from these women, then he had to have uncharted magical ability. Sure, Salvador had heard of the odd witch who'd successfully evaded one or more Elemental before, but never for this long.

Salvador supposed it was only a matter of time before the culprit was run to ground. Until then, though, he wanted to keep his head down around Diana, who was angry enough to heat the room around them without the benefit of the fireplace against the far wall.

Alec made that difficult with his frequent comments and questions. "I thought you said her soul would come back on its own?"

Salvador froze as Diana cocked her head in his direction. "I said it *should*—at least, I think so. Normally, when the soul is forced from a body, it's because of a shock or sudden trauma. From what I've been able to piece together, it hovers near the body. When that trauma passes, it takes up residence again, almost automatically."

Unless the body died. Then the soul moved on—permanently. But he knew better than to say so aloud.

"And what if the soul doesn't come back on its own?" Diana asked.

"Then it means it wasn't nearby...perhaps it wandered away."

"Can you call it back?"

Salvador winced. "If there's a way, I don't know how. Calling a *living* soul isn't like communicating with ghosts. I have no idea how to go about it."

"Then what are you doing?" she asked, gesturing to the candles and assorted accoutrements.

"I'm just trying to make her body as appealing as possible."

Diana raised a brow. He flushed. "I meant *healthy*. I'm trying to make sure her body as healthy as possible to make it a more tempting receptacle."

"A receptacle?" That one raised brow was insanely intimidating.

He fidgeted, but managed to nod. "For lack of a better word..."

"Where would her soul have gone?" Alec had whipped out a notebook and was jotting something down, presumably a list. "Wouldn't Gia stay close by? She had too much experience of the supernatural to just wander away like a confused human soul might. I have to believe she would have a touch more self-awareness than the average person."

Salvador set down the bowl he held. "Most people who get displaced don't remember their out-of-body experiences once they're back in their body—not beyond the standard *I-was-hovering-over-my-body* scenario. Perhaps the trauma was so massive it blasted Gia far away, and she's working her way back? That's just a guess, of course. We're in uncharted territory here."

Diana pressed her legs against the bed. "I don't feel her in the aether at all. I can't say for certain if I should or anything, but this feels wrong."

"Can't you go search for her?" Alec asked.

Diana frowned.

"I mean spiritually," he clarified. "Don't you have an astral-projection spell?"

She shook her head. "It's not really our thing. We can go formless when we travel in our medium, but we don't go running around bumping into displaced souls while we're there. It's a separate space."

"Do you think you can try?" Salvador asked. "I mean, I can keep doing my healing rituals over and over, but it won't do any good until her soul returns."

The Fire Elemental seemed uncomfortable, but she nodded. "I'll try."

And she did. But she failed...repeatedly. When she came back, so did Logan and Serin. No Elemental was capable of astral projection. They were too tied to their medium. Whenever they attempted to dissociate from their bodies, they automatically changed into their element—air, water, or fire.

That last had been enough of a hazard Sal had asked them to conduct their trials outside the clinic, but it didn't seem to matter where they did it. The Elementals appeared to be hard-wired to stay out of the astral plane.

After her last failed attempt, the Water Elemental kicked a boulder in his garden. Instead of breaking her toes—as one would normally expect—the stone shattered, blasted into smithereens.

The display of strength was startling. Ducking his head, Salvador contemplated making himself scarce, but his pride wouldn't let him retreat.

Serin wrapped her arms around her midsection. She was quiet

for what felt like forever. Logan and Diana didn't say a word when she eventually whirled around and pointed at him.

"What is it?" Salvador asked.

"You," Serin said. "You're a witch. That means you have the ability to astral project."

She hurried over, clapping a hand on his shoulder. "Consider yourself drafted. We're going to send you to find Gia."

6

———

Gia knelt in the rubble, cleaning the blood off the sword she'd just captured. The demon it had belonged to was a few feet away. Well, his *legs* were. The rest of Mammon's body was in a ditch.

Taking a deep breath, she pushed the demon's severed legs over the edge, watched as they slid down the dirt incline. Killing the demon who had pulled her into this pit should have been satisfying, but the small bit of revenge wasn't going to get her out of here.

Her memories of John's assault were vague. She knew he had rigged the sprinkler system of his lab to douse her with poison, but everything was blank after that. *You're not supposed to remember*, she reminded herself.

She was dead.

Grief welled in her chest. Gia had failed to stop John. The bastard had outwitted her. Now, she had passed into the other plane, leaving her sisters to deal with the mess John had made.

Unfortunately, Gia's numerous years of service hadn't guaranteed her a rosy afterlife. At the moment of her death, she had seen her body collapse in the basement, then there had been a swirling storm of color that had given way to darkness. When she opened her eyes, she had been here, surrounded by demons.

It had taken her a split second to get her bearings. The demons were only a few steps away, their weapons out and ready. Seven had set upon her—one whom she'd recognized. Not Mammon himself, but one of his lieutenants. That was when she knew exactly where she was.

Somehow, Gia had been pulled to hell.

Technically, there were a few places that could lay claim to that name. Currently, she was in the one she considered the worst—*Sheol*. The inhabitants had no love for their land either. That was why they were constantly trying to escape. Their hatred for those who sent them back here was beyond calculation.

And they waited for her now.

But Gia had served the Mother for centuries. It wasn't Gia's first time on the wrong side of an ambush. Many had tried to cut her down—many had failed.

Soon, Gia learned one benefit of being in hell. In Sheol, there was no distinction between body and spirit. Her Earth talent didn't work here, but she was still strong, still fast. And she had trained for this...

That first battle had been short, bloody, and hard. They tried to overwhelm her with strength in numbers, but, in Sheol, the rules were different. In their natural forms, demons were bigger than the lighter, faster humans they possessed on Earth. Thankfully, they were also slower. Plus, it helped Mammon's acolytes weren't too bright. Inevitably, each charged her like enraged bulls, their fighting techniques rudimentary. Even the better trained didn't know not to telegraph their next move as they fought.

Once it was over, Gia had won a slew of weapons. She stashed the majority before tracking the lone survivor to Mammon's castle. Gia knew too much about strategy to lay siege to it alone, but she didn't need to. Instead, she followed the example of her distant cousins, the Indian tribes of the Great Plains.

Her Counting Coup campaign was designed to infuriate the demon prince.

Gia started small, with the guards who patrolled Mammon's fortress, working up the chain of command to the prince's top lieutenants. She didn't kill anyone, but she sowed discontent until the order in the citadel was in shambles. Soon, the prince was enraged enough to leave his castle to deal with her himself. Once that happened, she did what she did best...and then had to repeat the act as the handful of remaining warriors came out of the woodwork to avenge their master.

Now what? Gia lifted the sword the prince had used, examining it closely. "Hmm..." She sniffed. Elven made, it was impervious to curses and spells. How had the demon prince come across such a treasure here?

The story was probably long and depressing. In her opinion, anyway, and Gia didn't need to dwell on the negative right now. But she was definitely hanging onto the sword.

At least I'll have a weapon that won't fall apart around here. Demon blood was corrosive to normal metal. She'd had to toss most of the arms she'd confiscated in her first round of skirmishes. Besides, the grip on this sword was almost comfortable, like it had been made for her.

She held the blade up, admiring the preternatural gleam. "You like me better than your former owner, don't you?"

The sword caught the dim light of the sky, as if it were winking at her. "Yeah, I know you do."

A throat cleared, sounding scratchy. The tiny demon who had been steadily inching toward her had finally decided to announce himself. "Excuse me, Your Highness?"

Her sword at the ready, she stayed her hand, waiting for the trick. Would he sprout horns and double in size? Maybe unhinge his jaw like a giant python in a misguided attempt to eat her?

"Err, excuse me, Most Exalted One," the wiry demon continued, panting. "Please don't remove my head from my shoulders. I am no threat to you. I am only here to serve."

Gia cocked her head when his bow deepened. He certainly didn't *look* dangerous, but she had learned the hard way the greatest dangers sometimes came in the most benign packages.

"Serve me how?" she suspiciously asked.

Bowing and scraping, he stuttered, "H-however you wish. Would you like to start with a tour of your castle?"

Gia blinked. "My what?"

The little demon waved at the distant stronghold. "According to the law of the land, that is yours now. It became so when you slew the old master."

"Is that so?" Gia murmured, sheathing the sword in the scabbard on her back.

She raised a brow, studying the skyline. The castle was the only structure in sight. "Well, I guess you better show it to me."

The demon broke into a grin that made Gia want to cringe in sympathy. With another genuflection, he turned, indicating she should follow.

It wasn't as if she had a better option, so she did.

7

When the vampire sliced into Salvador's palm with a silver blade, he tried not to wince.

"Should you even be able to hold that?" Salvador asked. Vampires were supposed to be allergic to silver. "Or is it yet another benefit to being mated to an Elemental?"

Alec leaned in, putting his hand over a collection bowl. "No, the resistance comes from being a Daywalker."

Unlike others of his kind, Alec had the ability to walk in full daylight, something even the elders of the Vampire Council were unable to do. Salvador wasn't clear on how Alec had managed the feat, but knew it had involved an elaborate ritual.

The bottom of the bowl was now covered in blood. "I hope this isn't making you hungry," Salvador muttered.

The vampire smirked. "I've fed, thanks."

Salvador peered behind him. The three Elementals were having a conference at the edge of the jungle. "And how does your mate react to your diet? The Fire Elemental doesn't strike me as the understanding type."

Vampire feeding was a notoriously sensual event.

"It doesn't bother her anymore."

"Seriously?"

"She's learned to enjoy it."

Salvador's eyes widened. "*Oh*. You feed from *her*?" he whispered, gesturing in shock at his own neck.

He couldn't speak from experience, but it was common knowledge that a vampire feeding was euphoric for the vamp *and* donor.

"I do if I can't hit a blood bank, but I don't need one very often. Her blood isn't like anyone else's. Even a minute amount can sustain me—even *energize* me—for days. Now that I've stopped combusting every time she shares with me, it's great," Alec said, wrapping Salvador's palm with one of the poultices he kept on hand for minor wounds.

"You *combusted*?" How was Alec even alive? Vampires were extremely flammable. For most, all it took was one spark before *boom* —that was all She wrote.

Alec reached for the bottle of quicksilver, adding a few drops to Salvador's blood. "Just my hands, actually. It stopped after a while. Being mates affords some protection. I travel in Diana's medium now."

"So, in addition to being able to walk in daylight, you can't be burned by fire and you're impervious to silver. If the Seven families were to find out about you, they would freak the fuck out," Salvador hissed.

Normally, Salvador didn't swear. In this case, though, he felt it was appropriate. The Seven families were the oldest and most powerful witch clans. His family—the Delavordos—were the most notorious. However, that didn't mean the others were any less dangerous. Salvador couldn't imagine the news that a Daywalker roamed the Earth would go over well with them. Not if they learned he was also impervious to fire *and* silver.

Alec smiled. "You don't have to be concerned about me. I can take care of myself. And as emasculating as it sounds—if anyone came after me, my girlfriend would kick their ass."

Salvador laughed, but the mirth quickly subsided. A pang of

sharp emotion passed through him, but it was only his old companion—envy.

When he was younger, Salvador used to wish for a different family, one that allowed him to have friends who weren't blood relatives. Now what he longed for was companionship. Something like what Alec had, although perhaps with someone less terrifying.

However, it wasn't in the cards. His family might have disowned him, but they still tried to exert their influence in his life. Any partner he took would be subject to their scrutiny. If his parents found out he had taken a wife without their consent, it would be bad enough. A partner they disapproved of would be even worse.

And Mother forbid I ever have children. His family would never let him live in peace if he fathered a child. That was why he'd decided never to marry. Salvador even avoided relationships where there might be the risk of accidental procreation. He had been celibate most of his adult life—he was *that* determined his tiny branch of the family tree would die out with him.

He had no illusions his little rebellion would make a difference. Not in the grand scheme of things. Salvador was an only child—the firstborn son of the sitting family patriarch—but the Delavordo family was extensive. He had relatives on every continent, enough to ensure their way of life would continue regardless of what he did. But it didn't matter. At least he'd spare his potential progeny the childhood he'd had learning to dance at the edge of the black.

"Have you ever astral projected?" Alec asked, breaking Salvador's reverie.

"Um... I'm not sure."

His friend raised his head, looking at him strangely. Salvador shrugged. "I tried it in my early twenties. It certainly felt as if it worked. I flew above my body—but I was pretty high at the time. I never tried it again."

"Well, I can get some weed if you think it will help... Maybe some LSD if you need it."

Salvador grimaced. "I think not. This is either going to work sober or not at all."

Alec hummed noncommittally, but his eyes appeared skeptical. "I think we're ready," he announced.

Salvador blinked, then jumped. In the space between seconds, he'd been surrounded by Elementals.

I didn't even hear them move. He cleared his throat, straightening his shoulders. A lesser man would have peed his pants, but his jockeys were dry as a bone. It was a small comfort, but a comfort, nonetheless.

Alec stood behind and a bit to the right of Diana, holding the bowl of *animae anchorum*, the spell mix needed to paint the sacred symbols over Salvador's head and heart, marking him on both the physical and astral plane. According to his research, this step was normally not necessary since most disembodied souls stayed close to their bodies. But after Gia's soul had gone missing, he wasn't taking any chances. If he got lost, the runes would act as a beacon, allowing him to find his way back home.

"Strip," Serin ordered, taking the bowl from Alec.

A flush crept up Salvador's neck, although he couldn't say why. Salvador swam and hiked on a regular basis—sometimes to gather ingredients, but mostly for recreation. There wasn't much else to do for entertainment in these parts.

He also chopped his own firewood. His lean body was nothing to be ashamed of, but the women surrounding him were some of the most gorgeous creatures he'd ever seen. The fact they were also the most dangerous only seemed to enhance that.

When someone pointedly cleared their throat, he coughed, unbuttoning his shirt. He tossed it aside, then stood with arms akimbo so Serin could start.

Grinning, the Air Elemental whistled. His blush deepened, and Logan smirked.

"Hey," Connell growled, poking her in the back.

"What?" She laughed. "He's pretty... *and* cut. His six-pack is almost as fine as yours."

That only made her werewolf mate growl louder. "I don't have a six-pack. Mine's a ten."

Serin ignored the interplay, dipping her brush into the *animae anchorum*. Lifting the paintbrush, she put the first whorl on his forehead, finishing quickly before lowering it into the bowl again so she could complete the more elaborate rune on his chest.

"Are we clear on the plan, *Sal*?" Diana asked.

"Yes," Salvador murmured, cringing at the shortened use of his name. Although his closest friends used the nickname, he hated how it sounded out loud.

When Diana noticed, she smirked, and he knew asking her not to call him that was a lost cause. "Provided you have something to serve as a talisman for Gia," he finished, trying not to sound sullen.

Getting to the astral plane was step one. Finding Gia was a whole other story.

"I sent Logan to Gia's ancestral home. I think we found something that will work."

The Air Elemental fished around in her pocket, then withdrew a necklace. Made of leather, it was woven with a brass-colored metal that might have been a dull gold.

When he took it in his hands, he immediately felt the history and a sense of quiet power. "This is extremely old, far more so than the condition of the leather would suggest."

Serin inclined her head. "Gia's father made this for her mother as a betrothal gift. And it *is* old. He was one of Cortés' men."

Salvador drew his head back, startled. "Cortés as in Hernán Cortés?"

"Yup," Logan said, leaning in to secure it around his neck. On him, the piece was tight, more like a choker, but he didn't find it constrictive. The pressure was oddly comforting, although he was having a difficult time processing what the women had said.

"The same Hernán Cortés who conquered the Aztecs?" he asked in disbelief.

"One and the same," Serin murmured, moving the brush over his heart. Diana observed them, her arms crossed. "His name was Leocadio, and he's been written out of history because he abandoned the cause when the plan to overthrow Montezuma was first suggested. He was an explorer, not a murderer, and wanted nothing to do with the conquest of an entire civilization. Leocadio wandered the countryside for over a year until he heard rumors of a healer of such renown that her abilities were considered magical. That was Gia's mother. We only know her by the name he gave her—Macaria."

Damn. Salvador took a deep breath, fingering the woven neckpiece. He'd known Elementals could live for a long time, but the scale was staggering. Gia was literal living history. And he was wearing a piece of it.

"There's a companion ring, too, crafted from the same metal," Serin said, adding a flourish to the design on his chest.

"Is it the one she's wearing?"

He'd noticed a small band of beaten metal on Gia's hand. At first, he'd thought it was a wedding ring, but it was on the wrong hand.

"Yes. Given the link between the pieces, we thought it would be a good way to connect the two."

"You are aware she 'left' the ring here when her soul went walkabout, correct?" he said.

"Gia has worn that ring since her parents died, more than three hundred years ago. Her connection to it goes beyond the physical."

That didn't seem long enough. Salvador frowned, doing the math in his head. "But didn't her parents live in the fifteen hundreds? Just how old were they when they passed?"

Witches lived a long time, but two hundred years was pushing it.

Serin's eye flickered. "Don't worry about it. Focus on your task. Hold on to the image of the necklace. Use it to find the echo of the companion ring in the other plane—wherever it is."

Salvador murmured his agreement. That would be easier said than done, but there was no point in saying so aloud. These Elementals weren't going to change their minds and let him off the hook.

Not long after, Serin finished. Salvador peered down, trying to see the details of the intricate design, but he would need a mirror to take it all in. He didn't ask for one. It would be insulting to suggest the Elemental didn't know what she was doing.

He tilted his head from side to side, stretching it. His body would be immobile for who knew how long. He may as well prepare it as best he could.

The Earth Elemental had been moved inside his antechamber, returned to almost exactly where she had first appeared. He'd asked for two cots, but Serin had nixed the idea of putting Gia on one. The ground would be her cradle.

"She's quite comfortable there," Serin assured him, then ordered a single cot be placed next to Gia.

Salvador circled the cot and Gia's body, making sure the spell runes they'd drawn on the floor would encompass them both. When he was satisfied, he stepped between the lines of the circle, careful to avoid mussing the lines.

He landed on the cot a little heavily. It made the metal frame squeak loudly in the otherwise-quiet room. The Elementals and their mates surrounded him. He supposed it should have been comforting, knowing they weren't there to kill him. Regardless, he couldn't help tensing. As long as he was unconscious, he would be vulnerable.

You're pretty damn defenseless now, his brain reminded him. but it didn't help him relax.

"How will we know he has actually left his body and isn't just asleep?" Logan asked, staring at him as if he were a colorful insect of some kind.

"I added a rune for that," Serin answered.

"You did?" Salvador couldn't hide his surprise. He hadn't known such a rune existed.

"It's on your forehead," the Water Elemental said. "It'll change shape, contracting in on itself when you leave your body. As long as nobody's home, it'll stay that way. Once you're back, it will unfurl again, but I'm hoping we'll know when you return because you two will wake up."

That last should have been obvious, but there had been cases where an astral projection went wrong. It had happened in the Delavordo clan actually—probably more than once. He'd heard the cautionary tale as a child. Before he was born, a distant cousin had become trapped in his own body for weeks after he failed to wake up on his own. If Salvador's mother hadn't brought the boy to Fulgencio, Salvador's father, he might never have been roused.

"Some people just don't have the talent," Fulgencio had warned, his lip curled. The fact the boy had been a blood relation only increased his father's disdain. A Delavordo should have known his limits, then broken past them. Failure was not an option.

Well, there's a first time for everything. He closed his eyes as Diana lit the candles wicks with a wave of her hand. In a low voice, he began to recite the spell. The words washed over him, vibrating in his ears until they became a hum, then a drone. The noise sharpened—a whine that climbed higher until it popped. And then, there was silence.

The next thing Salvador knew, he was gazing at his body, which was below him.

I'm floating. He had done it. Salvador had successfully crossed to the astral place—sober this time.

He tried to touch his neck to see if the necklace was still there, but he couldn't move his arm. In fact, he couldn't move anything. Salvador still had a vague sense of his body, but he wasn't able to control it.

Okay, this might be a problem.

He tried to control his limbs, flailing as if he were swimming. It took all of his focus to shift a few inches. Then he pictured the string of beads and brass around his neck, touching it with his mind.

All right now. Try to reach out to the ring.

That was all he needed. The anteroom of his clinic disappeared in a swirl of color. He hurtled through space, the ground rushing past him at supersonic speed.

Oh shit...

8

Gia ignored the weight in her stomach as she forced herself to pick up the dismembered head. Holding it with her fingertips, she set it on the spike, one of several conveniently embedded in the top of Mammon's fortress. Of course, she didn't refer to it as Mammon's place aloud, not since she'd beheaded the prince and taken over.

Aware of the many eyes on her, she pushed the head down on the spike more securely. It was smaller than the others, but she wasn't going for quality here. Quantity was what mattered.

Surreptitiously wiping her hands on her shirt, she stepped back as if to admire her handiwork. But her mind was a million miles away.

How long has it been since I died? According to lore, time ran on the same track in Sheol as it did on Earth, but it certainly *felt* different. A day lasted an eternity.

No matter, she thought, adjusting the last head. She had made the time count.

Gia had fought off wave after wave of demon attacks during those first few days after killing Mammon. News of the demon prince's overthrow had spread quickly. The neighboring powers wasted no time trying to take advantage, their goal being to claim his territory and the wealth stored in the treasury. But they hadn't known anything about *her*.

She had tried keep the body count to a minimum, dispatching only the demons who raised arms against her. But lower demons weren't too bright, so there had been a fair number. The ones who ran away lived.

Rather than allowing the inhabitants of Sheol to lay siege to the castle, she had opted to surprise them. Gia left the relative safety of the citadel, sneaking out to make a mobile camp. She'd taken the best weapons from armory with her. Some, she'd hid in the wastelands at landmarks she would be able to find again, keeping Mammon's sword as her primary weapon. Then, she'd circled back and took the fight to the bastards who had come to pick at Mammon's carcass…and she'd won. But there had been a cost.

A memory, distant and pale, rose to her mind. It was of her parent's village, when she'd found their bodies lying together in bed. They had passed at the same time…peacefully. Why their deaths were on her mind now was a mystery.

Perhaps because you won't go quietly yourself? How did this even work? If she died here—*again*—would she end up someplace else? Another hell dimension? Had Dante been right in some form? Was she trapped in the first circle of hell?

If I am, I really don't want to see what the others look like.

She wiped her hands on her pants, mentally disassociating from the gruesome tableau she'd just created. *You don't have to concern yourself with your humanity anymore. You're dead, remember?*

"Excuse me, Exalted One," Snagat interrupted. The little demon who insisted she was his queen skulked up behind her, forcing her mind to the present.

"Forgive me, Your Highness," he wheezed, his head low. "I just wanted to know if you would like me to put the other heads up here as well?"

"Please, would you stop calling me that?" Gia sighed. She may have been the de facto ruler of this principality, but she refused to wear the crown. She didn't care how many jewels it had.

Snagat had been an acolyte of Mammon, the factotum in charge of the fortress. Ever since she'd killed the prince, Snagat had been following her around, insisting on referring to her as his liege. Unlike Mammon and his warriors, Snagat was basically harmless, although his constant bowing and scraping was grating, to say the least.

You won't have to put up with it much longer. Gia had a plan. She had no intention of taking up residence as hell's newest queen.

Snagat cleared his throat—an awful nails-on-chalkboard scraping sound. "The heads, Your Grace?"

Gia glanced down at the trench below the battlements. It surrounded the castle like a moat, except it was empty. Well, it didn't have any *water*. Despite taking care of the large bands of demons, more kept coming, trickling in like rancid sewage. Consequently, the trench had been filling with bodies at a steady rate.

"Yes, go ahead and finish it yourself." She waved Snagat on.

Mounting the heads was a distasteful necessity. She needed to send a clear message to the neighboring princes whose lands resided farther from Mammon's territory. The new mistress of Sheol was not to be trifled with.

Of course, the heads on stakes wouldn't be much of a deterrent if two or more of the princes banded together against her. The demon princes of Sheol were notorious for their infighting, so she had a little time. Eventually, though, they would see her for the threat she was, then send their armies to deal with her.

Snagat bowed and bobbed in acknowledgment of her order.

"I'll be in the library," she continued. "Don't disturb me unless there's another incursion."

"Will you be wanting your evening meal served there?"

Gia wrinkled her nose. She didn't want to think about what people in Sheol ate or drank. But that was apparently one of the advantages to being dead. She hadn't been hungry or thirsty since her arrival. The demons born in this dimension required sustenance, but, so far, she was doing just fine without it.

"No thank you," she said, eagerly dismissing him. The demon smelled particularly pungent today. "Deal with the bodies, but make sure they're visible from a distance."

After he bowed again, she hurried inside to the library.

The minute she closed the door, her shoulders dropped. She took a breath, rolling her neck to loosen the tight muscles.

The library was the only place in the castle she could breathe. It helped the air was cleaner, free from the smoke and ash that filled the skies outside. Also, the presence of so many books was comforting, as long as she ignored their content. And what they were made of...

Sheol was a blasted wasteland. Few trees grew here. The only ones she'd seen around the castle were sad, stunted little things. There wasn't enough pulp in them for a pamphlet, let alone a book.

Gia gave herself a shake. It wouldn't do to examine things too closely while she was here. That way lay madness.

The library itself was an opulent space. It had vaulted ceilings at least twenty-feet high with elaborately carved molding that still showed traces of genuine gold leaf—a metal apparently valued everywhere. Strange-smelling candles filled an iron chandelier high above and the few wall sconces.

I wonder what Sheol was like before the demons?

From the ruins dotting the landscape, it appeared as if a more advanced civilization preexisted this feudal wasteland. Her cursory reads on the different hell dimensions let her put a moniker to it—Kasheoli, the name from which Sheol had been derived. But none of the sources mentioned whether Kasheoli had been ruled by other beings or by the demons who currently made this their home. Civil war could explain the status quo, but it could also have been an invasion from another dimension.

Gia pulled a book from the nearest shelf. *That's not my mystery to solve.* Her only objective was to find a way out of here.

Determination fueled her as she hunted through Mammon's texts. The demon had devoted most of his time and resources to getting the hell out of hell. In the end, he'd succeeded in the traditional manner—cultivating acolytes on the other side by letting them curry favor with him. He'd granted favors in exchange for flattery until they screwed up, accidentally releasing him.

Not being a demon, that path was closed to her. No matter what mediums told people, there was no way to summon a ghost from the underworld.

However, that wasn't the only way demons crossed over. Soft spots between the two dimensions were another option—if she only knew where any were. But Mammon would have known, or at least that was what she kept telling herself. He'd been too thirsty to get out of here not to explore every option.

She hit pay dirt a few hours later. Secreted between the pages of an obscure demonology text, she found a map. It showed the topography of the entire continent, with little X's marked on it. As maps went, it was an unprepossessing document were it not for one thing. One of the X's had been annotated recently with the words 'unknown witch' and a date—one she was familiar with. Mammon had marked the spot where he'd landed after she'd banished him back to Sheol.

X marks the spot... She'd sealed that opening well enough to know it wasn't the way back home, but what about the others? They couldn't all be the work of Elementals. Some had been done by witches, which meant there was hope for her. Not much—but a glimmer.

While there were some very skilled practitioners in her world, few could do spell work on par with an Elemental. *All I need is one scar.* If Gia found a weak point, she might be able to do what Mammon had failed to—open a door to her dimension *from* Sheol.

Rolling up the map, Gia tucked it into her pocket. She wasn't going to tell Snagat she was leaving. There was no need to advertise the fact the castle would be unprotected in case she failed. And if she got lucky right away, it wouldn't matter.

Briefly, guilt flared as she considered the fate of the servants once she left for good. *They'll be all right.* Once it was known the castle was without a ruler, it would be taken by another strongman in short order. Judging from Snagat's example, the servants wouldn't put up a fight. Their lives wouldn't change that much...she hoped.

You can't save everyone. Gia was good, but she wasn't *that* good.

She grabbed her new favorite sword and opened a window, dropping to the ground without a sound. Then she struck out for the high ridge in the east, the location of the nearest X on the map.

GIA HEARD the someone long before she spotted him. The demon had been trailing her for a few minutes now, ducking behind piles of garbage or fallen stone—as if he had a prayer of going unnoticed. He was making enough noise to wake the dead.

Crouching at the top of a shadowed boulder, she studied her pursuer. Trim and built, he had taken the form of a handsome human man in his late twenties.

Gia narrowed her eyes. She had to hand it to him...it. The glamour was nearly flawless. But the fiend had made a telling mistake. He was too attractive.

Most demons, the smarter ones, fashioned glamours that resembled regular people. It helped them blend in and stay off the radar. But someone this beautiful couldn't keep a low profile. His sheer prettiness forced eyes to him.

The man was shirtless, displaying a well-defined musculature across a tanned and toned chest. His stomach was even more flamboyantly rendered—his abdominal ridges were defined enough to scrub her laundry on.

Amateur. A glamour this elaborate was a waste of energy. Unless... He must be an incubus, the subclass of demons who specialized in seducing human females. It was the only possible justification for such an effort.

Gia sniffed, confident the blundering creature couldn't hear her. Below, he kept wandering, his head turning this way and that, as if he were searching for something. Every few steps, he would glance over his shoulder, going motionless as if listening. He appeared totally oblivious to her presence just a few yards away.

Pulling back, Gia counted a beat, then leaped, using the power in her legs to propel her forward onto the incubus' head.

The whistle of her sword cutting the air must have given her away. The demon snapped his head up, noticing her a split second before she jumped. He reared back, falling with a strangled yell.

"Argh—"

The noise cut short when he hit the ground, pushing the air out of his lungs. Not missing a beat, Gia rolled to the side in a single fluid movement, raising her sword for the killing stroke.

"Hey, wait!" The incubus put his hands up, pushing with his legs at the same time. Panic etched his features. "I was sent here by your sisters! Look."

He wasn't pointing at anything, but she saw what he wanted her to. The woven leather and handmade brass plate and small rings were unmistakable.

Baring her teeth, she lowered onto her haunches. Gia kept her sword pointed at his neck. A red rage misted her vision. "Where did you get that?" she hissed.

9

S alvador gulped, wincing and twisting away when the small movement made his Adam's apple graze the tip of the blade of the large sword Gia held.

He didn't know how that was possible on the astral plane, but this hellhole didn't work like any place he'd ever heard about.

"I, uh, I got the necklace from Logan—well, Serin and Logan."

The blade pulled back, but only by a centimeter. Gia stared down, her dark brown eyes boring into him as if she were staring directly into his soul.

"I was s-sent here to find you," he stammered.

Gia didn't respond, continuing to stand over him like the Archangel Michael, weighing his worth. Only she was fiercer and more beautiful than any angel Salvador had ever seen in a painting.

"Damn," he muttered aloud, immediately regretting it when Gia raised the sword higher, scowling.

"Sorry," he rasped, moving his head away from the blade. "I'm just irritated with Alec."

The vampire could have warned Salvador the Earth Elemental was stunning.

Yes, Salvador knew she was attractive. He'd been caring for the woman for almost a week. Even covered in those root-like threads, that fact had been obvious. But he was a professional healer. He'd done what he always did whenever a comely female came under his care—he compartmentalized. They weren't women or men, simply patients. He focused on their ailments and treatment to the exclusion of all else. Anything else receded into the background.

But the woman in front of him couldn't be ignored or put into a mental box marked '*untouchable*'.

The symmetry and striking architecture of Gia's face and figure was just the start. Salvador was sensitive enough to feel what was beneath. The surface beauty was nothing compared to the quiet power he felt radiating from her.

He remembered what Alec had said about the Elementals—that primitive cultures had worshiped them as gods. Salvador had scoffed at the time. He had been born into one of the most powerful witching families on Earth. A few of his ancestors had masqueraded as gods here and there throughout history. But standing next to an Elemental, they would have been exposed for the frauds they were.

Yeah, Alec should have warned him. If he had, Salvador might not be sitting on his ass with what was undoubtedly a stupefied expression.

Gia's death stare sharpened a fraction. "*Why?*"

Her tone was flat, but it somehow managed to resonate in his ears, sending a frisson down his spine. "Uh, for not warning me I'd end up here," he improvised. "Wherever here is..."

Salvador had been taught self-defense from the cradle, but he broke the cardinal rule now—*never take your eye off the enemy*. But he couldn't help himself. His gaze darted back and forth over the barren landscape.

There were piles of rubble all around them, making a narrow corridor. It had been relatively easy for her to ambush him, but Salvador hadn't had a choice. He had followed where the necklace had taken him, the copper and other metals warming progressively the closer he got to her.

"You're in hell."

"Excuse me?" Salvador blinked, whipping his head around again in disbelief before returning to Gia's face.

Those fathomless dark eyes took him in for a breathless moment. Ever so slowly, her arm moved to sheath her sword. "I said you're in hell. One part of it, anyway. This is Sheol, one of the seven known demon dimensions—the one closest to ours."

He took a deep breath, reaching for the protective charm he wore around his neck. It wasn't there. He belatedly remembered he had let Serin take it off in case it interfered with her spell. It wouldn't have worked on the astral plane. It might have worked in hell, though.

"How did I end up here?" he asked. "And why do I feel normal?"

He'd been on the astral plane before, and he knew how it worked. People may look like themselves, but their bodies didn't have form or substance. It's one of the reasons only seasoned witches could astral project. Being bodiless was jarring, to put it mildly. Without special training, it could destabilize a practitioner. He'd been prepared for the experience of being a ghost. But in Sheol, he could hear his heart beating.

Gia still watched him with that clinical, assessing expression. "I was going to ask you the same thing. Why are you here?"

Salvador got to his feet. "I, um, I was drafted. Serin and the others failed to astral project."

The corner of her mouth pulled down. "You're a witch."

His heart stuttered in his chest. *Stop that. You were prepared for this.* There was no way she wouldn't figure out what he was. He just needed to hide *who* he was long enough for them to get out of here.

Elementals policed all Supernaturals, but their history with witches—his family in particular—was complicated and bloody. If she found out he was a Delavordo, the fact her sisters had sent him might not matter. She could kill him out of principle.

"I'm a healer," he volunteered. "I've worked with Alec before. Your sisters brought you to me after you were poisoned. Well, technically, you just showed up in my clinic. You came out of the ground like monolith rising..."

Salvador trailed off as his simile went off the rails. "Not that you're large or anything. You're obviously quite fit—perfect, in fact."

Her fine ebony brow raised, and he coughed. "I've been treating you—your body that is."

Gia's lashes fluttered, betraying a hint of surprise. "I'm not dead?"

His lips parted. "*No!* Of course not. Although, considering where we are, I don't blame you for jumping to that conclusion."

She tilted her head. "Well, it *is* hell."

"Yeah," he breathed, still trying to take it all in. "I've been searching for you for I don't know how long. And I'm not hungry or tired, and I should be. I know I've covered miles in this search."

"None of the usual rules apply here." Gia gave him a final once over before shrugging, her muscles untensing.

"Most demons don't have form when they cross over to our world," she continued. "But the opposite happens to human spirits when they come here. However, I don't know why we don't tire or require food. Few people have crossed over to Sheol, then returned to tell the tale."

Salvador nodded, trying to stay calm. "How do we get back? Also—can we die?"

She gave him one more narrow-eyed perusal before turning on her heel, flicking her finger to indicate he should follow. "I'm working on an escape plan."

That did not sound promising. "I guess it wouldn't be hell if it were easy to leave...but the demons manage somehow."

Gia knelt, picking up a stone and studying it before tossing it aside. "That they do. But their way can't be replicated. We'll have to do it the old-fashioned way—by punching a hole through the barrier between our worlds and crossing back."

The use of the plural untwisted something deep in his gut.

"Does that mean you're not entertaining the idea of leaving me behind?"

She shrugged. "I can't very well leave you here. Not if my sisters were the ones who sent you."

Salvador heaved a silent sigh of relief. *As long as you don't tell her your name, you might actually get out of here.* Fortunately, she hadn't asked for it.

He cleared his throat. "Thank you."

"So, can you share this plan with me?" he asked, hurrying after her when she turned and began to walk away. Technically, his stride was much longer than hers, but she moved so quickly he had to jog to keep up.

"Sheol is one of the dimensions that intersects ours, but since it's a hell dimension, the barrier is not the same. It's thicker on this end, kind of like a gravitational field..."

He frowned. "Sorry. I didn't pay very close attention in physics class. I don't follow."

A flicker of something that could have been annoyance crossed her features, but it was gone before he could be sure. "You know how black holes are so heavy they pull everything inside?"

"Uh-huh." Salvador stepped around a fallen pile of stones that littered the path. Up ahead, larger boulders clogged the trail. The terrain seemed to be getting rougher. Gia didn't appear to be having any problems. She lightly hopped over the large stones, a ninja who wasn't subject to the normal rules of physics.

"Well, it's a bit like that. Think of Sheol as having heavier gravity than Earth. It distends the barrier, making it thicker on this side."

Interesting. "I'm guessing that's not accidental."

"No. It is by design," she acknowledged. "Just one of the many ways the Mother protects us."

"That would normally be comforting, but since we have to get out of here, I'm going to go ahead and freak out now."

Her eyes flicked to his. "Our best bet is to find a scar, a weak point for me to exploit. There's one a few klicks from here."

He brightened. "And you'll be able to open it?"

"Only if an inept witch closed it. If it was an Elemental, we're out of luck."

Any witch capable of banishing a demon and closing such a barrier was, by definition, an elite, but he supposed Elementals had a different yardstick to measure by. "I know I should be insulted, but I just want to go home."

Gia ignored him, pulling a piece of parchment from her pocket. She consulted what appeared to be a map, then pointed at a nearby ridge. "Can you climb that?"

He scanned the rise. It looked like a high hill, but he could see some recognizable structures in the mess. It wasn't a natural formation, but he couldn't make it out at first. He paused, recognizing a few architectural features—a lintel here and a piece of a pillar near the base.

"Yes. Were they all *buildings*?" he asked.

Gia nodded. "They were. And no—I don't know what happened here. Our records have nothing on Sheol before it became a wasteland."

Salvador stopped asking questions after that. He didn't need to eat, but it was still an effort to climb the steep grade of the hill.

He grabbed hold of a twisted piece of metal to climb around a considerable pile of fallen stones. "I forgot—you never answered my question. Can we die here?"

Gia twisted to glance over her shoulder. "Oh, most definitely."

THE SCAR WAS CLOSED TOO WELL. Gia insisted that meant an Elemental had sealed the barrier, but Salvador wasn't convinced that was the case. A highly skilled witch could have done the work, but he wasn't about to argue. There was little point.

Instead, he accepted Gia's word without question, and he was almost pathetically grateful when she invited him to accompany her back to her castle.

"You have a *castle*?" he asked in disbelief.

"It was Mammon's, the demon prince responsible for me getting sucked here. And now it's mine," she said, gesturing as they topped a small rise.

His sense of timing was impeccable. Gia had been leading him back to her castle.

He blinked like an idiot at the imposing multi-turreted fortress. "Exactly how long have you been in Sheol?" he asked, following her along the dirt track that led to the rear of the structure.

"Is it always this...full?" he asked as they crossed a narrow channel that might have been a moat had it contained water instead of bodies.

She didn't answer until they were inside. "I've made a few modifications. Just a few decorative touches."

He snorted, thinking nothing could surprise him. And then he saw the library.

Salvador wasn't sure how long he spent gaping at the shelves.

Up until that moment, he'd believed his parents had the most extensive collection of occult texts in the world. *They do. On Earth.* Salvador kept forgetting this was a different world.

Aimlessly, he perused the shelves, his eyes widening when he saw a copy of Agnodice's *Monograph of Rare Herbs and Poisonous Water Weeds.* After that, he was like a kid in a candy store, running back and forth but refraining from touching.

The shelves seemed endless. He spun on his heel to take it all in, biting his lip to keep from comparing himself to Belle in the Beast's library.

Gia got to work as he browsed. After a few hours—long enough for her to repeatedly decline her servants attempts to prepare a meal for them—he realized she'd never answered his question. "Does time move differently in Sheol? Have you been here longer than I think?"

Gia was quiet so long he wondered if she'd heard him. "I'm not sure how long you believe it's been," she murmured after a while, keeping her eyes on the piles of parchment in front of her. "For me, it's been roughly a week. I was pulled here almost immediately after discorporating."

"Then it's the same. Just a week," he muttered in disbelief. "And you already dethroned a demon prince and claimed his castle as your own?"

She raised her head, meeting his eyes with a stone-cold steady gaze. "I did what I had to do."

He straightened. "I didn't mean to sound like that. It's an incredible accomplishment."

"I know."

The silence that followed thickened, but Salvador wasn't sure why. Very few people could have done what Gia had. Anyone else would have needed an army, but she had won not just her life, but also an entire castle.

"Do you know how many demons I had to dispatch before I won this stronghold?"

He'd counted at least half-a-dozen heads up on spikes when they approached, but the bodies in the moat had been hard to count. Too many pieces...

Logic dictated the number was north of a dozen. But given the tension in the air, he didn't want to hazard a guess.

"Thirty-two," she answered, flipping through a leather-bound volume before lifting a quill to make a note.

"That's, um, very impressive," he said hoarsely. *Thirty-two freaking demons? By herself?*

He shifted uncomfortably as her dark eyes pinned him down. Apparently, Gia didn't like being commended on her skill, but shouldn't she have been used to that sort of thing? She was the senior Elemental, wasn't she?

Seeing his expression, Gia's lips compressed. She sat back in the wooden- and-leather chair. "I prefer to kill as a last resort. I am a soldier, a guardian of the Covenant, not a warmonger. I wouldn't have taken the castle if it hadn't been necessary, but Mammon would have just kept sending more demons after me. He had to go."

"Oh." Well, in that case, he could see why compliments were superfluous and unwelcome. Whoever said absolute power corrupted had clearly never met this woman.

Gia watched him a bit longer. "What is it?" she asked, her tone aggrieved when he lingered in front of her.

Way to go, Salvador. You've officially gotten on her nerves.

"Just thinking about how the patriarchy got it all wrong." He drifted away to study the shelves.

Most of the titles were in an unfamiliar language, but enough were in Latin for him to understand their rarity. If this place burned, it would be a greater loss to the dark side than the destruction of the library of Alexandria...

"My mother would give her eyeteeth just for a peek at some of these volumes," he muttered thoughtlessly, fingering the pristine spine of the *Codex Nabaha*. It rested next to a copy of Machiavelli's *Guide to the Dark Fae*, a work he'd never have guessed existed.

"And what would your father give?"

Salvador froze, his heartbeat slowing as his blood iced over. *Play it off. She can't know who you are.*

"Sorry, I didn't catch that." He pretended to be engrossed with the books, aware he had started to sweat. Eventually, his curiosity got the best of him, and he peeked over his shoulder.

Gia set down the quill, then folded her hands in front of her. "I asked what Fulgencio Delavordo would give to acquire these books on dark magic and the occult?"

Oh, crap. Suddenly enervated, Salvador dropped his arm to his side as he spun around to face his family's lifelong adversary.

10

Gia forced her face to remain impassive as Salvador Delavordo tried not to hyperventilate.

"You didn't give yourself away just now," she assured him. "I knew who you were from the start—well, almost. Once I realized you were human, I recognized you. You don't look like either of your parents, but you have a number of the Delavordo family features."

Although none had been combined in such a pleasing conformation before, she thought.

Salvador swallowed heavily. "I do?" he asked, unconsciously leaning away.

"The one you most closely resemble is Thiago."

That black witch had gone down fighting, but Serin had been able to deal with him with her usual dispassionate efficiency. If Gia had been the one sent after him, she would have been tempted to draw it out. Thiago had done a lot of damage in his day. In the end, it was better it had been her sister to dispatch him. Serin hadn't felt the tie as strongly as Gia had.

Salvador's face tightened. "That's err...that's unfortunate to hear."

She shrugged. "The resemblance isn't all that strong. Nevertheless, he is there in your face and form."

"I didn't know him as a young man," he muttered, turning back to the shelves. "So, I'll have to take your word for it."

She waited a beat. "You didn't mourn him when he died."

He sucked in a breath. "No. In fact, I was tempted to celebrate. Instead, I drank half a bottle of whiskey and passed out in my room… I know it was Serin by the way. She told me."

Gia raised a brow. "You didn't have a problem with that?"

"No," he answered shortly.

"I guess you wouldn't."

He blinked, shifting toward her questioningly.

"If you had, you would still be at Fulgencio's right hand, the heir-apparent to the Delavordo dynasty. Instead, you eke out your living in the wilds of Costa Rica, using all that expertise and training in the dark arts to help those who can't help themselves."

The undisguised horror in his features was almost entertaining, but Gia was beginning to feel a little bad for him. Her sisters had sent this man to find her, which meant—for better or worse—she was responsible for him now, at least until they found a way out of Sheol. Having him fear her was probably unavoidable, but there were limits.

Who would have believed it? She was concerned for a Delavordo's feelings. What her mother had repeated near the end of her life was true.

If you live long enough, you find yourself accepting things you wouldn't have compromised on as a younger woman.

It had sounded better in Spanish, the language her mother had adopted as her primary tongue after her marriage.

"How do you know this? How much do you know about me?" he asked after a short silence.

Gia shrugged. "We keep track of the major players."

He frowned. "I knew that. I guess I assumed that was for the family in general and not those who have left the fold."

She pulled another one of Mammon's horrid volumes toward her. "We don't distinguish between the family members in good standing and those on the outside."

"Then it's not just the disinherited you keep tabs on?"

"It's everyone we know about," she admitted. "But there have been cases when unacknowledged offspring fell through the cracks."

"But most of the time, you are aware?" Salvador had turned away, pretending to study the bookshelves again. His tone was far too casual.

Her lip quirked up. "What do you want to know?"

He pivoted to face her, clearing his throat. "Do I have any brothers or sisters I don't know about?"

Gia pursed her lips, trying to decide if she should answer. Salvador was an ally now, but it could change down the line.

"There are currently thirteen unacknowledged Delavordos in the world."

His family currently held the record. They had always been one of the more prolific witch clans.

"That's not what I asked," he pointed out.

Gia returned to her notes. "I know."

Salvador blinked at the foul-smelling little servant. His name was Snaggle—or something like that—a fitting moniker for someone with those teeth. For the last couple of days, the imp-like creature had taken to following Salvador around whenever Gia dismissed him —which was often.

"I'm sorry... what did you say?" Salvador asked, holding on to his manners by the skin of his teeth.

The stench was eye-wateringly bad.

"I asked if Your Eminence would like to dine in the solarium?" Snuffle repeated, hissing slightly through his long, uneven teeth. The sound was unnerving, but Salvador didn't think he was doing it on purpose.

I could make a killing as a dentist here. But then, he'd have to put his hands into these creature's mouths. He'd lose fingers, maybe his entire hand.

"I... no, but thank you." Salvador tried to smile, but it was too difficult.

How had Gia managed to interact with the beast so regularly without losing her lunch? Just last night, he'd seen her stand not two feet away from the creature for an entire five-minute conversation. There hadn't been even a hint of discomfort or disgust in her expression.

Supernatural lore held that the Elementals were the most powerful beings on Earth, beings whose power was directly derived from the source, the Mother. His family had always taken issue with that, preferring to treat them as obstacles to work around—always with the assumption they *could* be dealt with.

Now, he knew better. That brief conversation with Snaggle proved it. Gia was clearly a superior lifeform.

Snagat coughed gently. Salvador braced himself for the wave of noxious fumes that followed. "Then perhaps you would enjoy it in the formal dining room, oh Exalted One?"

"Thank you, but I'm not hungry," Salvador said, edging away. "Also, there's no need to ask me if I want anything every hour on the hour. I'm just a lowly guest. I don't require special treatment."

Salvador was desperate to downplay his importance in front of the servant. Anything for less one-on-one time.

Snagat almost vibrated with indignation. "But you *are* special. As the chosen consort of our new queen, there is nothing the staff—"

Startled, Salvador raised his hands. "Hold up. I'm not Gia's consort. She hasn't chosen me for anything."

The reality of that was surprisingly depressing—at least for him. Snagat, on the other hand, didn't attempt to hide his obvious pleasure at the news. He practically beamed—all yellow teeth and greenish drool.

Salvador crossed his arms. "Try not to look so happy."

Noticing his displeasure, Snagat subsided. "No offense meant, Your Eminence. It just seemed a trifle odd that one as powerful and skilled as our queen would choose someone like you—an entity so smooth-skinned with only one set of arms and legs."

Salvador blinked. "Naturally, Gia would choose a consort from among the worthy people of Sheol."

The beast nodded sagely, seemingly pleased Salvador understood. "Of course it would be one of the princes—whoever is wise enough not to tangle with her. I think Astaroth would be a fine choice. Even His Former Highness Mammon was afraid to cross him. Cernunnos, The Great Horned One, would also be a fitting mate. He has the finest poisonous spikes along his back. They're quite sharp, too."

Salvador stared, slightly aghast and a bit amused that a horned and poisonous demon was considered a better catch in this world than he was. But the urge to laugh died as he realized Gia probably *would* prefer a horned or six-legged mate to a member of the Delavordo family.

Buck up, buttercup. Once they got back to Earth, Gia would go off to save the world and he'd return to his *curandero* practice to heal. Only this time, he might be able to do it without looking over his shoulder all the time.

Witches and warlocks outcast from the Seven families were considered prey by certain players in the supernatural works. But Salvador refused to be easy pickings. He'd taught himself to fight, and he'd made allies by crafting spells and charms for certain supernatural beings.

In all likelihood, some big bad Supe would come gunning for him someday. With any luck, it wouldn't be one of the Elementals. This trip to hell might even serve to buy him a little goodwill with them.

If I could stockpile a favor from one or more, it would be huge. It would have to be the right favor or course. Something they could get behind.

"If there's nothing else?"

Salvador blinked, amazed he'd forgotten Snuggle was still there. *Don't tell me I'm getting used to this smell.* No, that wasn't possible. He was going to remember the stench even in his dreams.

"You can go," he said, dismissing the demonic servant. "Gia is expecting me in the library."

It was a big fat lie, but he had to get away. For the past few days, he'd been all over the castle, exploring the sprawling edifice and its outlying buildings. He'd even tried to go outside, but being under that stained orange and brown sky was too unnerving. Breathing in the air made him feel tainted, giving him the urge to take a scrub brush to the inside of his lungs. Now that he had a roof over his head, he could handle it only in short bursts.

Plus, the library was the most interesting room in the castle. At first, Salvador had hesitated to remove any of the volumes from the shelves. His concern had been a valid one. It was the most sizable library devoted to black magic he'd ever seen or even heard of. The sheer number of volumes made his own family's extensive collection look like one of those miniature free libraries people had started putting up like mailboxes in suburban neighborhoods. He didn't want Gia to get the wrong idea, but, after a day-and-a-half of vacillating, he'd decided to start going through the books and taking notes.

There were countless spells on hexes and poisons. Sure, ninety-nine percent were how-to manuals. He doubted the former king of this castle cared his books didn't include antidotes or treatments, but in Salvador's line of work, knowing the ingredients was half the battle. He couldn't let this opportunity to learn something new and helpful pass him by.

To his surprise, Gia hadn't tried to stop him. For a nearly all-powerful vigilante superhero, she was pretty reasonable. He shuddered to think how Diana or Serin would react. Pausing for a breath check first, he pushed open the door, halting as bright orange light nearly blinded him.

Adrenaline flooded his system as he prepared to run inside to save the books. After rapidly blinking, though, his eyes adjusted, and he realized the library wasn't on fire. What he was seeing was something else entirely.

It appeared to be a hologram, suspended over the central table, which was piled high with books. A golden vista glittered in the image. On closer inspection, he saw it wasn't the shining shores of

Earth. It was some distant vista of Sheol, barren with golden sand and more of that endless orange-brown sky.

When Gia flicked her finger, the floating image suddenly zoomed out like some sci-fi movie display.

"I thought there was no magic here," he said, entering the room.

Gia waved for him to come closer. "*I* don't have magic here. You don't appear to either, but it exists. It takes a while, but, with effort, it is possible to wield it—*if* you have enough skill." He stopped next to her, and she side-eyed him. "If something happens to me, you should know that."

Salvador stifled a scowl. He was suddenly irrationally angry someone might try to hurt her.

"No offense...but anyone who can take you down can plow through me without breaking a sweat."

"Not if you run," she said pointedly.

He narrowed his eyes. "What aren't you telling me?"

She lifted a shoulder, her gaze on the glowing vista. "Mammon isn't the only high-level demon in this realm with a beef against Elementals. Right now, they're too busy fighting with each other, but all it takes is one to call for a momentary truce. And they will eventually. Taking this castle was strategic, but it was better only in the short term. It proved to the kings that I'm a threat. When they come at me, they'll do it smarter than Mammon did, in larger numbers. We might get separated. In fact, if that happens, it would be prudent for you to take off before the first wave breaks."

Gia moved her hand, changing the scene on the floating image almost as if she were scrolling on a smartphone. "You should also start trying to call your magic. Your family included offensive and defensive spellcasting as part of your education, right?"

He nodded. "My spellcasting may be a little rusty, but I can still disarm the average armed attacker. Well, I could back in our world. I don't know if I will be able to here. I guess I should get on that."

Salvador started to move away when Gia's hand shot out, grabbing his arm in a vise-like grip.

"Do you see that?" Her eyes were fixed on the map.

Twisting around to see the glowing hills, he stopped and squinted. In the top left, there was a swarm of dots moving from east to west—fast. Extremely fast.

With a flick of her wrist, Gia zoomed in. The huge bat-like wings glittered with hints of iridescence he could see even at this distance. *Well, I guess not all demons are ugly.* These were majestic. The scales and snout shapes were uniform across the group. Their bodies were also elegant and symmetrical, something that couldn't be said for the inhabitants of Sheol.

"Wait—are those *dragons*?"

"Yes," Gia murmured. "The colors identify them as part of the Draconis Imperia. They're not native to this place. Rather, they come from a different dimension."

"There are dragons invading hell?" he asked incredulously.

A corner of Gia's lip curled up. "So it would seem. But they may not be doing it from their realm. They could be crossing over from ours."

His heart leapt. *What*? "That would mean they live on Earth."

Her expression seemed curious and contemplative. Not shocked in the least.

Well, damn. There were dragons on Earth, and she'd known the entire time.

Gia rocked on her heels, shaking her head. "If this is one of Earth's colonies, they're violating the Covenant by opening a portal to this world. Either way, we have to move quickly before they close it."

Hurrying around the room, she grabbed a bag and started throwing books and papers inside. When she was done, she went to the corner where she'd tossed a few of the swords and shields she'd brought up from the armory. Her hand hovered over the wicked assortment of weapons before she chose the largest sword, its blade painted black now so it wouldn't be seen in the dark. Strapping the huge weapon to her back, she picked up a lighter one shaped vaguely like a katana, then tossed it to him.

"Just in case you can't summon the magic of Sheol," she said before heading out.

11

———

Aswarm of flying dragons, no matter how far above it flew, was an awesome and somewhat terrifying sight.

He tried not to let that last part show, but he couldn't help ducking when the shadow of the front guard approached at sixty or seventy miles an hour.

"They can't see us," Gia assured him. He winced, chagrined she could read him so easily.

"I know. I can feel the spell you cast. It was simply a reflex."

Gia had cast an obfuscation spell to ensure they would remain unseen as long as no one looked too closely. He forced himself to stand up straight as the main body of the diamond-shaped regiment passed above them. The massive wings blackened the sky.

Salvador had never seen a dragon swarm before, but he could feel their sense of determination and purpose from where he stood. He clutched the sword tighter despite their relative safety. "They're sure as hell going somewhere in a hurry…"

He wouldn't have thought it possible for something to fly angrily, but the flock somehow managed to convey both indignation and self-righteous fury. There was something about their movement and bearing, like soldiers off to fight a war.

He turned to Gia. "It's clear they're spoiling for a fight. Someone is about to get a whole can of whoop-ass delivered via airmail."

Gia snorted as they watched the flock grow smaller, heading to a jagged cliff line in the distance.

"What's over there?" he asked.

"Another demon prince's castle."

"Which one?" he asked, but she didn't answer. When he glanced over, she was already some distance away. He ran to catch up.

"If they intend to return to Earth, they'll have left the doorway open. Otherwise, they'll be in the same position we are," she explained as she hustled him along.

They topped a small dirt rise. She slid down the other side with controlled grace.

"It better be guarded," she added as he awkwardly followed.

Confused, he tried to catch her gaze, but failed. She was moving too fast. "Wouldn't an unguarded door be better for us?" he panted, running after her.

"If the inhabitants of Sheol knew there was a gateway to Earth, every demon in the continent would be swarming to it by now."

Fuck. "And they're not exactly flying covertly."

"Precisely. They aren't trying to conceal themselves. The dragon's main advantage is in physical intimidation. They're not known for hiding their light under a bushel." She broke off to help him up after he slid and stumbled to the ground.

"The only thing in their favor is they're not native to Earth, so most demons won't assume that's where they came from. But some demon lords may know a few Draconai Imperia settled on Earth. It would be worth their while to send someone to check."

If that were true, then it was likely they'd already sent out search parties, a precursor to a full-scale invasion of Earth. Suddenly, this had become a race.

"They better have a damn good reason for coming here," she hissed as they arrived at a huge outcropping of boulders.

There was something here—an energy. The necklace around his

neck, which Gia had insisted he continue to wear, began to warm. The gate was near.

"And if they don't?" he whispered, wondering if a dragon was going to leap out, teeth bared.

"Then we close it for them."

"Good, good," he muttered. In a rush, he added, "From the other side, right?"

"Ideally."

Ah, hell. Salvador rubbed his eyes.

She regarded him, chin firm and resolute. "You know I'm right. The priority is closing the door."

"Yeah, I know," he said, ignoring the tightening in his gut. Leaving a portal to hell open endangered everyone on Earth. Even at his most selfish, he couldn't justify saving himself over saving the world. But there was some consolation—closing the door would be easier from the other side, provided they could get past whatever hurdle stood between them and the portal.

After a few minutes, the air changed, thinning. He started panting reflexively, even though his mind told him that he wasn't actually breathing.

Ears vibrating, the string of leather and brass around his neck became downright hot. "It's close. I can feel it."

Gia nodded and raised a hand, signaling to stay quiet. She halted at a crumbling stone rise that resembled the remains of a Grecian temple, complete with Ionic column. Cautiously, she poked her head around a damaged pillar. Then she twitched her fingers, signaling for him to follow.

He edged around the pillar, then promptly tripped. Scowling, Gia caught him, yanking him up to face the massive red-and-black dragon guarding the small stone arch. Behind the beast, the air rippled.

Salvador's stomach dipped and swelled, but not from the fear he should have felt at seeing such a fearsome creature. His reaction was due to their proximity to the opening. He could almost smell home.

"It's the way back to Earth. I can feel it."

The dragon swiveled its head, whirling on them with a roar at the sound of Salvador's voice.

"Well, there goes our element of surprise," Gia said in a flat voice. Her sword was out before he could blink, and she called out in a language he didn't understand. The dragon answered in kind. Swishing its tail, the beast called attention to the shining spikes. It chuffed, and a stream of flame rushed toward them.

Gia pushed him down just in time. Salvador hit the ground as the flame enveloped her. But she didn't try to evade it. She stood still, letting the fire cover her.

"You didn't burn," Salvador gasped, scrambling to his feet. The dust and dirt clouded his eyes, but he could still see that Gia was unhurt.

"This Draconis was born on Earth. Its flames won't hurt me," she replied.

There was a loud snort and a whoosh. The dragon disappeared. In its place stood a mountainous man. He was huge and dark, muscles rippling up his arms and thighs as thick as tree trunks. Although he was dressed in plain leather pants and a vest of the same material, his face and arms were covered in jagged designs and writing. At first, Salvador thought they were tattoos. On second glance, he realized they were painted on. *War paint.*

"Do you recognize me, Draconis?" Gia called to the dragon. "What is your name, and who do you serve under?"

The mountain of a man scowled. "You're not you. It's a trick."

Gia cocked her head. "Unfortunately for me, it's not. I was wounded and fell into a spell trap, which displaced my associate and me." She jerked her thumb in Salvador's direction.

"As you can see, I'm fine now." She twitched the blade. "What business do your people have in Sheol?"

The warrior's eyes were glued to the sword. "It's not your affair, demon."

"Again, I'm not a demon, and I want to know what the hell your leader was thinking by opening a door *to* hell?"

The soldier's head drew back, clearly confused at her insistence. But apparently, the critical thinking was too much for him because he scowled and lifted his sword. "You won't get through this door *moecha putida*," he spat.

Salvador winced. *Dirty slut?* Dragon man was in for it now.

"Okay, that's it," Gia muttered. That was the only hint anything else was coming. One second, she stood next to Salvador. The next, she was flying through the air, sword raised.

Salvador retreated a few feet as the warriors clashed. Gia was blindingly fast, but the dragon shifter was a trained fighter. He whipped around, twisting and raising his own weapon, one Salvador hadn't even noticed until it was in the soldier's hand.

"Where was he hiding that?" Salvador asked. That dude had been a dragon a minute ago. Where the hell had he tucked a four-foot sword?

No one answered, but he doubted the fighters could hear him over the crashing sound of metal on metal. The ringing vibrated in his ears.

Gia planted her foot for balance, then pushed the shifter with one hand. The muscled man flew backward, landing with a *thump*. His head hit the ground, kicking up a small puff of dust.

Salvador tried to cast a defensive spell, hoping the proximity to the gate would jumpstart his magical abilities. Although he did feel *something*, it wasn't the normal flood of energy—more like a trickle.

Damn. He needed to get closer to the opening. Maybe he'd be able to access his magic then.

As quietly as he could, he edged around the fighters. If he could just get to the door, he might be able to stick his foot through, accessing his magic while leaving his arms free to cast a few spells and help Gia.

Mentally, Salvador willed the dragon warrior to keep his focus on the fight. The door was only a few feet away. Salvador was almost there when the guy went flying again—due to another of Gia's killer roundhouse kicks. The dragon shifter landed next to Sal. Scrambling up, the shifter twisted to scowl in Salvador's direction.

"*Hey*. What the—" the warrior began, his nostrils flaring. He sniffed, cocked his head.

He didn't get to finish the sentence. Eyes rolling into the back of his head, he landed at Salvador's feet like a fallen redwood.

Gia wrinkled her nose. "Why did he just stop like that?" she asked.

"I, uh, I think I distracted him," Salvador said, putting his hands on his hips.

Exactly how was a mystery. "Perhaps my reputation precedes me?" he suggested, his chest puffing up a bit.

Gia snorted, then began to laugh. When the corner of his mouth pulled down, she subsided. "Oh, you were serious..."

He snorted, the sound only a touch self-deprecating. "Stranger things have happened."

Averting her eyes, she sheathed her sword before stepping over the prone pile of muscles.

"Wake up." Gia grabbed the dragon shifter by the hair, giving him a hard shake. She didn't let up until his dazed eyes cleared.

She squatted until they were face to face. "By rights, I should close this damn door behind me. Opening it was a violation of the Covenant. Your leader knows that. However, I'm going to be lenient in this case because it's my ticket out of here. You have twenty-four hours. After that, either I, or one my sisters, will be slamming it shut. It won't matter to any of us which side you are on. The door will be sealed regardless—*forever*."

The dragon shifter groaned in response, rolling to his side. Slowly, he sat up, regarding them with a mixture of disgust and resignation.

"Call your men. Secure this location. *Now*."

"It was fine until you showed up," the shifter hissed, although his voice sounded distinctly wobbly.

"Portals to hell are, by their very nature, insecure," Gia insisted. "Get some of the others back here to help you—half a dozen of your strongest warriors. Otherwise, you and your people will be held responsible if any natives end up on our side."

She headed to the opening, but paused. "And have your leader call on me when he returns to our realm. Your clan better have a damn good reason for coming here. I'm going to want to hear it."

Gia practically sauntered away, not even giving the warrior the courtesy of looking back to make sure he didn't mount a counterattack.

Salvador hurried to catch up, then reached for Gia's hand when she reached the portal. When she glanced at it, he realized what he'd done and felt his face start to heat. But he didn't let go.

Gia tilted her head to look up at him, wrapping her fingers tighter around his. Then she strode forward, pulling him through to the other side.

12

Gia was aware of the aching discomfort before anything else. It was unlike the sharp and more concentrated pain she'd experienced from the various wounds and injuries sustained from centuries of service to the Mother. This was more widespread, an insistent dull throbbing that spread from head to toe.

She took a cautious breath, drawing the air deep into her lungs. The tight band around her heart unwound, spinning into the aether as she inhaled the clean scent around her. There was an underlying moisture and fetidness she welcomed after the oily smell and metallic taste of the air in Sheol.

She was home.

Gia felt Diana before she saw her. Her sister's inherent heat was palpable, even from a distance. After the cold emptiness of Sheol's wasteland, it was a welcome sensation.

"Di," Gia whispered, belatedly licking her dry and cracked lips.

Warm strong fingers touched her face, prying her eyes open. Gia's vision was blurry, but she could see her sister's relieved expression.

"That's better," Diana's expression was closed, but Gia could feel strong waves of emotion coming from her like pulses of energy. "Welcome back."

Wincing, Gia sat up and surveyed her surroundings. She was in a rough cottage. A pair of camping chairs crafted from native wood set against one wall. Both appeared well-crafted and comfortable, but too mismatched to be anything but handmade. Gia had been lying on a makeshift bed of raised soil in the center of the room.

"It's good to be back," she said. She was surprised to hear the raspy sound of her own voice. *You weren't actually using it in Sheol.* It had been her soul in hell, not her body.

Gia touched the earth underneath her thighs, reveling in the granular and healthful vibration it gave off. Unlike the barren ground she'd been walking on for the past few weeks, this soil was alive.

She lifted a hand to her nose as if she were taking a hit of cocaine. After the disconnected aridity and desolation of Sheol, the effect was euphoric.

The land was so rich here in...Chiriquí? No, she was somewhere in Costa Rica. The distinctive mix of minerals and bacteria pointed a little more north of Panama.

Diana gestured at the packed-earth altar underneath Gia. "We tried putting you in a regular bed a few times, but the dirt kept rising to cover it, so we gave up and settled you back out here."

"Back?" Gia asked, still out of sorts. She ran her tongue along her teeth. They still didn't feel like hers, but the sense of alienness was slowly departing as her soul settled back into its chosen vessel.

"This is where you appeared once we decided to use Salvador for your treatment." Diana's nose wrinkled. "One minute, you were lying in the ruins on the Isle of Man. The next, you were here, in the clinic's waiting room."

Gia's lip quirked. "It was probably longer than a minute." The Isle of Man was some distance away. Normally, she did not cross beneath oceans due to the time and effort.

"Err...you do know where *here* is?" Diana asked. "This clinic belongs to Salvador. He's a...well, he's—"

Gia held up a hand. "Don't worry. I know who Salvador is—who his people are. Thank you for sending him after me. Given the circumstances, you chose well."

The line of Diana's shoulders dropped as she relaxed a little more. "I thought you'd be pissed. I know you have a history with the Delavordos. We all do, but Alec vouched for this one. He assured us that Sal is not like the others."

"Sal? I thought it was Salvador."

Diana smirked. "Yeah, he doesn't like it when I shorten his name, so I call him that at every opportunity."

Gia laughed before sobering. Her sister had never looked so tired. She imagined Serin and Logan were in similar states. After stretching her legs experimentally, she swung them over the side of the dais.

Gia patted the space next to her. Diana hopped up, leaning to the side until their arms touched. Her sister was careful not to push too much of her weight onto her, but Gia was having none of that. Gia pulled her sister in tight, encouraging Diana's head to rest on her shoulder.

Gia still wasn't feeling one hundred percent. Not even half that, but she was strong enough for this.

"Thanks," Diana murmured.

"For what?"

"For not dying."

Gia snorted. "I aim to please."

Diana laughed, but then she hung her head, her expression crumbling.

"Stop, my sister. There's no need for that," Gia said softly, wiping Diana's cheeks. Her sister needed catharsis, but Diana only tolerated weakness in others. She despised it in herself.

There was a moment of silence as Diana composed herself. She gestured to Gia's arms. There was a faint tracing of something, a spidery web of sorts, on the surface of her skin.

"It's a lot better now than it was. Sal appears to be a decent-enough healer."

"Judging by the evidence, he's nothing short of miraculous..." Gia muttered, not wanting to compliment Salvador loud enough for him to hear. "Where is he?"

Diana cocked her head, listening. "I think Alec must have taken him out. He woke a little before you did. He said he wanted to bathe, so they headed for the stream."

She turned back to Gia. "I thought it was weird he woke before you did, but he checked you out. He said there's still some poison in your system. It's working its way out, but you may be here for a few more days."

Gia scowled. "I have to find him."

She and Diana both knew they weren't talking about Salvador anymore.

Diana's shoulders slumped. She appeared exhausted. "John has disappeared from the face of the earth. I couldn't find him. Neither can Serin. Logan and Connell are trying their luck now."

"I should be out there, too," Gia said, rising. Unfortunately, even one step proved too much. A wave of nausea and dizziness nearly made her pass out.

Her sister helped her back to the mound of dirt, which adjusted automatically for her comfort.

"Not yet," Diana admonished. "You need to regain your strength. That poison was one for the books."

"I know. It took a long time for him to perfect," Gia said, her voice hardening. "I was foolish to trust John."

"You can't blame yourself. He was good enough to ingratiate himself to the T'Kaierian community. Serin grew up calling him *uncle*. Everyone trusted him. You can't fault yourself for not seeing what he was."

Gia wanted to argue, but there was no point. The only thing that would make a difference was catching and killing the bastard. "I suppose even we don't know what's in the heart of men. Although, I now realize why he would make himself scarce when you visited the island."

"You think I would have sussed him out?" Diana raised a brow.

"Perhaps. Perhaps not. Your built-in lie detector isn't infallible, but it makes sense John took steps to avoid you. He didn't last as long as he did in T'Kaieri by taking chances." Gia groaned as she flexed her arms and shoulders. "We can't be caught unawares by him again."

"We won't be," Diana vowed. She relaxed her hold, running her fingers over the faint marks on Gia's skin. "You know, I think I dreamt this."

Gia's sluggish mind began to work faster. "You dreamt of me being poisoned by John?'

"No. It was a very old dream, not clear at all. And there was nothing about John or his betrayal. It's just...it's the image of these," Diana said, tracing the marks. "I remember them."

As omens went, it was less than informative after the fact, but Gia had been in service long enough to know the Mother's ways weren't merely mysterious. Sometimes, they were downright perverse. "Prophetic dreams are rare for our kind. Yours was probably unrelated, but if you remember anything else, let me know."

"I will."

"What happened after I went down?" Gia asked.

Diana gave her a quick and concise rundown of events after the attack, starting with the booby trap at T'Kaieri and ending with the ritual that sent a disinherited Delavordo into hell to search for Gia. In turn, Gia told her about the spell trap and the open door to Sheol.

"Why the hell would *those* dragon shifters invade Sheol?" her sister asked. "It's nothing but a barren wasteland, isn't it? Do they expect to find treasure there?"

Like Gia, all three of her younger sisters were familiar with the major clans of shifters, but none had spent a significant amount of time with any of the Draconai Imperia, the oldest clan of non-native dragons.

The Draconai Imperia were refugees, the only survivors of a cataclysmic civil war that destroyed their civilization over a millennia ago. Compared to the small pockets of native dragon shifters, the Draconai were smaller and faster with a rigidly disciplined hierarchical structure.

There was still some debate among T'Kaierian scholars over which group of dragons first appeared on Earth. The most popular theory was Earth's native dragon shifter population took their form *after* the Draconai arrived. Noomi's great-grandfather, a former head archivist himself, was convinced the form was inspired by the Draconai *after* the first clans settled in North America. Some vocal authorities insisted the similarity in form was simple convergent evolution. However, after seeing the entire Imperia in flight, Gia was leaning toward the former.

"The Draconai have been around for an extremely long time, and we've never had any trouble from them," Diana observed. "I hope that isn't about to change. Could they have been on an invasion for gold or something like that? Those demon lords have been known to hoard wealth like humans."

"I suspect they were hunting treasure—just not gold or jewels," Gia murmured.

Given the way the junior Draconai had reacted to Salvador, Gia had a suspicion, but they wouldn't know the truth until the dragons returned. *If* they returned.

"Are these dragons anything like Serin's friend, Ed...he of the cookie jars?" Diana asked.

"No," Gia said. "The Draconai Imperia are another species from a different realm. They're a warrior caste that emigrated here a millennium ago, survivors of a war they never talk about. The Mother allowed them to stay so long as they kept the Covenant, and they didn't make war for riches. And they have honored that pledge—for the most part. But regardless of their relatively peaceful ways, they train every day, maintaining their rigid warrior ways amongst themselves."

"A life endlessly preparing for war, but not fighting one. Could that be why they went to Sheol? Could it be a training exercise?"

"Opening a door to Sheol is a clear violation of the Covenant. I don't think they would risk their place on Earth by doing so unless they had a damn good reason." She brushed her hair out of her face. "I don't know what that would be. Except for their leader, I've never spoken to them, although I know most by sight. They keep to themselves, an insular community. On occasion, one or two have even fought alongside earlier generations of Elementals, when certain threats arose."

Diana brightened. "So, they could be potential allies?"

Gia sighed. "I wouldn't count on it. Based on what I saw, they have their own war to fight. But we'll do as I told the guard. The door only stays open for twenty-four hours. Then we close it whether they are back or not—permanently. I also ordered the guard to send his chieftain to me when they return. If the answer is *unsatisfying*... then we may have to reevaluate the terms of the treaty."

Diana nodded. "I understand," she said, seemingly unconcerned that a serious battle with a dangerous shifter clan might be brewing on top of everything else.

If they had to leave, the dragons wouldn't go quietly.

"I'll cover the doorway until those dragon shifters get back," Diana offered.

Gia shook her head. "No, send Logan."

When Diana frowned, Gia patted her shoulder. "The inhabitants of Sheol have been conditioned to fire. I'm pretty sure one or more of those demon princes are impervious."

"Not to my fire," Diana sniffed.

"Maybe not," Gia conceded. Her sister's gift came from the Mother herself. It had never failed to destroy anything she'd wanted to burn. "But I'd rather have you on John's trail."

Her sister grinned. "Even better. Just know if I find him this time, I won't wait for you. The second I set eyes on him, he's toast."

Gia inclined her head. "Do whatever you have to do. No matter what happens, we can't let him accomplish his goal. But be careful. He's planned for this for years."

Diana's face softened, but there was a granite resolution in the tense lines of her back and arms.

On the historical Elemental badass scale, Diana was near the top.

"He's not going to get the drop on me or the others," she promised. "We're on our guard now, as are Alec's coven and the Maitland pack. Even Serin's new man Daniel pitched in. He put out a bolo on John on every human law enforcement channel there is. We are going to find him. He's going to be sorry he came for us."

That could be helpful, but Gia didn't set much stock in the

human's ability to hunt down someone as dangerous as John. No, they were going to have to take care of this themselves. The stakes were too big.

She forced herself to her feet, silently cursing her weak legs.

"I'm glad we have these allies right now, but you should know I don't think John is trying to kill the Elementals. I believe he's aiming higher—*much* higher. His goal is to kill the Mother."

13

Of all the Elementals Gia was the best-versed in healing. She knew how important rest was to the recuperation process. If it had been one of her sisters who'd been poisoned and nearly killed, Gia would have been the first one to insist they stay in bed for a few days—preferably a week.

Despite her knowledge, Gia was already out of bed, making herself walk around not ten minutes after Diana had left for her hunt. Gia couldn't stop herself. She was back in her body, breathing clean air, and surrounded by the scents of the Costa Rican jungle. Reasoning getting outdoors was what she needed, she grabbed a hiking pole leaned next to the door to use as a walking stick. Then she hobbled outside.

The energy hit her like an ocean wave. The trees and plants pulsed with life. She could feel the echo in her bones and her blood. After being cut off in a nearly dead wasteland, the sensation was almost overwhelming, a gentle bombardment. It was like a seed getting water for the first time—there was a storm of chemical activity as the shoots began to develop, pushing into the soil... connecting. That was what it felt like.

The farther she got from the cottage, the better she felt. Each step was healing. The jungle was restorative—almost as much as whatever Salvador put in his medicines and poultices.

A fire burned in the clearing in front of the house where a ring of stones had been carefully laid out. Two thin iron bars had been twisted into supporting arches to suspend a hook over the center of the flames. At the moment, there was a pot suspended over the fire. Some sort of stew bubbled inside. To the left of it, there was a rough mud-brick stove, also hot. Salvador was there, his back to her as he heated some flatbread on an iron plate that had been placed above the coals like a griddle.

He turned around, startled when he saw her. The morsel flew out of his hand. Gia took a few steps, faster than was advisable under the circumstance, but she managed to catch it before it hit the ground. Thankfully, there was no nausea this time, despite the abruptness of the motion.

Gia held out the bread, but Salvador shook his head, managing a winsome smile. "I was actually making that for you. Now that you're awake, I think we can start on solids. Alec said you enjoy all sorts of food, so I had him send out for some goat meat to make stew—one of my signature dishes. There aren't any restaurants nearby, so I've been forced to learn a few tricks in the kitchen," he said, waving at the makeshift cooking area.

"It smells very nice," she said before taking a bite of the bread. Despite his claims to the contrary, it tasted extraordinarily good— light, fluffy, and with copious amounts of butter worked into the dough. "And this is even better. Absolutely delicious."

"Thank you." He grinned. "Although we can't discount the fact it might be because you haven't eaten anything real for over a week."

"That could be it, too," she admitted, deadpan.

The flicker of the fire did interesting things to his features, she decided. Gia hadn't changed her mind. He *was* handsome enough to be a male succubus...

"Before you eat, Alec wanted to speak with you."

She raised a brow. "He's still here?"

Like most of her sister's mates, Alec disliked being left behind when Diana went on the hunt. He could travel in her medium. By extension, he could travel in those of her sisters as well. Because he didn't slow Diana down and was usually helpful, no one begrudged him tagging along. The only time Alec didn't go was when he had a new library to explore. The archives on T'Kaieri were his Mecca.

"I think he went to the stream," Salvador offered, removing the pot of stew from the fire and setting it on a broad flat rock next to the ring of stones.

"I'll be right back," she said. Maintaining a measured pace, she headed in the direction he'd indicated, despite the siren call of the stew.

She found the vampire right where Salvador said he'd be. He sat on a rock, typing furiously on a hefty military-grade cell. He'd given up the sleek top-of-the line models when he paired up with Diana. Her heat tended to short out the less-sturdy devices.

Alec whipped around as soon as she came into view. *"Gia."* Holding up a hand, he jumped up and ran with preternatural speed, stopping short a few feet from her.

It was to her credit that all she did was blink. If it were any other vampire, she would have put her arms out, decking him before he could get that close.

"I can't tell you how happy I am to see you up and around," Alec said.

"Yes, I can see that," she said, holding out her hand before he could hug her. His relief was somewhat out of proportion to the closeness of their friendship. Something else was up.

Alec took her hand, shaking it with jerky movements. She braced herself. "Did you discover something about John or his poison?"

"No, no. I'm afraid not." His hands came together, gripping one in the other tightly enough to make it white—well, whiter than normal. "This is about Diana."

She frowned. "What's wrong with her?"

Alex's lips parted, uncharacteristic indecision flickering across his face. "She's...not herself."

"I didn't notice anything wrong with her." Granted, Gia hadn't been *looking*, but if her sister were ill, she would have noticed—unless her ability to detect the resonance of other living beings was somehow compromised. *Which is a real possibility at the moment.*

Gia flicked her fingers at Alec, indicating he should continue. The vampire swallowed and opened his mouth, but nothing came out.

"Alec, just spit it out," she snapped.

"I think Diana is pregnant."

Relieved, she laughed aloud. "That's impossible."

"I heard it."

She rocked back on her heels. "You heard what exactly?"

Alec pointed at his abdomen. "The heartbeat."

The humor fell away, confusion taking its place. "No offense, but vamps don't breed. Not that way."

Vampire reproduction was a closely guarded secret, but Gia and her sisters were outsiders privy to the details. Few people were able to be turned. Once they did, their bodily functions slowed down enough to be almost negligible. Like shifters, they were creatures of magic, capable of great feats like super-strength and speed. However, in all their recorded history, none had reproduced after the turn. Not even the handful of vampiric Daywalkers had accomplished the feat, and God knew Alzeal Hussan had tried...

There was also the fact her sisters were like her. Elementals were perpetually fixed, their bodies remaining as they were at exactly the moment they took their vow to do their duty to serve the Mother and enforce the Covenant.

"You're wrong." Gia shook her head. "You have to be. We don't age or change. That means we can't conceive either. Not unless..."

She trailed off for the sake of delicacy. They both knew the only way Diana could fall pregnant were if she had given up the Elemental mantle, then lain with another man—a human or Supe who *wasn't* a vampire.

"It's not like that." Briefly, Alec's dark eyes heated into hot coals, but quickly subsided. "I haven't left Diana's side since before you were struck down. Before then really. The Elders of T'Kaieri weren't keen on my help doing an inventory of the archive unless she stayed behind to mind me. We were given a cottage there, near the beach, and well..."

Gia didn't need him to fill in the blanks. Alec and Diana were essentially still honeymooners.

"I'm pretty sure Connell heard it, too—the heartbeat." Alec rubbed his temple. "He didn't say anything, but he was giving Diana some pretty weird looks. Perhaps he detected a change in her scent, too. He must have kept it to himself, though. Otherwise, Logan would have been broadcasting it to the skies."

"Yes, she would have," Gia agreed in a quiet murmur. Her youngest sister wasn't indiscreet exactly. Gia preferred to think of her as exuberant.

"As I said, I don't believe Diana's aware of anything being *off*, but she's been consumed with worry ever since you were poisoned."

Gia nodded. Her sister had been orphaned at a young age. Diana had been alone in the world when Gia had gone to claim her and inform her of her legacy. Since Gia had been in service, she'd been unable to take young Diana in hand herself. Gia had done the next best thing by leaving the new recruit with extended family. But Gia had visited frequently. Consequently, her relationship with Diana had more of a maternal touch than the one she had with Serin, or even Logan, who was the youngest.

The Fire Elemental had already lost one mother. Gia could only imagine Diana's reaction when John ambushed her. For her sister's worry alone, John deserved to die.

"I've been doing some reading on embryo development," Alec continued after a pause. "Di's not far enough along for her to be carrying another's babe—not that she would ever do that. She wouldn't betray me."

"I know that." Gia had been grasping at straws when she'd suggested otherwise. When Elementals took a mate, it was for life... sometimes longer. It had been years since Gia had lost hers, but she knew she would never find anyone like Marco again.

"Perhaps it's something else. Maybe Diana has a parasite," she suggested.

Alec raised a dark brow, and Gia threw up her hands. "I don't know what to say. If you're right, then this is unprecedented."

"I'm hearing that too often lately," the vampire muttered. "I was hoping you would have answers. Perhaps there is record of an occurrence somewhere in your history, something before your time I haven't come across yet?"

"Don't bother looking. I can assure you no such information exists." If it had happened, she would have known. The Mother would have told her. Wouldn't She have?

Sighing, Gia sighed moved until she could lean against a tree at the water's edge. Resting her weight against the trunk, she took strength from its connection to the soil.

"We'll need to confirm this," she said eventually. "We should take her back to the island. The T'Kaierian healers are the most experienced with our unique physiologies."

Alec snorted aloud, then rubbed the bridge of his nose.

"They couldn't help Serin when she got poisoned." He paused, shifting his weight from side to side. "But what would you think if we brought her to Salvador? I think he's proven himself trustworthy and skilled. Maybe Di should come back here so he can confirm the diagnosis?"

"*No.*" Gia's answer was instinctive and immediate.

Alec frowned. "Why not?"

"Because..." she answered.

He stared. She crossed her arms, irritated he was forcing her say it aloud. "I know he is your friend and he helped me, but he is also a Delavordo."

Alec's expression showed his incredulity. "Salvador is a good man. He saved your life, for the Mother's sake."

"I know, and I'm grateful." Gia had no illusions that without Salvador's intervention, she might not have had a body to come back to. She couldn't forget the man had ended up in hell because of her, too... "But I am *one* Elemental. By definition, I am replaceable. If he had failed, you'd be talking to my successor right now. Diana conceiving while in service is something else entirely. What if the child were to inherit our abilities?"

"That's already how Elementals inherit," Alec protested, then added. "It's in your bloodline. Just ask Logan—she has more Elemental ancestors than anyone I've ever read about. And Salvador doesn't speak to anyone from his family."

Briefly, Gia closed her eyes. "He doesn't speak to them *right now*. But life is long, Alec. If an Elemental could be born without their mother having to give up her abilities, it would be considered blasphemous to certain ears. The news the rules were changing so fundamentally would alarm and upset every major witch and vampire house— even those we're on good terms with. Tell me honestly, how would the vampire council react if they learned your mate was carrying a child?"

Alec fell silent. But Gia wasn't going to leave it at that.

"Now you have to ask yourself this—and keep in mind the safety of your mate and your possibly unborn child are at stake. If the Supernatural community learned Elementals were able to breed, who do you think would be the first to move against us?"

The vampire's face tightened. He didn't answer, but he didn't have to. They both knew the clans who would be the most threatened were *the big Seven*—the major witch families. In her considered opinion, the Delavordos would be the first in line. However, for something like this, they might have help from the other houses.

At this rate, Alec was going to rub a hole through his skull. "Do you genuinely think our child would be born with Elemental abilities?"

"I don't know. But the Mother keeps us in stasis while we serve for a reason."

The vampire ran his teeth over his lip in an unnerving gesture. "Diana once implied it was because She feared an insurrection in your ranks. The Mother didn't want to be outnumbered."

"If She has reconsidered, it's because She has identified a bigger threat." The thought was not comforting.

The vampire looked grim. "John."

Gia considered that, but this madman's threat was just one in an endless line. "I wish I could definitively say that was it. But, honestly, I'm not sure—John is hardly the first person who has attempted to bring about the end of the world."

Alec snorted. "Don't I know it."

14

J ohn threw the empty ice bucket up in the air just so, making it spin before the flat bottom landed adroitly on his open palm.

He added a jaunty little hop to his step, wishing he could kick his heels together in celebration the way his favorite dancers did in the picture shows. *Movies*, he mentally edited. They called them movies these days...

Whistling, he set the ice bucket on the bench with a feeling he could describe only as giddy. Today's little experiment was going to go well. He could feel it in his bones. The ingredients were potent and powerful, but, more importantly, they were plentiful thanks to his stock of catalogs that sold scientific reagents. His chemist friend had recommended John take advantage of the suppliers when he made his umpteenth request for raw materials.

At first, he'd been annoyed to be rebuffed. John paid the man good money to be his supplier for the particular chemicals he required, but he soon changed his mind. The suggestion had been inspired. No more crawling on his hands and knees in the dirt to dig up a handful of weeds he needed to crush for an experiment. Now, most of what he required was a few mouse clicks away. Not all, but the majority. He was still refining his technique and formula, trying to find adequate substitutes for the few rare components, but this morning had proven fruitful in that respect.

Scaling up in volume was proving to be a challenge, but one he enjoyed. This was part was going to be fun. He was less sanguine about the move that followed, but his newest recruit was right. Successful deployment was all about location, location, location.

15

Connell's nostrils flared. The woods stank of dark magic and blood. "Do you smell that?" he asked.

"Yeah," Logan said, kneeling.

They were in the Canadian Rockies, at least a hundred miles from the nearest town. They'd come here directly after a detour to a patch of land near Blessing, Texas, where Logan had shut a door into hell.

Damn dragons, he thought as he scanned the trees around them. They could have gotten here much sooner if not for that errand, which had been anticlimactic, to say the least.

Connell had been pumped when Logan said they were going to be facing off with a bunch of dragon shifters, possibly slamming the door to hell shut on them. But by the time they got to Blessing, only one waited. The rest had already come through the door and gone home, wherever that was.

The dragon they'd left behind had presented Logan with a chest full of gold and jewels, calling it a tithe for their 'necessary' transgression. Connell had been tempted to bash the dragon over the head with his damn chest, but Logan beat him to it.

"Open another door to anywhere ever again, I'll shove that chest up your ass," she'd snarled.

"She can do it, too," Connell had said with a smirk.

The dragon—Jerik something—barely batted an eyelash. He'd simply inclined his head, informing them his chief would be at their disposal whenever Gia wanted an accounting. And that had been the end of it—for now. They had never found out what the *Draconai Imperia* were up to in *Sheol*.

Now they were finally back on the hunt for John. If that fucker was hurting Elementals, then Logan was on his list. Connell was going to make damn sure that POS didn't touch a hair on her head—preferably by breaking both his arms. And then shoving them down his throat.

Except for the excursion to Blessing, he and Logan had been bouncing around the world for weeks. In between wild goose chases, they'd stopped in Costa Rica to check on Gia and make sure the pair of freaks, the vampire and the Delavordo warlock, didn't do her in.

Well, that was what Connell was keeping an eye out for. Logan trusted the vamp. Apparently, the fact Alec was mated to Logan's sister meant he was above suspicion, but that hadn't been the case with Serin's first mate, so Connell was reserving judgment. As for that Salvador character, Connell trusted him about as far as he could throw him. Less than that really. As a werewolf, Connell could probably throw the witch pretty far.

The wind picked up, bringing a new brew of smells to dissect. The sting from the foul magic was the most prominent in the bouquet.

"Any tidbits from your little friends?" Connell asked. Logan heard spirits. They whispered in her ears, a mishmash of secrets and lies she had to sort through for intel. Those voices had led them here in their search for John. From the smell of it, they were late to the game...

"Nothing useful," she replied.

Logan didn't attempt to keep her voice down, but it didn't matter. The wind didn't carry it far, just enough for him to hear. Otherwise, it would have given her position away to their enemies, and the element knew better than to do that.

His mate's expression was serious, but also a trifle smug, which was her right. She had won their wager. Before they got here, Connell had insisted the latest hint from long-dead things was going to be yet another dead end, and he'd been willing to put his money where his mouth was. Or, rather, his pride. He didn't know exactly what kind of forfeit Logan would demand, but it would be colorful. *And satisfying.*

Connell rarely won their bets, but it didn't matter. After her wicked sense of humor had been assuaged, Logan made losing feel like winning.

"Get your head in the game, wolf-man," Logan murmured. "And stop checking out my ass."

"I wasn't." *This time.* But he had been leaning in that direction, which was unwise given the hint of death on the wind.

The suggestion was faint, but even a trace was enough to make his hackles rise. It didn't smell of decomposition. This was fresh. In his head, his wolf growled—at him. It was a reprimand, reminding Connell to protect his mate. Even if she didn't need it most of the time.

Logan was still fixated on the ground, where the spoor of some spell had fallen. She stood, lifting stained fingers. "It's shifter blood. Wolves."

He scowled, scanning the woods as he examined the panoply of scents again.

"Are you sure?" he asked, his words a whisper. The wind wasn't always so sanguine about not carrying *his* voice. "I'm not getting anything like that. Nothing recent anyway."

"The magic is overpowering it, but I can separate them. Just takes a little molecule maneuvering." She straightened the fine features of her face, setting it in grim lines. "Whatever spell this is, its covering everything like a blanket over a flame."

So, this *was* related to John. A coven associated with him created a spell that suppressed the vital signs and scents of whoever cast it. Even a werewolf wouldn't have known a practitioner masked by it was in the same room unless they happened to be looking at them. Variations of the spell had proliferated. One even masked the user's aura, which had led to no end of grief in his pack.

He took her finger and brought it to his mouth, taking a tiny lick before she could stop him.

"*Hey*." His mate smacked him with an open palm. "What did I tell you the last time you did that?"

"Something along the lines of 'don't ever do that again'."

Logan tapped her steel-toed boot on the ground. "*Because*?" she growled, elongating the word into three syllables. Lengthening words was a new habit of hers, one she indulged in when he was driving her up the wall.

"Because the black magic might infect me," he finished with a shrug.

When Logan threw up her hands, he patted her on the back. "Babe, you know that's not going to happen from such a small taste. I'm an alpha werewolf who happens to be mated to an Elemental. No trace of a spell, no matter how evil, is going to overcome that. But now I can smell the wolves under the spell. The poor bastards can't hide now."

His mate's narrow-eyed glare alone would have felled a lesser wolf, but she knew he was right. Connell's innate immunity was bolstered by their bond.

Her nose wrinkled. "It's still gross. Don't even think about kissing me until you brush your teeth."

He snorted, then shifted to four legs. His sense of smell was better in wolf form, and there was a hunt to begin.

The change was faster than normal, another advantage acquired since taking an Elemental mate. Some wolves had a difficult time transitioning form. In his pack, the time it took to shift was roughly correlated with the wolf's position in the hierarchy. Since Connell was second only to his father, that meant he was accustomed to a fairly quick shift. However, since he'd hooked up with Logan, the change happened between one breath and the next.

As an added bonus, he didn't have strip anymore. Logan simply magicked his clothes away. And unless he truly annoyed her, she magicked them right back when he reclaimed his human shape...usually.

When he was done changing, he shook himself, taking a second to make sure his brain caught up with his four-footed form. Glancing up a Logan, he gave her a wolfish grin. She tsked, waving him on.

His mate kept her legs, keeping pace with him as he loped along, his nose to the ground. Unwilling to risk losing the scent, he kept his pace measured and even. Despite what he'd told Logan, the trace was faint, hints of it playing hide-and-seek in the cold moonlight.

The night creatures didn't react as they passed. Before he met Logan, that would have been unheard of. Rabbits and deer recognized him as a predator. It was instinct, but not one a werewolf minded. Giving chase was half the fun.

Now he could float right past a doe and her young without either batting an eyelash. It made grabbing a midnight snack a lot easier, but also a little boring, too. Fortunately, his instinct for the hunt was more than satisfied by nights like these.

Logan held up a hand, pausing mid-step. She signaled with two fingers, telling him to follow her as she broke left. Silently, they topped a rise, shielded by a clump of bushes as they peered down at a clearing. Two people, a man and teenage girl, stood close together in a shaft of moonlight.

The girl was little more than a child. Her tears shimmered, dripping down her chin, but she was barely making a sound despite the deep shudder that ran through her tiny body.

Connell's attention turned to the man, her brother judging by the resemblance. There was something off with the way they just stood there. Why weren't they moving? Their relative stillness was unnatural, especially given the cold. Both were coatless. The threat of hypothermia should have kept them moving.

His lupine eyes studied the young man's averted head. The tendons of his neck stuck out in stark relief. *They're bespelled.*

That was why they were frozen in place. Nudging Logan, he tried to call her attention to the man's neck, but Logan was way ahead of him. She'd found the source of the dark magic.

Connell almost missed the witch in the shadows. Swiveling his head, he followed Logan's line of sight, belatedly spotting the creature who had her arms out, pulling at nothing as if she were drawing in an imaginary net.

The witch's sinister whisper rose and fell with the breeze, barely audible despite his superior hearing. Logan reached down, and he stifled a whine of surprise that would have given away their position.

A shimmering net of gooey-looking black threads covered the man and his sister. A curse held them prisoner, sapping their strength. The male fought it with all he was worth, but the girl was almost spent. The only thing holding her up was the last shreds of her brother's will.

Anger exploded inside him. Logan's touch on his head firmed, holding him back when he would have leapt down, teeth bared.

"Allow me," she said. Her tone was clipped, almost formal. Yeah, she was pissed.

Her next move was a blur. Connell saw the silver flash of her sword, but only for a second before he ran full tilt down the hill, snarling.

He didn't know what Logan was doing, but the threaded net of the curse was glowing now, the bright orange of heated coals, as if it were fighting back. But it was no match for his mate's determination. The net flew off the huddled pair, releasing them. It blasted backward, covering the witch in her own curse.

The creature didn't have time to react before he barreled into her, knocking her to the ground. Out of the corner of his eye, he saw two bodies fall. The brother and sister hit the soil with twin cries, but he didn't glance in their direction. Leaping off the witch, Connell rounded on her.

The creature stank of blood and dead raccoon, the animal she'd killed to curse the shifters. Black magic required sacrifice. The strongest spells needed death to power them.

Connell dropped back with a snap of his jaws before the witch could get to her feet, blocking her with bared teeth from advancing. He could feel his mate at his back, wondering for a second why she didn't come forward to take the bitch's head off. That was when he scented the second witch—a male this time.

Damn spell, he thought, following it with a monologue of swear words Logan would smack him for saying aloud.

"Get them out of here," Logan called, drawing his attention back to the boy and girl.

He didn't need her to tell him twice. As satisfying as eviscerating a couple of black witches would be, saving the innocents came first.

Connell's paws dug into the dirt for traction, letting him twist his body to shoot in the opposite direction. He pounded after the two wolves, who'd managed to get to the edge of the clearing despite their weakened states. But they wouldn't get farther without help.

The girl fell on her knees at the edge of the clearing. Connell chuffed approvingly as the brother took her in his arms, lifting her before trying to make a break for it, but the kid stumbled as he reached their side, the second witch hot on their trail.

Connell thought about shifting to human form, but his teeth made better weapons than any sword at the Elemental safehouse. He snapped and feinted forward, distracting the second witch as Logan's sword sang. There was a thump right before a head rolled by.

That was around the time the second witch realized he was screwed. The man had been raising his arm, a spell vial in his hand, when his partner's dismembered head smacked into his shoe. Screaming, he checked his motion, dropping the vial and running away like a little bitch.

Connell was on him before he reached the trees. A quick snap of his wolf's jaws severed the witch's jugular, and it was over.

Shifting back to human, he rolled his shoulders as the tendons slid into place over his wide frame. He spit out the taste of black witch, wiping his mouth with a scowl.

"Damn, they taste like shit," he muttered to no one in particular.

He was trotting back to the strange wolves when he realized his family jewels were swinging in the breeze. That and the wind was blowing hard now. "Um... babe?"

Logan was busy searching the witch's corpse. She turned out the pockets, her hands working quickly.

Finally, she lifted her head and blinked, absently wiping her hands on the witch's pants.

His grin was slow and easy when Logan's eyes grew slightly glazed. They ran over his muscled form as if she just couldn't help herself. His mouth went dry when her gaze lingered on his ten-pack, but the sound of someone else's stomach growling disrupted his increasingly dirty train of thought.

Pointedly clearing his throat, he gestured to his naked body, then to the huddled pair of skinny wolves. Belatedly, his clothes reappeared. He scanned the woods, wondering if there were a third witch.

"There aren't anymore," Logan said, reading his mind. "I would feel the gap created by their bodies."

When she gestured, he realized she meant the wind. Logan was employing it to do a bit of reconnaissance, using it to measure the negative space around them. How had she separated a body from a tree that way?

The shape, of course.

"Cool." He hadn't known she could do that, but it didn't surprise him. Nothing his mate did shocked him much anymore.

He turned to the battered wolves at the edge of the clearing, hailing them with a big 'hello,' but the sound of his baritone made them shrink in on themselves.

The shivering girl burrowed deeper into her brother's arms. The boy—young man—kept his eyes down, instinctively acknowledging Connell's dominance as an alpha male. Except having these kids too scared to look at him wasn't going to get them anywhere.

"He's not going to bite. I promise," Logan said.

The shivering wolves continued to stare at him as if he were licking his chops. That reminded him...

"I'm starving," he announced, pitching his tone to a higher and hopefully more friendly register. "Who wants a burger?"

16

The fluorescent lights at the rear of the diner flickered like a strobe light. Logan knew it was driving her man bonkers, so she pushed a sharp gust in the general direction of the fixture, knocking it hard enough for the long bulb to fall out of the socket. Next to her, Connell relaxed, taking a huge bite of his second triple-decker burger. The young werewolves were working on their first with slow, careful bites—the kind taken after not having eaten in a while, so the stomach couldn't take more than a bit at a time.

Since Connell's mouth was full, she decided to take the lead. "You guys are Russian, right?" she asked.

The hungry pair stopped chewing, exchanging worried looks. Connell glanced at her, raising a brow at their obvious reticence. Scent wasn't her thing, but the kids' sudden fear and desperation were more pronounced now.

On closer inspection, they were even younger than she'd initially thought. The girl was around thirteen, maybe fourteen. Her brother was only a few years older. She'd be surprised if he were over eighteen.

They're still babies. Sure, wolves were equipped to be on their own at much younger ages than most Supes, but these kids seemed too young to be running around on their own without a pack.

"I heard you call her *sestrichka*. That's Russian for little sister. So where are you two from?" Logan punctuated her question with a big bite of her own burger. It was pretty damn good, but she was always hungry after a fight, so anything that took the edge off was going to hit the spot.

The older boy took a deep breath. "My name is Ravil. This is my sister, Sabina. We are from Georgia."

It was a lie, but so well done she couldn't call them on it. Connell, however, smirked with patent disbelief. "Where'd you boost that SUV?"

The kids had been driving a cherry-red Range Rover, last year's model. They'd abandoned it at the edge of the woods when it ran out of gas.

Given their obvious hunger and the shabby state of their clothing, there was little chance the vehicle belonged to them. For now, they had parked it up the street, since Logan couldn't whisk the entire group through the air currents.

"We borrowed it." Ravil's voice was firm, but his pulse flickering at his neck visibly sped up.

Logan decided to let it go, nudging her mate in the ribs when he opened his mouth for what would no doubt be another sardonic remark.

"How did the witches get you?" she asked.

It took Connell and Logan a lot longer to get the answer to that one, mainly because the kids weren't sure when the witches had targeted them. A few days ago, from what it sounded like. And it was becoming increasingly clear they'd been on the run even before then.

After their garbled explanations, Connell coughed, softening his expression. "You've entered the northern edge of the American coalition—that's what we call the loose confederation of *Were* packs in North America. I'm from the Colorado Basin. My dad is the chief. His name is Douglas Maitland. I'm Connell. You've met my mate here, Logan..."

She touched his thigh under the table, squeezing it until he trailed off. It was better if these kids didn't know exactly what she was. They were squirrelly enough. Adding a Supe's innate fear of her kind wasn't going to help anything.

The kids' sudden stillness told her that they had recognized the Maitland name. And they would. Her mate's father and grandfather were legendary among their kind. Hell, even Connell's name was probably known to them.

When they didn't say anything, Connell raised a brow. She shrugged, but pinched him under the table.

He cleared his throat. "I know things are pretty different in the Russian—excuse me—Georgian packs. But here, we follow a certain protocol. We always let the local alpha know when we're entering his territory. The alpha in this area is Rafe Hawkins. His territory is pretty big, but the pack is small, just twenty or so wolves. None your age, really. And my da has rules about underage wolves." He paused to demolish the rest of his burger.

"Rules like what?" It was the first time the girl—Sabina—had spoken. She sounded even younger than she looked. Her voice trembled slightly, but she sounded curious.

Connell shrugged. "If you stay in the territory of North America, you have to go to school. Not college, of course. Not if you don't want to, although that would be the chief's preference. Regardless, even if school is not your thing, you still have to graduate from high school or get your GED. Maybe vocational school after that—basically, you have to have a plan on how you're going to make a living. The pack will help with cash and a place to crash if you need it while this is going on. Of course, all that depends on whether you're planning to stay under the Maitland purview. No one is going to make you if you'd rather move on."

He picked up a French fry, dipping it in a truly excessive amount of ketchup. "Now, Rafe is a reasonably decent guy, although he acts like he has a stick up his butt most of the time. But the wolves under his protection don't have many complaints. He's a hard man, but fair. You're welcome to stay and appeal to him, ask to join his pack. But I can tell you right now that you'd be better off heading south to my da."

He leaned back in the booth, throwing a casual arm over Logan's shoulders. "It's a bigger pack. That means more wolves your age. We're not hurting for cash, so you will have time to figure out your situation and get back on your feet."

"More wolves also means more people watching out for you," Logan added softly.

"Not all packs are like that," Ravil muttered.

There was a dictionary's worth of history in those words. Unfortunately, they didn't have time to wheedle out the kid's life story. Douglas would take charge. She trusted Connell's father to do right by them.

Logan stole one of Connell's fries, then popped it into her mouth. "The Maitland pack is different," she said, infusing her words with truth. Wolves could smell a lie. "You're going to be fine there."

Ravil's lips parted, but Sabina put her hand over her brother's. They regarded each other for a moment, having a long conversation without words.

Logan watched the interplay, specifically the way Sabina squeezed her brother's fingers until they blanched white despite her superficial fragility. *Now there is a kid who wants to stop running.*

An hour and two cheeseburgers later, the young wolves were ready to head to Colorado. Logan exited the diner, sniffing the night air as Connell pressed a wad of cash into Ravil's hand.

"Get another car with this. There's a used car lot a couple of blocks south of here."

"No one will miss the Range Rover for a few more days," Ravil replied, dropping the pretense he'd borrowed the vehicle.

"Maybe, but we don't know if the two witches in the woods were all there were or if they're part of a larger coven, so you should dump that car and get your ass to Colorado as fast as you can. Drive in shifts if you have to."

The wolves didn't need to be told twice. Ravil pocketed the cash and hustled Sabina away, heading in the direction of the car rental lot.

Connell waited until they were out of sight. "All right, what was it?"

"What was what?" she asked innocently.

"I want to see whatever it was you took off the witch's body."

Sighing, Logan fished the small totem out of her pocket. It was a ghastly little thing. Connell took it, then sniffed. His expression darkened, and he swore explosively.

"I guess those two had a lucky escape," he said from behind gritted teeth.

"Yes," she murmured, taking the totem made of the entwined hair, bone, and fur of a werewolf. "We'll burn it. That'll release whatever tainted magic it holds."

He shifted away, taking a moment to compose himself before turning back to her. "This is related to John, right? These witches were more of his acolytes."

She paused, listening to the whispers on the wind for confirmation. "I'm ninety-five percent sure they are. But they were prepared to kill themselves rather than talk. In this case, they chose death by werewolf."

"*Fuck*," he swore. "How many more of these assholes are we going to trip over before we find the man himself?"

Logan rolled the totem between her finger, feeling the faint lines between her brows deepen. "I don't know. A lot, I think."

17

Salvador twisted as Alec emerged from the jungle in a blur.

"I have to go," he called, whipping to his makeshift workstation on the wooden picnic table. He began sorting and packing with blink-of-the-eye rapid movements.

"Where's the fire?" Salvador asked, snorting at his own joke.

"What?" Alec blinked, pausing to stare with the unnerving stillness peculiar to his kind.

"Nothing, never mind," he said. "Did your talk go well?"

Salvador didn't want to admit it, but he was eaten up with curiosity. What did Alec have to talk to Gia about that he couldn't ask his mate?

"It was...fine." The vampire's attention had wandered back to his bags. He pointed to a stack of texts at the end of the table.

"I'm going to leave these medicinal plant books here for now," Alec offered. "One of the T'Kaierian archivists will be by to pick them up in a day or so. I'm afraid you won't be able to duplicate them—they're spell-proofed to prevent that, but you can take as many notes as possible between now and then. If you want, I can teach you a spell that will help you transcribe faster."

"Oh, I'm good," Salvador said, caught up in Alec's haste. The vampire's urgency was infectious. "I know that spell, or one like it."

That probably didn't trump the vampire's photographic memory, but Salvador's normal human memory was boosted by specific charms of his own design. The time and ingredients were costly, but he didn't skimp when it came to his healing practice.

"Are you staying for dinner?" Or would he and Gia be dining alone?

His friend murmured something Salvador didn't understand as he whipped out his phone and speed-typed a message.

"You must be anxious to get back to your mate," Salvador said, stating the obvious. "But if anyone has a built-in defense to that poison, it's Diana. All she has to do is set herself on fire before contact, and the chemicals would evaporate and break down."

Alec actually lifted his head this time. "That's a good point, but it's not our chief concern anymore. Gia thinks her attack was just the warm-up. John is after bigger fish."

"Bigger than the Elementals? But that only leaves—" He broke off, scowling. "Wait... He's not that crazy, is he?"

"Apparently, he is." Alec shrugged, a tiny tremor betraying his disquiet. "Don't worry. I can't think of any way for him to administer his slurry of toxins to Her. I mean, how would you even get to Mother Nature?"

"I'm sure I don't know," Salvador said weakly. He staggered over the picnic table, then collapsed with a thump.

"Well, even if he can't accomplish his main goal, he can still do a lot of damage to our world. But then again, I never underestimate human stupidity."

Salvador hummed, nodding his agreement. He was glad Alec's mind was elsewhere, or the vampire would have noticed his sudden tension.

Alec continued to talk, ranting about mad alchemists as he prepared his departure. Salvador only listened with half his attention. His stomach roiled. *Aw hell, I'm going to have to talk to Gia about this, aren't I?*

"Where is the Earth Elemental?" He'd expected Gia to follow Alec out of the jungle. Had she left?

A pang of something unpleasant coursed through him, but he stifled it. Gia had seemed content to break bread with him. They had been to hell together. At the very least he'd thought she would say goodbye.

"She's still by the stream," Alec answered eventually, looking around to take stock of his progress. "There's a little ritual to accelerate the healing process. Gia said to go ahead and eat without her. I'm sure she'll be along shortly."

Salvador picked up a scroll the vampire had overlooked, then handed it to him. "Good...I would tell you to give my regards to your girlfriend, but she scares me and I'd rather she forgot I exist."

Alec nodded as if this were sensible. "Not an uncommon reaction. Get in touch if there's a problem with your payment."

He was gone before Salvador could ask if he could collect a favor from the Elementals instead.

Well, that plan was out the window. After learning the alchemist's true intentions, the best he could do was ask Gia to spare his life. Once she found out about Ciro's pilgrimage to the Mother, she was going to want to kill him.

SALVADOR TRIED to be patient and wait for Gia at his cottage, but his curiosity got the better of him and he went looking for her.

A mysterious Elemental healing ritual? How could the *curandero* —the healer—in him resist?

Also, if she got mad at him for spying, at least she wasn't at full strength yet. The chances of her hitting him with a huge boulder or dropping him in a vat of quicksand was low.

He found her in a small clearing a stone's throw from the clear mineral stream that was his main source of water.

He had no idea where she found the clothes she wore. Her old clothing had been damaged and stained, so her sisters had changed her into one of the hospital gowns he kept for patients when she was still unconscious. When they'd woken after Sheol, she had still been wearing one, but now her outfit was leather, all black. It more closely resembled the clothing her sisters had been wearing than the buckskin-colored pants and maroon leather top she'd arrived in. But her ensemble wasn't the most startling thing about her at this moment.

Gia sat cross-legged on the ground, her hands up, middle finger and thumb touching in a classic meditation pose. All around her, the ground rippled as if she were sitting on the surface of a windy pond instead on solid ground.

The reaction of the local flora was almost as unnerving. Fresh green shoots and runners snaked out of the undergrowth, creating a circle around Gia. There were even some tree roots mixed into the bunch. As he watched some ran up her body, touching her almost reverently.

His mouth dropped open. Salvador had never seen plants grow that fast. And the energy coming from them was palpable.

Were they feeding her? Shit. They were. Mother Earth was using the jungle plants to restore her chosen one to battle-ready form.

Salvador knew he would never see the jungle in the same way again. He'd lived in Costa Rica for years. The growth and decay rates of the local flora and fauna were spectacular. It was a fact he'd noted and was comfortable with. But before now, he hadn't realized the jungle could be both alive and *aware*. It suddenly felt as if every tree and shrub had grown eyes.

Shake it off, idiot. You have a very uncomfortable conversation to get over with. However, he should probably start it later—after Gia was done getting pumped up by the greenery.

A surreptitious retreat was easier said than done. He stepped on a dry leaf. The resulting crackle wasn't loud, but Gia's lids flew open, her amber-colored eyes pinning him to the spot.

"Hey," he said, holding up the plate he'd brought as an excuse. "I, um, made a few *chile rellenos* to go with the stew. I figured after not eating for so long you could do with a feast, but I don't want to disturb your ritual..."

As he continued to stare, one of the runners near her shoulder popped up and twirled toward the sound of his voice. When Gia cocked her head, the runner followed suit as if it, too, were studying him.

Okay, that isn't at all creepy, he thought, lying to himself.

Gia rose in a single fluid motion. It was smoother than her first halting steps after her coma. God, had that only been a few hours ago? Her recovery time was off the charts.

"It's no trouble. I can continue later," she said as the tree roots and runners retreated.

For a minute, he just stood there. Despite the time they'd spent together in Sheol, having her attention fixed on him now made his mind stutter and nearly stop. Damn, she was beautiful. Somehow having her here, interacting with him in his insignificant corner of the jungle, made her more real than before.

"It's no trouble," he said when he remembered how to speak. He lowered the plate a fraction. "I can heat them up for you later if you'd like. I don't want to disturb your meditation. It's, ah, a very healing practice."

Wow, that was lame. Salvador was typically a confident man. He didn't understand why he felt so awkward. He was never like this with his other patients...

Well, they hadn't had Gia's amber gaze, the one that melted his insides into a useless pile of goo.

"They're better fresh," she said.

"What?" He blinked, caught off guard.

"The *chile rellenos*. In my experience, they don't reheat well."

She sauntered past him with a hint of a smile. If he didn't know any better, she almost seemed to be enjoying his discomfort.

Great. Gia the Elemental, sworn enemy of my family, knows I have a crush on her. Perfect... just perfect.

He trailed her to his cottage, then served their meal.

Salvador decided being self-conscious was a waste of time. An Elemental realizing he had a crush on her was hardly the most embarrassing thing that had ever happened to him. True, he couldn't quite think of anything worse, but he would. He had faith it would come to him.

Gia didn't ask him what he was laughing about when he took the seat across from her. She just seemed to accept his strange behavior as par for the course. And why wouldn't she? To her, he was just another Delavordo. *And that reminds me...*

He waited until she had finished the meal he'd prepared before broaching the sensitive topic.

"Alec left some wine," he offered, holding up a Bordeaux that probably cost more than his healing practice made in a decade.

She held up a wooden cup, then indicated the pitcher with her other hand. "After Sheol, clean water is the most decadent thing we can possibly drink."

"I suppose that's true." He put the bottle down with some regret. Alcohol might have helped, but could an Elemental even get drunk?

Gia set her cup on the table. "What's wrong?"

Damn. Where did he start?

"Actually... a lot." Salvador rubbed his temple before forcing his hands flat on the wood's surface. "Alec told me more details about your attacker and his plans for the Mother."

"Attempts like this have been made before, but you don't need to concern yourself," Gia assured him. "We will find him."

"I have no doubt of that," he said, truly meaning it. "But it's one of those previous attempts I need to speak to you about."

"I already know about Thiago and his plans for world domination."

The words were tinged with humor that didn't match the events she referred to. But he appreciated her attempt to lighten the mood. It also reinforced his belief she didn't know Thiago had almost killed him all those years ago. His parents had hushed that up rather well.

"I, um, was actually referring to Ciro's staff...and how he used it to reach the Mother."

Astonishment widened the Earth Elemental's eyes. Then her lovely face hardened. "Ciro did *what*?"

18

———

It could be worse. Gia's expression was cold, but at least she hadn't crushed Salvador with a boulder or sucked him into a makeshift grave.

"Well, it wasn't exactly a staff." Salvador held out his hands as if gripping two imaginary bars. "Have you seen a divining rod—the kind used for water witching?"

"Dowsing," Gia supplied shortly, her normally full lips compressing into a thin line. "Yes, I'm familiar with the method."

Dowsing rods and the practice of water witching were phenomena humans had trouble explaining. Using a forked stick or metal rod, a skilled witcher could find underground water sources with roughly ninety-percent accuracy. In fact, Gia was aware of some who had been right every time.

"Let me guess," Gia said, leaning forward to put an elbow on the table. She was starting to appear weary. "Ciro used his special divining rod to find weak spots in Earth's surface in his attempt to get to the Mother."

Wincing, he corrected, "His *successful* attempt."

Gia held her hand up, closing and opening her eyes in an exaggerated fashion. "Debatable."

Uncomfortably, he shifted while she continued to visually dissect him. "The event was well before my time, of course, but it's family lore."

"Ciro was never on our radar."

Salvador cleared his throat. "Yes, well, he died young. Personally, I believed his absence was the reason Thiago turned out the way he did. Ciro was his father, but I probably don't need to tell you that."

"Your family tree is required study for new Elementals," Gia acknowledged.

Of course... He continued. "According to my grandmother, Ciro was a savant, a genius when it came to spellcraft, but he was socially inept and awkward. He used to put deodorant on the outside of his clothes because he never bothered to learn where it was supposed to go. His mind was completely consumed with magic and methodology."

Gia raised a brow at that, but she didn't comment.

"Anyway, he crafted a few objects with magical properties, charms, and other stuff."

She nodded. "The broom."

"*Oh.* You know about that."

Ciro had somehow managed to imbue a wooden broom with the ability to fly. In itself, that wasn't unusual—most kids under the age of ten tried to make a broom fly at one point or another. It was a sort of a rite for members of the Seven families. But the best most could do was levitate for a few minutes. Ciro's, however, could actually bear a person's weight and hadn't run out of steam—literally, because he'd added that as an effect—since it had been made, roughly sixty or so years ago.

"I also remember when your cousin took the broom joyriding one Halloween."

Smugly, Salvador smirked. Risking exposure was a violation of the Covenant. "Analia was grounded for the rest of the year."

"I bet. So, why do you think Ciro's divining rod worked?" she asked, picking up another piece of fry bread.

"He said it did."

Her other eyebrow reached for the sky.

"He wasn't trying to end the world or anything like that," he qualified. "According to family legend, Ciro simply wanted an audience with the Mother. I think he meant to ask for a boon of some kind, maybe more magic—I'm not really sure. It might have just been a challenge he wanted to overcome. He was that kind of practitioner. If it had never been done, then he would try it, regardless of the risk. He *needed* to know what would happen."

Gia's sigh was long. "I'm familiar with the type. How did the divining rod work?"

"According to legend, it found soft spots in Earth's crust, the ones that led to passages your kind used to utilize to commune with Her."

The existence of those mythical tunnels wasn't a secret precisely —more like a myth no one believed in anymore. Except for Ciro, of course.

There was a lengthy silence.

"I take it you're not going to confirm those exist," he muttered.

Gia's impossibly thick lashes briefly screened her eyes. "They used to—once upon a time. The Mother sealed them up over a millennia ago."

Damn, this was excruciating. "Err. Yes, well, Ciro's hypothesis was that She had overlooked a few. He believed a skilled practitioner with the right tools could find such a passage."

"And he settled on a divining rod to help him find one?"

He nodded. "Dowsing is where he got the inspiration. Something similar works for leylines, so I guess he figured it would do the job. It took him over a year to come up with a prototype he was satisfied with. One day, he took it out to test it. He came back weeks later claiming he'd been successful—to an extent. He said he'd reached Her, but she'd paid him no mind. He tried to get her attention with a demonstration of his magic, but Ciro couldn't explain what happened next. One minute, he'd been there with Her. The next, he'd been topside, lying in the middle of a clearing somewhere in the American Midwest without any knowledge of how he got there. He'd lost over a week of time... Although, honestly, that part wasn't unusual for him. Ciro hadn't been a linear thinker, and it spilled over into every aspect of his life."

She ignored the last part. "What proof did he have that he reached Her?"

It was only natural Gia would be skeptical. "None, really. Just his word. But my grandmother swore it was true. Ciro wasn't the kind to lie or exaggerate. Deception was beyond him. His mind just didn't work that way. If he'd been born later, I think he would have been diagnosed as neuroatypical."

Salvador broke off and reached for the water, suddenly parched. "Ciro returned to the family seat after his attempt—the house where my parents now live. He needed more supplies as he'd decided to craft a second more potent divining rod. He'd left the original prototype behind when he went back out to try again. No one ever saw him after that."

"Did anyone try to use the prototype after he disappeared?" she asked.

"My grandmother did, but she used it to search for Ciro, not the Mother. However, he had disappeared from the face of the earth. Truthfully, Ciro's wife didn't mind much. She was a Patel by birth, and it was an arranged match. She remarried into the Burgess clan a couple of years later."

And she hadn't looked back—not even to periodically check on the child she'd left behind. Despite his tender years, Thiago had stayed with his grandmother. Any children from a Delavordo union always stayed within the family. That was what marriage was like in the Seven families.

Gia crossed her arms. "Is there any chance your grandmother fabricated the story for Thiago's sake?"

The unexpected question made him snort with laughter. "Did you ever meet my grandmother?"

Another flicker of her lashes. "Once or twice."

"And did she strike you as the kind of woman who would make up stories to spare someone's feelings—even a child?"

Gia tsked. "Okay, you have a point. What about the divining rod?

Who has it now?"

"It should be in the family vault. Anything Ciro made and left behind is in there, with the possible exception of the broom."

Her nose wrinkled. "Your parents keep that vault locked down tight. It would be a suicide mission for a rogue practitioner to break in it. There is, however, the possibility they could simply hand it over to a collaborator."

He wanted to laugh. "*No*. My father doesn't do alliances. Even if a skilled practitioner approached him, he would never deign to work with an outsider. I doubt he'd even give him an audience."

Gia considered this. "That may well be true, but the vault is open to members of your family, isn't it?"

He shook his head. "Not without my father's leave, or at least that was how it worked when I left."

She drummed her fingers on the table. "You have many cousins who can gain access to the vault on another pretext."

"I do have many stupid relatives," he acknowledged.

Gia slapped her hands on the wooden surface, pushing up. She began to pace behind the bench. "John specializes in finding people —young and old—who are unsatisfied with their lot in life. He feeds their discontent, weaponizing it so they cause the most amount of damage. In that way, John is quite masterful."

Praise coming from an Elemental about how evil someone was, and, in a cosmic twist, it was not a member of his family. *This does not bode well for the fate of the world.*

Damn, he did not want to do this, but what choice did he have?

"Look," he began. "I haven't spoken to my parents in years. For this, though, I can get in touch with them. At the very least, I can make sure the divining rod is still in the vault."

The corner of Gia's mouth turned up. "I'm afraid you will have to do much more than that."

A sinking feeling started in the pit of his stomach. "What did you have in mind?"

Her smile grew devious. "I think it's time you took me home to meet your parents."

19

———

Alec hurried through the sodden city streets, the yellow light of the streetlamp reflecting in the puddles. He was glad it wasn't raining, not because he felt the cold, but because his mate was out there somewhere.

Technically, Diana didn't feel the cold any more than he did. Sometimes, though, the rain steamed off her innate heat. It wasn't enough to obscure her vision, but he didn't like the idea of her having any handicaps when she fought.

She'll be fine. She always was.

Alec had no shame in admitting Diana was the superior fighter. During one particularly heated battle, he'd actually *hidden* behind her. Well, he was a bit embarrassed about that, but he'd been holding a precious one-of-a-kind Shakespearean folio when they'd gotten ambushed. Letting it get damaged would have been a travesty of biblical proportions. His mate understood that, and she only teased him about it occasionally.

A cold blast of wind flattened his hair. It smelled of more rain. He hurried his steps, his mating bond pointing the way.

Something slithered out from behind a dumpster. He stopped, sensing something Otherkind. The creature finally slid into view.

A furry little Fae, some kind of subspecies of brownie, grinned at him with its razor-sharp teeth before skittering past.

Briefly, he considered following it. Those particular creatures were sometimes taken in by hapless humans who thought they were cats. Brownies loved to mess with humans. For the most part, they enjoyed living like domesticated animals...until they subtly took over their human's lives. Entire families were bamboozled. He'd heard plenty of stories, but none of the vicious little Turks had been known to harm human children, so Alec gave them a pass. Besides, Diana was expecting him.

Alec continued, streaking through the wet city streets as fast as he could when unobserved. When the water from an awning dripped a particularly fat stream of water down his collar, he took out his phone, texting his car service to meet them at the edge of the park. That was where his mating sense told him he would find Diana.

He hadn't expected the park to have a fence. However, the edge bordered a small ravine. The leap from the bottom to the top of the fence was around fifteen feet, but he made the jump with only a single step in between for leverage. He cleared the bushes on the other side by a few inches.

Thankfully, due to the weather and the time of night, there was no one to witness his superhuman feat.

The action was in the northern edge of the park in a wide, tree-bordered clearing and the hedge that marked the boundary on this side.

Alec ran, wondering why the hell he could only hear one heart-beat, yet make out many pairs of feet. *Fuck.* Diana was surrounded... and her adversaries were vampires. And that wasn't the worst part. Although they all appeared to be different ages and nationalities, they were all roughly the same age—newborns hot off their tran-sitions.

A chill ran through him. Even for the magically endowed, becoming a vampire was an arduous process. Normal humans had no way to sustain the change. Most died in the attempt. Only a few had enough of a predisposition to the supernatural to survive the attempt.

Six... seven... eight. To have this many survivors pointed to an exponential body count. And these left were too thin, literally half-starved despite their fine clothes.

Eight was too many mouths to feed, even for his coven. It wasn't impossible, but it required double or triple that number of vampires to act as guardians—to keep the newborn under control —and *many* more willing blood donors. *Or slightly fewer unwilling ones.*

Like a rabid pack of wild dogs, the vampires surrounded his mate, making a wide circle around her. Slipping off his coat, Alec rested it on a nearby bench—no sense in ruining his new Stefano Ricci— ready to charge if Diana needed him. She rarely did. But he always got ready, just in case.

However, it appeared as if tonight might be the night. The circle of hungry vampires silently closed in on his mate.

Trained. They had been trained. Most newborns didn't have the wherewithal or control to accomplish that. *Damn. She has to kill them all.*

So many newly turned vamps with training spelled big trouble. He had hoped... but no. They couldn't afford to spare any. Without resentment, Alec accepted their fate.

The leader's voice was raspy, but he could still make out what she said.

"We are going to kill you, witch."

Well, if that was what they thought his mate was, the poor bastards didn't stand a chance.

Diana ignited her hands, startling the underlings. The leader didn't panic until his mate clapped her hands behind her, then clasped them in front, forming a sustained ring of fire.

Di raised her hands, pushing her palms out. The move sent the flames hurtling forward—a full three-hundred-and-sixty degrees of fiery death.

Only two or three of the newborns managed to escape the blast. The slow ones tried to scramble out of the path, but the fire caught them anyway—stray sparks catching and igniting their clothes. The flames spread like hellfire, burning their adversaries to dust as he watched.

This part was easier when it wasn't other vamps.

Dian's sword flashed as a survivor launched himself at her. The big motherfucker was fast, but his mate bent backward in a Matrix-worthy movement. She braced her weight on her hands, using her feet and his own momentum to send him flying over her. The heavy asshole crashed next to where Alec waited with a silver knife. It only took a moment to remove the head.

He picked it up, then showed it to his mate.

"You and the heads," Diana groused. She didn't roll her eyes, but she wanted to. He could always tell.

In the meantime, the last vampire had picked up something from the ground. She removed two weapons, one for each hand.

"Is that a super-soaker?" Diana asked incredulously.

"Diana, stay back," Alec yelled. Flashing in front of her at full speed, he threw his arms up in an effort to shield her. A water gun could only mean one thing—it was full of the venom John had created.

"You're one of us," the female snarled, her tone disbelieving.

Alec did a double take. He hadn't looked at this female closely enough on his first assessment. This one wasn't a newborn. He'd put her at nearly twenty years after her turn. And she was strong. Any coven would have been proud to claim her.

"It's too late," Diana murmured. "Her aura is nearly black."

Fuck.

"You actually side with this bitch?" the female spat.

"Were you going to kill her?" he asked, jerking his head in Diana's direction.

"Yes."

"Of course I do, then."

"Fine," the vampire seethed. "You both can die."

She raised the water blasters, intending to soak them with the deadly poison.

Alec went to grab Diana to get her out of the way when he felt her arms move up his side, effectively caging him in place.

The streams flew toward them in slow motion. He opened his mouth to shout a warning for Diana to let him go and run when a wall of flame rose, the brightness so intense it nearly burned out his retinas.

Alec heard a sizzle as he blinked rapidly to restore his sight. When he had, there was nothing left of the black-aura vamp aside from a vaguely human-shaped scorch mark and melted plastic. After another quick blast of flames, even that was gone.

"I'm so glad I got here in time," he breathed, relieved.

When he spun around, his mate wore a sardonic expression. "Really?" she drawled. "Because I would have preferred you show up to get in my way *after* the fight was over."

"Well, you're finished now, right?" he asked with his most winsome smile. "How about dinner? The car should be pulling up right about now. We can be downtown in ten minutes."

His mate wasn't paying attention. "Seven...eight," she counted aloud. "I could have sworn there was one more."

Diana rotated in a circle, her arm bent at the elbow. When she came to a clump of bushes, she pointed her finger like a gun. "Bam."

Belatedly, Alec heard the last vampire in the bush, rustling the leaves. There was a sharp intake of air before it bolted. Alec only caught a glimpse, but it was enough.

"Oh my God," he breathed.

Diana nudged him. Taking off after it, she called, "It's getting away. Hurry up."

"But... Di—"

The small form had disappeared beyond the fence. It had to have somehow managed to wiggle under it through a gap an animal must have made.

In a blink, both the small vampire and his mate were gone. *Damn it*. He pounded after them, running over the fence. This side of the park bordered the bad part of town. The neat and quaint brick buildings almost immediately gave way to industrial concrete and dilapi-dated wooden shacks.

He hadn't even been aware Canada had bad bits like this. In his mind, modern cities here were clean and bright. However, before meeting Diana, he'd never sought the underbelly of any city. His old life had been filled with opulent wealth, five- or six-star hotels, and richly appointed apartments interspersed with some very dusty libraries.

Alec finally caught up with his mate at the edge of a dingy neigh-borhood. She was disappearing into worn three-story apartment building that had seen better days.

"Hey," he whispered when they met in the hallway. Diana had slowed down quite a bit, showing an uncharacteristic amount of caution.

"What's up?" he asked.

"There's a witch in play now."

"What?"

"A witch swept up the vamp in the alley, then brought it here."

"Is it John?" Could this finally be it?

Diana shook her head. "I didn't get a good look, but the body mass is off. This person is too small."

"*Damn.*" Well, that would have been too much to expect—not to mention this place was nowhere near as atmospheric as what their adversary would have chosen for a final confrontation.

"Diana, I have to tell you something about the last vampire."

"I understand." Diana waved dismissively. "Its aura is reasonably clean. We'll spare it if it stands down."

"No, that's not it," he said urgently.

His mate stayed his hand, pressing a finger to her lips to indicate someone was listening.

She started up the rickety flight of stairs that led to the second floor. They moved down the hall past empty rooms. He would have heard the heartbeats behind the doors. The rent had to be dirt cheap, but the fact no one was home at this hour said something about the building's desirability as a residence.

He heard one racing heartbeat behind the last door. Diana stood in front of it, nodding once to indicate the little vamp was in there, too.

"Please wait!"

But Diana had already ignited her hands. One kick, and the door-jamb splintered. The thin particle wood gave way like it was made of paper. She disappeared through the threshold without pause.

"*Damn it.*" Alec bolted after her, trusting his reaction and superior speed—or his mate—would save him if he were rushing into a firefight.

Diana stood in the middle of an empty living room. A beat-up couch and loveseat were crowded into the too-small space. There was no television. A lot of books stacked in crates had been tied together with fishing line to make a bookshelf.

There was also a fair number of vials and spellcraft paraphernalia laid out on the only table, which he guessed wasn't used for eating—not unless the practitioner wanted to poison themselves.

He couldn't hear any heartbeats anymore, so he guessed the witch had activated some sort of masking spell. It wasn't a good one, however. Its energy was leaking all over the place.

Diana narrowed her eyes on the door next to the kitchenette. At her direction, he yanked it open and stood back. A bathroom was revealed, complete with rusted claw-foot tub. Diana extinguished one hand to pull back the shower curtain.

Inside the tub, a young woman huddled over the vampire child.

His mate huffed in surprise, caught off guard.

"Please don't hurt him," the woman pleaded, holding a hand up. She pressed the child's face down with the other. "I'm begging you—it's not his fault. They did this to him."

The witch was quite young, with dark skin and eyes. Her features were Indian, from the subcontinent, but the accent was high-society London—too posh for their surroundings.

Diana's head drew back, her nose twitching as she studied the vampire child. It stank. The stench wasn't eye-wateringly bad, but it was close.

The boy's face was pressed into the witch's side as they huddled together, but there was no scent of blood, so at least it wasn't biting her.

"How old is it?" Diana asked, assessing the child.

"*Jason,*" the woman hurried to correct. "His name is Jason. He's only seven."

The witch enunciated every word as if she were talking to a kidnapper. *Always humanize the victim…*

"And you weren't a part of…" Diana wiggled her fireless fingers in the directions of the park.

"No! I would never do something like this."

The witch had tears in her eyes now. They appeared genuine. Di must have thought so, too, because she let the other hand's flames go out.

"He didn't ask for it." The witch still shook her head.

"At seven, I doubt anyone would. Immortality in a child's body would suck… Literally, in this case." Diana snorted.

Alec winced. Under the circumstances, the joke was in poor taste.

"So, do you know what happened?" he asked.

Still trembling, the woman shrugged helplessly. "It started a few weeks ago. People began disappearing. Sometimes, the bodies would turn up. At first, I didn't realize what was going on. I thought it was some sort of crime spree. But then Jason disappeared."

"Is he your son?" Diana asked.

"*No.* He lives down the hall. His mother—she's a drunk. I don't think she's even noticed he's missing."

His mate crossed her arms. "But you did."

The woman nodded. "I, um, I don't have family here in the city. He comes over here to eat when his mother forgets to buy groceries."

Fuck. The gut punches wouldn't stop coming. The witch obviously loved the child. And he was going to have to kill it. And her… if she got in his way.

He rested his hand on his mate's arm. "Diana, go outside."

His mate scowled. "Why?"

He tugged her around to face him. "I don't want you to watch."

Inside the tub, the witch whimpered.

"What in the hell are you talking about?"

"Turning children is against the Covenant."

"I'm aware." Diana sniffed. She was, after all, the expert in the room.

"In theory, turning a child isn't possible. However, if one does survive, they have to be destroyed. They simply can't control themselves. So, please, go outside—this is not something you should ever have to see or do. Not in your condition."

Diana's frown deepened as the child burrowed closer to the witch. The realization it could understand him only made this worse. But once it got hungry, that would change. All reason and vestige of humanity would vaporize in the heat of its hunger.

His mate smacked him again, hard enough to hurt. "He can hear you."

"Di—" he began.

His mate ignored him. "Can you stand him up, please?" she asked the witch.

"Please don't!" The witch sobbed freely now.

"He'll be fine." Diana waved dismissively. "It's just going to get a little hot in here. And you shouldn't be touching him if you know what's good for you."

The witch made a visible effort to get ahold of herself. "All r-right. I've heard of you. You're supposed to be fair."

Nudging the boy, she urged him into an upright position, keeping hold of his hand. "It's going to be okay, Jason," she told him. Then she let go, huddling into a ball at the far end of the tub.

Diana rolled her eyes. "*Farther.*"

Reluctantly, the witch got out of the bathtub. The little boy hissed in reaction, showing his tiny fangs.

Alec hard to force himself to keep watching. The vampire child was a crime against nature.

Diana put her hands on the boy's shoulders. A nearly imperceptible lick of flame ran down from each of her hands. They swept down his body, burning his clothes—his hair, as well—away.

And just like that, it was over.

Thoughtfully, Diana regarded the boy. He watched her back, eyes glazed and jaw slack.

Join the club, kid.

"You're going to look weird for a little while, but the eyebrows and head hair will grow back. The body hair might not, but consider that a plus. Just tell your future girlfriends you're really into manscaping." Diana shrugged. "Or boyfriends. Whatever. I don't judge."

At that, she pressed her thumb to Jason's forehead. Immediately unconscious, he slumped over.

She caught the boy before he hit his head on the ceramic. Picking him up, she handed the sleeping child to the witch, who hurried to cover him with a towel.

"You stripped him," Alec said, dumbfounded. Intellectually, he had always known Diana had the capability to remove magic, including vampirism. It was one of the major weapons in the Elemental arsenal. In spite of this, his mate hadn't stripped anyone since they'd met. Most of her cases had strictly been the kill-the-bad-guys variety. The rest had been the equivalent of a supernatural cleaner mopping up the various messes Supes got themselves into.

"I suppose this falls into that category," he muttered. The child was human again. There wasn't a whiff of magic anywhere. The kid didn't even smell bad anymore. The fire had cleansed him in every way.

Scowling, Diana rounded on him. "What exactly did you think I was going to do? And what was that other crap about?"

"Uh, something else," he hedged. "Let's get out here before we discuss the rest," he added, aware the witch watched them like they were her evening's entertainment.

Gia had said it was necessary to keep the pregnancy a secret. Alec didn't even know this witch's lineage—although she slightly resembled the Patel clan.

Fishing into his breast pocket, he withdrew a silver card case. Opening it, Alec handed one of the thick vellum cards to the woman. "Call this number."

Bewildered, the woman took the card. "For what?"

Alec shrugged. "Whatever the child needs."

"Like a hell of a lot of therapy," Diana suggested, tugging on his arm.

"And a new door," Alec called on their way out. They were out in the street before his mate spoke again.

She put her hands in the pockets of the fur-lined parka she'd chosen for their wet winter travels, just over her belly. "It's not a parasite, is it?"

Alec swore under his breath. "You know you're...*expecting.*"

"I'm not an idiot. I could feel it." Di let out a long breath through her nose. "Are you sure it's not a parasite?" she asked hopefully.

He shook his head. "I can hear the heartbeat."

"Already?" Diana frowned down at her stomach. "I figured it out because of the growing temperature differential."

"But you hear it now, right?" Diana's hearing was almost as good as his own.

"I'm actively trying not to listen. It's distracting."

"Oh. Of course." He understood that. An Elemental on the front lines couldn't afford to let her focus stray.

"And how do you feel?" he asked, unable to hide his anxiety.

"The same." His mate sounded as confused as he was. "It's not supposed to happen this way."

"I know. Please don't be mad, but one of the reasons I stayed behind in Costa Rica was to ask Gia about this. Unfortunately, she didn't have any answers. This is unprecedented for your kind."

Diana crossed her arms, lips pursing. "I could have told you that."

"I just wanted to be sure there wasn't anything I'd missed. I've been reading every record of previous Elementals and their offspring. But conception while in service has never happened. Or, if it has, it was never recorded. I brought Gia into this to make sure."

He rubbed his temple. "Gia didn't want me to ask Salvador about it, but we should find someone—maybe a healer in T'Kaieri. We're going to need some sort of prenatal care."

Her expression darkened. "Well, haven't you been a busy bee

buzzing in everyone's ears?" He didn't need to be told she was angry at him. The extra heat in the air made the slight drizzle steam up.

"We were never going to be able to keep it a secret," he pointed out. "Connell could smell the change in your scent in Costa Rica."

She grimaced. "You still should have discussed it with me before you spoke to my sister."

He hung his head. "I know, and I am sorry. I was just hoping to have something positive to tell you—at the very least an answer as to how this happened."

Diana snorted. "I have the only answer I need—that the rule book is out the window. From here on out, we're in uncharted territory. Do you have a problem with that?"

Given their *union* was also an unprecedented novelty, he could hardly argue. "No. As long as you're happy about the babe... *Are* you happy?"

"I'm still processing. That's allowed, isn't it?" she asked with a touch of sarcasm.

He inclined his head. "Of course. And, for the record, I'm also still processing. But I'm pleased, too. Since I turned so young, I didn't think I would get a chance to have one you know...a child."

"I didn't want one," she confessed. "I never wanted one."

He knew that. Diana had despised the vulnerability of her childhood. She would never inflict that on someone else. But her life was exceedingly different now. She was strong, and she had him. They had each other.

A thousand promises came to his lips, reassurances he would always be there for her—that he would never let anyone hurt their baby—but he stopped before he made them.

Uncharted territory. The rules were changing too quickly. Making promises he might not be able to keep wouldn't make her feel better.

"And now that we're going to have one, do you think you could learn to be happy?" Or would she decide not to continue the pregnancy?

Apparently, Diana had no such ideas. She nudged him with her hip, slinging an arm around his waist. "As long as you change the diapers, I can deal."

He laughed in relief before taking her in his arms. She leaned against his chest, melting into him. "I'm serious about the diapers."

"I know you are. Don't worry. I already bought several instructional books on the subject."

20

———

Gia didn't have to carry a watch to tell the time. Her internal chronometer was more accurate than most timepieces. Which was why she knew Salvador had spent thirty-seven minutes choosing what to wear. *And now he says he has to find shoes...*

Sighing, she tried to hold onto her patience. After all, this was her fault. She was making Salvador walk into the lion's den because it was more expedient for her. Guilt flared as the man in question passed by the window in a three-piece suit.

*Wow. Not bad...*Gia told herself it would be unseemly for an Elemental to wolf whistle. And where had he been hiding that suit?

In the back of the closet, just in case.

Delavordo men gravitated strongly toward bespoke suits unless they were part of the younger set, in which case they wore designer clothes fresh off the runway—whatever was fashionable.

Ten more minutes passed before Salvador emerged from the cottage. He was wearing a lightweight linen shirt and a pair of khakis —an outfit almost identical to the one he'd insisted he needed to change out of. The only concession he'd made to their upcoming visit was the shoes.

"So...you only changed the sandals?" she asked skeptically.

Salvador glanced at the loafers he wore. They appeared expensive, no doubt a pair leftover from his pre-exile days.

He put a hand on his hips. "My mother would have a heart attack if I walked over her Persian rugs in earth shoes."

The sad part was that was probably true.

After a pause, Salvador held up a cell phone. "I can have one of Alec's drivers pick us up."

She shook her head. "I wasn't planning on an overland route."

Salvador's handsome face scrunched. "I was afraid you were going to say that. But, as your doctor, I have to advise against this. It's got to be taxing, traveling that way."

"We will be fine," she assured him. The Delavordos had property all over the world, but they were creatures of habit. At this time of the year, Fulgencio and Lucia could always be found at their compound in Belize. "Crossing under an ocean might be a bit much, especially with a passenger in tow, but I can handle anything on this continent. Probably. Definitely..."

Salvador stopped breathing.

"I'm kidding!" Gia held out her hand. He studied it for a moment before taking it. Unexpectedly, his fingers moved to intertwine with hers, tightening reflexively.

"It will be fine."

"You already said that."

"And I meant it." Waving her hand, Gia made the ground go soft, letting it absorb them without further delay.

SALVADOR CLUTCHED Gia's hand as the ground opened above their heads—except, until a moment ago, they didn't *have* heads.

At first, the ride was exciting. He'd taken Gia's hand, and they'd sank into the ground as if they were in an elevator platform lowering into a top-secret superhero lair.

But then the ground had closed over their heads... and his skin had dissolved. The line of demarcation that marked the end of him to the rest of the existence had suddenly vanished. Dust to dust. In a snap, they'd started moving—the essence of him and Gia propelling through solid matter like a tremor rolling through the ground during an earthquake.

It was the sort of mind-bending trip that could threaten one's sense of self. A lesser mind might break. But even though he didn't have a hand, he could still feel Gia holding him the entire time.

No sooner had he gotten ahold of himself, then bam—the ride was over. They'd shot up, then the ground spit them out. Staggering, Salvador caught himself before he fell flat on his face.

It was as if they'd been on a lift that came to a sudden stop... or like standing on top of a freight train that had crashed into a wall.

Gia, of course, didn't stumble. She continued to hold his hand until he recovered his equilibrium.

"That—that reminds me of the time I did ayahuasca *after* mushrooms," he said once he was sure he wasn't going to hurl.

Gia actually winced as if this was a memory she shared. "Not a combination or sequence I'd recommend."

Neither would he. That lesson had been learned the hard way.

"It was during the experimental phase of my healing practice," he explained. "I was exploring the possibility of using those as treatments for trauma. I decided on micro-doses of the mushrooms and nixed the ayahuasca."

"Wise, but you could have read that in Dusay's *Guide to Healing Hallucinogens* without the self-experimentation," she said, referring to a native text popular with practitioners of alternative medicine.

Salvador pivoted, checking out their surroundings. There were in a clearing between a bunch of trees—deciduous this time, not tropical. "I don't give my patients anything I wouldn't take myself."

He turned to find Gia studying him. It wasn't interrogation-mode scrutiny, more like she'd just realized something.

"You're very unusual for a Delavordo."

Was that a compliment? Yes, it had to be.

"Thank you." He gestured around them. "This looks like the woods around my parents' house."

"We are across from the property," she confirmed. "Most of the surrounding land is warded except for a narrow strip leading up to the drive."

"Can't you deactivate them?" He'd always been warned that no ward—no matter how well-crafted—was Elemental-proof.

"Yeah, but I didn't want to be rude. Speaking of…"

She extended her hand. A plant popped up beside them. As he watched with wide eyes, it grew, the stems bifurcating and sprouting leaves. Then buds appeared, blooming into lush blood-red flowers. They intertwined, forming a bouquet. When Gia put out a hand, the bunch landed in it, the knot of stems severing at their base as if the bush had shed it.

"Remind me to have you visit my medicinal herb garden when this is over… Is the bouquet for my mother?"

The unusual flowers were in her favorite shade.

Gia inclined her head. "It is customary to bring your hostess a gift before you raid her vault."

Despite his trepidation, he laughed, which was probably what she'd intended. But he stopped when she put a hand on his arm. "I know I'm putting you in a difficult position, but I don't intend to let you trade any promises for the artifact. According to the Covenant, I can confiscate anything that poses a threat to the Supernatural world. This one does, in more way than one."

"Yeah," he drawled. "Somehow, I don't think flowers, no matter how lovely, are going to make up for confiscating Ciro's divining rod."

At least he was already an outcast. His father couldn't disown him twice.

Gia nodded toward the flowers. "This particular flower is the species Arabella used to cure her beast in the seventh century."

Salvador stared. Somehow, it didn't surprise him to hear the fable was true. Most legends were. "That wasn't the version of the story I heard."

Her careless shrug did interesting things to the bodice of Gia's shirt. "Yeah, that one is wrong. It wasn't roses."

She pushed the bouquet into his hand, then nudged him forward. They began to walk north.

A few minutes later, the house appeared behind the ornate wrought-iron fence. They weren't in front of the main or south gate, but somewhere in between.

His eyebrow rose. "Are we supposed to jump the fence?"

As if on cue, the metal bars gave way like theater curtains.

"Show-off," he muttered.

Giggling, Gia waved him through the opening. The infectious sound wrapped around him, giving his internal organs a pleasant buzz. Behind them, bars closed with a flap, settling back into the ground noiselessly.

They circled around the side of the house, coming up the long gravel path to the front door. In front, the sprawling three-story mansion loomed like behemoth rising out of the water.

The house was a recent addition to the family holdings—only about a century old, which was practically new compared to some of their European properties. Everything about the house, from its fresh coat of stucco to the meticulously maintained flower beds, spoke to wealth and a level of control and oversight that bordered on the maniacal.

"Home sweet home," he muttered. The place hadn't changed much in the last decade. The cars in the driveway were different, newer models of luxury cars. Someone was even driving a Tesla, but one unlike any he'd seen before. This car had to have been custom made. It had sleek space-age lines and a muted sparkle, almost as if someone had embedded precious metals under a layer of smoky acrylic.

He rubbed his eyes. "Is that even street legal?" Sure, an effort had been made to mute the brilliance of the finish, but the car would still blind other drivers. It was a highway pileup waiting to happen.

He turned back to the house, wondering if his parents had been informed of their arrival.

"Not yet," Gia answered.

"So now you're a mind reader on top of everything else?" he asked.

"Nope." She patted him on the back. "But I don't need to be. It's all over your face. I can tell no one in the house is scrambling to arm themselves with defensive weapons. They're all either at rest or moving at a leisurely pace."

He wondered what kind of spell she cast to be able to read everyone, then realized one was unnecessary. Gia had probably read their locations via the composition of their bones.

Hmm... that would be handy to test osteoporosis in my older patients.

"You know with my masking spell, we can stand out here all day, but it rather defeats the purpose of our visit," she said after a minute.

"Right..."

Salvador offered his arm. With a courtly nod, Gia took it, handing him the bouquet.

Taking one last look at the house, he sucked in a deep breath before leading her up the front steps. He straightened his shoulders, then pressed the doorbell.

"You are acting like this is a social call to put me at ease, right?" he asked as they waited for the butler to answer the door.

"Is that what I'm doing?" she asked, cocking her head to the side.

He glanced at her from the corner of his eye. Why had this woman—who by rights should consider him her mortal enemy—become the rock he was holding onto?

"I wish it were real," he whispered, seized by melancholia.

Gia snapped her head around to study him quizzically. Her lips parted, and he prepared for a blistering set down or at least a question for clarification. Instead, she closed her mouth and patted his arm.

Ouch. Pity from an Elemental. Definitely time to get ahold of yourself.

Salvador turned back to the door as it opened. The shock on the butler's face was cartoonish.

"Hello, Gerardo," he said, inclining his head.

"Señor Salvador!" Gerardo staggered back as Gia marched forward, dragging Salvador in her wake.

They entered the grand foyer. Doric columns surrounded the polished marble floor. Embedded in the center was an elaborately rendered Delavordo family crest edged in gilt. Above them, the vaulted ceiling was painted with a fresco done in the style of the Renaissance masters. At the moment, it showed a long-distant ancestor hunting down a stag. The animal had just crashed to the ground. It stopped when he focused on it.

Gia glanced up. "Bespelled?" she asked.

"Yes. But it only moves when you're not looking at it. The scene changes periodically—great moments in Delavordo family history."

He was grateful she didn't laugh or make a cutting remark in front of Gerardo. The butler would have been wounded. When someone was in service to one of the Seven, the family's pride was their own.

Gia took the bouquet, then handed it to the servant. "For the lady of the house," she said.

Gerardo barely looked at her as he accepted the bouquet. His rheumy eyes were still fixed on Salvador. "May I ask if your parents are expecting you?"

"No. I didn't know I was coming until today," he said. "It was a spur-of-the-moment decision."

"I see." Gerardo's gaze fell on the bouquet. He blinked, drawing the inevitable conclusion. "I'll go inform your mother and father that you're here...with a guest."

He left with the offering, having failed to recognize Gia. But then... how many people actually knew what she looked like? For many black-magic practitioners, the Earth Elemental was probably the last thing they ever saw.

Insert 'what a way to go' joke here...

"You know he's up there suggesting I finally came home to introduce a prospective bride," he told Gia as she studied the decor.

"I don't think they'll be suffering under that particular misconception for long." She patted him on the back. "Why don't you go up and explain? I'll wait here."

"That might be easier," he agreed. It would be a short reprieve, but if he could postpone the fireworks long enough to explain to his parents that he was trying to save all magic, they might not come out with guns blazing.

With heavy feet, he followed in Gerardo's wake, trudging toward the infinity-spiral grand staircase at the far end of the foyer. The artwork on the walls had changed, but so had the configuration of the doors leading out of the room. Mother had been redecorating again.

Using magic to rearrange the structure of the building took a lot of juice, but that had never been an issue in the Delavordo household. Wholesale rearrangements didn't happen at the same speed or scale as the stairways at the fictional Hogwarts, but Salvador had grown up accustomed to having to hunt for the kitchen's new location. At least the position of the master suite never changed. It occupied the central space behind the stairs on the top floor.

Salvador half-expected one of his cousins to jump out at him the way they had as children, but it was strangely quiet. Well, they were old enough to be bored by hanging out at the Grand Palais. They were probably abroad in more exciting places like Barbados or Transylvania.

Small blessings. But he knew better than to expect his parents to be totally alone. His mother and father were both from large families. Fulgencio was the oldest of thirteen, his mother was one of seven, both numbers with occult significance. It was no secret why their families had arranged the match. As far as the Seven were concerned, it was considered only partially successful because they produced only one gifted child—him. An heir and a spare were *de rigeur* when one was the head of a family, but his mother had trouble conceiving after he was born.

Unlike Delavordos of days past, Fulgencio hadn't divorced her for a younger, more fertile model. His mother would have been far better off if he had. He reached the top-floor landing when the door to the master suite swung open. His mother appeared in the doorway, closely followed by his father.

Fulgencio Delavordo was as tall as Salvador, but he was much leaner. Salvador barely looked at him. He couldn't tear his eyes from his mother.

Lucia Delavordo was a well-preserved petite woman with fine aristocratic features. Salvador had his mother's nose and chin, but he got his height from his father's side of the family. But discounting Lucia because of her size and delicate appearance was a mistake, possibly a fatal one.

He was frozen with shock at his mother's appearance, but for an entirely different reason.

Pushing away his shock, he rounded on his father. "What the hell?" he burst out, waving at his mother's burgeoning stomach. "After everything that happened, how could you do this again?"

His childhood had been far from idyllic, but the worst moments had surrounded his mother's many miscarriages.

"Hello to you, too," Fulgencio said sarcastically, drawing himself up to his full height.

"You *promised* you would stop trying. I thought this madness was over."

"As if you cared about your mother's health and welfare," his father snapped. "You abandoned your family."

Salvador gave his father's accusation the attention it deserved, which meant he completely ignored it. "How many times do we have to go through this!"

"Anyone who abandons their family the way you did doesn't get to lecture me—"

"She almost *died* the last time," Salvador interrupted, shouting now. "She almost died *every* time!"

"*Enough*," Lucia said crisply. "This was my decision. I did what I had to do to secure our family's legacy. In case you forgot, according to you, I no longer have a son."

Unbelievable.

"Our house is in no danger of dying out." The Delavordo family tree was so thickly branched it resembled a bush.

"Is that because you've finally forgotten your foolishness and have decided to come home?" Lucia asked. "Does the woman you brought with you have anything to do with your decision?"

"What woman?" Fulgencio asked, apparently late to the game.

"The one who brought me those lovely flowers," she said, pointing to the bouquet. Sometime during the argument, Gerardo had found a vase for the bouquet. He'd set it on the antique Hermes table in the entrance of the master suite. Afterward, he'd wisely disappeared.

His father frowned at the display. "So, after all this time, we're supposed to believe he's brought someone home for our approval?" Fulgencio put his hands on his hips, throwing Salvador a disparaging glance. "I don't think so. What the hell are you up to?"

"Nothing much. Just trying to save magic."

Lucia's patrician nose wrinkled. "What is that supposed to mean?"

Salvador closed his eyes, shoving his fingers through his hair. "I mean I didn't come home with a girl. I came home because the Earth Elemental needs something from the family vault, and I accompanied her."

His father's face contorted. "*What*?"

Lucia's recovery was quicker. "You brought one of those *things* here?"

Salvador took a deep breath. "Actually, she brought me, and she has a name. I believe you know it—Gia."

"What could she possibly want? Our family is not in violation of the Covenant."

"Not at the moment," he muttered. *That we know of...*

His father swore explosively as he made for the stairs.

"Where are you going?" his mother called.

Fulgencio paused. "That thing wouldn't need him to come here for access to the vault," he said, pointing an accusing finger at Salvador. "The only use he serves is as a distraction. It's *already* inside."

Salvador wanted to argue, but his father was right.

"She can't do that," his mother scoffed, following at a more sedate pace. Sighing, Salvador fell in step behind her.

His mind went back to the iron bars parting like the Red Sea. "Of course she can."

"How?" Lucia scoffed. "Our vault is the most heavily warded room in the hemisphere. The door has over twenty different spells ensuring no one gets in without your father or me, as we are the current keepers."

He followed her down the stairs. "She's not going in through the door, Mother. Gia is the Earth Elemental. She can just walk through the wall."

21

Salvador offered his mother his arm on the way down to the basement.

"How far along are you?" he asked. Prenatal care was a big part of his practice.

"Six months." Lucia's tone was crisp. "And before you ask, it's going well. No problems at all."

"It's different this time," he finished as they reached the basement landing. "Where have I heard that before?"

Stopping, she rounded on him, but she didn't speak. She didn't have to. Lucia could say everything with her eyes.

"Mother, I know we don't agree on a great many things, but this was supposed to be one we did see eye to eye on." He lowered his voice. "I just don't want you to go through something terrible again."

Lucia looked down at her stomach, vulnerability creeping into her expression. "It *is* different this time," she whispered.

Salvador took a deep breath. He hadn't seen his parents in years. Yet, less than ten minutes into their reunion, and it felt as if he'd never left.

His mother was one of the most uncompromising and

demanding people he'd ever met. It had taken a lot to get them to stop trying for a second child.

Lucia had been a terrible parent, second only to his father. Salvador had believed for years he'd reached the point where he no longer cared what they did. But seeing her now—pregnant and prepared to put herself through hell again—and he wasn't so sure.

Tears stung his eyes, but he knew better than to let them fall. Lucia hated tears. "I hope so. I truly do."

By silent agreement, they walked down to the vault together. There was only one way in and one way out.

His father was still undoing the wards that secured the entrance. "I think we beat her here."

"I doubt that," Salvador said with a shrug.

"The walls are two feet thick," Fulgencio scoffed as he undid the fire-repelling ward. "This vault is the most highly fortified room on the continent. It's more secure than any bank in the world."

"Maybe... but Gia is already inside," Salvador repeated.

His mother rolled her eyes, but the argument was pointless. His father had undone the last ward.

Lucia did the honors. After nudging Fulgencio out of the way, she stood in front of the double doors and held up her arms, chanting briefly in a mix of Italian and Latin.

The heavy stone doors swung toward them. Soft luminescence lit the chamber full of shelves, small cells, and the odd pedestal.

"You got rid of the torches," Salvador observed. His parents had always been traditionalists, but he was glad to see they were moving with the times.

A curved shelf blocked the view of the rest of the chamber. It was one of many. From a bird's eye view, the arrangement of shelves and cupboards formed a celestial pattern—the outer edges a rough circle. Priceless antiquities and works of art were stored down here. Never-before-seen paintings from the old masters lined the walls, interspersed with cubbies that housed museum-quality antiques. They were all on the outer edges because they were the least valuable items in the room.

Magic was the currency of the Seven families. The outer rings held the lesser charms and talismans, along with occult books of middling significance. The farther inside, the more magical the objects became. They were also more dangerous.

They found Gia in the center. One of the pedestals to the left of the haunted Rodin statue was empty.

Formally, Gia inclined her head. "Fulgencio, Lucia, greetings," she said, almost conversationally before gesturing in the direction of the empty pedestal. "Is something missing?"

When he was growing up, Salvador had been quizzed relentlessly on the items in the vault. *Knowing one's history is the key to innovation,* his tutor had repeatedly said. *We stand on the shoulders of giants.* He should have known what belonged there, but the contents of the central ring had shifted placement while others had been removed since he'd been here last.

"Nothing is missing. An artifact is out for cleaning," his father acidly bit out. "Now explain why you are violating my family's vault and inner sanctum?"

Gia didn't respond. She studied his mother. A flicker of pity and concern crossed her face. Of course she would have known about his parents many failed attempts to have a second child.

The Earth Elemental approached Lucia. Alarmed, his father stepped in front of her, trying to shield her.

"It's okay," Salvador said. The Elementals might consider his parents a threat. Unlike some members of his family, though, Gia would never harm an innocent...

The Elemental held up her hands, her expression benign and open. "May I?"

His father snorted, but he twisted to Lucia with a glance that asked what she wanted. Lucia flicked her hand, gesturing for him to move aside. When Gia put her hands on Lucia's burgeoning stomach, his mother held still.

Salvador held his breath. Everyone did.

Gia lifted a brow. "Healthy," she pronounced. "With a strong heartbeat. The baby's development appears to be on track."

She put her hands down. "Congratulations. I expect you'll be adding another leaf to the family tree around the Equinox."

Salvador's mouth dropped open. *Shit.* He was going to be a big brother after all.

Salvador's mother and father stared at each other. His father blinked rapidly. Lucia gazed down, putting a hand on her stomach. "Thank you," she said hoarsely. His father ran a hand down his face, quickly giving them his back.

After sucking in a deep breath, his father turned around to face them. "We know the child is female."

With a nod, Gia lifted her hand. She waved it across his mother's stomach. "May the Mother's blessing be upon her."

Salvador frowned as a muted luminescence in the Elemental's hand faded.

"*Oh.* Well, thank you for that." Seeming uncertain, his mother touch trembling fingers to her mouth. It was an emotion he wasn't used to seeing her express.

His father cleared his throat. "Yes, we are grateful for the blessing." It was to Fulgencio's credit that he only sounded a little hostile.

The corner of Gia's mouth lifted. Salvador doubted she had ever heard such a sentiment from any Delavordo—well other than him. "You're welcome."

Reaching out, she patted the empty pedestal. "And I hope you finish... *cleaning*... this artifact soon. Its absence is throwing off the dampening effect of the Solis configuration," she said, referring to the celestial pattern the family used to make sure the artifacts didn't react.

Magic was inherently unstable. When an object was imbued with enough of it, they were able to affect the space—and sometimes even the people—around them. With more than one truly powerful piece, things got interesting.

Cross-reactivity was a big problem with collections like this, which was why they organized artifacts into specific patterns with occult properties. When aligned properly, the harmonic resonance of the objects were muted. It required maintenance because the energy of magical objects fluctuated, sometimes unpredictably. If one of the anchor points—like an item powerful enough to be on one of his family's pedestals—was missing for too long, then the buffering effect of the design broke down. The results could be catastrophic.

"Do you want me to adjust the pattern?" Salvador asked. That had been one of his chores growing up.

"No, I'll do it," his father said, a touch snappishly. "Can you tell us why you came?"

"Ciro's divining rod," Salvador said.

His mother frowned. "That *stick*?"

Fulgencio's nostrils flared. "Excuse me, that is one of the family's most precious artifacts," he snapped.

"Please," Lucia said. "It's a worthless stick that does nothing."

"Just because you couldn't get it to work—"

"*We*," his mother interrupted. "*We* couldn't get it to work. If we couldn't, then no one can because it's a *stick*. It doesn't do anything."

In his head, Salvador agreed with his mother, but he could see his father winding up. Fulgencio put his hands on his hips—a sure sign a long, drawn-out argument was coming.

"Nevertheless," Gia said, stepping forward to forestall the disagreement. "We need it."

Lucia scowled. "Why?"

"A purely preventative measure."

"You hope," Salvador muttered.

Gia sighed, flicking her thick lashes at him. "Yes, I do. Where is it?"

He turned to his parents. "Is it still in the epsilon closet?" he asked. Certain objects that didn't fit in the configuration were given their own space, tiny closets in different corners of the room.

"Yes, although there's not much point. It's *inert*." His mother glared at Fulgencio as if this were an old argument.

Salvador walked over to the closet, ignoring his father's scowl. The epsilon closet was technically a bunker, one of several. The door was between rings two and three, and it was opened by a genetically keyed spell.

He drew the charm he wore out from under his shirt. It had multiple purposes, but the one he needed was the simplest. Flicking open the end, he revealed a tiny needle. He pushed his index finger onto the point until a drop of blood appeared. Kneeling, he swiped it across the floor.

The detailed rune design engraved on its surface began to glow an iridescent teal color, his mother's signature spellwork color. The luminescence flared, spiking before it gradually faded. Once it was gone, a door slid open, revealing a steep set of stairs.

The bunker was a bit more crowded than he remembered, but that was to be expected. Delavordos loved to experiment.

He found the divining rod in the rear, hanging unceremoniously from a hook.

If this is an occult tool capable of reaching the Mother, then it should be hidden behind lasers and motion detectors. Or his mother was right, and it just was a stick. He took the stairs up two at a time, making sure to clean the blood from the floor to reseal the door.

The scene when he returned reminded Salvador of a Mexican standoff. His father fumed, face tight with a familiar expression of indignation. His mother studied her nails, affecting airy unconcern, as if whatever Gia wanted was beneath her.

The Elemental stood with her hands behind her back in a classic *'look how harmless I am'* pose. She wasn't moving much, just slightly pivoting on her heels, but that small motion gave her a nearly two-hundred-and-seventy-degree view of the room.

Of course. Gia was in the lion's den. What Elemental could resist cataloging the Delavordo treasury? She had probably already committed the contents to memory before he'd even arrived with his parents.

Salvador handed the divining rod to Gia. Her expression blanked as she examined it. It had been sculpted out of a single piece of walnut, the blunted end split a few inches from the base, forking into the polished ends. Runes and occult symbols covered it the entire length, which was roughly a meter.

A tiny pucker appeared between Gia's brows. "Interesting."

"What is?" Lucia asked. "Don't tell me that thing works."

"I don't know if it does, but it's very...balanced."

"In what way?" Salvador asked.

Gia bobbled the rod. "The wood was chosen with care—walnut, equally balanced between male and female, as well as Earth and Water. Carving it up should have destroyed that, but it was done so carefully the balance was maintained. It's finely crafted."

Hmm. Both informative and simultaneously cryptic. And with that somewhat unnecessary compliment at the end. The Earth Elemental was surprisingly politic. But then his family's history with their kind had generally been beyond the point where diplomacy was an option.

"I don't like this," his father said, drawing himself up to his full height. "No one has used this artifact for nefarious purposes. I don't think it's fair for you to preemptively confiscate it on the off chance someone might try to steal it. If that were to become a precedent, you could empty this room—a gross violation of the Covenant. As long as they aren't being used for harm, we get to *keep* our objects of power. I'd hate to have to contact the other family heads over this."

Briefly, Salvador closed his eyes, searching for patience. "Please don't make this any more difficult than it has to be."

Fulgencio glared. "Of course you would say that. You have no concept of family loyalty!"

He held onto his temper with an effort of will. "I'm not going to listen to this again—"

Gia cleared her throat, pivoting to face his father. "Perhaps you'd consider loaning it to us. It's important."

"How can we possibly trust you with it when you can't even secure your own precious archive?" Fulgencio peered down his nose at her. "We know about the theft at the Water colony."

Gia didn't even blink. "Good. Then you know the threat is significant. But I can assure you this item won't be lost or harmed in any way."

Lucia had recovered enough of her equilibrium to remember she was also supposed to be throwing up roadblocks. "I don't see why we should help you. It's not like the Elementals have done anything but make our lives more difficult."

Salvador restrained a snort. "It was more than a theft. T'Kaieri could have been destroyed."

His father's lips flattened. "Forgive me for saying this, but why should we care if Elementals are being attacked? We aren't exactly allies. In fact, our lives might be a bit easier without the constant threat of their interference in our affairs."

"Because our adversary's goal isn't to kill Elementals," Salvador huffed, the last thread of his patience unraveling. "It's to kill the Mother. If he accomplishes his goal, he'll kill *all* the magic along with Her."

His mother and father didn't have a snappy comeback to that.

"Or John could be trying to reverse the spectrum," Salvador pointed out, putting his index fingers up and inverting them. "He could be trying to remove magic from Supernaturals to give it to people like himself—to humans."

"That is also a possibility," Gia acknowledged, inclining her head. Her measured response told him that she'd already considered that scenario. A good tactician operated two or three steps ahead of everyone else. *That's probably why she's so pissed.* She hadn't considered a threat from within the T'Kaierian community, and she'd been caught unawares.

"Perhaps under these circumstances, you would reconsider loaning us the artifact?" she said, rephrasing her request.

"I don't think we can let Ciro's staff leave Delavordo custody." His father sniffed.

Gia smiled brilliantly, holding out her free hand. "Condition accepted."

Fulgencio's head drew back as the Elemental took his hand, pumping it up and down. "What?"

"And I have the perfect Delavordo for that," Gia continued as if she hadn't been interrupted, then handed the staff to Salvador.

Belatedly, the light of realization dawned on his father's face. "I didn't mean my son. He's been outcast—exiled."

Gia shrugged. "Then you should have said so before. Come along, Salvador."

Flabbergasted, his father gaped, his face going from red to purple.

Salvador wanted to laugh aloud. He'd never seen his parents outmaneuvered so easily. The Elemental was completely throwing them off their game.

His mother waved her perfectly manicured nails. "He's just going hand it over to you once you are out the door."

"I promise the rod won't leave his custody," Gia offered. "Even if I need to use it, it will stay with him."

His father rounded on Salvador, about to interject.

"And it won't leave my sight." Salvador sighed, walking to the door. He was done. "Gia and I are old traveling companions."

"And where did you two go together?"

"Nowhere special," Salvador said, tugging Gia toward the door. "Just hell."

22

Salvador had no idea where they were. He'd walked out of his parent's house on his own steam, confident he'd handled the confrontation as best he could, but his mind was teeming, too full of facts and memories. Overloaded, he blindly followed Gia, trusting she would lead them... anywhere else.

When the ground covered them again, he barely noticed, not until it spit them back out again in an unfamiliar clearing. Salvador staggered to sit on a rock under a shade tree while Gia examined the divining rod, turning it over and over in her hands.

"Are you all right?" she asked after a minute.

He glanced up. Her eyes were uncharacteristically soft on his face. "I know that must have been a shock for you, finding out your mother is with child again."

Salvador took a steadying breath, blinking to ease the strange dryness in his eyes. "You must know about their earlier attempts, all the rites and fertility rituals they pursued, along with the many miscarriages that followed."

He had watched his parents explore every option under the sun and a few that had only worked in the dark of night. Despite their expertise in magic, they had been so desperate for a second child that they'd visited every witch doctor and second-rate shaman rumored to help with infertility. Some of the things they had done—the lengths they had gone to—those had stayed with him.

"I used to have dreams," he said without meaning to. But once he got started, he couldn't stop. "I dreamt that one of their rituals succeeded, and Mother carried a second child to term. But it always turned into a nightmare. What she ended up giving birth to wouldn't be a baby—it would be a monster."

Gia lowered the divining rod. She sat cross-legged in front of him. "I heard some of the rumors. They weren't just trying to conceive another heir."

"No," he whispered. "They wanted to improve upon nature, to ensure the child's magical potential was off the charts. It backfired. Human beings weren't meant to hold that much magic. Mother kept miscarrying. I thought it had permanently ruined her chances of getting pregnant. The last few attempts nearly killed her. Yet, they *still* kept trying even though I begged them to stop."

He suppressed a shudder. "I can still remember every second of that last attempt. It was terrible. The house is so large, but I could her screaming in every room—I know because I ran through each trying to find somewhere I couldn't."

He broke off, startled, when Gia covered his hands with her own. But she didn't say anything. She just squeezed his fingers, silently comforting him.

"If you hadn't made me come here today, I wouldn't know they tried again," he said. "The fact they succeeded..."

She could still die. His mother wasn't out of the woods yet. All Gia could assess was the babe's health up to that moment.

"You were right that their measures to concentrate magic were the reason they failed to conceive," she said, squeezing again. "The fact she's carrying to term means they gave up that particular quest."

"Apparently, enough time must have passed for some of the damage they did to repair itself, too," he said, absently rubbing his thumb over the top of her hand.

Her skin felt like silk, which seemed strange. He would have thought they'd be hard and rough like her element. In the flesh, however, this big bad Elemental was soft and yielding.

Damn, he wanted to sleep with her. Just one time. If he got to, he'd happily return to celibacy until he died.

"It took a few decades, but Lucia's system must have normalized enough to carry to term," she continued. "It may still be difficult given her age, but no more than other women who choose to pursue a late-in-life pregnancy."

Her words should have been a comfort, but Salvador was having trouble processing the news. "I don't know how to feel about it. After all this time, I'm going to have a sister…"

Something he couldn't decipher flickered across her face before it went blank. Gia let go of his hands, then stood.

"If you'd like to return to Costa Rica, I can send you back now."

"What happened to the divining rod never leaving my side?"

She shrugged. "In their time, the Delavordo family heads have lied and broken countless promises to my kind. A little tit for tat won't hurt my karma if you'd rather return to your practice. I'm sure you have patients waiting."

"There is another healer in the area they can see."

Gia raised a brow. "One as good as you?"

Was she trying to flatter him?

"I touched the divining rod."

Her brow scrunched. "And?"

"It's keyed to Ciro," he said. "He did that with most of his experiments. Only a family member has any hope of activating it."

Gia kicked a pebble, pulverizing it into dust. "I see…"

"I am happy to stay to help you with it," he offered.

"If the rod even works, I don't know how long this will take," she warned.

Hopelessly outmatched, he rose so he could at least be taller. "You can count on me for the duration."

Her eyes closed briefly, but then she schooled her face into a benign expression. "Well, then I would appreciate your help."

Salvador grinned. "That was hard for you, wasn't it?"

She surprised him by smiling back. "You have no idea."

Gia was about to turn away, but he forestalled her with a hand to the arm. A fine line appeared between her brows, but she allowed him to pull her closer.

"Eventually, I hope you will trust me enough to tell me the truth about whatever it is you're hiding—about my parents and what they did in their efforts to give me a brother or sister."

"Salvador..." she began.

"What?" he asked when she didn't continue. For the first time in their acquaintance, Gia appeared flustered.

"I know there's something. I can see it in your eyes." He pressed closer until they were actually touching.

Sal expected Gia to push away, but she merely shook her head. "As long as they do no harm, your parents are entitled to their secrets. It would be a violation of the Covenant for me to intervene."

Questioningly, he cocked his head. "Is telling me what you know really intervening?"

She winced. "It could be seen that way."

They stood still, pressed against each other. Against everything that was right and rational in the world, he was the one who backed away.

He could feel Gia watching him, but he didn't turn around. *You need to focus. Whether she likes it or not, Gia needs your help to save the world.* Salvador picked up the divining rod.

"I wonder if blood will help?" Picking at the spot on his finger, he rubbed off the scab sealing the pinprick wound. He squeezed his finger until a bead of red welled at the tip.

Gia pointed to the joint where the rod handles split. "Try there."

He smeared the blood on the wood, pulling his head back in case of a reaction. "Nothing." The wood didn't absorb the spot, nor did a spark ignite the magic.

"I guess it's not a blood artifact."

"No." She took the rod back, then closed her eyes, but popped them open after a second. "You could have asked me to tell you what your parents have been hiding as payment for healing me and coming to get me in Sheol."

"I know that," he said quietly.

"Why don't you? Honor would compel me to answer if you demanded that as payment."

At first, he didn't know what to say. But then it came to him. "That particular piece of knowledge shouldn't be currency."

She would tell him eventually, but it wouldn't be because he bargained with her. He wanted her trust.

Gia scowled. "Don't do that. Don't make me like you."

This time, it was his turn to give her a slightly smug, all-knowing look. "Too late. You already do."

23

Daniel hung up the phone with a grunt. He squinted at the horizon beyond Biscayne Bay. Sunset was doing creative things with the light. Soaking up the last rays, he let his frustration wash away with the breeze.

"Any luck?" his mate asked. Serin leaned over a rock, using her hand to swirl the water in an infinite loop.

The setting sun reflected off the bay, making her face glow. His heart stuttered involuntarily. She was so damn beautiful it actually hurt sometimes.

Being mated to an Elemental was certainly giving his cardiac muscles a workout.

Serin raised an expectant brow, and he forced himself to focus on the matter at hand. "Nothing on the APB so far. I'm going to send John's description to my buddy with the Marshall's service. That should get it circulating more widely."

She nodded, then resumed swirling.

He grinned. "Thank you for not thinking this is a stupid idea, or at least not saying so aloud."

Serin rose in a fluid motion, coming to rest next to him. "Well, I admit it is unconventional for us. At this point, however, I'm more than willing to try it your way—a human hunter for human prey. But don't feel bad if we don't get a bite. John may not even be in this country."

"I know, but it can't hurt." He gestured around them. "Remind me why we washed up here?"

"Just chasing down a lead. There's a siren operating in these parts who was approached by a man who made some rather specific promises. I heard it secondhand, so it may or may not be true, but we need to follow up."

Daniel's head jerked up. "A siren as in a *mermaid*?"

Serin shrugged. "A siren is a type of water Fae. Cold-blooded. Only some stories are true."

"Let me guess... The part where they lure men to their doom with their songs is a factual bit?"

His mate rewarded him with a smile. "The parts with the body count do tend to be based in fact."

He snorted softly. "Of course they are. What makes you think this siren is going to come here?"

"Because she said she would. Nerissa is nothing if not reliable— the Fae are predictable that way. They have their own code of conduct and rules of governance."

"Can they really not lie?" he asked. That was something he'd always heard about fairies, but he'd never believed it. As a former member of law enforcement, Daniel knew lying was like breathing.

"They can't if they are upper-caste Fae," Serin confirmed. "A few millennia ago, the Seelie and Unseelie Courts were in turmoil. There were countless insurrections and plots against the throne and between the courts. Too many of their most powerful were dying. The monarchs of the time feared they would end up wiping them-selves out or diluting their power so much they would be easy prey for enemies from the outside. In an unprecedented move, the heads of both factions collaborated. They bound their followers with a powerful curse—one that keeps them from lying on penalty of death."

"Wow," he muttered. "That must have taken a lot of mojo."

"It did. In fact, the Fae had to sacrifice one of their most powerful artifacts to pull it off. A fair amount of their magic went with it. Today, the Fae are still dangerous, but there aren't any among their ranks who could be classified as world-breakers."

He turned that last phrase over in his mind. How many *world-breakers* had this world seen? Was John one? Nah. Daniel would let that happen over his dead body.

"So the Fae can't lie, but I bet they can massage the hell out of the truth," Daniel observed. "Like most politicians."

"That's right." Serin laughed. "The average member of the Seelie and Unseelie can put your human leaders to shame with their skills."

He grunted. "They sound like a ton of fun," he added, squatting next to her. "I'm guessing your friend Loki isn't high caste?"

"No, and thank the Mother that he's not. The higher you go, the more concentrated the power. Could you imagine the trouble he could get up to if he had that kind of juice?"

"I'd rather not," he said, wondering what the trickster Fae was up to. Daniel had expected to hear from him by now. He made a mental note to ask Noomi. The pair had gotten close during their last adventure.

"Underhill is their home, right?" he continued, determined to cram as much knowledge into his head as he could.

"It is now. That's where the Fae Courts are located."

"Have you been there?"

"Once or twice. Our kind can't open the door to Underhill."

"I thought you and the other Elementals could go anywhere?" Daniel asked with a frown.

"We can—anywhere on Earth. But Underhill isn't on Earth. It exists in its own pocket universe. However, it has many tendrils to our world. Some scholars think they may have been one at some point, but they diverged. Personally, I think it latched onto ours, like a parasite."

"Huh," Daniel said with a sniff. She put a hand on his shoulder, then rubbed. When Serin had told him about the spot of Fae blood running through his veins, he'd been a bit alarmed. What she told him wasn't making him feel better.

"An Elemental can enter Underhill by invitation of the ruling monarch—and the current Seelie queen is not likely to issue one unless it amuses her, or if we find an unsealed passage. Underhill creates them on its own from time to time."

"It almost sounds like T'Kaieri—alive and with a mind of its own."

Serin sat up, then stretched out on the rock beside him. "Well, to my knowledge, T'Kaieri has never tried to kill anyone. The same can't be said for Underhill."

"Groovy," he muttered.

His mate snapped to the right as if she'd heard something in the distance. "The siren is incoming. Look alive."

In the distance, he caught a flash under the water. The localized swell moved toward them fast. It reminded him of a scene in Jaws. He half-expected a fin to pop up, but the tiny ripple stayed beneath the surface, an unseen menace.

A head emerged, followed by a shapely set of shoulders. The siren was stunning, but the beatific smile she gave him reminded him of a predator—like a praying mantis contemplating her next meal... alien and calculating.

"Serin!" Nerissa squealed at his mate before switching her attention to him. She looked him up and down as if she wanted to devour him whole. She flashed him a smile, proving she could do it if she wanted to. She had the equipment for it—sharp, almost needlelike, teeth.

The siren raised out of the water with a hand on the stone, then touched his pant leg. "What a delicious specimen. Did you bring me a present?"

"I'm afraid not," Serin said, her voice flat and discouraging.

Daniel shied away from the siren's touch, trying not to let how creeped out he was show on his face.

"Oh." Nerissa was crestfallen. She dropped into the water with a little pout. "Is he a gift for the queen?"

"Another no. He's with me." Serin reached out to pat his pocket, reminding him to take out his phone. "I wanted to ask you about the man who approached you a few months ago."

Daniel held up the screen, displaying the sketch of John.

The siren narrowed her eyes, scanning the likeness. "Who said anyone approached me?" she asked in a cloying sugar-sweet voice.

"A little birdie mentioned it," Serin deadpanned. "Was this the man who sank the cruise ship?"

"John *sank* a cruise ship?" Daniel exclaimed. "When did this happen?"

"It was last year, but nobody died." Nerissa sneered, her tone clearly conveying no deaths was a bad thing. "Humans are far more prepared for disasters at sea these days. And they have much faster rescue vessels. All hands were saved—well except for an old man who had a heart attack. Sadly, he was not buried at sea."

Her regret over that fact was palpable. Daniel smothered a grimace as the mental image of Nerissa munching down on a human leg popped into his mind.

"He was trying to get your attention," Serin continued. "John wanted in with the Fae, and he risked thousands of lives to do it. My source told me that you were there when the vessel sank."

"And you believed them?" The siren practically batted her eyelashes.

"My source wasn't lying—*it* can't." With her fingers, Serin drew something in the air. A symbol appeared, glowing briefly before sinking into the water. The light flared, and a ghost of an image appeared on the reflective surface—a massive cruise ship in distress. Just off to the side was a telltale shimmer. Nerissa's head bobbed in and out of view for a second, just long enough to identify her.

Serin had told him the ocean had many secrets, but a Water Elemental could discover them if necessary.

"Fine," Nerissa snapped. "I saw him on a small craft near the sinking vessel. He was playing a recording of a siren singing."

"So, he was trying to get the passengers to jump off the vessel to what...feed you?"

Nerissa scoffed. "A facsimile doesn't have the same power as a siren's voice. He wasn't even close enough for them to hear him."

"But a siren has excellent hearing," Serin observed. "How else would you be able to hear all those drowning sailors? What did John want from you?"

Daniel didn't think the Fae was going to answer. She flicked a drop of water in his general direction. "He offered to sabotage every Coast Guard vessel on the Eastern seaboard for me, in exchange for an audience with the queen."

Serin was starting to lose her patience, but it was hard to tell by her deceptively bland expression. "And did you carry this message to your regent?"

Nerissa was incensed. "As if I would ever do such a thing! It's against her dictates. The queen does not consort with upstart practitioners—or Elementals if she can help it."

The siren turned away as if bored. "Is that all you wanted, Serin? I have things to do..."

"Did you make your queen's policy clear to the suspect?" Daniel asked.

Nerissa turned, batting her long lashes. Her hand snaked out again, touching his shoe this time. "Are you very attached to the human, Serin? I have all manner of treasure I could trade for him."

"Excuse me, but I am not up for barter." Daniel was starting to feel objectified, like a piece of meat. *This must be what those Magic Mike guys feel like...if they were going to be eaten at the end of the fun, that was.*

"I just love the sound of his voice. It's so deep and rumbly, like an earthquake under the water."

"Glad you like it," Daniel growled. Not being addressed directly was starting to get on his last nerve. "Did the suspect mention anything else? Something that suggested where he was going or who he was going to speak to next?"

The Siren ignored him, putting both hands on the rocks and resting her head on her arm. Behind her, an ornately finned tail rose out of the water, flicking him and Serin with drops of saltwater.

"If there's nothing else, I should get going."

"Seriously, you're not going to answer my question?" Daniel was getting pissed.

"She can't," Serin guessed. "The Fae have standing orders from the queen—minimal compliance with our inquiries."

His mate knelt, squatting in front of Nerissa. Unlike most Supernaturals they'd met since he'd started running with Serin, the siren didn't blink. "But this man isn't wanted by us because he's a danger to Elementals. We're hunting him because he's a threat to the Mother... and I don't have to tell you how uncomfortable life would be for the Fae if something happened to Her."

Nerissa ran sharp teeth over her full lower lip, contemplating Serin's words.

"This man is looking for a way to get to Her, but there is no path to the Mother. There are, however, a number of entrances to Underhill popping in and out of existence all the time. Not all lead to the Seelie Court, but some do. You might want to consider that."

The siren made a little smacking sound. "I will pass that along."

She retreated a short distance from the rock.

"Pity you didn't sing for John," Daniel called. It wouldn't have solved all of their problems, but it could have saved them a whole lot of legwork if the siren had just eaten the bad guy.

"What makes you think she didn't?" Serin asked.

Annoyance flickered across Nerissa's face.

"He would have been prepared for that," his mate finished.

"No comment." The siren was petulant now.

Serin glanced down at her, raising one fine eyebrow.

"It was a charm," the siren admitted grudgingly. "I don't know where he got it, but I couldn't undermine its hold."

"How would you do that?" he asked curiously.

"The way most spells are undone—with saltwater." Nerissa's expression was wicked. "Like this."

A wave built behind her, heading toward them. It flew over the edge of the rock to slap them down or sweep them over the edge—or at least that was what the flesh-eating mermaid intended. Daniel put his hands up in reaction. He felt a push as if the pressure dropped, and the water fell away from him almost as if it hit a wall.

It didn't touch Serin, either. The water danced around her, settling into the ocean like an obedient puppy dog.

Nerissa huffed in disdain before disappearing under the waves. This time, the surface of the water wasn't disturbed by so much as a ripple. There was no way to tell where she'd gone.

Daniel turned to his mate. She frowned. "Did you do that?" she asked.

"What?"

"You pulled on my power to deflect the water."

Daniel blinked, then grinned. "I can do that?"

Serin wrinkled her nose. "Apparently."

He beamed. "I didn't know that was a benefit to our relationship."

"It's not supposed to be."

Daniel prided himself on being a no-nonsense and helpful mate, but this time he was beside himself with glee—for all of two seconds.

"That didn't hurt you, did it?" he asked, concerned.

"Relax, I'm fine." Serin still observed him like a bug under a microscope.

"But you felt it? If it happens again, will it compromise you? Like does it suck away some of your power?"

That would be bad in the middle of a firefight.

"I didn't feel drained. I channel my gifts from the Mother. I just channeled a bit more is all."

Daniel's mood swung back to jubilant. "That is awesome! I bet the damn werewolf can't do that."

Logan's mate Connell was like a lot of guys he'd met while in the DEA—brave and brash in addition to being smug and arrogant. And a showoff. Daniel was a fairly tolerant man, but the only person he allowed to emasculate him was the woman in front of him.

Alec was okay for a bloodsucking creature of legend, but the werewolf was a bit much even for him.

"As far as I know, Connell can't use Logan's talent."

Daniel threw his arms up. "Yes!"

Serin continued to frown.

"I won't do it again, I promise. I wouldn't want to distract you in a fight."

"No." Serin reached out to grab his shoulder. "I want you to do it, *especially* in a fight."

She backed away. "Who knows? Alec and Connell are powerful Supes, weapons themselves. Perhaps this is the Mother's way of evening the score."

He threw her a bright grin. "I'm all for that."

But Serin didn't smile.

"What's wrong? Isn't this good news?"

"Of course it is," she said after a moment. "But if the Mother is expanding your abilities this way, it must mean that whatever is coming is big—more than She thinks we can handle on our own."

"Oh." Daniel's excitement faded. "Well, that is...unfortunate."

There was a beat of silence, then Serin gestured at the rocky beach. "Don't let me rain on your parade. You are allowed to enjoy this new development. Go nuts."

His grin was so wide it almost hurt his face. "Show me what to do."

24

"*Don't do that. Don't make me like you.*"

"*Too late. You already do.*"

Gia wrinkled her nose, replaying those words in her mind. It had only become more true in the days since, but she wasn't ready to acknowledge it. It would only give Salvador ideas.

She adjusted her grip on the divining rod, poking it into the liquified earth between two massive tree trunks. After weeks of experimentation, Gia thought she knew how it worked now. The rod needed to resonate not just with the user, but also the land they stood on. They just needed to find the right soft spot. Thus, their current location. They were in the redwood forest somewhere between Klamath and Clear Creek. It was one of many locations they were testing with the rod.

They hadn't heard anything from John in weeks, but time was running out. She could feel it.

Salvador hadn't complained when their quest stretched from days to weeks. He'd been an ideal traveling companion, never objecting when they hopped from Elemental safe house to camping in the woods and back again. Very little seemed to faze him. Despite the shock of learning he was going to have a sibling, Salvador continued being genial, almost Zen.

He was well versed in spell lore, and he had quite a few interesting things to say about cursed and bespelled artifacts. Since most of the worst ones had been made by his ancestors and extant relatives, she hadn't been surprised by that, but neither had she expected him to be quite so helpful.

Salvador also prepared meals without being asked.

Gia loved food in all its forms—gourmet, fast, healthy. Her favorite, though, was junk. Salvador was also a fan. He could cook like a professional chef, but he was just as content to drop everything and hunt down a greasy hole in the wall that made the best zeppole in Little Italy.

His fine qualities and charm were worming their way past her defenses. *You are not developing feelings for a Delavordo.* Not those kinds. Friendship was possible, of course. She had lived long enough to know that the knife's edge she and the other Elementals danced on made for strange bedfellows.

Now was that a Freudian slip or was that a Freudian slip?

"Are you hungry?" Salvador asked from behind another redwood.

She gave herself a shake, giving up on her task. This place was close, but it was not receptive to the divining rod. "You read my mind," she said, coming around to where Salvador arranged wood in a ring of stones.

No, not in a million years. And even she didn't think she'd be doing this job that long.

Then stop picturing what he looks like without that shirt...

Salvador stood, his impressively wide shoulders on display in a V-neck woven shirt. "I should gather a bit more firewood if we're going to be cooking here—and, before I forget, *where* is here again?"

"Pacific Northwest."

"Ah." He pointed to the redwood trunk. "I should have guessed that. Any luck with the rod? This isn't our final destination, is it?"

"Not yet. The rod is responding, but not in sync yet. We should keep looking around. There is another leyline cluster less than twenty clicks away." She waggled her brows. "But first, dinner."

He laughed. "Gathering enough wood for the meal may take a while. These trees are protected, so it's limited to what I can pick up from the ground."

Salvador stopped speaking as the trees around them dropped some of their smaller branches on the ground. He jumped when one landed less than a foot away.

"Sorry," she apologized. "Didn't mean to startle you."

He sniffed. "I'd believe you if you weren't smirking."

Bending, he picked up the branch that had nearly brained him. He held out the meter-long length of wood. "I don't suppose you can cut these into usable pieces?"

As if on cue, the wood severed in three places, making four conveniently sized logs.

Salvador wasn't prepared for that. He tried to hold on to them, juggling, but ended up dropping one on his foot.

He shut his eyes, moving his foot to roll it off. "Ouch." He cleared his throat. "Maybe a little warning next time?"

Pursing her lips together to avoid laughing, she nodded, hissing in sympathy when he began to limp. "Nothing's broken," she told him.

"I don't think...hey, you have X-ray vision for bones?"

"In a manner of speaking."

He stopped, pivoting to face her. "Why do I feel naked now?"

"I have no answer to that."

Salvador absorbed that for a minute. He put his arm out, bracing his legs apart in a classic figure-drawing pose.

"What are you doing?" she asked, her head pulling back.

"I'm making it interesting for you."

Suppressing a giggle, Gia held her hands above the ground. Beneath them, a spring appeared. A mound rose in the center with a round bush. It ballooned and sprouted branches, then senesced, leaving an assortment of gifts behind before the rapidly withered away.

"Cool," Salvador whistled, lifting up a dark purple fruit. "What are these?"

"Seasoned black apples. They're pretty good. I think you'll like them."

"Are they real? I mean, can you still find them around?" he asked, lifting one and smelling it. "Or are they extinct like the flowers you gave my mother?"

"They're not that common, but I think you can still find them in Arkansas."

She held up a fleshy thing that looked like an oversized purple strawberry without seeds. "These, however, are extinct. As far as I know, they never had a name, but they taste like a cross between plums and cherries. The rest include some non-native species of fruit and vegetables." She picked up a particularly thick and fleshy golden chanterelle. "Some are choice specimens that can be found here."

He marveled at the size of the mushroom. "That thing must weigh more than half a pound. I know a restaurant in Berkeley that would give you a free dinner in exchange for a few mushrooms like this."

"I think we can manage something better than Chez La Loup."

His face lit up. "You know it?"

"Food appears to be an interest we have in common. I'm surprised you know it, having spent the last few years in the wilds of Costa Rica."

"I did take the occasional vacation," he said before getting down to the business of cooking.

She soon discovered that when it came to mushrooms, Salvador was an artist. Considering he prepared the entire meal without the benefit of pots and pans, he did an admirable job.

"I may have to keep you around," she said when she was done eating.

He beamed. "Okay."

Blinking, Gia met Salvador's eyes. He seemed perfectly serious. For some reason, shooting him down didn't even occur to her.

"Are we going to head out to the next leyline cluster now?" he asked.

"Uh, sure. If you're not tired. Alternatively, we can head out in the morning if you'd rather call it a night."

"I can make it," he began saying before jerking his head sharply. A rending sound filled the air as the earth split right where she'd been poking the ground.

Gia groaned as a massive and roughly hewn hand appeared, clawing its way out of the earth.

"*Chingado*," she swore. "We woke it up."

25

Salvador didn't consider himself a coward. He was the type of man who ran out of his house when there was a cry in the night, picking up a mallet or something else suitably heavy along the way.

But when the creature roared, wiggling its bulk to widen the soft spot to dig itself out of the ground, he didn't object when Gia pushed him behind her. The fact he didn't run away screaming was enough to soothe his masculine pride.

His mind belatedly noted the curled horns atop the creature's head. It gurgled, dripping saliva from jaws filled with jagged and broken teeth that resembled bone tusks. Fumes emanated from the rotting moss hanging from its head.

"What the hell is that?" he asked as a distinctive 'ting' vibrated in the air. A sword had appeared in Gia's hands, called no doubt by the spell he hadn't heard over the hammering of his heart.

"I don't know," she replied with a grimace, obviously unable to stop from reacting to the smell emanating from the pit.

"What?" he asked.

She shrugged, her mouth pulling down. "Never seen one before. My guess is it's one of Underhill's forgotten. I think—"

There were more words Salvador desperately hoped were details of her attack strategy or a 'I know just the spell to deal with this' but the beast chose that moment to roar again, drowning out whatever she said.

The ground shook as the creature banged its tree-like limbs—and at this point, four were visible even though it appeared to only be a third of the way out—on the ground.

Gia ran faster than he'd ever seen anyone move, Alec included. She circled the creature, drawing a rapid circle with the point of her sword. Embellishments appeared, runes and symbols forming a containment spell. As the circle widened, the soil began to churn, forming a sinkhole. The beast disappeared with a final roar.

"Well, that was easier than I thought." Salvador heaved a breath.

"I'm afraid it's not over," Gia said, sheathing her sword. "Using the divining rod unsealed a prison I doubt anyone in the Seelie Court remembers is still there. I just buried it. We might get lucky. It's possible it'll suffocate."

"What are the chances of that?"

"Not very good," she admitted. "Otherwise, it wouldn't have been buried at a leyline nexus. The energy currents must have been twisted to make a net around it."

"One we disturbed," he finished. "So now what?"

"Now, we fight. Get ready."

Surprised she wasn't trying to shoo him away, Salvador spun around, searching for anything he might be able to weaponize.

Fae, she said it was Fae. It might be sensitive to iron, but he doubted it. The trolls weren't, and this creature was closer to that than the dryads he treated once in a blue moon. What else did that leave? Lemongrass—for some reason trolls didn't like it. But this was the Pacific Northwest, not the tropics.

Mugwort? Shouldn't there be some in these woods?

Crap. There was nothing like that around. He half hoped Gia would want to run, but even as he thought it, he dismissed the idea. She was an Elemental, and it was her job to make sure the creature didn't get loose. They were miles from civilization, but that thing would tear through an army like tissue paper. Not to mention that letting it be seen by non-magicals was a violation of the Covenant.

Well, there's no help for it. He rolled up his sleeves, checking to see his finger was still bleeding. *Or was that a bad thing? What if it smelled blood like a shark? Never mind that.* He needed his strongest defensive spells. Without his medical bag, he was short of supplies. *Blood would have to do.*

Taking the pendant off, he cut himself wider before removing his shirt.

Gia paused, taking in his bare chest in confusion. "What are you doing?"

"Need more surface area," he bit out, tracing his bloody finger over his chest.

"Oh," she said. She whirled away, swishing her sword as if to test its sharpness on the air. The sword continued to sing as the runes on the ground multiplied, growing into an ever-widening series of ornate and concentric rings.

"Will those help?" he asked, adding an additional protection sigil on his arm next to the one for acceleration. *If the beast got loose, he was going to need to move very fast.*

The ground rumbled beneath them ominously.

"I think we're going to find out."

Okay. Expecting comfort from an Elemental had been rather stupid under the circumstances.

Forget it. He lowered his head and started muttering, focusing on his fists and the line of sigils running up his muscled forearms.

The lines drawn in blood flared, then started to glow. The iridescence was thickest where the blood was visible, but even the bits with only a trace lit up. *Good.* His enchantment had taken.

The air around his fists shimmered, heating it until it resembled the space around a campfire. But this was no optical illusion. It was magic... twisting and pushing against the fabric of reality.

Another sword had appeared in Gia's hands, giving her a matching set. She walked backward until she almost touched him. Snatching his hands away, he bent to pick up a stone. It began to sparkle, the glow transferring from his palms. When he threw it, it would detonate on impact with a force stronger than C4. He could supercharge over a dozen more before his magic was spent.

"Not bad," Gia said, scanning the glowing stone. Several more rolled across the ground, neatly stacking themselves near him. She was giving him more ammunition. "Don't do more than ten—you'll need the energy to run if we don't put it down in the first few minutes."

She was right.

"I could tap into the leyline," he suggested, wincing as another roar made his ears ring.

"Sorry," she said, shaking her head. "I might need the cluster's power to reform the prison if we can't kill it."

He was having difficulty following her again. The rumbling earth was getting loud again. Subtlety was not in the creature's repertoire. He spared a moment to thank the Mother for that.

"Here we go," Gia warned, her hips widening into a battle stance.

This time the creature burst out of the ground like the colossus Shai-Hulud of science fiction.

Dirt sprayed over him. Shielding his eyes briefly, Salvador started running, stooping to pick up an armful of stones along the way.

Gia leapt straight into the fray. He caught one glimpse of her sailing body, a sword in each hand. She was a few feet from the head when a thick redwood trunk obscured his vision. Clearing the tree, he pulled back his arm and hurled the rock. Gia had gone high, so he aimed low, hoping to take out the legs.

There was a thud and a roar. The rock hit its target—he was sure of it. However, there was so much dust and shrapnel thrown into the air by then, he couldn't confirm the hit.

But then he heard the stomping footsteps. By rights, the creature should have been a legless wonder. Salvador had put a lot of juice in the stone, but it hadn't been enough. Dropping back, he charged another stone and ran, flinging it as the haze cleared to give him another shot.

He caught a glimpse of Gia running and leaping through the air.

His heartbeat seemed to track her movement, stopping and restarting when she landed on the creature's back.

When it started beating again, he raised his arm, but so did the monster. A thick vine shot out at head height. Throwing himself on the ground, he scrambled away as the end of the vine split, grappling at the tree trunk behind him. The slimy creepers ripped a chunk out of the tree.

Gasping, he pictured his head being crushed like a grape as he crawled away. But he'd have to run to the next county to get out of range. It seemed those vine appendages were capable of growing to unspeakable lengths.

Scrambling, he backed up, watching Gia dart back and forth. He held his breath as those deadly vines lashed out, trying to wrap around her. They came within a hairsbreadth of her head. He opened his mouth to call out a warning, but she was already moving out of range. Whatever freak spatial sense Elementals had was working overtime.

Gia sank into the floor, popping up on the beast's other side. He almost cheered when she sheared off two vine appendages before scolding himself. *Stop gawking and help, you idiot.*

He bounced from foot to foot, searching for his opportunity. Picking up one of the stones, he found his moment when everything in front of the beast cleared, revealing its upper torso. Rearing back like a Major League pitcher, he let go, aiming for the monster's head.

"Incoming," he yelled. His heart stopped as the creature shifted, bowing to the ground just before the glowing stone hit. The explosive sailed over the beast, toward Gia's chest, as she swung her sword at the creature.

"No!"

His cry made her head jerk up. At the last moment, she lifted her free hand, deflecting the stone at the creature. Then she kicked it in the back, causing it to fall over the rock. The beast's own bulk protected her from the blast—which was large enough to throw stinging shrapnel up. He twisted to protect his eyes, but not far enough. A piece cut his cheek before glancing off.

The direct impact seemed to stun the creature. It moved slower now.

Gia turned, scowling. "Pro tip—if I can hear you, so can the bad guy."

"I didn't think it would understand English," he apologized lamely.

But Gia wasn't listening anymore. She started chanting a spell, one that seemed to encompass both containment and something else —a draining curse, something that would deplete what strength the monster had.

If the opponent were human, this would have been the most horrible way to die. He made a fist, empathy enervating him. His grip didn't have the strength it normally would.

"What is happening to it?"

The creature's sound was both pitiful and enraged. But it wasn't loud, not anymore. It grew quieter as the beast became weaker.

Sadness crept over Salvador at the wretched sound. "I guess we're not trapping it anymore."

Gia was going to kill the creature. Despite the fact it had been trying to cut them down and possibly eat them, pity welled in his heart.

He crept closer to where the beast writhed on the ground. Up close, it resembled a distended Swamp Thing, vines and trees branches wrapped around boulders. "Do... do we have to do this? Couldn't we imprison it again?"

She shook her head. "That would be a far crueler fate. It wants to die."

"How do you know that?"

Her face was somber and drawn. "Can't you hear it?" she whispered, her eyes a well of pain and compassion.

The plaintive cry was desperate yes—but he couldn't make out any words. Then he gazed into the beast's face. The eyes. They were intelligent and tormented.

Gia knelt, heedless of the writhing vines. She touched the creature's head, then glanced over her shoulder. "I'm going to need your help."

"What?"

"You must know a spell to kill plants, yes?" she asked

Salvador lifted his foot, untangling it from a still-twitching creeper. "Uh, can't you do it?"

"That's not how my magic works," she said, a thread of impatience entering her tone. "I can try to tear them off, even send them far away, but they will just regenerate. But a Delavordo is taught how to kill everything under the sun—I'm counting on that now."

Not knowing how to feel about that, he knelt, half-expecting the limp vine to be playing possum. Any second now, it would lash out and wrap itself around his neck.

"Faster if you please."

Salvador steeled himself, then put his hands around the nearest vine. "Uh, okay, I'm not proud of this one, but here goes."

"*Mortifer obnitor.*"

It was a curse he'd known for years, ever since he'd gone exploring the wilds of the Congo at thirteen with his father and cousins. Instead of hacking their way to the dreaded temple of Baphomet, his father had taken a shortcut and used a dark curse to defoliate the jungle instead. It was a spell equivalent to agent orange.

At first, he didn't think it was going to work. But then Gia put her hand over his. She didn't touch him, but he felt the jolt anyway. The strength of his spell got a boost.

The vine began to shrivel and wither away. He was right about it being wrapped around stones. The boulders and rocks were exposed as the greasy vines retracted, turning to dust.

With a flick of her wrist, Gia sent the stones rolling away. Salvador drew back. He'd expected the stones and vines had been an avatar powered by magic. But he'd been wrong.

"It was a suit," he breathed, staring at the man on the ground.

"Yes." Gia's voice was clipped.

The man before him was a Fae warrior, or what was left of him. Pieces of his original army uniform still remained—a brace on his arm and most of a shin guard. The flesh around it was still muscled but desiccated, like jerky strung and wrapped around the bones. His skin was pallid and grey. The man was next to dead, but his face was hauntingly handsome. His appearance was not a Fae glamour. This had been a nobleman.

The man whispered something, Fae words in dialect so old Salvador couldn't decipher them.

"I understand," Gia whispered. When she opened her hand, a knife appeared. She gripped it tightly.

Salvador grabbed her hand. "But what if we can save him?"

"Too late," the Fae man rasped in plain English. "Every breath is pain. There is nothing left without the enchantment—the spell took everything. I served my regents faithfully, yet they still did this to me."

"That war is over," Gia said. "The kings and queens who fought it are long dead and buried. A new queen sits on the Seelie throne."

"And the Unseelie?" he wheezed.

"Hidden from this realm."

Salvador started, dropping his arm. He hadn't known that. He'd assumed the Unseelie Court was up and running—same as the glittering one.

The man said something else, but Salvador couldn't understand him. It was then he realized the man hadn't been speaking English at all.

It's because I was touching her. Like demons, Elementals had the gift of tongues. They could speak every language there was. Demons used that gift to ensnare unsuspecting humans. Elementals needed it to do their jobs. Perhaps he'd heard the translation because she'd shared some magic with him to boost his spell. He wasn't sure.

More words were exchanged, then Gia nodded. Salvador started to close his eyes as she brought the blade down, but he forced them open. To look away would have dishonored the warrior.

The blow sliced the man's neck at the jugular. After so long under a black curse, the blood didn't run out of his body. He'd been right about that. The enchantment had used him up, turning his green blood—Fae blood tended to have an emerald tint when exposed to air—nearly solid. It oozed a bit around the cut, but didn't run over his chest the way his blood should have.

The little strength left in the warrior gave way. His face went slack and began to crumble, falling into dust. Salvador coughed as some of the brownish-gold powder made its way into his lungs.

Hurriedly, he got to his feet, then staggered. "Whoa. Head rush."

Salvador glanced down. A spot of blood on his shirt blossomed outward. "Or not."

Gia shifted, then scowled at his shirt. "Hey, what happened?"

Belatedly, Salvador felt the pain. "This is wrong. It was a tiny piece of shrapnel. I barely felt it."

"*Mierda*," Gia spat, lifting his shirt to examine the wound. "It's working its way in."

"What?"

She swore under her breath. "Those ancient Fae kings and queens didn't mess around. Every bit of that suit-shell was designed to destroy. The vines were poisonous, and the stones within were enchanted. Even a shard or pebble is lethal. Whatever shrapnel hit you is burrowing deeper, trying to find your heart. Our only advantage is that the spell is old, so it's going slower than it would have when it was first cast."

Fuck. "How do I get it out?" he asked, falling to his knees. Despite what she'd said, he could feel the rock moving. It felt as if it were going plenty fast to him. "It's a rock. Can you call it out?"

Gia crouched, putting up her hands. Her nose wrinkled, her mouth hardening with effort.

"Anytime would be great," he urged, gritting his teeth. Sweat had sprouted on his brow, starting to drip down his temple. But he tried to hide how much it hurt.

She inhaled with a hiss. "It's not working."

"But it's a rock."

"Apparently, it's not from these parts."

"What?"

Gia blinked, swallowing. "Shut up."

"But—"

"I said shut it." She rose, then began waving her hands over his body.

"What is that?" he asked.

"A stasis spell. And a complicated one, so stop interrupting."

"But—"

"Not again." Gia gritted her teeth, placing her hand on her chest. "Okay, well, nothing else but to do it, I suppose..."

She held up a finger. "This is going to hurt me more than it hurts you."

Unable to help himself, he opened his mouth to ask what she meant, but closed it when her fist reared up. That was the last thing he remembered before she knocked him unconscious.

26

———

Salvador woke up staring at the benign and nearly toothless smile of an old hag.

"Um, hello?" he said, rubbing his head as he scooted into a sitting position. He was crammed onto a double bed. It was a standard, which meant he was too tall for it. His legs hung over the edge, but someone had covered him with an embroidered blanket.

"That should be thank you."

Squinting, he peered over the old woman's shoulder. Gia leaned against the far wall in the fire-lit semi-darkness.

His head was still swimming, and his limbs felt too heavy to lift. "All right. I'll play. Thank you."

The old woman beamed. "*Que lindo*," she cackled, reaching out to pinch his cheek. "*Debes de quedarte con este.*"

"Nana, stop." Gia chided. "*Puedes preparar algo de comer para el? Va necessitar toda su fuerza.*"

"*Si, si.*" Gia helped the old woman to her feet before ushered her out the door.

"Nana? As in grandmother? By the Mother, how old is she?" he asked in disbelief as the door closed behind the crone.

Practitioners were longer lived than humans, but this was

pushing the boundaries of all reason. And her nana thought he was cute... and that Gia should keep him? He blushed, trying to push *that* thought out of his mind. Instead, he focused on what Gia had said. H *was* hungry, and they did need food to keep up their strength.

"No, of course she's not my grandmother," Gia said, rolling her eyes. "Although she is one several times over. Everyone here calls her nana, even me, although I'm old enough to remember her in swaddling clothes."

Wincing, he held the spot where the shrapnel had hit. There was a bandage over the wound now.

"It's gone. Nana helped me get it out. She also purged the poison and reknit the flesh. It's almost all healed."

"Who is *we*? Where are we?"

Gia appeared uncomfortable. "You are in Telerin village. My family's home."

Salvador nearly gasped, but he stopped himself because he thought it might hurt. "That woman is your actual grandmother?"

"Of course not. I said she wasn't. The woman who birthed my mother is long dead. But my family lives on. Nana is my younger sister's descendant—specifically, she's her great-great-great-great-great-great-great-great granddaughter—give or take a few greats."

"You had a biological sister?"

"I did," she said slowly. Salvador suspected Gia did not share these details with many people. "Her name was Isadora. She was fierce and only minimally annoying the way sisters are supposed to be. Isadora had only one surviving daughter, but that daughter had three children. Successive generations have been even more prolific. I have relations all over the globe. But this is the place I call home," she said, gesturing to the window and presumably the village at large.

"And Nana is the best healer in the world, although I admit you do give her a run for her money, at least when it comes to poisons and curses."

"She healed me?"

"She did," Gia murmured. "I did help a bit. But then, I owed you one."

He peeked under the bandage. The wound was still red, but it was no longer open. "That's debatable. I should have let you deal with that Fae berserker on your own. I just got in your way."

She shrugged. "You helped. Some."

It was subtle, but there was a slight clipped quality to her words.

"Are you angry at me?"

"*No.*"

His eyes widened. Gia was lying to him. "You are." And he knew why. "It's because I almost died. *Aww.* You would miss me."

"I would not." She scowled, rolling her shoulder awkwardly.

"Admit it. You like me."

"That's not it," she insisted.

He snickered. "I've finally grown on you."

"Maybe a little," she grudgingly admitted. "Like a fungus."

Now he was ready to dance a jig, or he would if he could stand. "We've had mushrooms with practically every meal. You *love* fungus."

Gia's mouth firmed into a thin line. Deciding to let it go, he examined his surroundings, silently marveling she had brought him home.

Now that his eyes were getting used to the darkness, he could make out that the rough walls of the room were adobe. A wooden bureau polished to a deep shine set flush against the wall. The surface was covered in small porcelain figurines and other knick-knacks every woman over the age fifty seemed to accumulate.

And the old woman was Gia's descendant. It was mind-bending. This wasn't like the vampires whose little cliques were mostly static. Gia was like a great stone in a shifting river of time. It flowed past her while she remained unchanged. But she still immersed in it, surrounding herself with her loved ones.

"Do they know what you are? Your relatives, I mean?"

Gia sat on the stool Nana had vacated. "Of course. I don't have to hide what I am here. That would be ridiculous. The people of Telerin are my family."

Unbelievable. "But it's not like T'Kaieri, the Water Elemental's home. This place is open. Anyone could come here. Anyone could leave. It's not a closed community, is it?"

"It's not," she said. "I wouldn't want that for them. This is the same land my mother and father walked—a pocket of magic hidden in plain sight. Everyone here has magic in their blood. It's a repository of learning as well as a home. The Mother's love is strong here—although if I were you, I wouldn't make the mistake of believing us to be doves and diplomats. I also wouldn't share your last name with anyone here. Not even Nana, unless you want her to spit in your food."

"Of course," he muttered. The Delavordo name was supposed to open doors. That was what his mother always said. But that depended on the places a Delavordo wanted to go. Lucia couldn't know how many of those doors had slammed in his face because of his family name.

Salvador supposed it could have been worse. He could have lived centuries ago when the seven families were in open warfare, instead of the tense alliances and clandestine conflicts of today.

I could have been like the Fae warrior, unwilling cannon fodder. "Did they truly do that to their own people? The Fae, I mean."

Gia leaned back with a sigh. "When the battles raged between the different Fae kingdoms, nothing was beyond the pale. There were more then, too. Fiefdoms, really, but some were quite powerful. Now only the two strongest remain, Seelie and Unseelie, yin and yang. They'd destroy each other if they could, but then the other would fall as well—a result of the Great Curse."

Salvador's fuzzy brain supplied the knowledge. In addition to imposing certain restrictions on lying, the Fae's Great Curse was supposed to have done a few other things, but those had never been detailed in his history books. "Let me guess. It guarantees mutual destruction?"

"In a word, yes."

He nodded, sympathy for the fallen kingdoms of the past overwhelming him.

His growling stomach pushed him past his reverie. "By chance is Nana a good cook? I'm starving."

"She's a better cook than she is a healer."

He brightened, but her continued serious expression put a damper on his enthusiasm. Assuming it was because they failed, he sat up straighter.

"I'll be ready to head out to the woods after I eat," he promised. "Since the berserker is gone, we can try again."

"It's all right. We don't have to go back to the woods. I figured out another way."

"You did?" Shouldn't she be happy about that? Gia was sober as a judge.

True, he wasn't a specialist on women's moods. His few girlfriends had remained closed books, but he wasn't completely dense when it came to Gia.

Which was why a sinking feeling had started in the pit of his stomach. "Why do I get the feeling that I'm not going to like this?"

He finally got a smile, but this one did little to comfort him. "Because you're smarter than you look."

27

Gia swallowed the last sweet raisin and pineapple *tamale*. Nana smacked her on the arm, warning her she was going to choke if she didn't eat more slowly.

"Ow, not so hard, Nana," she chided, rubbing her arm even though it didn't hurt. It was a game they'd played since Nana was little.

She ate some more, savoring the warmth of the kitchen. Before Nana, it had been Celestina cooking here. Before Celestina, this had been Renata's domain. Her sister's descendants had generously opened their home to her for centuries. And, fortunately, they had all been good cooks.

Nana's steady stream of chatter worked its usual magic, soothing the ragged edges of her soul. The fight with the Fae warrior had bothered her more than she had let on. What had been done to him—that kind of depravity and desperation left a mark, even when a person only bore witness to it.

Bussing Nana's cheek, she hugged her goodbye before taking Ciro's rod and walking to the village square. The cluster of houses in the center of town had their lights on. Inside, her relatives went on with their lives, uninterrupted by her visit. Even Nana stayed behind in her kitchen, pleased to have a man to cook for again. And as long as that man didn't share his family name, he would live to see another day.

Gia reached the open space in the middle of town, taking a seat at the base of the statue dedicated to the Mother. Like many in this part of the world, it more closely resembled the Virgin Mary than the Mother, but it was all in the eye of the beholder. The bird she held in one hand was a dead giveaway.

Salvador appeared a few minutes later. He had showered and changed clothes, and he held a *pan dulce* in each hand. "I brought one for you," he said handing her one of the breads. "They're still warm, hot out of the oven."

Shaking her head at his boundless appetite, she took the bread. It did smell good. They ate in silence, leaning against the base of the statue.

"I'm surprised Nana didn't insist on coming to see you off," he observed between bites.

"She's old, and her arthritis is acting up," Gia replied, polishing off the last of the sweet bread.

"And your other relatives?" he asked, gesturing at the clearly occupied houses.

Her mouth pulled up at the corner. "You act as if my visit here should be a big event. But as you pointed out earlier, this isn't T'Kaieri. We don't stand on ceremony here. We don't even sit on ceremony."

Gia licked her fingers, then gestured at the benches she'd passed over in favor of the statue base. But he shook his head, squatting at the base of statue.

"So, they don't make a big deal about you coming around?" he asked.

"No, and thank the Mother for that." She snorted. "My relatives have their own lives, their own struggles and triumphs. Some are big and some aren't. I come from a talented line of practitioners. That talent lives on in the current generation."

"Well, I know all about magic begetting magic," he acknowledged, looking around him contemplatively. "There must be some pretty interesting stories in this village. But you're still the center of it, aren't you? I feel like there should be fanfare or a spotlight on you and what you're doing. Isn't this an extraordinary situation with the Mother being so directly threatened?"

"If the world was ending tomorrow, would you want to know?" Gia wrinkled her nose. "I don't sound the alarm every time the world comes under threat. It would be selfish...and repetitive."

That finally seemed to sink in. Salvador stopped glancing around as if expecting the villagers to surround them—in his case, with pitchforks.

"So what dreaded fate is in store for me?" he asked with a significant look at Ciro's rod, brushing the sugar off his hands.

"I figured out a shortcut, one that doesn't require being at the perfect place." She lifted the rod, then pushed it into his hands. "We're going to turn you into the perfect user instead. We are going to make the rod think you are Ciro."

Salvador frowned, limply holding the handles of the divining rod. "And how are we going to do that?"

He could tell from her expression that he was going to hate this part.

"I am going to alter your aura's wavelengths to match his—or close enough to his to make the rod work."

"Okay...I thought you didn't know Ciro. How do you know what his aura looked like? Also, how the hell do you 'alter' them?"

Her hesitation spoke volumes. "Well... I don't have a clue what Ciro's aura looked like. But I'm familiar with the resonance and specific frequency unique to Thiago's."

He scrambled away so fast he almost fell on the floor. "Wait, what?" He put his hands up. "I don't know what the hell you are planning, but *no!*"

He was nearly shouting by the time he was done.

Carmen, Nana's niece, poked her head out of the window of the house across the way. "*Quien handa haciendo todo este ruido?*" she asked, annoyed. "*Estoy mirando mi novela.*"

Gia waved. "*Todo esta bien.*"

Carmen's head retreated, but not before giving Salvador the stink eye.

"Keep it down," Gia muttered in an aside. "You interrupt her soap operas at your peril."

"Sorry, but you can't be serious," he burst out.

"I assure you I'm quite serious. Carmen can turn you into a frog faster than you can blink."

"That's not what I mean, and you know it. You can't make me like Thiago. He was a monster. His aura was darker than Vantablack."

She frowned at him. "Vantawhat?"

"It's the darkest shade of black there is," he supplied. "Manmade."

"I see." She lifted her hands. "Look, I'm not going to make you evil. Or, at least, I don't think I am."

He hung his head. "You have no idea, do you?"

Gia pressed her lips tightly together. "I admit I haven't done anything like this before. But it's our best shot. And if you happen to get all stabby, I will keep tweaking your aura until you're not. We have to keep adjusting it until the rod works for you."

"Assuming you chance on the right frequency." His face twisted as if he'd smelled something foul. "None of this sounds even the slightest bit appealing."

"It's not supposed to," she said honestly. "And you're going to do it because neither of us wants to deal with the alternative. Besides, we don't have to add the black. Or not a lot of it. I did run into Thiago when he was young enough for him to be relatively clear of most of the darkness that eventually consumed him. But it's a starting point. Aura patterns are based our parents—combinations with variations, just like genes for hair or eye color. Honestly, you're more than halfway there. I wasn't kidding when I said you were most like Thiago in appearance."

"So, it's not just my nose and striking cheekbones," he grumbled. "The family resemblance extends to my aura?"

"Are you surprised?" She gestured for him to sit on the ground.

"Not anymore." His expression was so downcast that she put her hand on his shoulder before she could think better of it. When he cocked his head to put his cheek against it, she pushed him down until he rested on the ground.

"Is there a leyline nexus here?" he asked as he arranged his long limbs to sit cross-legged, his face resigned.

"Yes."

Nodding, he placed the rod in front of him. The point dug into a crevice between the cobblestones. "All right. Do your worst."

Gia ignored the sneaky voice in the back of her mind that told her this was a bad idea.

As the Mother's warrior, she was used to putting her life on the line on a daily basis. True, she did have some experience protecting others, but it was usually an abstract act—i.e. kill the bad guy so others could live. If it were direct, it was usually because she stood between someone and the monsters who wanted to eat or dissect them. Having a person entrust their life to her in this manner wasn't normal.

She moved behind him, then put her hands on the back of his head. He jerked, twisting to peer up at her.

There was a hint of a smirk on his face. "I thought you didn't like touching me."

"I never said that," she admitted before she could stop herself. "And for the record, I have to touch you to do this."

He faced forward again, taking a deep breath. "If the worst happens, promise not to leave me dark. I'd rather be a vegetable."

Gia patted his head. From his sudden scowl, she could tell he hated it. "If the worst happens, I'll probably have to kill you."

"I never doubted it for a second," he said easily, making her laugh.

Then she ran her hand from the top of his head to the nape of his neck where his hairline met smooth supple skin. She blinked, letting her second sight take over. Salvador's aura flared, a rainbow of light spilling over into her hands.

Most of the Delavordos sat firmly on the red end of the spectrum —they ran around flaring crimson and orange as if they were on fire. But like Thiago and presumably Ciro, Salvador was a kaleidoscope of cool tones, the shades of green indicative of his healing talent, along with more indigo than she would have guessed.

Thiago's had been quite a bit darker than this, of course. Gia bit her lip before she could confess that she didn't precisely know where to start. In theory, this was similar to mending an aural tear like Logan had done a few years back. It was also *nothing* like that.

Mother guide my hands. Gia studied the shifting waves of his aura. Mentally, she gave it an experimental push.

"Ow."

She pulled her hands away. "Did that hurt?"

"Uh, no. Not exactly. It was more...shocking and creepy. Like someone walked over my grave."

"Hmm. Let me try again." She put her hands back on his neck. The muscles underneath corded like iron as he braced himself.

"You can't be this stiff."

Salvador jerked his head up. "You can't possibly tell that."

Confused, she frowned. "What?"

His eyes cleared, then he blushed. "What?" he echoed.

Realization dawned, and her face heated. "I mean you have to relax if this is going to work."

The burst of laughter was unexpected, especially since it came from her. Straightening, she cleared her throat as Salvador studiously avoided her eyes. He faced forward again. Resuming her position, she closed her eyes, picturing herself surrounding Salvador's aura with her own.

Yes, that was the key. She couldn't poke and prod here and there, and expect his wavelength to shift. No, what she had to do was far more intimate...

He was reacting to her physical touch. What she was about to do to him was more invasive than a proctology exam. *Damn.* Gia hadn't expected this to be so embarrassing.

Swallowing, she shook herself, then shoved her feelings away. Stretching her ability, she wrapped her essence around Salvador until she had totally enveloped him.

Salvador tried to hold still, but he almost vibrated under her hands. When he threw his head back, she suddenly knew exactly what he would look like during a sexual release.

Blushing madly despite herself, she slid her hands to his shoulders, trying not to let his response distract her. She redoubled her efforts, using her own aura to recalibrate his.

It was more difficult than she'd thought. Every time she got close, his natural aura would rebound, fighting to reassert itself. She poured more energy into her hands, shifting and nudging. The effort required considerable effort and precision.

Sweat broke out on her brow. That hadn't happened in a while, but then this wasn't her normal kind of fight.

"Does this hurt?" she asked after a big push made Salvador groan aloud. His head fell back again, and she stared into his glazed eyes and slack features.

The man felt no pain. Quite the opposite. It was startling enough for her to stop.

"Keep going," Salvador urged.

Gia hesitated, clearing her throat. "*O-kay,*" she said, unsure whether to laugh or douse him with cold water. Or herself. Maybe them both.

His aura was resonating, the colors distinctively different now. "Well, the good news is you don't appear to be growing homicidal," she reassured him, resuming her work.

Even if it didn't hurt him, she was quickly tiring. Gritting her teeth, she ignored her growing exhaustion. She had to remind Salvador to keep trying to use the rod, but if this went on much longer, she was going to have to take a break.

Except she didn't. Gia couldn't remember the last time she quit at anything. So, when the edges of her vision began to darken, she powered through because she didn't know how to do anything else.

Failure is not an option, Gia kept thinking as she began to lose consciousness. In the distance, she heard Salvador's voice calling to her. It no longer had a languorous hint. That had been replaced by panic. And then she fell forward, carrying him with her. Together, they kept falling.

28

John scowled. His goggles were too damn tight, but he'd learned from experience not to adjust them outside the shelter. His fingers didn't work that well in the cold. And despite all the high-tech cold weather gear he wore, John was freezing his bollocks off.

Antarctica—the mysterious realm. Many of his countrymen had explored this place with the intent of planting their flag in the name of their king. Personally, he couldn't see the appeal. To his eye, this was a wasteland, full of ice, snow, and not much else.

John tapped his glasses to clear the buildup of snow. *Britain has a queen now,* he reminded himself. And with her ascent, the dominance and prominence of his home nation had predictably waned. *Pity.*

After failing to discover a natural passage to the Mother, John decided on another course of action. If he could find a way to get his formula down to Her, his purpose would be served nearly as well as going down to take care of business on his own. Not as satisfying, of course, but he would have to make do.

John had tried the hot springs in Yellowstone, trusting one to be the conduit he needed, but his efforts there had failed when no clear passage down to the earth's core materialized, despite the research claiming there was one. He'd even tried the volcanoes and hydrothermal vents of the Kamchatka peninsula, but after almost falling into a steam vent, he'd decided Antarctic drilling was the way to go.

He sniffed, then squinted. The wind was up, whipping the tattered flags over the buildings. The defunct research station had changed hands many times. At one point, America, Russian, and Norwegian flags had been flown here. Hell, that light blue bit up there was Argentinian, if he wasn't mistaken.

The buildings had been empty for over a year. Fortunately, most were still sound. They would hold the *elements* at bay until the job was done.

John guffawed aloud at his brilliant pun. The isolation of the station had made setting up this operation a bitch, but now the heavy equipment was here, the isolation was in his favor.

He knew he was being hunted. But this was literally the last place those Elementals would search for him. And his little project? It resembled every other drilling or research operation out there. He could be digging for oil or getting ice-core samples. Little did the men working for him know he wasn't interested in taking something out of the ice. He was interested in putting something in.

When he heard a shout, he turned to see Han Cho, the deep-core drilling engineer he'd hand-picked for this leg of the project. Cho waved him into the main office, so they could talk inside.

It took him a full minute to pull all the gear off his face. The air inside was recycled, but at least it was warm.

"I'm afraid I have bad news, sir," Cho said regretfully.

"You didn't hit the drill depth I wanted. Did the damn drill bit break again?"

Equipment failure had become the norm out here, but he had been told the new drill was top of the line. "I told you it was too small," he bit out.

"It's not the drill, sir. We hit the depth you required, then tried to lower your...err...your device."

John was thrilled. "The sensor." That was what he'd told Cho it was—a prototype that would collect scientific readings for research purposes.

"Uh, yeah. The sensor..." Cho's voice sounded skeptical. "I'm afraid the casing cracked, and some sort of liquid spilled."

A bit premature, but as long as it was at the right depth, they were golden. The poison would be disseminated along the leyline that ran all the way down to the earth's core. "The fuel?" he said, attempting a cover-up. "I think that's fine. The electronics shouldn't be damaged. We can try again."

"Well, there was a lot of fuel, sir. We were going to pull the sensor back up, but I'm afraid the liquid froze. Now the entire apparatus is stuck."

He stilled. "It froze?"

"Yes, sir."

"*Fuck*. That shouldn't have happened." His poison had plenty of antifreeze components. He wasn't a complete idiot. Apparently, his preliminary tests had been insufficient to capture the harshness of this extreme landscape.

It needs to stay liquid to saturate the leyline. Damn. Not to mention adding more chemicals at this stage would alter his perfect formula, destroying the potency.

John felt rage simmer in his chest. In earlier days, he would have strangled Cho to death, but he was past such immature displays. That and a body dropping among such a small group would definitely be noticed. He could see the headlines now—*Murder in Antarctica*.

So, he simply shrugged and forced a grin. "Back to the drawing board."

29

It felt as if her eyelids were weighed down with stones.

"Please say you're awake."

Five more minutes.

"If you don't wake up, I'm turning this car around and taking us back to the surface."

Ugh. "What the hell are you talking about?" she asked with a groan, keeping her eyes closed.

"By car, I mean Ciro's rod," Salvador supplied. "And by wake up, I mean open your damn eyes because I don't know where the *F* we are."

"Are we not swearing now? I know you can," she said, reluctantly lifting her lids. "Are my eyes still closed?"

"Nope," Salvador said. "It is actually this dark."

"Where are we?" she asked, making out his outline above her and to the left.

Belatedly, she realized the things underneath her were Salvador's legs. He'd gathered her body to him in the darkness.

His concern was obvious. "I don't know exactly where we are, but I believe it's where we're supposed to be."

Gia sat up. Their surroundings were still fuzzy. They were below ground. That much she knew. "It's a cave."

She didn't mean to make it sound like a question, but her senses hadn't caught up yet. There was the sound of running water, but it was faint. Just a trickle running down the walls.

"It is, and it isn't," he answered cryptically. He helped her up. A brief impression of rough walls drifted by, then there was a sense of space, as if they were hanging over a great chasm—because they were.

When he whispered a small rhyme, a light appeared, expanding between his hands. He tossed it up. It stayed above them, hovering like a tiny sun.

Gia and Salvador stood on a precipice. Below them lay a twisted warren of walls.

"A labyrinth," she groaned aloud. If she weren't so tired, she would have thrown up her hands.

"I guess She wouldn't be the all-powerful Mother if She made things easy for us, but at least there is a set of stairs."

He was right, of course. The long and twisting staircase began to the right. It snaked down into the darkness without an end in sight.

"I guess we should get going," she said, heading for the stairs.

He reached out to stop her. "Not yet. Getting us here took a lot out of you. We should wait until you've regained your strength."

Suddenly, the reminder she wasn't in top form irritated her.

"I'm fine," she said, tugging her sleeve out of his grip.

Salvador shook his head with a superior expression. "I'm afraid I'm going to have to pull rank."

"A witch doesn't outrank an Elemental."

"I know. I'm not speaking as a practitioner, but as your physician." He put his hands on her shoulders. "Listen to your doctor. You need to rest. We either do it here or halfway down those stairs. Personally, I prefer up here."

Damn, she hated when he was right. But Gia had too much self-possession to let it show.

"Fine," she growled. Well, it showed a little.

He offered his hand, and she took it. He guided her to the top of the stairs. They were more than wide enough for two people to sit on.

"Who built these stairs?" he asked

"The same entity that built the maze, I would guess." Gia leaned against the wall. Salvador's arm settled over her shoulder. He pushed her head the other way until she leaned against him.

She shifted her head just enough to see his face.

"You shouldn't be afraid to touch me. I mean, we've practically had sex," he pointed out.

Gia didn't know why that was so funny. "I'm afraid it was only good for you."

Salvador put a hand over his heart. "*Ouch.* Well, this may be incredibly inappropriate, but I hope to change that someday."

She opened her mouth, but he nudged her lightly and shook his head.

"Later. After this next leg of our long, strange trip."

Gia was too tired to scowl, so she gestured to the maze. "This will be our last journey together."

She meant to discourage him, but he only smiled. "Really? Because I'm getting the impression this is just the beginning."

"More like the beginning of the end," she said repressively. But Gia was still tired, so she moved ever so slightly, resting her head more solidly on his shoulder. She inhaled deeply, drawing in the scent of soap and sugar that was mingling with his scent.

"Are you smelling me?" he asked.

She could hear the smile in his voice.

"Shut up," she said, snickering softly. Then she closed her eyes for a while.

SALVADOR ONLY GOT to savor holding Gia for a brief time. The Earth Elemental's batteries recharged quickly. After less than an hour of rest, she dragged him down the stairs to the mouth of the labyrinth.

The walls were made of stone, a polished volcanic rock that made the most of what light there was in the place. It was too massive to call it a cave. He and Gia had entered a subterranean world, one so large that starving to death before they found their way out would be a real possibility if he were with anyone else.

"I should have taken Nana up on her offer of a doggy bag," he said, losing track of their location after a few too many sudden turns. "Of course, if that sweet roll was my last meal, it was an excellent one... I don't suppose you can grow one of those magic bushes with a few plums or maybe a steak?"

Gia muttered something under her breath.

"I'm sorry, what was that?"

She pivoted, then blew a stray hair out of her eyes. "I said my powers don't work down here. Neither do yours. They disappeared when we entered the labyrinth proper."

He could have sworn he wasn't moving, but Salvador managed to trip over his own feet anyway.

"Oh... So we *are* going to starve to death." He sucked in a breath through his teeth. "Cool."

Gia reached out, then squeezed his arm. "Don't worry. The dehydration will kill us long before starvation becomes an issue."

Yeah, he'd walked into that one. "You know, when my family issued its many warnings about your kind, they never mentioned how annoyingly snarky you were."

Gia batted her long lashes. "Really? Because that's the first thing they should have told you." She nudged him hard enough to make him trip again. "It's just a puzzle, and I've always been good at those. Now, c'mon."

She led the way, rounding yet another ninety-degree turn. A second later, she shifted and held up a finger. "I, um, I don't suppose you'd consider closing your eyes for the next minute and a half?"

Her hesitancy was unnatural. Gia didn't do uncertain.

"Is there some sort of monster you can't look in the eyes around that corner?" he asked.

When her nose twitched, his arms fell to his sides.

"Oh God, there is." His voice dropped to a whisper. "Is it Medusa? It's Medusa, isn't it?"

"Not quite."

Salvador took a deep breath before marching around the corner.

"It's a pile of old bones," he said, almost relieved. Sure, someone had died there, but at least it wasn't a mythical creature that turned people to stone or flesh-eating monsters. "Granted, it's not a good sign for us survival-wise, but it could be worse."

"All right, then. Why don't we move on?" she asked, hustling him past the bones. They had almost cleared the next corner when he stopped her.

"Wait, why did you think that would bother me?" Curses could take some twisted forms. As a healer, he was used to some grisly sights. Skeletal remains didn't qualify.

Gia avoided his eyes. "I just didn't want you to get discouraged about succeeding in the maze."

Briefly, he closed his eyes. "Those are his bones, aren't they?"

"I'm afraid so." He knew Gia felt bad when she wrapped her arm around him. She gestured to the remains with her free hand. "Meet your great-uncle Ciro."

Salvador walked to the pile, staring at them as if they would suddenly rise and start spilling their secrets. "I feel like I should say something. My grandmother talked about him as if he was supposed to be the second coming—our family's biggest lost opportunity."

Gia's shoulders drew up. "Do you pray?" she asked.

"Not since I was twelve," he admitted, wondering where he should start.

Kneeling, he crouched by the bones. He reached out to touch the remains of what must have been a shirt.

"Hey, look at this," he said, seeing a brown puffball mushroom near the shoulder. "I guess some things do grow here after all."

Gia bent to inspect it closer. "Hey. Don't touch that."

But it was too late. He'd already plucked it from the ground.

As soon as he lifted it, the mushroom shot out a spray of spores, covering them both. Coughing, he dropped it to the ground, a wave of dizziness overwhelming him.

Somehow, he managed to catch Gia before she hit the ground, but that didn't help her much because he lost consciousness right after.

_____

30

"*Mi amor*, that dish isn't going to finish itself."

Gia startled, wondering how long she had been sitting at the kitchen table.

The morning light filtered through the yellow curtains she had chosen because they made the room warm and cozy.

Marco, her mate, stood over the frying pan. "You're the one who made the wager. Are you crying uncle already?"

"Uncle?" She scowled, wondering why the hell that word bothered her so much.

Marco's handsome face creased. "What's wrong?" he asked, setting the frying pan on the brick he'd carved runes on. It was the last one he'd baked in the kiln in the backyard. The rest were in the walls of this house, the home he'd built for them.

"You were always doing things like that," she whispered, holding her temple. "Sentimental touches that made everything perfect."

Her head didn't hurt, but it felt as if she'd just woken up from a long sleep.

"Gia, are you okay?" Marco asked. "I've never seen you turn down a *sopapilla*."

That was what was in the frying pan. Gia reached out, then took a piece of the sweet fry bread. It was still warm, the scent making her stomach growl. "I would never turn one of these down. They're your specialty."

Pleased, Marco sprinkled powdered sugar on top before passing her the honey pot for good measure.

"I'm fine. I think," she said, still feeling oddly disconnected. "I just have the nagging feeling I'm forgetting something."

Marco turned the chair around, sitting in it backward so he could rest his arms over the backrest. His face was lit with that warm, loving expression she knew so well. The man liked to watch her eat, but she didn't mind or feel self-conscious the way she did with others. Marco wasn't just her mate. He was her oldest friend.

She polished off the *sopapilla* while he filled the silence with stories about his work. He was in the middle of an anecdote about his friend and the trip they were planning when she suddenly remembered something.

Gia grabbed his hand. "Marco, you can't go to Ecuador with Josue. It's not safe to go there right now—"

Marco frowned. "*Mi amor*, I already went to Ecuador. Josue and I finished the relief operation early and returned last month, don't you remember?"

"What?" She shook her head, her heart working overtime.

Gia pressed her hands to her head. It felt as if her head were stuffed full of cotton wool, but she wasn't wrong about this. She had to stop him from going on this trip. "No, no, we had this exact meal and we discussed your upcoming trip. I should have told you not to go because the area is unstable—"

"Gia, love, we make *sopapillas* every Sunday when we are both home. And we *did* have this conversation. I also told you everything would be fine, and it was." He put a hand on her forehead. "Are you feeling all right? I mean, I know you can't fall sick, but you mentioned your last assignment was difficult. Perhaps you're feeling some after-effects?"

"I said it was bad?" she asked, shock and relief making her fingertips tingle. Or was that his touch?

It had been so long. Except it hadn't.

Her head spun. Gia tried to get to her feet, but Marco urged her back down, hovering over her attentively before making her a cup of her favorite tea in a mug he'd fired and glazed himself.

I still have that mug. Her vision swam in and out as memories overlapped and tangled. She gazed up into Marco's worried face. A tear slipped down her cheek, and she released a shaky breath.

"Okay, now I know something is wrong," he said, the line between his brows deepening. "Should I call Serin?"

"Can you please sit?" she asked, patting the table in front of his chair. When he continued to make a face, she took his hand and pulled him down.

"*Mi—*"

Gia covered his mouth with her hand.

"I'm choosing to see this as a gift instead of the less-than-kind trap the Mother has set for the unwary." His beautiful face wavered slightly as tears filled her eyes. "For so long, all I wanted was the chance to look into your eyes again and tell you about everything."

She gripped his hands tightly. "And even though you're not truly here, I want to say how much I love you. Part of me will *always* love you." Gia blinked back the tears, determined not to miss a second with him. "You were the best thing about my day—even after you weren't there anymore—and I will be grateful I knew you and you loved me until the day I die...which is hopefully not today."

Nodding, she stared at the ceiling. "This can be over now. I passed."

When Gia looked back down after wiping her tears away, Marco was gone. Salvador sat in his place, reading a book. "Or not..."

He looked up, his smile warming the entire room, the features of which had dramatically altered. It wasn't her and Marcos' kitchen, but another one in some other home. This was a glimpse of the future, a life that could be hers if she were willing to set aside her prejudices and misgivings long enough to seize it.

Sal set aside his book, reaching for her hand, but she shook her head.

"I understand what you're trying to tell me," she said emphatically. "Seriously, Mother, we don't have to do this."

"So, should I just go?" Salvador asked, a corner of his lip quirking. He gestured to the door. Even in her delusion, he was both self-effacing and a little sarcastic.

"Yes, Salvador the hallucination, you can go. I'll see the real one in a minute."

She stood, then closed her eyes. Thankfully, when she opened them, she was back in the labyrinth. Salvador was crumpled on the floor next to the bones.

"Okay then," she said, rubbing her face. "I don't suppose you're going to wake yourself up..."

He stayed still next to the remains of his great-uncle.

"Yes, that's what I thought," she muttered, leaning over him. "Well, I hope your delusion is not as interesting as mine was, for your sake."

"Darling." Someone handed him a glass of champagne.

Blinking, Salvador shook his head. He was sitting at the head of a long, and unfortunately familiar, table.

"No," he rasped. He was *not* in the formal dining room of Mammon's castle... and that was *not* Snagat serving Fulgencio, Salvador's father. His mother, no longer pregnant, sat next to him, engrossed in conversation with his cousin. Behind her, another demon servant shuffled past with a tray laden with hors d'oeuvres.

"Did you not hear me?" The long, blood-red fingernails were the tipoff.

"*Analia?*" he asked, his mouth twisting.

His cousin's dark eyes flashed. "What is wrong with you? Snagat asked if you wanted another drink."

"Why?" he asked blankly. His head swam, his eyes watering. Damn, what was wrong with him?

"Because..." Analia's gaze was dagger sharp. "It's our anniversary, and I can't drink with your parents watching me."

When he scanned her, his gaze caught on her burgeoning stomach.

Bile rose in his throat. "Okay, that is very twisted."

In whatever gruesome reality he'd landed in, his mother was no longer pregnant, but his cousin was expecting... and, apparently, it was supposed to be his.

"I did not marry my cousin." Salvador felt every inch of his skin begin to crawl. True, she was his second cousin, but he was still close to vomiting. It did not get better when the servants wheeled in the stuffed pig on a trolley. At least it looked like a pig...with disturbingly human-like appendages.

"Honestly, Sally, you are such a beast until you drink," Analia spat, using the version of his name that he despised the most. "Please finish that drink now, then have another before our mothers finish it all. You know how long it takes these damn demons to get up and down the stairs to the kitchen."

Salvador pushed away from the table. "And that's my cue to get some air," he ground out. Nodding tersely, he hurried out the door.

The castle was laid out exactly as he remembered. Rushing through the corridors, he turned down the hallway with the collection of skulls mounted on the wall before bursting free of the castle ramparts. The night was cold, and the air was heavy with particulates that made breathing more work, but he didn't care.

Somehow, he had ended up in hell again—this time, without Gia. How was he going to get out of here without her?

The dragons! Were the dragons still here?

Suddenly, his father clapped him on the back just as Salvador was staving off a hyperventilation fit. He didn't quite catch his words.

"I'm sorry, what did you say?" Salvador asked.

"I said with the baby on the way, it really makes you think about the future. I mean, someday, all of this will be yours..."

His father waved at the distant vista of darkened hills and distant fires.

Okay, that did it. Salvador whirled around and took his father's hands, shaking them briefly. "Would you excuse me for a moment?"

"What—"

Salvador didn't wait for the rest of Fulgencio's response. He ran inside, tearing through the castle as he shouted Gia's name.

31

Gia was actually sweating. She may have strained a tendon, but she had finally managed to drag Salvador's tall and toned form down three turns of the labyrinth—away from Ciro and his spores.

Of all the times to not have super-strength or my normal endurance.

"You know, Sal, those muscles look very nice, but they make you damn heavy," Gia told the prone body as she stretched her aching back. "Right now, I'm wishing you weren't quite so...fit."

He continued to be dead weight, unconscious and handsome. "It would be far more helpful if you resembled your third cousin twice-removed Rodolfo—who was cadaverously thin. Or course, that might have had something to do with the fact he was constantly brewing potions to enhance his powers and a particularly potent one burned most of his stomach lining off."

She closed her eyes, replaying the image of the labyrinth as seen from the top. Most of it had been hidden in shadows, but she'd been able to see the center. Unless the twenty-foot walls had rearranged themselves—and after her hallucination, she wouldn't put it past the Mother—they were only a turn or two away.

Salvador murmured something. Bending, she caught her own name. "Good," she said, fully expecting him to rouse, but when he didn't wake up, she pushed him over and whacked on his back, anything to get the spores out of his system.

The smacking sound was loud in her ears. He was sure to have bruises later. "This hurts me more than it hurts you," she said, continuing to hit him.

Should she drag him out of the labyrinth? Would the divining rod work in reverse?

"I will leave you if you don't wake up," she lied, hoping the threat would do the trick. When it didn't, she sighed. Wracking her brain for a solution, she sighed and slid down the wall.

Gia had an eidetic memory, enabling her to remember thousands of spells. However, most were defensive. The healing rituals she knew required magic to kindle them.

Except for one. Gia knew a way to break a sleeping curse that didn't need magic. What it needed was love.

"You may be out of luck, buddy," she muttered.

But the man had come to *hell* to find her. She had to give him that. *And you know you want to.*

Berating herself, she scooted closer, bending to press her lips to his.

Nothing. He didn't even twitch.

She waited a bit more, studying his face, but there wasn't so much as an eyelash flicker.

"Right," she said, mentally kicking herself. *Why had I thought that would work?*

"What happened?"

Gia jumped despite herself. Bewildered, Salvador scanned their surroundings, his slack features firming as he sat up.

Catching sight of her, he grabbed her arm. "Oh, thank God. For a long and horrifying minute—or hour, I have no idea how long it was —I was back in Sheol, but you weren't there. However, my entire family *was,* and I don't want to get into the gruesome details, but I am so extremely glad my parents have no ambitions to rule a hell dimension because I think they would be way too skilled at it."

He scrubbed his face with his hands. "I thought it was real, but then I heard you calling my name. Thank you." He touched his lips, realization dawning in his eyes. "Did you—how did you wake me?"

"I slapped you really hard," Gia lied, trying not to laugh. "Now get up. We haven't even hit the halfway mark of the maze."

Salvador got to his feet with effort. "I don't suppose there is a fruit-filled garden or nice gastro-pub in the center of the labyrinth?"

With her assistance, he limped around the final corner.

"Or a giant monster," he whispered, stopping short. "I guess it wouldn't be a true labyrinth if there wasn't a giant monster in the middle."

Gia felt her blood run cold. "Not a monster," she whispered back. "It's a minotaur—Ariadne."

SALVADOR GRIMACED. "I thought the minotaur was a male... and Perseus killed him. Wasn't Ariadne monster-adjacent in Greek mythology?" he whispered as they edged around the sleeping creature.

In life, the beast was close to the creature of myth depicted in Greek legend—with the addition of a set of huge pendulous breasts. They were obvious, as Ariadne slept on her back. The rest was spot on—a muscled, two-story-tall body and cloven feet—*check*. Massive horns—*check*. Also, they appeared much pointier in person.

Visions of the time he had almost been gored by a bull in Pamplona in his wild youth flashed through his head. *And I thought that was scary.* Being run through by one of those would hurt. *A lot.* He doubted the minotaur would even notice his lifeless corpse impaled on one of those.

"The Greeks got the story wrong," Gia hissed, tiptoeing as the minotaur snuffled in its sleep. Its breath was rank enough to make his hair curl. "Now please be quiet until we're clear."

She had a point, but Salvador was too fascinated for caution. Plus, Ariadne snored so loudly it would drown out a marching band—a big Texan one. As long as he kept whispering, there was no way she would hear him.

"But wasn't the minotaur supposed to be her brother? Or are they a family of minotaurs? What about Perseus?"

"It was *Theseus* who slew the minotaur in the Greek tale, but that obviously didn't happen in real life—quite the opposite."

"You mean she..." He pointed at the minotaur, then mimicked being gored.

"More like..." she began, opening her mouth wide before snapping it shut and pretending to chew.

He made a face, but she shrugged dismissively. "He had it coming —trust me."

"Did you know them?" he whispered, almost vibrating with excitement.

"*No.* Now shut your damn beautiful mouth or I will slap you," she said, her frustration cresting over.

"My what?" Salvador laughed.

They grew aware of the silence at the same time. "Crap." He closed his eyes, afraid to look.

"Ariadne, girrrrl! How are you doing?" Gia asked, shoving him behind her.

The chilling sound of hoofbeats on stone rang out. He twisted to see the monster rearing up on its hind hooves. It started to stand... and it kept going and going until it towered over them. The snout, horns, and teeth were shiny with mucous that glowed faintly, as if it had bioluminescent algae inside.

"The better to eat you with?" he wondered.

There was an unintelligible growl, and Gia shook her head. "No, no. He's not a snack. Just a traveling companion."

More growls. "Sorry, no. I wasn't visiting. I didn't know you were here. I was just on my way to make a report to Her. There's a situation aboveground... No. No. Of course not."

"What is she saying?" he asked, less surprised than he should have been to realize Gia could understand Ariadne.

Gia rounded on him, frustration filling her brown eyes. Belatedly, he shut his mouth, but now she growled something at him. "What did you say?" he asked from behind gritted teeth.

She gave him a hard shove. And then the message became clear. "Run!"

32

Ariadne's roar was finally growing fainter. Gia was grateful that hurdle was behind them, but Salvador was limping now. He had been trying to hide it for the better part of a day, but she knew he'd landed wrong on his ankle after they scaled the wall of the labyrinth when the minotaur had trapped them in a dead end. They had only just escaped by the skin of their teeth, but Gia didn't begrudge Ariadne her effort. She had just been doing her job.

Thankfully, Salvador was still mobile, which was saying something because she was pretty sure it had been at least two days since they'd entered the maze. Or at least that was what her empty stomach told her.

A few more challenges had come and gone after they'd escaped the minotaur. A few hours after that, they had run into a door locked with a mystical combination. It had been the very devil to untangle, but she had managed—with Salvador's help.

Then there had been a challenging bit where there hadn't been a floor for several hundred meters right when the maze walls had grown too high to scale. The pit below had been endless—at least, they hadn't been able to determine how far down it went. None of the stones they had tossed in had hit the bottom.

They had been forced to scale the walls sideways, using tiny finger holds and cracks to cross to the other side. Eventually, they had made it across, although their fingers had been bleeding by the time they had. And so it continued.

We must be getting close to the end of the labyrinth. If Ariadne's area was the middle, then they should be at the end, shouldn't they?

Somehow, their circumstances hadn't dampened Salvador's irrepressible optimism or his *many* questions.

Naturally, he had insisted on hearing the entirety of Ariadne's tale, including the bit about Dionysus and what a colossal douchebag Theseus had ended up being.

"But you didn't know them personally, right?" he repeated at one point as they felt their way in near darkness.

His continuous chatter was a handy way to track him in the gloom, so she answered his questions, even the repetitive ones. "No, I told you I wasn't around. It was Itzel, my predecessor."

"Another Earth Elemental?" he asked in surprise. There was a grunt, then a scrape. She suspected he'd stumbled in the dark, but he didn't let on. "Sometimes, I forget there were any Earths before you."

"Yes, Itzel was the one who passed her mantel to me. She was my mother's distant relation."

"I thought there wasn't a generational inheritance," he said. "I always believed it was more like *Buffy the Vampire Slayer*, you know, the whole... one-is-randomly-chosen-by-destiny thing."

"Elemental lineages don't have a clear line of descent like a normal witch family does. Our children don't necessarily inherit our abilities. It's rare if they do, but the predisposition has to be there, in the blood."

Was that going to be the case with Diana's offspring? Gia had no idea. An Elemental hadn't fallen pregnant while in service before. *One of the many questions I have to ask Her.*

"Why do you think the Mother is making this so difficult for you?" he asked offhandedly. "I thought She would roll out the red carpet for you. Aren't you Her favorite?"

She'd hoped he wouldn't ask about that. But he'd come all this way, and she knew he deserved an answer... Gia could trust him with it.

"An incredibly long time ago, the Elementals of the earliest age rebelled against Her. She had been sleeping, and they grew discontented and unhappy with the constant warfare that kept breaking out within the human and supernatural populations. Sometimes, even between them."

"Your kind actually rebelled?" Salvador was shocked.

"It was more of a strike than a full-blown insurrection, but a lot of damage can be done when we lay down our arms. The Elementals came down here to see Her, all four together, to air their grievances—ignoring their duties to do so. Chaos broke out above. But She did hear them out. She ended up triggering an ice age to end the fighting."

"An ice age? Isn't that overkill?"

"Not in Her mind, I guess." Gia shrugged. "In any case, the Mother put safeguards in place to ensure it would never happen again. That was when the Supes had to agree to the Covenant or face being stripped of their powers. As for the Elementals, most willingly retired, then new ones were chosen. Except they found their ability to convene circumscribed. Afterward, all four Elementals could never be in the same place at the same time ever again."

"I didn't know that. How do you have staff meetings?"

"We don't." She laughed, then sobered. "But I do wish we could all be together." She paused. "I love my extended family, but my Elemental sisters are closer than blood. It took me a long time to accept the fact our squad was never going to be together like that. But it's all right. It's not like I don't get to see them, just not all at once."

His hum of acknowledgment and sympathy vibrated in her ears, and Gia realized he was much closer now than he'd been before. She turned and put a hand on his chest, landing over his heart by chance.

"There is something I want you to know," she began. "Can I count on your discretion?"

There was enough light to see his nod. "Of course."

"I'm serious. You can't tell anyone—especially your family."

Salvador put his hand over hers. "Gia, listen to me. After I was disinherited, I had plenty of opportunities. Well, at first, I partied a lot, but then I decided to dedicate myself to righting some of my family's wrongs by healing. I didn't make myself hard to find. A lot of powerful people came to me over the years, seeking alliances or partnerships. This includes members of the other Seven families. Hell, it includes members of my *own* house. Other Delavordos wanted to band together to overthrow my parents. Needless to say, I wanted no part of that. When all was said and done, I didn't want to owe allegiance to *anyone*."

He squeezed her fingers. "But if *you* wanted me to make a vow—to swear on a stack of parchment—I would do it. I will keep your counsel, whatever it is."

His words rang with truth and sincerity. Gia took a deep breath. "Things among the Elementals are changing. According to Alec, Diana is pregnant."

There was a short silence. "Uh, did... did she retire and not tell you?" he asked uncertainly.

"No."

His mouth dropped open. "Wow. Er, sorry, Alec didn't mention it. It's a surprise."

"I told him not to tell you," she admitted.

"*Oh.*" He drooped a bit, crestfallen.

She ran a hand through her hair. "At the time, I wasn't sure if we could trust you. Your family—"

"Might go ballistic." Salvador waved away her unnecessary justifications. "And if by some miracle they kept their cool, then it would be one of the other Seven getting their panties in a twist. I get why you didn't tell me—I do—but why are you sharing now? Aside from the obvious."

"What is the obvious?" Gia would like to know because she felt lost. The sense of being unmoored had been with her since before the labyrinth—before Sheol—and she hated it.

She couldn't see him, but she felt his hand when it covered the one still resting on his chest. "I know you didn't slap me awake," he murmured.

Gia didn't deny it, but her thoughts were in turmoil. "I'm worried about Her," she confided, knowing he would understand she couldn't talk about them just now. "I shouldn't be. Heaven knows She's seen worse, but something feels off. The closer we get, the more wrong this all feels."

Salvador wrapped an arm around her. She let it stay there, even leaned in a bit. The strong beat of his heart thrummed under her fingers.

"Are you worried She'll ignore you or push us out? Because I admit I've been a little concerned since we found Ciro."

"I don't think that's the fate She has in store for us," she said, aware the outline of his form was growing clearer.

There was a light at the end of the tunnel—literally. Only it wasn't a fixed point in the distance. Whatever it was—it was getting closer. Turning around, she pushed Salvador behind her. She tensed, preparing for the next challenge the labyrinth would throw at them.

But then the world went white. After a minute, she heard the Voice...and it was telling her that it was sorry.

33

Salvador was holding Gia one moment, then his retinas burned as light returned to the world.

He stood in a vast cavern lit by unknown means. And it was empty save for him and Gia. She was in the center of the open space, her hand up.

Was she? She was... Holy crap. "Gia, can you hear me?" he shouted as he ran across the open space.

She didn't react at all. Her eyes were open, unseeing. The rest of her was in suspended animation. Even her hair was motionless, the thick sable locks frozen in free-fall. He touched it, knocking it to her shoulder, but the gravity-defying conformation of the curl didn't change.

He spun around, taking in the empty cavern. They weren't in immediate danger, but he knew she'd been correct. Everything about this was wrong. He could tell by the way the hair on the nape of his neck stood on end.

And Gia. Something was happening to her. Someone was hurting her right in front of him. She wasn't moving, her face frozen in surprise, but he knew she was hurting. He felt it in his soul. And there was nothing he could do about it.

"Fuck," he muttered. What was he supposed to do now?

There wasn't much to do except wait. He put his hands on either side of Gia's face, lowering his head until their foreheads were touching. "I'll be here until you tell me not to be... because I love you."

Gia had never felt so alone.

"Why?" she asked over and over again. But there was no answer. Just the echo of that message—the one permanently burned into her brain—and the question that had followed.

It felt like she couldn't breathe, but she was panting, desperately trying to catch a real breath. Drawing her pain inside, she tried to pull herself together.

She knew this pain—had felt it when Marco died. Had that been *Her* way of preparing Gia?

She shuddered, the world swimming with unspent tears, and she inclined her head. *I understand.* "Your will be done," she breathed. *"Release me."*

And the world restarted.

"Gia!"

The tears finally fell. Her vision cleared as Salvador grabbed her arms, pulling her to him. But she held something in her hands. It pressed between them, warm and smooth, almost a perfect sphere of clear blue crystal.

He backed up, gazing at the smooth oval crystal in her hands. "That wasn't there a second ago. What is it?"

Gia glanced down, perplexed. "I don't know."

"What about the Mother? Did you warn her about John and his poison? What about—"

Holding the crystal up, she shook her head. "My... our discourse is over."

Relieved, Salvador's shoulders dropped. "So, it worked?" He gestured to the endless and empty cavern. "She's not here because She moved. She got to safety, didn't She?"

"Not exactly." Gia swallowed hard. "She's not here because She left."

"What?"

Fighting past the lump in her throat, she forced the words out. "The Mother is gone. She... She has abandoned us."

HER HANDS FELL, but Salvador caught the crystal before it fell to the floor. And then he caught Gia as she broke down and sobbed.

Pressing the stone back into her hands, he lifted her into his arms, cradling her close.

"It's going to be okay," he lied, wondering how the hell this had gone so wrong.

The Mother was the Mother. She was all-powerful and eternal. She wasn't supposed to pack her bags and go. He didn't believe it was physically possible. The entity that was the Mother was integrated into every part of the world. How could they still be alive in that world without Her?

He was not going to get those answers in this damn desolate chamber. Face hard, he cuddled Gia closer, heading for the entrance he could no longer see anymore.

Salvador took a step. With a dizzying flash, they were above-ground again.

The Mother's cavern had disappeared. They were in a flat open space with nothing in sight for miles. Spinning around with Gia in his arms, he saw a carpet of stars behind a familiar desert skyline, the wind drying the tears on her face.

"We're in Monument Valley," he breathed in disbelief. But the shale and sandstone buttes were too distinctive to mistake.

Salvador closed his eyes, pressing his face into Gia's hair "Why did She go?" he asked, his voice hoarse.

"She said She was tired. She said She was...done." Pulling back, Gia gazed up at the sky. Slowly, she pushed away, and he set her on her feet.

Gia's face began to lose that blank, shell-shocked expression. She pointed at the sky. "That's where She is. She went back to the stars, back to where She came from."

He frowned. "But wasn't the Mother from *here*?"

Gia shook her head. "No... It's all confused now. She was trying to tell me so many things. Staying here was Her penance. A self-inflicted punishment."

Gia gasped, enlightenment and horror on her face. "I remember now. She showed me. There was a war here. A terrible war..." She broke off, clutching his arm. "The poison it wrought you can't even imagine. The sheer destruction of it—the carnage and pain."

Staggering, Gia sat, leaving the strange, mildly luminescent stone in his hand. The earth rose to make her a seat.

At least that hasn't changed. But *why* hadn't it?

"The poison threatened to spill over, and Her people came here to end it. When She and the others like Her were done, everyone on both sides of the conflict were dead. Her people left, calling it a day. Their job had been done, but She was devastated to have caused so much wholesale destruction. So, She stayed and remade the world, repopulating it by using bits of herself to start again."

"Supes or human?" he asked.

"Supes I think... We were supposed to be made in Her image. But then, the humans followed soon after—they evolved naturally, almost exactly like the ones who were here before. The planet shaped them once. It did it again."

"Really? Why did She allow that? Why have two kinds of people on one planet?"

Gia pursed her lip. "I don't think She meant it to happen. When the humans came back on their own, She let them be, figuring it would all work out. Or perhaps She'd simply lost her taste for genocide. Regardless, this new world order was supposed to be a hierarchy with our kind on top, but the conditions here were such that humans proliferated more freely."

"Well, if the Mother wanted to prevent war, that was not the way to go."

Gia rubbed her temple. "In the normal course of things, the engine runs on its own and becomes self-sustaining. She meant to get it going and leave. At least, that was Her intention."

"What happened?"

"She grew invested in Her creation."

"Yay us," he offered lamely.

Gia's brow creased, and she studied her hands. "She never meant to stay so long."

"*Okay*. So, the world engine got rebooted, then She watched over us for a few hundred millennia. Why would She leave after all this time? Was it John? Was he the straw that broke the camel's back?"

He buried his hands in his hair. "But that doesn't make sense. She's faced so much worse than a trigger-happy human with a beef against Supernaturals."

"I don't think it was John." Gia's voice was hollow. "She'd already been setting things in motion. This had been planned for a long time."

Light filled her eyes, and she twisted to gape at him in wonder. "I know why you're here," she whispered.

Salvador's brows drew together "In like an existential sense?"

"*No*. I know why you're all here." Leaping up, she took the crystal stone from him. "And this. I am supposed to choose, to set the new cycle in motion."

"A new cycle as in a whole new era?"

"Basically, yes."

It made sense in a twisted kind of way. The crystal sphere was the key, and it was Gia's to do with as she pleased. Who else could be trusted to decide the fate of the world?

Gia put her head in her hands.

"Are you all right?" he asked, leaning over her.

"I just can't believe I lost Her. It happened on my watch."

"No..." Salvador leaned down to clutch her cold hands in his. "You can't think of it that way. She left now because She trusted you. She chose you to make the right decision—whatever that is."

The last words nearly ripped him in two. He wanted to tell her not to go, to stay with him, but he knew he couldn't be that selfish. The best he could do was memorize the lines of her face. He never wanted to forget what she looked like right now.

Gia put her hands around her stomach, staring at him dubiously.

"Does this era reboot require some sort of big cataclysm to initiate?" he asked, sucking in a breath through his teeth. "Like an extinction-level event?"

Sweat broke out on his brow when she didn't answer. "What were your choices?" he asked.

"I abstained, at least for the moment," she confessed, taking a shaky breath. "I can't make this decision alone. It has to be all four of us. We have to find my sisters."

When he stepped back, he staggered a bit. He waved at the ground. "Then you're not supposed to go back down there again?"

Her brow creased, but it wasn't from pain. It was confusion. "Why would I do that? She's not there. I received Her message and the catalyst."

Salvador regarded her helplessly. "I assumed you would have to take Her place."

"*Oh.*" Gia blinked, then shook her head. "No, I...I don't think anyone could. No single being could encompass all that She was. Not if they weren't of her kind."

"Good. Good." He surreptitiously wiped his eyes. "Can I ask you something else?"

"What is it?"

"Are we going to live through whatever that crystal does?"

Gia stared into the stone's depths. In the few minutes since they'd surfaced, the muted luminescence had changed. A light inside had kindled, and it got brighter by the second.

"I wish I knew."

34

The rocky hill Gia had designated as the meeting place was savagely steep. Salvador felt the burn in his thighs on the way up, but it had been worth it when they reached the top.

It was as if the Mother herself had designed it. The rocky outcropping rose from a forest of pines that stretched as far as the eye could see. The top appeared as if it had been sheared off by a giant blade. Stones lined the edge like jagged teeth.

It was a fitting place for what was coming. If only he knew *what* that was...

It hadn't taken them long to track down Gia's sisters. Alec and Diana had been consulting the texts in Talos, the vampire council's library. Gia remembered Serin and Daniel had been recalled from the Gulf while the Air Elemental and her mate had come down from somewhere up North, but Logan had sent the wolf ahead alone.

The news the Mother had left Earth to its own devices had been a shock to all the Elementals, but it was their mate's reaction he was having an issue with. He much preferred Alec's flabbergasted silence and Daniel's calm wait-and-see attitude.

The wolf, on the other hand, had been pacing and muttering nonstop since he got here. Salvador wanted to nail Connell's tail to the floor. Unfortunately, the wolf was in his bipedal form, so he didn't have that option.

"I can't believe She's gone," he kept saying.

Daniel caught his eye, and they exchanged a commiserating look. *Who would have thought the human would be the steady one?* Because if vampires could sweat, he'd be standing in a puddle right now. *And forget about the shifter...*

"Where is your mate?" Salvador asked with a grimace when the wolf's pacing kicked a stone into his ankle.

"She's coming," Connell growled, checking his watch.

"You okay?" Salvador asked, giving Alec his attention. The vampire appeared paler than usual.

"I'm fine," Alec rasped. "There are just a lot of changes in the works."

Oh, yeah. He'd almost forgotten. This news on top of his concern for his mate made this a double whammy.

A pregnant Elemental. The biological implications alone were troubling. "Yeah, I heard. How is that going?"

"Uh, fine. Fine. At least, I think it's fine. Still early days."

"Is Diana still in control of her talent?"

Alec whirred to face him, a question in his eyes.

"I mean, her heat isn't a problem for the fetus, is it?" The doctor in Salvador couldn't help but be concerned.

"I don't think that's an issue. She's only a little above the normal human range."

"Really?" He hadn't known that. Salvador would have expected a Fire Elemental to be much higher. If she was on par with a werewolf, that would probably work out, especially if the child had inherited some of his parent's magic. It was all in the blood, wasn't it? That was something he'd been hearing his entire life.

The curiosity was eating him alive. "So, if there's still a fight, is Diana going to partake?"

Alec blinked. "Of course. Why wouldn't she?"

How the hell was he supposed to answer that? "You're not worried about the baby?"

Alec ran a fang over his lip. "I'm worried about all of us."

Exchanging another quick glance with the silent Daniel, Salvador nodded. "Yes, that's...fair."

"I don't understand why we're waiting." Alec frowned, gesturing to the trio of Elementals at the center of the summit. "It's not like Logan can join them. Only three can congregate at one time. Even then, it's uncomfortable for them. Diana says it's like chewing tinfoil."

Salvador had forgotten about that. "Good question," he acknowledged, scanning the trio. A whiplash of wind passed over his head, then Logan was there, standing next to Connell.

She gazed at him the way Salvador wished Gia would look at him. They exchanged a few murmured words, and she handed him something. He slipped it into his pocket, slinging a casual arm around her.

The Air Elemental settled in his arms as if she were going to wait there, but Gia turned and beckoned her.

Diana stepped back as if she were going to trade off so Logan could take her place, but Gia stopped her with a hand to the arm. He didn't hear her telling Diana to stay, but he could see the bewilderment in the Fire Elemental's expression.

The same confusion was all over Logan's face as she approached her sisters. And then she was next to them.

Salvador smacked Alec on the arm. "Hey, isn't there supposed to be some sort of built-in self-destruct to prevent them from getting together at the same time—something to do with keeping them from insurrection or stopping them from taking over the world?"

Alec's wide and startled eyes were all the answer Salvador got.

Connell snorted. "Not anymore, I guess. New game. New rules."

35

———————

The wind whipped Diana's red hair. She picked a stray lock out of her face. "Are we sure about this?" she asked, her face grave.

Di had shared her special news with their other sister. Serin was surprised, but it didn't shock her. Not compared to Gia's report.

The Water Elemental's expression was carefully composed. "Is it possible the Mother has simply moved?" Serin asked. "The empty cavern could be a ruse. Perhaps She fears insurrection again?"

"I wish that were the case, but I don't think so." Gia stroked the crystal sphere. Its inner fire had taken on a mystical glow, an indescribable gold-and-purple medley.

"The disconnect we've been feeling in recent years... It's not because She was falling into one of her long slumbers. And it's not because of John, or at least not just about him. Her time here was always going to be limited. She has been divesting..."

Gia had told them about the images she'd seen while locked in the chamber's aether—the war from before time and the empty desolation of the land afterward. Then the repopulation and surprise return of the humans.

"Do you feel, I don't know, a little weirded out?" Diana scowled.

"Like She was just messing around, and the planet is her fiendish laboratory? Otherwise, She would have just brought the humans back and not added something of herself in the Supernaturals."

"C'mon, Di, I'm sure it wasn't like that," Serin said. "Whoever and whatever She was, I believe She was trying to make amends for those terrible things that happened. Her long period here alone speaks to how deeply that weighed on Her conscience."

Diana scowled. "But now She's gone, and we're left holding the bag. This world is a hot mess."

There was more than a small ring of truth to that, but there was more to it. "This world is what we make it," Gia whispered before raising her head to meet Diana's eyes. "The truth has unsettled me as well. But let's wait for Logan. We can hash this out once she's here."

Serin twisted to scan the sky behind them. "Here she is now," she said as their sister landed next to her mate at the edge of the summit. Gia waved Logan over.

"All right, why don't I take a powder? I need to cool off anyway," Diana offered, backing away. But Gia shook her head, then reached for her. She needed all four of her sisters close.

"No. Stay."

"But—"

"Listen," Gia said.

"I don't hear anything," Diana said.

"And you don't feel it either." Gia gestured at her sister. "I don't either."

The Mother's failsafe—the unpleasant ringing sensation in her ears, the one Gia felt down to her bones whenever she was this close to her sisters—it was gone.

Gia witnessed the moment of epiphany. It washed over Serin first. Her sister blinked and grabbed Diana's arm, linking them. Logan became aware when she was halfway to them. Her expression nearly brought Gia to tears.

Slowly, Logan closed the distance. "Where is it?" she asked, gesturing to her ear.

"It's not needed anymore." Gia held out her hand to her sister.

The Air Elemental took her hand, sending a shooting thrill down her spine like electricity.

For the first time in her life, Gia was with all of her sisters at once, touching them, breathing the same air.

Diana broke the circle first, shielding her face to hide the fact she was crying, unlike Logan, whose eyes were openly streaming. Gia pulled her sister back into an embrace, reconnecting them.

Even the mates seemed affected. Connell seemed slightly dazed. Daniel was stoic. Alec, like his mate, was also teary, the effect slightly ruined by the fact his tears were blood, but it was still sweet. Alec knew better than anyone what this meant to Diana.

Salvador flashed her a bracing smile before giving her a thumbs-up. *He has to stop doing that...*It warmed her too much, almost making her believe everything would be okay. She of all people knew better.

What she had to tell her sisters was difficult. The beginning, at least, she had to tell them in private. "I'm sorry, but this first part is for their ears alone."

With a wave, she crafted a circle. It was large enough to encompass her and her sisters, but not the men on the periphery. She and her sisters could converse inside it without being heard.

She faced the women, staring at each in turn. "My brave and beautiful sisters. I have served Her for many years, and I knew all of your predecessors. They, too, were brave and strong warriors, but when I met each of you, I knew you would outshine them."

Diana flushed and blinked rapidly while Logan bit her lip. Serin threw an arm around their youngest sister, pulling her in tight as Gia continued. "Each of you inherited the mantle from a worthy predecessor, but your potential to excel beyond them was there from day one. It was boundless, and not one of you have *ever* disappointed me. Not once."

Diana wasn't the only one who cried now. Gia wiped her eyes.

"I know it's difficult to accept the Mother is gone, but She did not leave us completely alone. We have each other." She opened her hand to indicate the men. "And we have them..."

Serin's lips parted. "Are you suggesting She orchestrated Daniel and me and the others—that our meeting our mates—was no accident? It was by Her design?"

Diana schooled her expression, but Gia could feel her sister's anger by the spike of heat coming from her direction. "I don't buy that. Nothing about us was by design. Do you have any idea how close I came to setting Alec's ass on fire those first few weeks?"

"I don't think She handpicked him for you," Gia said. "I don't believe She was all that cognizant of what She was doing at the end. But I do think she set things in motion so what was destined to happen was accelerated. Elementals have never found their mates so quickly for a reason. She abhorred change. But it was there in the images flooding my brain in Her chamber. The message was muddled, but these precipitous meetings were meant to be a gift, some solace in the face of Her abandonment. She knew we would feel betrayed. And She never wanted us to feel alone."

Logan nudged her. "Does that mean what I think it means?" she asked with a waggle of her eyebrows.

Diana frowned, then wrinkled her nose as she caught on. "*Really*? A Delavordo?"

Gia sighed. "The Mother works in mysterious ways. It doesn't mean we have to take what is offered but as odd as it sounds, I'm glad the opportunity is there—even if it doesn't work out." She shrugged. "Does that even make sense?"

Serin nodded. "I'm glad you're open to new possibilities after all this time. Even if that possibility comes in the form of a Delavordo."

Logan was skeptical, but she finally nodded. "At least he's hot. But the long hair in the man bun has got to go—like yesterday."

Diana laughed. "I second that. Every time I see it, I want to hack it off with my sword," Subsiding she took her hand. "But if you go down that route, I have every confidence you'll be able to keep him in line. We'll still be watching him like a hawk. One false move and he's getting the ass whipping of his life."

"Nah, have you seen the way he looks at her? He's like a widdle puppy," Logan interjected. "Besides, he may be an outcast, but he's still a Delavordo. He's probably into that sort of thing."

Gia snorted. Despite the gravity of the situation, she could always count on her sisters for levity and perspective.

"The world The Mother left behind may not be the one we would have designed. Hell, it's not the one *She* intended. But we're still here, and we have a decision to make."

Gia lifted the crystal. In the presence of all four Elementals, the light flared brighter than ever before.

"The Mother left this," Gia said, raising the stone between them. It stayed suspended in the air, revolving slowly.

"What is it exactly?" Diana asked.

"A trigger." It was the closest description Gia could come up with.

"And what does it trigger?" Serin asked.

Gia took a deep breath, staring into the crystal's depths. The stone was perfect, beautiful, and also terrible. "A new world—if that's what we decide is best."

"I believe She intended for the choice to be mine alone, but that isn't fair. The sheer magnitude of this decision means it can't be made by a single person. I think She knew that. Otherwise, I wouldn't have been able to leave her chamber without making a choice."

"On that note, I don't think it was for *us* four to make alone," Serin said. "If there are no accidents, then the fact that our mates are representatives of each of the major races on Earth—shifter, vampire, witch, and a human with a touch of Fae blood—means something. How did that come about if we weren't meant to weigh these options together?"

Gia huffed. She should have seen that for herself. "A very good point," she conceded.

Raising her arms, Gia erased the spell circle, gesturing for the men to join them. Connell stalked to Logan's side while Alec hovered protectively over Diana. Serin and Daniel exchanged a telling glance as he stationed himself next to her until their shoulders touched.

Salvador didn't have a choice but to step into the empty space next to her. "What did you decide?" he asked, trepidation in every line of his body. "What is the new era going to look like?"

"I don't know. We had a few personal issues to discuss first. And it was decided that given the diversity of backgrounds you men repre-sent, you should have an opportunity to voice your opinions."

"But we don't even know what that thing does," Connell said, staring askance at the brightly glowing sphere.

"I don't know what Salvador told you about the events in Her chamber. She left one of Her convoluted messages. Much of it is unclear, but one thing I did come to understand. She never intended for there to be two classes of beings on this world." Gia gestured to the crystal. "And now we get to decide who will prevail—the Super-naturals or the humans."

"What?" Logan's face crumpled. "What does that even mean?"

Gia held up the stone. "This crystal triggers some sort of hard reset. I think She believes everything would be simpler if the playing field was level."

"So that's what this boils down to?" Diana asked "Us versus them? That's the same as John's game."

"That is seriously fucked up," Connell growled. Logan put a soothing hand on his arm.

A shiver that had nothing to do with the wind ran down Gia's spine. She agreed, but that didn't change anything. The choice still had to be made.

"How does it work?" Serin asked.

Gia touched the sphere. It pulsed ominously. "We can remove humans from this plane. I think She wanted to at the end, but she couldn't bring Herself to do it."

"How do you know that?" Salvador asked

"She showed me..." Gia rubbed her hands over her face. "All the crap—the pollution poured into the atmosphere has derailed normal climate patterns. It was within Her power to stop the effects, but She didn't... She was going to use them to set off a cataclysmic storm. Maybe more than one."

"Which would kill a lot of Supernaturals as well. Not everyone is as hardy as a *Were* or a vampire. Some of the Otherkind are quite fragile," Alec said, giving Salvador the side-eye.

"That may be the only reason why She hesitated. I can't really say."

There was a pause as the group absorbed this.

"Is picking one side over the other even feasible?" Serin asked. "Even my family, who are as far removed from humanity as any could possibly be, are mostly human. We're intermingled with them on the most fundamental level."

"I don't know how, and I don't know who, but there must be a line because if we deploy the crystal as a weapon, then the humans would crumble to dust. She showed me what it would look like—how the earth would reclaim them."

There was a universal grimace at that one.

"What's behind door number two?" Logan eventually asked, crossing her arms. "Are we supposed to wipe out ourselves instead?"

"No." Gia frowned as she mentally picked through the images she needed to answer. "If we side with humans, the outcome is different. If we trigger the crystal with the intention of removing magic, it would evaporate, much like when we remove it from bad practitioners today."

Connell and Logan recoiled.

"Once the aether is gone, that would be it. We would all be human—permanently."

"Some Supes might wish we had killed them outright instead," Diana said.

Salvador snorted. "You're not kidding. My mother and father would rather die than be human."

"Diana is right. Isn't this playing into what John wants?" Logan frowned. "His poison is meant for Supernaturals. Once they're gone, El Douchebag gets to rediscover magic—or that's his intention. He's been stockpiling enough occult books and objects of power to do it."

"He wouldn't be able to. The aether would have burned up, so it could never return."

Connell growled. "Magic or no magic. Isn't this the Mother just giving that piece of shit what he wants unless we choose Supes?"

"So, we rule against humanity to spite him?" Alec asked incredulously. "I don't know about you, but I don't want to do that. Entire branches of my family are still human. So are my colleagues—the many scholars I've worked with over the centuries. Most are, at any rate."

Connell nudged Daniel hard enough to push him forward. "And you—don't you have anything to say on behalf of your species?"

Daniel appeared more composed than anyone else in the circle, but that didn't surprise Gia. Serin's mate was more levelheaded than most Supes.

"According to Serin, I have enough Fae blood where it counts," Daniel began "Not that I am advocating ruling against humans. But I'm not worried about this magic crystal ball."

Everyone looked at him curiously. "Why not?" Alec asked.

"Because I think you're going to take door number three."

As you thought, full of surprises. Gia inclined her head.

"What is this third option?" Salvador asked.

"The other option is to do nothing," she replied. "The Mother may have been severely myopic toward the end, but She was not blind, and I think She knew we would be too invested in this world to take such a drastic step. Otherwise, I doubt She would have cared to match us with our mates."

"*Mates? Us?*" Salvador's ears perked up.

Gia held up a finger. "Not now."

She could tell he wanted to argue. He was practically bursting, but he nodded, moving closer until they were touching. "So, we let the world continue as it is. What's the harm?"

"Unfortunately, that has a cost, too. A high one."

"Because of how everyone sucks?" Diana asked.

Gia was getting tired, but they needed to know everything. Of the people here, only Serin had an inkling of what else was out there.

She scanned the circle of faces, trying to find the right words. "The Mother came here from across the stars, and She was not alone. Her people fought a war here, and I don't think it was the first. She stayed to repair some of the damage they had wrought. When She stayed behind, Her presence had another effect—She shielded us."

Gia dropped her head back to look at the stars. "There are other beings out there, entire civilizations. Some are peaceful, while others are not. We are not unknown to these beings. A few are already here."

"Which ones?" Daniel asked. "I thought the Mother created all life on Earth."

"She set it in motion, provided a guiding hand, but even She was not so prolific. Others came, some similar to our Supernaturals in form but also completely different."

"Those dragons," Connell said, tapping Logan on the arm. "The ones who invaded Sheol. You said they weren't from around here."

Gia nodded. "That particular clan of dragons sought sanctuary long ago. It was before my time, but I saw their arrival in Her memories. The Mother allowed them refuge after their home was destroyed."

"And not just them." Diana rubbed her head as if she were getting a headache. "So if we maintain the status quo, what are we looking at? A bunch of small revolts, attempts to grab power and territory, or a full-blown insurrection?"

"It could be either or none. Followed by an invasion somewhere down the line. I have no idea. Prognostication is not one of my gifts."

Briefly, Diana squeezed her eyes shut. "If something comes for us, it may not be in our lifetime. It may fall on our children to deal with them."

"Fuck," Connell muttered. He rolled his neck, then grunted. "Well, I don't know about you, but it sounds like the threat will come regardless. However far out these hypothetical threats are, do we really want the earth to be filled with defenseless humans? Can the sphere make humans magical?"

"Again, giving John what he wants," Connell growled.

"If it's possible, we have to consider it," Gia said, struck by the idea.

"As the only human—mostly human, anyway—I feel I have to interject here," Daniel interrupted. "It is a spectacularly bad idea to give the average man or woman magical powers. You've seen what they do with a little bit of power and a gun. Imagine giving them the ability to shoot lightning bolts."

"None can do that." Connell sniffed.

"Well, actually…" Serin murmured.

Diana and Logan raised their hands.

The werewolf dismissed that. "Oh, well, whatever. I know I can trust my mate with that kind of power. Diana, too, I guess. And I actually agree with you, although I am a little surprised. I thought you'd be all for humans leveling up."

Daniel raised a skeptical brow. "You forget I was DEA. Before that, I was in the army. I've seen firsthand what humans can do to each other. Letting magic loose on them will lead to carnage. People are already too good at killing each other."

"True. I'd say we just wait until they off each other, but if it didn't happen in the last few millennia, we shouldn't hold our breath," Connell added.

Daniel's face screwed up. "Like shifters don't love to kill each other. Didn't your father—the uber Canus Primus boss-of-all-were-wolves—need Gia's help to end the endless warfare between packs and unite them under one banner?"

Connell shot him a dirty look. Daniel rewarded him with a smug smile. "Yeah, I've been doing my homework on this bright and shiny new world I am now a part of."

He addressed the others. "In my honest opinion, magic plus humans equals bad—unless your short-term goal is lots of death and destruction. But I know you're playing the long game here, so I'm going to go with the majority rule."

Someone groaned. Gia thought it was Alec.

"Can we destroy the crystal?" Diana asked.

"I don't know," she said honestly.

"Should we even try?" Logan poked the stone with a finger, sending it spinning.

Connell snatched his mate's hand away. "Hey, hey. Let's not trigger the magic-destroying weapon on accident."

Logan clicked her tongue in agreement. She put her hands behind her back, taking a step away from the brightly glowing stone.

"It wouldn't be that easy," Gia assured everyone. "I suppose we could take a stab at destroying it... We'd have to obliterate it, so nothing remained. Given its nature, I don't know if I could do it alone, but all four of us have never been together like this before, so..."

"We could hide it instead," Logan suggested. "Connell may be right. If someone comes along, gunning for the world, we might need to use it. Maybe in time, we can use it to give humans magic—when they're ready."

Was there ever really another option? They were silent for a moment, staring at each other, then Serin nodded and put her hand on Gia's forearm. Diana followed suit, holding Serin's arm. Logan completed the circuit, sealing the pact.

"The agreement is made," Gia declared.

Serin winced. "But where would we hide it? After the theft at the archives, we know no place is safe. And we won't be around forever. We can't risk anything happening to it after we're gone, especially since we have a new generation to consider," she said with a nod toward Diana's still-flat middle.

Gia's head swam. There were so many details to consider. "I suppose... I could try to take in the crystal. It is a terrestrial stone."

"*Whoa...* what?" Logan asked, putting up her hands.

Gia didn't like this option any more than the other two, but it had to be shared. "The crystal is pure magic potential, but it is also a stone. I might be able to absorb it, to keep it safe."

"What are you going to do? Eat it?" Connell asked sarcastically.

"No, she's not going to eat it, dufus." Logan scowled before turning to her sister. "But that thing is huge—you can't possibly keep something like that inside your body without it affecting you. It would be like being permanently pregnant or something."

Alec sucked in a sudden breath, then choked on it. Next to him, Diana rolled her eyes.

"You okay, buddy?" Logan asked, whacking Alec on the back hard enough to knock him over. Connell generously caught him, but he did wipe his hand afterward.

"He's just freaking out because I'm pregnant," Diana muttered.

Daniel's head jerked up at that. "What?"

Logan was less restrained. She flew at her sister, already shrieking. Thankfully, Alec checked her progress, catching her in midair with his preternatural speed. "Gently. She's pregnant, remember?" he reminded her.

"Congratulations!" Logan called as Alec handed her to her mate. Connell set her on her feet with a grin.

"Guess we have to start talking family planning," the wolf said, effectively wiping the mirth off his mate's face.

Gia cleared her throat. "Yes, it seems the barriers to having families while Elementals has been removed. Also, if Diana has conceived, it's possible we'll start aging as well."

"Do you feel older?" Serin asked curiously. Of all their sisters, Gia knew exactly how old everyone was. It was an aspect of her gift, like having a radioactive carbon-14 test built into her eyeballs.

"Not really," Gia said, taking a closer look at herself.

"What about me?" Diana asked, her shoulders straightening as if she were bracing herself.

"You haven't aged a day since you came into your powers, but that fetus has."

Diana's face scrunched. "That's too weird, even for me."

"Anyway," Gia said, clearing her throat. "Getting back to the stone... I believe I can manage with it. I'm sure I can get used to holding it, as it were."

Alec bent over so his eyes were level with the sphere. "What if it were smaller? If you can digest it, can you break it? Or slice it up?"

"Are you suggesting dividing it between us?" Serin asked.

"It would work, right? You can share abilities to some extent, right? If the piece were divided into four, would you each be able to hold a piece?" He glanced at Diana, then his face clouded over. "Better make that three."

"Hey, if my sisters are going to do their part, so am I."

"But—"

Diana held up a finger. It got warmer for few seconds before the Fire Elemental tamped down her anger. "We've discussed this," she ground out.

"Excuse me, *this* is not what we discussed." Alec began waving wildly at the stone.

Gia made a stop gesture. "First, let me see if I can even divide it."

With a flick of her fingers, she beckoned the revolving sphere closer, then wrapped her hands around the stone.

I hate this thing. The thought rose unbidden. For a moment, guilt flared. For so long, Gia believed everything that came from the Mother was a gift. But Gia did hate this thing, especially because it felt as if it belonged to her.

She focused her talent on the stone. It flared again, much brighter than before. The tension in the circle jumped.

"Don't, um, don't set it off," Salvador leaned over to whisper.

"She knows what she's doing, healer," Diana snapped before she lowered her voice. "Babe?"

"Yes," Gia answered, not taking her eyes of the stone.

"Don't accidentally set it off."

Pressing her lips together to keep from saying something she'd regret later, Gia closed her eyes. Her talent could feel the crystal's resonance better this way.

If she wanted to divide it—safely—all she had to do was find the right frequency.

In the end, it was easy. The frequency was hers, the same one she used to break rock and bend the earth to her will on any normal day. Gia rolled her hands over the stone. When she removed them, there were four equal spheres.

Well, at least She hadn't made it difficult. Not physically, at any rate.

Serin picked up a sphere. It flared and then quieted, pulsing gently.

"I think it likes you," Daniel muttered.

"It has adapted." The internal resonance pattern had altered slightly, tuning itself to Serin's special frequency, the reverb of the aether she used to manipulate water.

"All right, so how do I do this?" she asked, looking to Gia for guidance.

"Wait. It's still too big for Diana," Alec protested.

Connell was overcome by a sudden coughing fit. Everyone but Logan glared at him until he turned his back, his shoulders shaking until he composed himself enough to rejoin the conversation.

"I'm sure it's fine," Diana said, reaching out. Alec caught her hand, expression heart-wrenching.

"What if it were more than four pieces?" Daniel interjected quickly. "Would we explode if we had a piece inside us?"

"Uh... I have no clue," Gia admitted. "Probably not."

"I don't think that's a good idea." Serin eyed her mate with concern.

"Why not? We've established that I can tap into your powers."

"Wait, you can do what?" Connell asked.

At the same time, Alec made his own surprised exclamation.

"Anyway," Daniel continued, ignoring the interruption. "That rock should be just as happy in me as it will be in you because we vibe on the same wavelength now, right?"

"Only one way to find out." Gia took one sphere. With careful effort, she pinched it in two.

Daniel stepped in front of Serin, spreading his arms wide. "Okay, hit me."

"It might actually be best if it were Serin first," she said, handing her sister the two stones.

"Okay, how do I do this?" the Water Elemental asked.

"This is a bit complicated," Gia began.

"We don't have time for complicated," Daniel said, plucking a stone out of Serin's hand. At first, Gia though he was going to try to absorb it on his own, but he was simply making sure Serin was only holding one before he slammed his mate's hand across his own chest.

Serin's eyes widened. Her hand was flat across his rib cage.

Daniel's neck corded, but he instantly relaxed when Serin removed her hand. "That felt weird."

"Are you all right? Do you feel it inside you?"

He shook his head. "It's like nothing is there."

"My turn." Serin gripped the second stone in her hands. The sphere dissolved with a shimmer that ran up her arm, dissipating with a ripple of iridescence that reminded Gia of the sun setting over her favorite lake.

Logan and Connell were next. Gia pinched the remaining stones down their middles, and they each took one piece inside. Like Serin, both the Air Elemental and the shifter shimmered slightly.

Gia took her eighth next. The stone melted into her, attaching itself to her bones with barely a whisper.

There were three stones left.

Salvador met her eyes. "I understand if you don't trust me enough for this. I can—"

Gia took a stone, unceremoniously slamming it into his chest. Gasping, he bent over.

She winced. "Sorry, that was a tad harder than I intended."

He waved her concern away. "Not a problem," he wheezed, managing to look inordinately pleased to be in pain.

"I should have asked first—you can't go off with it. I'm afraid it can't leave my side." She held her breath as she waited for his response.

Salvador stared at her blankly for a second then broke out in a huge grin. "That won't be a problem."

A tight little knot inside her relaxed and she gave him a nod. There was a lot more to say...compromises would have to be made but that conversation would have to wait.

When Diana took the final two stones, Alec sucked in a ragged breath, holding her hands when she tried to press it against her ribs.

"Can we just hold off until the baby is born?" he asked, staying her hand.

Diana regarded him for a moment before nodding slowly. "What should we do with the extra in the meantime? Even an eighth could do a lot of damage in the wrong hands."

The vampire held his arms out just like Daniel had. "Put it in me. It's not like I'm using my organs. There's room in there."

"If you insist," Diana said with a laugh. She pressed one stone in, then the other. This time, the shimmer reaction was *much* stronger.

"Oh, oh, oh!" Logan crowed, nearly beside herself. "He looks just like those sparkly vampires in that movie."

Gia watched as the vampire stared down at his hands. Logan was right. He resembled something straight out of *Twilight*.

Alec raised his head, his face the picture of distress. "Please tell me this isn't permanent."

Gia couldn't answer him. She was laughing too hard.

36

———

hould I try to kidnap one?

John stared at the blinking cursor on his tablet, trying to think of a scenario where he could grab one of the remaining Elementals and still live to tell the tale.

He couldn't. Taking Gia by surprise had been a wonderful stroke of luck, but he didn't think he would be so fortunate a second time. Even without witnesses to the actual event, the others would adapt. They would be wary of him now, and John knew one underestimated an Elemental at his own peril.

Since serendipity was not a solid battle plan, he had to come up with something else. It was time for some out-of-the-box thinking. He'd always excelled at that.

Setting his tablet down, he clapped his hands and stood. The door of his office led to a small gangway. Branching off to the left were stairs to the ground level of the vast one-room warehouse.

The building was a recent purchase, something made under one of his many aliases. His enterprise required space and privacy. No doubt the commercial real estate agent thought he was storing toxic waste here, but the premium he'd been paid would ensure his silence.

With satisfaction, John stared down at the rows of bright green barrels, but it only took a second for his enthusiasm to dim. Having so much of his potion on hand was like being all dressed up with nowhere to go.

He'd been searching for a way to Her for years. Decades, truthfully. Few of his contacts in the Supernatural world had known of the forgotten paths, and those who did hadn't had a clue where to find one. Those Supes who might have had a prayer of such deep knowledge—the old witch houses and the Fae—they had shut him out. Repeatedly.

His fist tightened at the rail. That rejection would be their undoing. When he was done, all those self-satisfied Supes would be completely irrelevant. He just needed to figure out how to make a big splash because his plan B, trying to inject the liquid into the earth's core blindly, clearly wasn't going to work. Too haphazard.

John lifted his brows. His warehouse was on the outskirts of a large city. He could always introduce his concoction into the local water supply. Titrate it *just* so in the right amounts, and only the weakest of humans would be affected.

But the Supes? Their numbers would be devastated.

To make his effort worthwhile, it would have to be more than one city. How many could he hit without arousing suspicion?

The idea itself was simple. A municipality's water supply was surprisingly vulnerable, but knowing when and where to drop his additive required extensive research and proper preparation. He had to hit the Supernaturals were it hurt.

But John was a consummate scholar. He had always excelled in his studies.

37

D aniel couldn't believe his ears. He motioned to Alec, who sat across the room at the wide oak table with a pile of books in front of him. "Was there an old guy with him?" he asked. "He would appear to be on the wrong end of his fifties, paunchy and bald?"

It had been weeks since the summit on the hill—at least, that was what he called it.

They were in Minneapolis at one of the vampire's many apartments. He and Serin had met up with the Fire Elemental and her mate after discovering their parallel investigations had brought them within a couple of hundred miles of each other. They had met up at the posh penthouse to regroup and share notes, but the ladies had taken off to 'do a circuit,' which usually meant going to find random bad guys to beat up. It was an Elemental's preferred method of blowing off steam.

Alec was on his feet now, but Daniel forestalled him when he started to ask a question.

His man at Homeland hadn't had good news. "No one by that description," Lester said. "The guys were local talent, and not the brightest bulbs either. Honestly, they're just stupid kids pretending to be criminals. For fuck's sake, they were hired off Craigslist. I know Bioterrorism wasn't something on your list of weird things to search for, but there is a bunch of green goo—a barrel of it—and goo *was* on your list."

"Hold the evidence and the kids, and do it quietly," Daniel said, widely waving at the vampire. "I'm flying in ASAP with some consultants."

He hung up, prepared to launch into an explanation, but Alec held up a hand, typing furiously with the other.

The vamp tapped his ear. "I heard everything. I'm pinging the girls and having the jet fueled."

Daniel blinked. "You have a jet?"

"I have a few. Where are we headed?"

"Some no-name town in Colorado," he replied, switching his phone to the map application to find the nearest airport.

He glanced up to find the vampire watching him intently.

"*Where* in Colorado?"

GIA KEPT her distance when the wolves opened the barrels.

"Be careful not to touch it," Douglas Maitland growled at his men.

The instructions were a bit redundant, given that his wolves were in full hazmat gear. But she appreciated his concern for his people—and how he was reining in his temper at this attempt to poison his pack's water supply.

She had thought he was more subtle than this. And less suicidal.

How had the alchemist found out about this well? Given the high concentration of shifters in the area, the Maitland compound and surrounding area were, by necessity, on the municipal grid, but what wasn't common knowledge was they used two different wells as their primary water sources. One was very close to the main house. That one was too close to the inner sanctum, but the other was just inside the woods. Their existence and exact location weren't public knowledge.

Daniel, their most experienced interrogator, had already spoken to the kids who were supposed to dump the barrels in the water purification plant, followed by the well. The pair hadn't known who hired them, taking half the cash up front. They'd also been under strict instructions to wait for the last day of the month, but a video game tournament had conflicted, so they'd decided it wouldn't hurt to do it early.

The three industrial-sized barrels of toxin were proof of how badly she had underestimated their adversary's manufacturing capacity.

I should have known better. It would have taken a vast amount to rig up the sprinkler system the way he had in the castle ruins.

"I had no idea John could make this much," Gia muttered, rubbing her head. She didn't get headaches often, but her entire brain felt tight.

"I had no idea he had such brass balls," Diana replied with a snort. "I definitely didn't have this on my *John-is-a-tool* bingo card. Imagine thinking he could take on Douglas' wolves."

"You give him too much credit. He sent minions to do his dirty work, sneaking poison like this—it was a cowardly act."

"But one with consequences," Diana argued. "He has to know the Colorado pack won't let this stand. There won't be anywhere he can hide after this."

"I don't think he has any plans to hide at all. If these boys hadn't been premature, we would have discovered that the month would have ended with a bigger bang."

"You think he's planning to hit more locations? Some sort of statement?"

She nodded. "Followed by a last stand."

He'd have no choice. After attacking the wolves and Mother-knew-who-else, he would have to prepare for the end. And she knew better than anyone that a good defense was a good offense.

"Shit," Diana muttered. "Where do we start?"

"Anyplace there are large concentrations of Supes. Minus the vampires. They wouldn't drink the water. He will have figured out some other way of getting this crap to them."

"Like an army with water pistols?"

"It's a possibility."

Diana twisted until she could see her, eyes wide. "Shit, really?"

"He'd want to do it up big. A battle—after our numbers are decimated—would be the biggest bang he could think of."

"Well, shit."

"Can you burn the liquid? Or will the fumes do us in?"

"As far as we know, they don't have any effect," Diana said. "So, we won't need to keep our distance when I torch it."

"Good." Gia nodded, then sighed.

"What's on your mind, toots?" Diana asked, studying her from the corner of her eye.

Gia sucked in her lip, chewing on it. It was a childhood habit she'd stopped doing long ago. "We got lucky this time. We owe this opportunity to Serin's man Daniel and his human methods of investigation. For too long, we've depended on the Mother to determine when and where to act. But She's not here to guide our hands anymore. In fact, I think we handicapped ourselves by following Her directives so blindly."

Diana frowned. "That's harsh. And inaccurate. We follow the shifts in the balance. By and large, it's a method that still works."

"It does, and it doesn't. We've known the system is faulty for a while now. How else could John continue to hide from us?"

"Cause he's a sneaky-ass alchemist using our own secrets against us?"

Gia pursed her lips. "Regardless, we have to start doing the legwork. Calling in favors among our people—in addition to checking human businesses like storage places and private security firms."

"I hate mercs," Diana grumbled. "I swear they get more *ugh* with every generation. Give me a good old-fashioned Hessian, Sleepy-Hollow-style, any day."

"Bite your tongue," Gia chided. "You're not old enough to have fought a Hessian, so I'll overlook your ignorance on this matter. The modern ones are much easier to deal with."

"But as plentiful as fleas on a rat," Diana pointed out. "And they'll be armed with those toxin-tainted bullets."

"Yeah, we're going to have to think about some kind of deterrent for that. In the meantime, we need to search for spaces where John can make and store large volumes of his poison—storage units in manufacturing districts and the like. And start canvasing the modern-day mercenary companies. Humans sell those services out in the open these days. That should be to our advantage."

"I'll put Daniel and Alec on that," her sister promised. "We're going to need all hands on deck."

Gia nodded, watching Salvador bend over one of the barrels.

"Maybe keep some of it?" he suggested, having overheard the entire exchange. "I'm also going to need access to Alec's suppliers."

"What are you thinking?"

Salvador scratched his nose, then took out a notepad. "It won't be easy. With some help, I can work up more of the antidote I developed for you. Maybe we can even tweak it to make up a pre-inoculation that would confer immunity."

Gia was intrigued. "You think that's possible?"

"I won't know until I try," he said, staring at the barrels. He touched a spot on his chest, right over where she'd shoved the trigger stone, and rubbed absently. It was his new favorite unconscious mannerism. "It will be a challenge. But consider me motivated."

38

D ouglas pulled on a shirt, then ran downstairs. He'd been shoring up the pack's defenses last night. He had ended up crashing just after dawn, intending to get at least a few hours of shut-eye. However, knocking on the door had woken him after forty minutes, and he was *not* happy.

He tugged too hard, swearing when a button popped off his flannel shirt. It went rolling down the stairs ahead of him. Apparently, for once in his life, the house was empty of other wolves.

What the hell are they doing? There were at least half-a-dozen wolves in residence, including Mara, his daughter and fill-in enforcer while his son Connell was away.

Of all the days for her to get an early start—but then, that wasn't generous of him. Mara was taking the pack's security seriously, and he couldn't fault her for that.

The pack had been readying for battle for days. The compound was heavily fortified, but once his wolves had discovered the incursion on the water supply, they had redoubled their efforts, going over every inch of their territory in search of weaknesses.

The warriors of his pack were getting ready. Once Diana and Gia had raised the possibility that this John character meant to raise an army against them, the Colorado Basin Pack had volunteered to stand at their back. Whatever he threw their way, they would be ready to tear down.

That so-called alchemist had struck at their home. For that reason alone, he deserved to die. But securing the compound came first. They had to be sure their children and more vulnerable members—those too young or too old to fight—would be protected in their absence.

The knock sounded again, and Douglas tried to tamp down his annoyance. They were in Defcon one, so whoever this was had passed their security checkpoints. Douglass knew it wasn't one of his wolves. None would have knocked, which could only mean one thing. It was the witch.

Logan, his Elemental daughter-in-law, had promised to send someone to help them detect any intruders—no matter what masking spells were used. It went against everything in him to let a practitioner walk on these grounds. For his people, though, he would swallow his bile and let the witch work. As long as they kept the magic on the side of the light, he would put up with it. But the Canus Primus didn't kowtow to magicians, no matter who had sent them.

Pulling a face, he yanked open the door, ready to intimidate the hell out of whoever Logan had sent, but then froze. *Fuck. Why didn't I comb my hair?*

"Hello," Hope said brightly. She was dressed in all black, looking for all the world as if she were about to grace Vogue Asia. At her feet was an oversized black leather apothecary bag.

She wasn't alone. Mai, incongruously dressed in gauzy pastels, scowled. She pulled her sunglasses down. "Well, aren't you going to invite us in?" she groused.

Clearing his throat, he stepped back. "My apologies. You caught me unawares. Logan didn't mention who she was sending." Or when they were arriving. He would have showered.

The women entered, following him past the mudrooms into the vast open space of the living room, up to the grand staircase that led to the second floor.

Douglas held his breath as Hope turned around in a circle, taking it all in. She stepped into the sunken living room area, setting her bag on the polished wood table.

As the pack leader, his home had to be big. Though most of his wolves had their own homes, he had to be able to accommodate a dozen or more on a moment's notice. In fact, the pair Connell had sent to him, Ravil and his sister, had just left, taking up residence in a cottage near the high school.

When he built the house, all he'd cared about was making it functional and comfortable. But now he couldn't help but take pride in the space he and his pack had made into a home.

"It certainly has your stamp on it," Hope said with a note of approval.

"Well, I did put a lot of man-hours into the place," he admitted, rubbing a hand over the nape of his neck.

"It shows." Hope's approving expression was starting to make him blush.

He hadn't realized he was smiling back until Mai cleared her throat. "If you two are done making googly eyes at each other, we can get started."

Flushing like a teenager, he pivoted to scowl at Mai. Undaunted, she glowered right back.

Hope tsked and fluttered her lashes, her serene and genial countenance unperturbed. "Logan brought me samples. I've been working on the puzzle of the masking spell ever since your trouble started." She indicated her bag.

Before he could offer to take it for her, Mai slapped something into his hands. Fragrant herbs assaulted his sensitive nose. Coughing, he held the bag away from him.

"Are these for a spell? What do I do with them?"

"You boil water." Mai smirked. "It's my tea."

"*Jie Jie*, you can't order the Canus Primus around," Hope chided, poking her sister.

A door slammed.

"Dad..." Mara, his daughter called, running up from the back hallway. She came to a stop as she caught sight of her dad.

"I heard our guests had arrived." Mara glowered at Hope and Mai, suspicion darkening her countenance.

Like Logan, the Li sisters were both of diminutive height, so Mara towered over them. And like him, his daughter shared his prejudice of witches.

"Manners, Mara," Douglas reminded her with a sigh. "Logan sent her mother and aunt to help us."

Mara's face immediately dropped its sullen aspect. "Oh-my-God, really?" she almost squealed, putting her hand to her mouth.

She held out her arms. To his shock, Mai smiled graciously, approaching to give the taller woman a squeeze.

"It's so great to meet you in person, Mai," Mara gushed. When she caught his incredulous glance, she shrugged. "What? We've been emailing."

His brow creased. How had they even connected? Well, through Logan obviously, but how had his little girl so obviously bonded with the prickly Mai?

Asked and answered. Both his children were wonderful, strong wolves, of course, but as the chief's only daughter, Mara felt the need to be just as aggressive and forthright as her brother Connell. It went without saying that it didn't make things easier for her.

"Emailing about what?" he asked.

"This and that," Mai grumbled. "Come, Mara. Show me where your kitchen is because obviously this one isn't going to fetch me a hot mug of water anytime soon."

The pair disappeared into the kitchen before he could think up something civil to say in reply.

Hope didn't bother to hide her amusement. He gave himself a little shake. "I apologize for not being prepared for your visit. I wasn't expecting Logan to send you."

"I've been working on those masking spells since my daughter shared the details with me. I was able to examine most of the spell vials she found at Bishop Kane's house. The residue on the discarded ones was most informative."

Douglas nodded, briefly closing his eyes. Hearing his former friend's name still stung. Bishop's betrayal had rocked their pack. Kane's children still dealt with the aftermath. But Douglas was fixing it. Or he was trying to.

Delicately, Hope averted her eyes. *Logan must have filled her in on the details of what happened.*

"Did you crack them?" he asked. The masking spell Bishop had received from John was one of several variants. The original had been invented by a Burgess by-blow and her black coven a few years back. The alchemist had taken the formula and tweaked it, giving it a special hellish twist that had enabled a traitor to mask his intentions toward the pack.

Hope lifted a shoulder. "Most permutations. I'm reasonably confident I can set up a perimeter alarm that would detect anyone crossing your borders. We just have to make sure we type everyone who belongs here in order to exclude them from the spell. Otherwise, whatever alarm we set will be going off all the time." She paused. "With a little effort, we can make it permanent if you like."

He sighed, passing a hand over his weary face. "I hope that won't be necessary."

Douglas hated the idea he couldn't protect his own without a spell. However, with the Mother gone, these were perilous times. He didn't want to make a decision he would later regret. "Can we table the talk of permanence for later?"

Hope grimaced, her delicate nose wrinkling. "It would be better to know now, before we get started, but—if you decide to keep such a safeguard up, we can simply start over. For now, we can focus on tagging your people, so the spell doesn't react to them."

"That's a lot of wolves," he muttered. Even restricting the number to the local pack, that was over three dozen wolves. If he counted those outside county lines, then he had to start multiplying exponentially.

Hope put her hand on his arm. "I know it is. That's why I brought Mai. With her help, we'll be done in no time."

His answering smile was a trifle stiff. "That's very generous of her —of you both. Mai is great."

"She is, isn't she?" Hope beamed. She held out a hand. "*Come.*"

Douglas blinked. For a second, he thought she'd was talking to him, but he was on the wrong side to take her hand. Then the bag she'd left on the table began to float in her direction. Wide-eyed, he watched the heavy parcel drift like a feather until it paused in front of her, waiting.

"*Damn.* You didn't even say bibity-bobity-boo," he said. He doubted even the most seasoned practitioners in the Seven families could pull off a trick like that.

Grinning, Hope grabbed the leather handles, patting it as if it were an obedient pet. "Let's get started."

39

———————

Gia found it difficult to take her own words to heart. She knew she had to find a new way of conducting her work, but it was far from easy to change of habits honed over centuries.

Magic had taught her a lot of shortcuts. While she could apply some to the research—they had to in order to find the alchemist—it wasn't *her* way.

Diana seemed to be doing okay with the changes. At first, Gia assumed her younger sister let Alec do all the grunt work, but Diana had surprised her, rolling up her sleeves and pitching in. Her scholar mate had definitely rubbed off on her.

Logan would be fine, too. She was the youngest, and she relied less on the balance than her older sisters. The Air Elemental also had her voices to guide her, provided she could get them to behave.

And Serin has Daniel. The human detective would guide her sister into this new era. Which just left Gia stuck in in the old ways. *Oh God. I'm the dinosaur.*

Groaning at that realization, Gia allowed herself to wallow in self-pity for two minutes before gathering her composure and taking stock. She would not fade into irrelevance now—not when the world was in such dire need.

Forcing herself to set aside over a half-millennia of the magical training that had been a touchstone for her, she made and fielded calls, learning to decipher property records and do what Daniel affectionally called, *'following the money'*. Her efforts bore fruit, identifying a warehouse in Arizona that was likely a poison repository.

Alec and Daniel had been substantially faster with the research, finding two other likely storage places in isolated parts of Michigan and Southern Florida. The one in Arizona hadn't been as likely a candidate, but Gia hadn't been willing to leave any stone unturned.

And wouldn't you know it… when we got here, we found an army waiting. Well, not waiting exactly. But they must have had this place under surveillance because once she and Salvador had started poking around, they had come in force.

Gia felt the rumble in the earth when the vehicles were still miles away. But the distinctive vibration of heavy vehicles coming one after another was unmistakable. They drove single file up the road, minimizing the target they presented.

Climbing to the roof of the single-story warehouse for a better vantage point, she huffed, blowing her hair out of her eyes as she spotted the two large vehicles. Both were full of men and women in high-tech tactical armor. *Great.*

Salvador scrambled after her, his face falling as he counted the SUVs. "Was there a tripwire I somehow missed?"

She shook her head in confusion. "I didn't detect anything, no hidden cameras or spell traps. I checked thoroughly. There must be some kind of masked surveillance I'm not familiar with."

Gia had taken precautions, training herself to search for any variations of the Burgess masking spell. She should have been able to detect anything remotely like it. *This must something wholly new.* Crap, just how innovative had John become?

"They could be using satellite surveillance."

"What?" Gia twisted toward him.

"If these are human mercenaries, most have served in at least one branch of the armed services," he explained. "There are a fair number of military satellites. The people who run these soldier-of-fortune companies have ties to the upper echelons of government. They can get those feeds through backchannels and favors."

Gia swore under her breath. This *was* a whole new ballgame.

"Satellites? Well, that's just peachy," she snapped, breathing out before reaching into her pocket. She pulled out a seed the size of an almond.

"What is that?"

"Something I prepared. Think of it as a power cell."

When she squeezed the seed, it disintegrated in her hand, coating it in a luminescent gold-and-green powder that looked like finely ground glitter. Gia activated the cloaking spell, boosting it with the energy she'd trapped in the seed. When she was done, she blew the dust into the air, sending the web of her enchantment as far as she could.

The air above began to sparkle as the breeze carried the spell out, covering the area as far as the eye could see.

Salvador tipped his head up, staring at the sparkle. He took a deep sniff. "Smells like concealment. Do you think it will work on the satellite feeds?"

"I have no idea," she said honestly. "But it's not as if we have another option. No sense in giving the human military-industrial complex fodder for war—more than John has already given them."

Suddenly, Salvador grinned.

"Weird thing to be happy about," she groused.

"You said *we*."

"You're incorrigible." She pushed him affectionately toward the edge of the warehouse, indicating he should climb down. "Don't get all sappy on me now. Prep your defensive spells. We should try to keep as many alive as we can. These guys are just pawns."

"Pawns with automatic weapons," he called as he climbed over the edge.

At least John had chosen an isolated warehouse in the middle of nowhere. It would make less of a mess. Which led to her next question—did these people even know what John had gotten them into?

Not that it mattered. She couldn't afford to treat them as complete innocents.

Hopping down from the warehouse roof, she landed on the ground, connecting with the earth below her feet.

The line of cars was almost there now. Waiting a beat, she counted her breaths. *One, two...* On three, she raised her hands, lifting the ground under the asphalt just in front of the lead armored car.

The SUV flipped over as the remaining three vehicles squealed to a stop behind it. Soldiers in full tactical gear swarmed out, some immediately taking cover while those in the front ran to the flipped-over car to get their people out.

The soldiers lifted their weapons, then the bullets began to fly.

Gia pulled a chunk of concrete out of the back wall, levitating it toward Salvador to give him cover. As for her, the bullets were made of metal. She allowed them to get close, stopping them about a yard out. Then she released them. They fell to the ground like fat raindrops.

Abruptly, the bullets ceased. She could feel the confusion wash over the assembled soldiers. At some signal, though, they resumed shooting.

"C'mon, already," Salvador shouted. "You know the bullets aren't going to work."

At that moment, a chunk of concrete broke away from the edge of the piece covering him, spraying him with concrete dust and shrapnel.

"Maybe just keep quiet?" she suggested.

She only took her eyes off the humans for a second, but it was enough time for them to rearm themselves.

"What the hell?" she asked when three soldiers slid out a wheeled contraption complete with canon.

"You could just let them fire it," Salvador suggested, still wiping his face. He threw out an arm, tossing a spell ball with a chant that sent it into a curving trajectory. It hit the left flank, stunning the humans into immobility. "The point is to destroy the warehouse, isn't it?"

She stopped to throw a chunk of asphalt at the canon assemblage, crushing it and sending the humans scrambling.

"Not before we go through every inch of it for evidence of John's location," she said. Only after that would she call Diana here. Together, they would burn this place to the ground. "Now stay there while I take care of this."

Gia decided it was time to get her calisthenic on—she ran toward the group, the hail of bullets dropping out of her path like rain. Darting forward, she took the gun off the biggest man before decking him. She made sure to pull the punch. Gia didn't want to kill him— not unless he asked for it.

Stirring the ground next to the road, she crafted dust devils for cover so she could check the gun's composition. Good, all terrestrial ingredients. It was mostly metal. John hadn't provided them with anything special, although she didn't know how one would go about making a machine gun out of a meteorite in any case.

Pushing with her talent, she dismantled the gun. It fell into several pieces, but that wasn't enough for her. Another push and the fragments melted into pools of metal that were quickly reabsorbed into the ground

A slight noise alerted her to a presence. A woman had breached the perimeter of the dust cloud. She pointed another of those guns right at Gia's head.

"Thanks," she said, waving. The gun flew out of the woman's hands, dissolving into a big puddle at Gia's feet.

She lifted her hand, freezing the sandstorm and slowly putting it down so all the grains settled at once.

Putting on a show never hurt anybody.

"Holy *shit*," the woman cried, falling and scooting backward until she hit her head on the door of the nearest SUV. "What the hell are you? Magneto?"

"Who is Magneto?" Gia asked before peering into the woman's aura. "Hey, you're a shifter."

Scanning the other soldiers—who were continuing to fire despite keeping their distance—she noted their signatures. Over half were shifters. But they didn't seem to recognize her, which meant they were pack-less and had never caused enough trouble to get on her radar.

She tsked and focused, pulling in with her talent. One by one, the heavy guns flew out of her adversary's hands, disintegrating as they did.

When she was done, she was surrounded by over a dozen weaponless men and two women. She clapped her hands. "Attention, soldiers. Attacking me is a violation of the Covenant, which every Supernatural is bound by at birth. *So. Stop. Trying. To. Shoot. Me,*" she said, punctuating every word with a clap, shaking the ground under her feet. She was annoyed.

"The only excuse for this is ignorance—but that's all. Ignorance does not absolve you."

"What the hell are you talking about, lady?" the woman near her feet hissed.

"The fact you don't know tells me that your pack leader is either a pretender or one in a long line of wolves outside the fold."

"I don't have a pack leader, you crazy—"

The woman blinked, drawing her head back until it banged on the door of the SUV, because Gia was in her face, having moved too fast for the woman to see.

"I don't let anyone call me what you're about to call me. Not even another woman."

Salvador sidled up next to her. "Well, you know you were right about John hiring entire mercenary companies," he said as Gia backed away. Belatedly, she let his concrete shield crash to the ground.

"Yes, I'm very insightful," she said dryly, surveying the wreckage. The soldiers had regrouped. A man inched toward the door of one of the vehicles.

She put her hand out and made a fist, crushing the SUV into a ball.

"Like it was tinfoil," Salvador muttered. "Cool."

"How are we going to get out of here now?" the woman near them protested, apparently feeling brave enough to get to her feet.

"Sit in each other's laps," Gia snapped. "Since you don't have a copy of the Covenant, here it is."

She waved her hand, inserting the long string of words directly into the woman's brain, a spell Gia hadn't had to use in decades.

The woman collapsed to her knees, crying out, "*Hey.*"

"I could have just emailed it to her," Salvador said, waving his phone. "Or we *could* and probably *should* wipe their memories."

Gia rubbed her head, mulling it over. Technically, she *had* been in this position before, having to choose to wipe a mixed group. She had done it without compunction, but as this shitshow had just demonstrated, this was an all-new ballgame.

"Just the humans," she finally decided, rubbing her eyes.

"Wait," the woman cried, but it was too late.

Salvador had prepared for this. He reached into his pocket, pulled out a vial, and unstopped it. Throwing it wasn't necessary. The smoky white fumes rushed out like a giant snake—as if they were eager to escape.

But it was Salvador's guiding hand that made sure they only enveloped the humans.

As one, three men and the other woman dropped to the grounds.

"What did you do?" the female soldier asked, whipping around to gape at the fallen.

Gia held up a hand. "I take it your compatriots know your true nature," she said, nodding at the female and the remaining three shifters. On closer inspection, only two were wolves. One was a cougar while the other was something small and furry.

"Your badass mercenary crew has a *rabbit*?"

"How did you know?" the huge muscled soldier who shifted into a floppy-eared bunny said in consternation. He spoke with a thick Bavarian accent.

"How do *you* not know who *she* is?" Salvador asked, waving his hands to encompass Gia.

"Sal," she said, touching his arm.

"To be this old, they must have run into other shifters," he grumbled. "They *should* know."

Gia shrugged. "The world is a big place, and they are still young."

The shifters were under thirty, probably recruited from all corners of the globe judging by Peter Rabbit's accent.

"What do you know about the guy who hired you?" she asked the woman.

"Nothing," she replied, throwing up her hands. "Just a bank account. It was supposed to be a simple job—secure the warehouse. Collateral damage acceptable."

"Wow, did you get set up," Salvador muttered. "Someone is tossing professional soldiers and hapless Supernaturals at an adversary they don't have a chance of defeating—namely her and her sisters," he said, pointing at Gia.

"Do yourself a favor," Gia said. "More of the same is coming. Convince whoever signs your checks to sit this one out."

She turned back to Salvador, gesturing to the prone humans. "How much did you take?"

"A day or two," he replied, crossing his arms. "It depends on biochemistry."

"A touch excessive," she conceded. "I will have to ask Dalasini to work up more precise charms."

Gia turned back to the shifters. The woman had gone to one of the fallen men, gathering him into her arms.

"Under most circumstances, exposing the Supernatural to a human is a violation of the Covenant. Exceptions for close friends and family have been made, but your trust in them must be absolute. So, carefully choose whom you decide to tell about yourself and what you are from now on. Knowledge of us cannot spread—for now," she added

Even as she said the words, she began to doubt herself. The Mother was no longer here. What impetus would any Supe have to keep Her most sacred laws now? *Other than I said so.*

Sighing heavily, she conceded the truth. The Covenant would have to be amended to reflect their new reality.

"I suggest you pile into the car you have left and go," Gia told the female wolf. She thrust her thumb at the warehouse. "Because I'm going to tear that place up to find whatever I can on the man who hired you. Then I'm going to burn it and its contents—which is buckets and buckets of poison intended for domestic bioterrorism by the way."

She shifted, prepared to send a pulse into the ground, a message for Diana to join them.

"It's okay. I texted Alec," Salvador said, reading her mind. "They'll be on their way when they wrap up their business. Alec's warehouse and the one Daniel found were also real. They got similar receptions."

"Mixed groups again?" she asked.

"No. I checked. Theirs were all human."

Good. "Then tell him to wipe their memories. If there's nothing leading to John, raze the warehouses to the ground. Then we need to put those two on another task."

"Which is?"

"Tell Alec and Daniel to do what they do best. Follow the money. This time, though, follow it to the bank accounts these mercenaries were paid from. It's our best shot."

He nodded and got to work, taking a moment to help the shifters load their unconscious people into the remaining vehicle, stacking them like cordwood in the back. And despite the fact those same soldiers would have shot his ass, he did it gently—because he was Salvador.

Gia walked into the warehouse, heading for the stairs leading to the office above the ground floor. From the vantage point, she could see the rows and rows of barrels, each full of enough toxic bullshit to take out a legion of Supernaturals.

Well, it would never touch them now.

Her hands fisted on the rail, and she felt him. John's imprint was on the wood. "Can you feel me, alchemist?" she asked. "*Because I'm coming for you.*"

40

"Well, I'll be damned." John brushed off some of the glass that had fallen on his shoulder. He hadn't taken the news that his warehouses were gone all that well.

The wreckage of his laboratory was proof that even after all this time, his temper still had a cutting edge. But the picture that was attached to the end of the email had just turned his world upside down.

No word from the team yet. I don't expect they survived if these creatures are as dangerous as you say. The feeds caught a single image of the assailant, and only from a great distance. Once the team was in range, all the cameras cut off, so this is the best image we are likely to get. I've blown it up for you, but there is a substantial loss in resolution. Nevertheless, you can make out a man and a woman standing on top of the warehouse, waiting.

. . .

BUT THE PICTURE quality didn't matter. He would have known that head of lustrous dark hair anywhere. As a bald man, he'd always envied it.

Gia had somehow survived his toxin. It shouldn't have been possible, but she was stood next to the disgraced Delavordo heir—the healer. It was explanation enough.

I should have tried to recruit that one myself. Oh, well.

Glass crunched beneath him as he made his way to the rear of his trailer. He'd attached an extra storage unit to the hitch in the back. It contained a half-a-dozen barrels of his toxin, the last he had left in the world.

For a minute, he debated starting again, but the idea made his balls itch. *Make more, try to wreak havoc, and almost get caught.* It was a vicious circle.

Except the Elementals would find him before he could produce the amount he'd had stored.

Belatedly, he noticed he was bleeding. A shard had caught his finger. Sucking at the drop, he shook his head. He was forgetting himself, who he really was...

It was his own fault. He'd changed his appearance, lived under an assumed name for so long, he'd forgotten just how *bad* he was.

No, it was time to write the end of this saga. But how?

Suddenly, it came to him. Of course. He knew when and where to finish this—even how to deliver the message. The Earth Elemental was the key. He knew her history—knew everything about them.

Alistair Crowley, the wickedest man in the world, rubbed his hands together. If he had to go out, he would do it with a bang.

41

Logan busted into the safehouse library, running with Connell nipping at her heels.

Gia looked up from her place at the computer, rising when she noticed her sister's urgency.

"Did one of the others find a lead?" she asked.

Logan stopped short and opened her mouth, then clamped it shut as she held up a finger. She appeared ready to explode.

"What is it?" she asked, concern creasing her brow.

Logan's delicate features tightened. Her hands fisted, crumpling a card she held in her hand.

Gia's head drew back. "Logan?" she asked, brows raised. But her sister was impotent in her rage. Connell cleared his throat, but his growl was thicker than Gia had ever heard it.

"The asshole is calling us out," he said, plucking the card from his mate's hand and handing it to Gia.

Frowning, she took the card. "An engraved invitation?" she asked in disbelief.

The card was a heavy cream stock, with gold letters. The first line read: *The honor of your company is requested...*

"It's not so much an invitation as a summons to the battle," Connell growled. "Complete with hour and place."

Frowning, she scanned to the bottom. When she read the location, her expression hardened. Then, she laughed. Logan frowned as if Gia had gone crazy.

"You okay?" Logan asked, recovering her voice, although her face was red.

Of course she doesn't know. She's too young, and I never told her the details.

Gia shook her head, putting her hand on her sister's shoulder. "You know, I don't think I've ever said this about anyone before, but I'm going to really enjoy killing this man. *A lot.*"

MARA NARROWED her eyes at her father. He held his arms out while Logan's mother Hope added a final flourish to the sigil she'd just painted on his chest. Personally, she thought it would have been easier without all the hair on his pecs, but that didn't seem to bother the woman much, mainly because as soon as she finished painting the rune, it disappeared, melting into his skin as if the mix was pure alcohol and not eleven magical herbs and spices. The chest hair didn't affect the absorption one way or the other.

Mai was doing the same with Derrick, who, in Connell's absence, was the pack's third—after her. A long string of shifters, both male and female, were lined up along the wall, waiting for their turn.

"Is this really going to make us bulletproof?" Derrick asked skeptically.

Mai, who had been doing his sigils, popped her gum in his face. She waved her brush in the air. "Don't be stupid," she scolded. "If you run into a hail of bullets, they aren't going to bounce off you like you were Superman. Quite the contrary. They will be attracted to the sigils."

"Wait, what?" Derrick growled, grabbing her wrist. Mai glared, whispering something. With a yelp, he let go of her arm, shaking it as if it stung.

Mai smirked.

"Sister, behave." Hope tsked before turning to Derrick. "But Mai is correct. They won't make you bulletproof. Even my Logan can't do that. Only Gia wields that power because of her affinity to metal. So, we're doing the next best thing." She waved a delicately manicured hand over Douglas' chest. "The bullets will be strongly attracted to this region here, pulling away from your head and extremities."

"Yeah, that sounds great, but what about our hearts or vital organs?" Derrick asked sarcastically. "Or do we not need those anymore?"

"The sigil-covered area will be protected by your body armor," Douglas said in a warning tone.

"But then we won't be able to shift," Salome pointed out from somewhere near the end of the line.

Mara took a deep breath, calling on her small reserve of patience. The fact Salome was allowed to go to this battle, but Mara had to stay here to protect the homestead, was a major bone of contention between her and the chief. But she couldn't continue to argue with him about it because as the pack's interim number two, it was her job. Or so the chief kept telling her. Somehow, she doubted he would have told Connell to stay home, but she couldn't point to their history to argue the point. This upcoming battle—in Ecuador according to the fucking invitation—was an unprecedented situation.

"That is where Hope's long study of war comes in," Douglas said, breaking into a grin that warmed exponentially when it lighted on the woman in question.

Hope backed away with a benign nod. She left the room but returned a few moments later with a set of the new tactical armor in hand.

A pack as large and as old as theirs had a lot of resources. Shifters were protectors. Most had done stints in the military or various law enforcement departments, but as her brother's attack a couple of years ago had proved, they weren't bulletproof. Body armor that could adapt to both their human and lupine forms was the holy grail. A few decades back, her parent had founded a company for the sole purpose of creating it. But there had been a number of setbacks.

However, Hope studied war as a profession. She was a much-lauded professor of the subject who was invited all over the world to give lectures. Hope was familiar with every general in the world, even the most obscure. She knew more than tactics, however—she knew about their customs *and* their arms. Being a kickass witch meant she could apply what she learned in new and innovative ways.

Hope held up the armor. It looked like a thicker, padded version of an eighties-era bodysuit—the kind that snapped at the crotch. "This suit is spelled to conform to you, transitioning to fit both your forms. Mai has also contributed, imbuing their fibers with extra-absorbent powers. Any impacts should be muffled."

She broke off, then addressed the chief. "How many of these did you say you had?"

"Enough. I would like Mara and the older children to be fitted for one as well. Just in case."

"Yeah, I wish," Mara muttered. She could only hope she would need one. Not that she wanted the pack children to be in harm's way, but it chaffed she was being sidelined from the action.

Hope threw her a commiserating glance, but her father ignored her as usual.

"We can do that," Hope assured him.

Mai appeared next to her, blowing a bubble that popped with a snap. "Well then, we better get our butts in gear. This line isn't going to finish itself," she said, waving at the waiting shifters.

"Of course," Hope said, affectionately squeezing her arm. Mai moved back to the line after giving her what was—for Mai—a friendly nudge. "Next time, it will be your turn, I promise."

Mara nodded, wishing it were true.

She watched the sisters work for a while, moving with that same airy grace their daughter possessed. Her father did the same, but his attention was restricted to one sister.

Mara wasn't the only one who noticed. Wolves were the nosiest of all the Supes, and many an eyeball tracked Hope as she worked.

The rumors had started the minute they arrived. The pack wondered if the father would go the way the son had. And despite Logan's obvious status and power, not everyone was happy about her and Connell's union.

If her dad seriously pursued an outsider like Logan's mom, there would be a lot of unhappy wolves. Even a defenseless human woman would be preferred—they wouldn't threaten the established pack hierarchy.

The woman in question didn't seem embarrassed or put off by the collective scrutiny. In fact, nothing seemed to faze her. Hope continued, a bright and open presence so incongruous with the steely inner strength she so obviously possessed. Just like Mai, who was a bundle of razors and knives wrapped in gauzy butterfly wings.

A few minutes later, Hope passed Mara's father, giving him a smile. But to Mara's eyes, it was no more personal than the ones she gave anyone else.

Maybe the pack grumbles and complaints weren't going to be the problem after all. Perhaps the bigger issue would be something else entirely. Like the most powerful wolf in the Americas getting his heart broken...

Well, look on the bright side, she told herself. They could all still die.

42

The bright full moon illuminated the thickening ranks of the opposing army. What had been an empty field just an hour before was quickly being filled by human soldiers and Supes bent on killing them.

There were more than Salvador would have guessed. According to Alec and Douglas Maitland, some were known quantities on the side of the black. A coven from New York, some Russian shifters, not to mention the crew from the Fae Black Darrig. There were others, too, but his stomach had started to hurt so he'd decided to stop counting and asking for names.

"What is the point of letting them assemble and line up again?" he asked with a grimace.

Gia didn't answer. She stood alone at the peak of a small rise. Just behind her were Serin and Logan. A few feet away, Diana stood next to her mate.

The air felt oppressively heavy. He nudged the vampire. "Um, I get this is a showdown to the death, but why is everyone so grim?"

The Elementals were trained warriors. From what he'd seen, they enjoyed their work. And the wolves—they freaking loved fighting. Yes, he understood the importance of this particular fight, the gravity of the situation. But the Elementals should have been pumped to mete out justice to the man who had betrayed them *and* the misguided idiots who followed him.

"It's this place," Diana murmured.

"What about this place?" The hills were picturesque, like most of the land in this part of Ecuador, but there was nothing special about it that he could see.

Diana sighed. "There was a village here once. It was overrun by insurgents. Marco, Gia's mate, came here to help. He was shot by someone, a case of friendly fire. This is where he died."

Holy fuck. His eyes flew to Gia. She faced away from him, but he could see her tension. It was in the line of her shoulders, the way she held herself. John was a master in psychological warfare—the piece of shit.

"Man, I really want to kill this guy," he muttered.

"You'll have to get in line. A very long one," Alec replied. "Besides, didn't you take an oath to do no harm?"

"That is for doctors. I'm a *curandero*, which is also a witch." And he believed in justice more than he believed in keeping his hands clean. True, he had never been in a battle like this, but he'd had plenty of hand-to-hand fights. He'd even fought off a trio of muggers intent on assaulting one of his distant neighbors. This couldn't be that different. He just had to pick an opponent while staying aware of his surroundings. How hard could it be?

"What happened to the village?" he asked, scanning the empty hills and fields. Marco hadn't died that long ago, a few decades at most. There should have been derelict buildings or at least foundations, but there was no trace of anything now.

"Serin moved the stream that provided the water to the villagers," Diana volunteered. "The people followed it. The Mother quickly reclaimed what was here, leaving it like new, untouched."

"*Okay.*" He hoped Gia had found that therapeutic instead of a heavy-handed attempt to erase her pain...

"Are you ready?" Alec asked. Salvador nodded, stretching his fingers. His hand ached after having finished the arduous task of giving six or seven dozen wolves toxin-proofing injections, but his pockets were loaded down with spell vials. His arms were also prepped with protective and defensive runes. "It's almost time."

"Do you really think he'll show?" Engraved invitation or not, Salvador was skeptical. *That would qualify as terminal stupidity.*

"Despite the impressive assortment of malcontents he has assembled, I don't, not really. It would be suicide," Alec murmured.

Salvador opened his mouth to agree, but he was forestalled when Gia turned, having heard their entire conversation.

"John is already here," she announced. "He's behind the others near the trees."

"The one shielded up the wazoo?" Serin asked. "I noticed him, too."

"Are you sure?" Logan asked. "I just read Fae from that guy."

"Yes, he's disguised as one of the gnomes."

"Like that'll help the fucking coward," Diana growled.

Logan asked the question Salvador wanted to. "If he's back there, what are we waiting for?"

"I didn't want anyone to be caught unawares," Gia said, pointing to the sky.

Scowling, Salvador glanced up, catching the strange whine for the first time. "What is that?"

"Drones." Gia put her hand on Logan's shoulder. "Take care of them, then circle back. There are three choppers coming up right behind them."

Stunned, Salvador froze, expecting death from above, but the Air Elemental was on it. She disappeared, too intent on her task to acknowledge the order.

Ahead of him, Gia nodded to her other two sisters. She and the other Elementals ran forward as the world exploded in light off to the right where the bombs crashed less than half a mile from their position.

"Shit," he muttered, running as fast as he could. He was quickly overtaken by their wolf allies, ending up somewhere in the rear guard.

A wall of fire rose as the choppers appeared, complete with men belaying down from tactical ropes, enough for it to rain hell down upon them. Logan blew them off course. The helicopters spun out of control, the armed personnel swinging from them like an enthusiastic stripper's tassels. He didn't see where they landed.

After that, the adrenaline fragmented his perception. He caught snatches of breathtaking scenes that were like something from an action movie—Serin washing away a squad of camouflaged soldiers, clearing the path for the wolves to get to the Black Darrig. Those deadly Fae ran straight down the middle of the field, leading dog-sized...err... somethings. The animals had short torsos, and they were earless with huge jaws and smooth round heads. They tore into the wolves with snarls and crunches that sounded too much like bones breaking for Salvador's peace of mind.

"*Hey,* look alive, dufus." Logan appeared out of nowhere. She snatched the spellbomb he clutched, chunking it behind him. Whirling, he heard a strangled scream as a man fell. One of John's allies had snuck up behind him.

"Thanks," he called, but Logan was already gone. Small tornadoes followed in her wake.

On his left, Diana threw fireballs at a group of vampires he hadn't known was there. The ground thrummed under his feet. He spotted Gia, arms out, as a river of dirt crashed into a line of camouflaged soldiers, carrying their weapons away and leaving them floundering in the dirt like unbalanced toddlers in a sandbox.

Salvador tried to do his part, but he was slower and less experienced in battle than every other person in the field. Grabbing more spell vials, he spun in a circle, trying to find a viable target. He didn't locate one until an opposing wolf leapt on him, sending him crashing to the ground.

43

The snarling jaws were inches from Salvador's neck when Gia rose from the ground next to him with a pop. She grabbed the wolf's rear leg, twisting it until it popped out of the joint. The wolf turned on her with a snarl, so she punched it in the muzzle, tossing its unconscious body over her shoulder.

"Thank—"

Gia held up a hand, pointing down the hill. "We've got injured, and you are far more valuable as a medic. Douglas will lose wolves if you don't get your ass down there. Go triage."

He looked as if he wanted to argue, but he simply closed his mouth with a sharp nod and ran down the hill.

She grabbed his arm before he got too far. "Watch your ass and *don't get dead*," she ordered, letting him go.

Salvador beamed. "I love you, too," he said, bending over for a short, searing kiss. Then he pulled back, turning away.

"That's not what I said," she shouted after him as he sprinted down the hill.

"Then why did I hear it loud and clear?" he yelled back, laughing.

Grinning despite herself, Gia twisted to survey the field. Serin had done a good job of washing away John's toxin from the soil. He'd tried to work it into the earth, tying it to the same plague curse Jordan had detonated in T'Kaieri, but his attempt to incapacitate her and the others had failed. They'd foreseen this and figured out how to sequester the contamination with impermeable rock, pulling it down and away from the living soil. Even now, a specially rerouted underground river carried it away to the ocean where it would be diluted to the point of harmlessness.

I have to hand it to the bastard. Even under their noses, John was doing a magnificent job of hiding. He'd shed the gnome identity as the helicopters flew in, sliding into another disguise before she could blink. It took her a number of minutes before she found him again— as a Fae burkin this time. The camouflage was intricate and must have taken him years to learn how to do, but Gia was angry and determined. She knew how to peel away the layers of magic to get to his underlying bone signature.

But the de-masking took time, and she had to examine every man and woman on the field. No sooner did she spot the little worm than he would dive into the melee, slipping on anther disguise like he was changing coats. By the fourth one, she gritted her teeth, telling herself she was going to grind his bones into a paste.

Not to mention, John wasn't the only one she had to worry about. It must have taken him years, but he had managed to collect the worst of the worst—witches, Fae, and shifters she would hesitate to send her sisters against, preferring to take them on herself.

At one point, she saw Diana go down, thrown to the ground by one of the Black Darrig. Reacting, Gia softened the ground, pulling Diana down and under her adversary, then raising her behind them.

"Thanks, babe," Di called after her fire lit up the Durrin from the inside out.

Gia saluted, then swiveled only to find a new adversary in front of her. *Well, well...* She inclined her head. "Seska."

The witch bowed with a flourish. A product of the ill-fated union of the Morgan and Patel clans, Seska had been on her and her sisters' watch list for years, but she'd stayed under the radar for the last decade. Gia was disappointed to see the witch here now.

"Aren't you going to tell me it's not too late to return to the light and forge my own path?" Seska laughed, a hysterical sound tainted with madness.

That's new. "No," Gia said slowly, adding '*Gladio*' in a whisper. The sword she'd claimed in Sheol appeared in her hand. It gleamed bright blue in the moonlight, its edge sharper than ever. "You've had ample opportunity to change course. Eventually, there are no more chances left."

She threw the sword just as Seska released her arsenal, hurling half-a-dozen spell vials at once. Gia deflected most, but one vial hit her. She brushed away the burning mix from her arm as her sword flew out. It arced like a boomerang as she called it back with her talent.

A normal blade shouldn't have been able to slice through Seska's many protection spells, but the Elven blade was still rejoicing its liberation from the demon king in Sheol. There was a slight hesitation as it hit the witch's dark aura, but only for a second. Then it kept going, eager to please its new master.

The witch collapsed into two pieces, bisected neatly at the waist. Gia decided to leave the body where it lay. Seska had clearly been busy in her decade of silence because her corpse was too tainted for Gia to feel comfortable sending it into the ground. Also, thanks to John, this patch would have to absorb a lot of blood and black magic tonight—too much. Instead, she'd ask Diana to burn the body later.

Farther away, a wall of flame crashed into the web of sticky vines some unknown Fae had thrown toward the wolves. Jumping in, she peeled one of the creepers off a male—she thought his name was Terrance—when it wouldn't respond to her magic at a distance.

"*Serin*," she called as the skin on her hand started to burn. A sticky substance covered the twisted vines, like an acidic mucus. She felt the vibration in the aether distinctive to her sister, but it was Daniel who skidded to a stop next to her.

"Should I?" he gasped, panting rapidly.

She waved him on, guiding his relatively untrained hand as he blasted the vines covering the wolves with a spring he called himself.

Helping, she called sharp stones from the deep, bringing them to the surface by pushing and twisting her hands together. The stones tracked her movement, crushing and shearing the appendages off.

"Not bad, rookie," she told Daniel, helping peel them away from the wolf. Terrance's fur—or was it Derrick?—had partially protected him, but the vines had worked into his hip, exposing muscle where it cut the deepest.

The wet wolf twisted out of its last restraint. He jerked, as if determined to head back into the fray, but Gia grabbed him by the muzzle and pointed him sharply in the other direction. When he wouldn't go on his own, she addressed Daniel.

"Take him down to Salvador," she ordered, softening the ground and sending them both down the hill, bypassing the fight.

Adrenaline kept her hopping all over as she ran back and forth putting out fires, or, in some cases, helping start them. At one point, she twisted around to find a human mercenary behind her, but he was too frightened to do anything. He couldn't even point the weapon he held at her.

"Hey, guy, think fast," she said, tossing a fist-sized rock at him. Yelping, he dropped his automatic weapon. Tsking, she rushed him and threw out a fast jab, knocking him unconscious. Keeping the hapless humans alive made her job a little more difficult, but she did it anyway... up until she spotted her real prey.

John wore a damn fine illusion of an attractive woman, one of the human mercenaries.

Gia tore through 'her' buddies, the cluster of male soldiers the faux female hid with. She tossed soldiers twice her size out of the way, making sure the spot they landed in was muddy and extra slippery so they couldn't get back up.

Using her booted foot, she kicked the last man soldier in the backside, sending him sliding away. Belatedly, the John-woman lifted his weapon. Snatching it out of 'her' manicured hands, Gia bent the AR-15 down the middle, trying to twist it like a pretzel. The metal's tensile strength was too weak, and it ended up snapping in half.

She grabbed the asshole by the collar as he tried to run away. Gia raised her hand, blasting the layers of magic away to reveal the pudgy and sweaty form of their enemy.

One of the soldiers who'd managed to crawl up to them stopped short, his face twisted when he got a look at John unmasked.

The sheer horror on his face told her that there was a story here, but she didn't have the time or the patience to hear it. Gia let the ground swallow the soldier up, spitting him out near the tree line.

"The breasts were a nice touch," she told John, who still tried to break her grip. "But this ends now."

"On that, we agree," he said, lifting a spell vial that had suddenly appeared in his hand over his head.

"Simple sleight of hand," he grunted as he threw it at her face. "Sometimes, the oldest tricks are the best."

44

Letting him go with a push, Gia put her hand out, sending the vial rushing back at John with her talent.

"You're not supposed to be able to do that," he grunted. "I carved that myself—from a shooting star that fell on sacred land in the Yukon. Your magic doesn't work on non-terrestrial stones."

She raised a brow. "Let me guess. You bought this meteorite online?"

His face tightened. John drew himself up to his unimpressive height. "I purchased it on eBay from a reputable vendor. Or so his ratings said. Is no one honest?" he asked, totally without irony.

"Well, I guess there's only one thing left to do." John unstopped the vial. For a moment, she thought he would try to throw it at her, but he surprised her by upending the entire mess on top of his own head. The sickly green dripped down his neck and ears. He bowed, mockingly holding out his arms. "I'm all yours."

She fluttered her lashes, lifting one shoulder. "I accept your unconditional surrender."

Screwing his face into snarl, he lunged for her, trying to wipe the excess liquid on her.

"It's not going to work this time," she snapped, lifting her hand.

The mud under his feet responded, drying and growing coarse. It rushed over his hand, sanding off the top layers of his skin.

"*Ow...*" John whined. He put his hand on his head. The shiny round melon pulsed red, bleeding in half-a-dozen spots. Then he lifted his hand to his mouth, nursing it.

Disgusted, she grabbed his arm and shook him, confirming there were no more hidden vials left. Around them, the sounds of fighting dimmed. The battle was winding down.

John cleared his throat. "For old times' sake, I'd appreciate it if Serin did the deed. I wouldn't mind going out like Jordan. In a few thousand years, maybe scientists will find my mummified corpse and put it in a museum."

"The fact you think you're important enough for a museum is just..." She swallowed, bile in her throat.

"But I am," he insisted. "Allow me to introduce myself—"

She held up her hand. "Stop right there. I don't care."

"But my name is—"

"*I. Don't. Care.* There's one of you in every age. But, in every age, there is one of me to stop you," she interrupted, punctuating every word with truth.

As for his *request*—that wasn't happening. Gia wasn't letting this turd anywhere near her sister. Not that Serin couldn't handle the confrontation, but this kill was Gia's.

John didn't even try to break free. Instead, he rubbed his hands together in anticipation. "Fine, so what shall it be? Will you pull my bones out of my body? Or just grind them into dust in situ, as it were? Will I spend the rest of my days as a formless lump, like the prover-bial blob fish?"

His laugh grated on Gia's ears.

"I've actually been giving this some thought," she admitted, "weighing my options. I had the list narrowed to a few favorites, but I just thought of something better."

Gia let the ground soften, flying them down into the bowels of the earth as fast as her talent could carry them. When they arrived at their destination, she let him fall to the ground as the travel disorientation knocked him off balance.

She backed up a step. "Congratulations. I've decided I'm going to give you exactly what you want."

Gia raised her arms like a game-show hostess, waving at the empty space around them. "Welcome to the Mother's chamber."

It had been fairly easy to return now that she knew where it was. Also, there were no elaborate safeguards in place anymore. Why would there be? There was nothing here to protect.

John twisted around, examining the vast blank space. "It's empty."

"I know."

He shrugged, then stood. "Did you move Her... for Her safety?" His tone was smug, almost flattered.

"No. The Mother has left us."

"What?" He threw back his head and laughed, fanning his red face.

Briefly, she closed her eyes. "Yes, the Mother has left this world. But before you get excited, She didn't decide to leave because of you."

Part of Gia still wanted to blame him, but she had long accepted the truth. The Mother had one foot out the door for years.

John scowled. "But magic still dies now, right?"

Gia suppressed an eye roll. "Of course not."

John's face went from a pleased gloat to a sneer. "She gave it all to you, didn't She?"

"The Mother did what She has always done—She left the world in Her chosen's hands." And what Gia and her sisters did with it was not his concern.

John's round face scrunched. "What does that mean? Are you the Mother now? Do you get to pick and choose who is magical and who isn't?"

"It doesn't matter. Not to you." She flicked her fingers at the cavern. "This is your world now. But I have good news."

Gia beckoned, calling the hyphae to come to her. All around John's feet, the psychedelic mushrooms that had put her and

Salvador through the wringer sprouted. As one, the puffballs ejected their spores, covering him.

"What the f—" Coughing, John wiped his face and arms. He swore, his puzzled expression fading as his mouth slackened and his eyes glazed over.

"Now the world will be exactly what you make it," Gia whispered.

Then she pivoted on her heel and left him there, alone.

45

Gia rose from the depths, shaking off her encounter with John. In her mind, the punishment fit the crime, but a tiny part of her regretted not lopping off his head. *That would have made Alec happy.*

The remnants of John's ragtag army had run away—those who could. The rest, mostly humans, were being treated by the Maitland pack medics. The black shifters were mostly dead, along with one of Douglas' own, an older wolf she'd met years ago but couldn't name. No doubt there has been other losses, but she would seek that knowledge and get a true accounting later.

She had no idea what happened to the black Fae, but it had been messy.

Dalasini and Caiman floated through the litters that held the human mercenaries, wrapping whatever limbs were free with their special memory-altering bracelets.

When Dalasini saw her, she broke away. "Is it over?"

"Yes," Gia assured her, touching her shoulder. John had deceived the T'Kaierian elders for decades. They had believed he was one of them. She didn't need to ask any questions to know how deeply Dalasini had been hurt.

Dalasini swallowed. "Thank you. Again, I'm sorry for letting him get so close, for trusting him."

Gia shook her head. "It wasn't your fault. It was no one's fault. I don't want you to worry about him anymore. It's done. It's taken care of."

Nodding and blinking back tears, Dalasini whispered her thanks, resuming her work.

Gia started searching for Salvador and her sisters. She spotted Diana's bright hair at the top of the hill where a knot of people stood or knelt. Mara and Douglas were there with her sisters and most of their mates. Concerned to see them so close together, Gia hustled up the hill, letting the wolves and assembled T'Kaierians do their work.

"Oh, cr—" Gia bit her tongue to keep from swearing aloud when she got to the top.

Connell lay on the floor, his leg below the knee gone. Logan, who was covered in blood, stared up at Gia anxiously. "He's going to be fine," she said in a hard voice.

"Of course he is," she said, widening her eyes emphatically at Salvador, who was on Connell's other side, tightening a tourniquet over the stump. He fished an envelope out of his pocket, then sprinkled the contents over the ragged tissue. His expression was grim.

"How did this happen?" she asked.

Connell answered, his voice thin and strained. "One of those fucking witches got a lucky shot." He side-eyed the man treating him. "Sorry," he added with a pant.

"I'm fine," Salvador said. His tone was cool and matter of fact, but his eyes were stark.

She glanced at Douglas. "Can you..." she began.

"*No.*" The chief's face was set. "Pack magic can heal, but it can't regrow entire limbs."

Fuck. Then it was real. Connell had been compromised.

Losing a limb wasn't the death sentence it was in the old days, but Connell's position as the next pack leader was now in jeopardy. Other wolves would see his missing limb as a sign of weakness. He would be challenged again and again. Sure, most challengers would hesitate to take on a wolf mated to an Elemental, but pack politics prohibited a mate from interfering in fights for dominance.

Gia knelt. Her hand shot out, grabbing Logan's fingers, the ones covered in her mate's blood. This was *not* happening. Logan had come close to losing Connell once. Gia would be damned before she let it happen again.

"Don't worry," she said. "I think She owes us one."

Logan blinked, trying not to cry. "How—"

Gia waved her into silence. She had no idea if this would work, but she was seeing something unbidden—as if the idea hadn't come from her own mind.

When she held out her hands, the Elven sword appeared. Someone sucked in a loud breath.

Gia winced. Damn, she was going to hate this part. Connell wasn't going to love it either.

No help for it now. Gia dropped Logan's hand, then latched onto the stump with a hard grip while holding up the sword in her free hand. She closed her eyes, blocking out Connell's strangled scream. He stopped almost immediately, but it didn't help.

"Gia? What the hell are you doing?" Salvador hissed, holding the patient still.

"Other than hoping someone is holding Mara back, you mean?" Gia asked, not opening her eyes.

"*Yes.*" The anxiety in his voice told her the female enforcer wasn't the only one having a problem with what Gia was doing. Connell's breath came fast and hard enough to feel it spilling over her hands.

Someone put a hand on her shoulder. From the heat, she thought it was Diana, but Gia nudged her off. "Sorry, love, but I have to focus."

"*On what?*" Salvador whispered.

Making something from nothing. Except that wasn't strictly true. Tightening her grip on the sword, she focused on it.

You have only served me a short time, but I need your help. This is a just cause and a just man... and you will probably enjoy this.

The metal of the Elven sword was imbued with magic. It would be malleable enough to do what she asked—*if* she could convince it to cooperate. That and Connell was one of the crystal's repositories, so pure magical potential rested in his body. Combined, those would be more than enough.

It has to be. She peeked at the stump. There was no change.

Okay, any time now.

Sweat began to drip down her spine. Time passed. She was starting to have serious doubts, but Gia finally felt a change under her hands.

There was a startled exclamation. But she knew she wasn't getting it right. The leg lacked the proper conformation. "Salvador, a little help here," she said, not opening her eyes.

"What do I do?"

"Help me shape it," she said. He might not have been a traditional doctor, but he had more knowledge of anatomy than anyone else here.

"Well, you need—"

"Not out loud," she cut him off, reaching for his hand. She didn't need to see it to know where it was. "*Picture it.*"

There was a beat of silence, but their connection was already there, very new but oh so strong. The mental images began to trickle in, strengthening and smoothing. When she finally opened her eyes, it was to see a shiny new leg where the stump had been.

"It's..."

"*Awesome,*" Logan finished in a whisper. The leg wasn't as bright as the Elven sword's metal. The surface was duller, something that wouldn't catch the eye in the moonlight. But the magic was still there, humming in tune with the crystal in Connell's chest.

"Thank you," Gia said aloud, tipping her head toward the newly formed limb.

"Are you talking to the foot that used to be a sword?" Salvador asked.

"Yeah, don't worry about it," she said quickly, hurrying to stand. Connell didn't need to know that his new appendage was over a thousand years old and sentient. There would no doubt be some issues later, but that was tomorrow's problem.

"Uh, no offense, but how is this metal foot supposed to help?" Mara asked, peering at it with a frown. "Won't it break or drag behind him when he shifts?"

"*No*," Connell burst out excitedly. "I know it looks like metal, but it's alive. I can *feel* it. I think I can work with this."

"Really?" Douglas' face mirrored his daughter's skepticism.

"*Shit*. It doesn't even hurt anymore." Connell wiped the sweat and blood from his face. He started to stand but hesitated, giving her a questioning glance.

Gia waved him on. "No sense in waiting. Give it a whirl."

Everyone stepped back as Connell rolled, shifting as he went. Gia held her breath, but then Connell shook his muzzle, twirling to display his lupine leg and paw.

"Damn, it worked," Alec whispered under his breath.

"Like I said, She owed us one."

Salvador's handsome face appeared serene and confident. "I never doubted you for a second."

She laughed at the outright lie.

"Yes!" Logan jumped, leaping onto Mara's back. Holding on with her knees, she threw her arms in the air, whooping in victory.

Smile growing vague with fatigue, Gia sat on the rock that had cropped up for her convenience. Salvador squatted in the dirt next to her. She leaned to the side, allowing some of her weight to rest on him.

Drifting slightly, Gia tracked the movements of everyone around her, but she let the others take the reins. New arrivals from T'Kaieri brought in supplies. The hired soldiers and allied Supernaturals were taken away. She was too drained to ask where.

Once they were gone, the atmosphere changed, kindling into celebration. Serin and Logan gathered broken branches, which Diana lit to make torches. Someone cracked a barrel of T'Kaierian ale, and Alec made a call. Expensive bottles of wine appeared and were passed around as if they were beer, along with food that smelled incredible, but she was too tired to eat.

Connell played with his new limb. He soon discovered it

responded to him in either of his forms, turning into whatever shape he wished.

A snort escaped her when he turned it into a pirate's peg leg. He imitated a rum advertisement, posing like pirate over the barrel of ale, before chasing after Logan, threatening to make her walk the plank if she didn't kiss him.

After that, it only took him a few minutes to realize he could fashion it into a weapon. "I'm the freaking *Terminator*," he shouted across the hill as the peg leg morphed into a spear. He kicked out at a tree, promptly getting the point stuck in the trunk.

Logan hurried past her. She shook her head and shrugged, laughing. "At least he's pretty."

Salvador rose briefly, going to fetch them both drinks. She took the bottle from him, not bothering to ask what it was.

"You took John to the Mother's chamber, didn't you?" he asked as they watched Caiman pull Serin into an unfamiliar Caribbean dance.

Content to watch her family, Gia merely nodded.

He nudged her. "The spores?"

She huffed. He knew her so well already. "The spores," she repeated.

"I like it."

She shifted, watching his face. "I thought you would."

"So, what happens now?" he asked.

"Besides a massive cleanup?" She gestured at the battlefield below.

"Yes, besides that."

Gia tipped her face to the stars. A star streaked past. *Where is the Mother headed next? And what would She do when She got there?*

"We get ready," she replied. "We get everyone ready."

46

───────

Rhys, the Draconis Imperia clan leader, had unwittingly chosen one of the Mother's favorite places for their meeting—the Coyote Buttes in northern Arizona. The local government allowed very few people to visit these days, intent on preserving the unique and delicate conformation of the sandstone that made it an out-of-this-world landscape here on Earth.

She and Salvador had arrived early, but the dragon was already there. Rhys waited at the top, of course. Below him, the swirling sandstone 'wave' undulated.

The dragon smirked, as if he were daring her to scramble up there, potentially damaging the stone. Rhys could never let anyone else have the high ground, even if they weren't enemies.

Salvador gazed up the hill, laughing under his breath. He still traveled with her—probably would for the rest of his life.

Surprisingly, it was working out well on multiple fronts. Gia encountered many people who required a healer in the course of her work. Salvador's skill was constantly tested by these cases, but he was rising to the challenges. And if it took her a little longer to wrap up each case... that was fine with her. Having company in the form of a handsome man who could cook had restored something in her nomadic life she hadn't realized was missing.

Salvador had even found another *curandero* to take over his Costa Rican practice when he wasn't there, so his regular patients weren't left without care. His consideration of others was unfeigned. She knew that now and appreciated it. She appreciated *him*. And returned the sentiment ten-fold.

She and Salvador were the strangest of bedfellows, but her many years of service had taught her to accept the gifts she was given. Gia was feared by her enemies and loved by her sisters, but now she felt cherished again.

"Someone likes to put on a show, huh?" Salvador remarked, the corner of his mouth pulling up as he took in the hyper-masculine figure highlighted against the full moon. The dragon was bipedal. His wings weren't out, but his aura blazing like a torch, projecting testosterone and machismo, and yes... the pose looked staged.

"He can hear us, you know," Gia warned her mate. A dragon's hearing was as good as a wolf's. Maybe better.

Salvador grinned. "I don't care. As for the rest of our audience..." He gestured to their empty surroundings. "I guess bumping into the odd hiker isn't a big concern at this time of night."

"Not at this hour, or when it's this cold," she conceded, eyeing his outfit critically to make sure he was warm enough.

Salvador had made a few concessions to the freezing January weather—namely boots and a down parka. But he insisted he wouldn't need those once his blood 'got all the Costa Rica' out of it.

"Why don't you wait here?" she suggested, rubbing the leather and bead string around his wrist. It was the necklace her father had crafted for her mother. Gia had given it back to Salvador a few weeks ago—permanently this time. He wore it as bracelet, looping it around his wrist instead of his neck.

Salvador's face tightened, clearly unhappy at the idea of her going alone. "Only because it would get us out of here faster," she assured him. "I did promise you a wood fire and bottle of cognac at the stash house, didn't I?"

"Well, if it helps get us home faster, go give him hell," he relented with a grin, waving her on.

Turning to her last task of the night, she hailed the dragon, who had no doubt flown to the top of the butte. Sinking into the ground, she rose up through the rock,

She appeared next to Rhys with a whisper of stone, taking extra care not to disturb a single undulation.

The shifter's innate heat made him impervious to the weather, and he'd dressed accordingly. He wore a vest the color of dried blood with black pants. Both were leather, although she suspected the hide wasn't domestic. It looked like something that would have put up a fight.

"Gia." The dragon lord inclined his head. "I trust you are well."

His deep voice rumbled along her spine. It was a sound that would have intimidated a lesser soul, no doubt by design. *I bet he practices the frequency.* "I'm quite well, thank you," she replied with equal formality.

"So, is what I'm hearing true? Has your Mother abandoned you?" He didn't tack on 'little girl' aloud, but she heard it, nonetheless.

It was why she hated dragon shifters.

"The Mother has… retired," Gia confirmed. "But She took steps to ensure her legacy before she left."

"What does that mean?" Rhys asked, eyeballing her from under his stupidly long lashes.

"It means don't test me, asshole. I can still take you."

Laughing, Rhys threw back his head. "I have no doubt that is true."

Subsiding, he stared up at the sky. So far from civilization and the light of the nearest city, it was a blanket of stars as far as the eye could see. But the beauty held peril, too. No one knew that better than Rhys.

"There will be trouble," he said.

"I'm sure there will be," Gia acknowledged. "Are you going to be a part of it?"

Rhys retreated a step, putting his hands behind his back. He began to slowly pace in a circle. Gia tapped her foot, resisting the urge to roll her eyes as she waited for him to say what she already knew—the dragon shifters would remain neutral.

"Should the worst come to pass, the Draconis Imperia will be ready to fight alongside you, should you call our banners."

"*Ah.*" Well, that was a surprise. In a way. "I see. I guess that answers my other question about why in the hell you were in Sheol. You obviously found what you were searching for over there."

And it had given him something he'd lacked for the last few millennia—a reason to stay on Earth. Sure... he'd *had* to before, but now he *wanted* to. It had taken her a while to put the pieces together, but she was ninety-percent sure now. Rhys had someone to protect.

The dragon stopped pacing. "What do you know?" he growled.

"I know that someone we watch regularly fell off our radar for a while. I also know *she* is back now."

Rhys grunted, giving her the evil eye. "If you were tracking her so closely, how in the hell did she end up in Sheol?"

Gia lifted a shoulder. "Some stuff went down. I maybe got a bit dead, but good news—I'm back now, the apocalypse was averted, etcetera, etcetera."

The dragon shifter snorted. His eyes fell on Salvador. "Interesting choice of a companion."

She huffed. "I'm aware—and I could say the same thing to you about the company you keep."

Rhys said nothing. He simply continued watching her.

Sighing, Gia decided to stop beating about the bush. "He's going to want to meet her."

The dragon bristled, invisible scales raising and settling just beyond her sight. "*She* is mine."

Gia put her hands in her pockets. "Valeria is her own person. And she thinks she's alone in the world. But she has family, including parents who have been searching for her for years, not to mention a brother who has been denied all knowledge of her," she added with a nod down the hill.

"You weren't exactly concerned for Valeria when she was out on the streets on her own," Rhys snapped. "And she isn't alone now. She has *me*."

Gia had expected a much longer macho tirade, even a little Tarzan-like chest beating. However, after the single outburst, Rhys clamped his lips shut.

Gia sighed. "Look, we did what we could for her. For the most part, though, our hands were tied. They frequently are with that family. Not to mention that too much of our attention would have put a bigger spotlight on her. But circumstances have changed. Salvador is outside his family's sphere. As long as first contact is limited to him, Valeria should be safe enough."

"*No.*"

Gia raised an eyebrow. "Don't you think you should let *her* decide? From what I hear, Valeria possesses a strikingly decisive mind and manner. And I don't think she would like you making this decision for her."

With that, Gia left him stewing. She waved, sinking through the rocks to join her mate at the bottom of the ridge.

"That looked like it got interesting," Salvador observed.

"It did." She gazed into his handsomely earnest face, grimacing slightly as she made a decision. *So much for not interfering.*

Taking his arm, she began to lead him away. "Salvador, I have to talk to you about something. It's about your sister."

Concern shadowed his face. "What is it? Did Lucia get in touch? Did something go wrong with her pregnancy?"

"No. Everything is fine as far as I know. That isn't the sister I'm talking about."

Salvador frowned. She slipped her arm into his, leading him away from the bluffs. "This is going to be a long story..."

EPILOGUE

Gia tried not to laugh as Diana nearly brained Alec with the Egyptian fertility statue he had brought to serve as a focal object during her delivery.

Fortunately for everyone in the room, the vampire had excellent reflexes. He snatched the heavy stone figurine out of the air before it crushed his temple, admonishing Diana with a gentle. "It's okay, love. I completely understand your frustration, and I'm here for you."

It was the hundredth or so time he'd said something like that, supportive and endlessly patient. It would have been only mildly annoying, but the fact he made these pronouncements while zipping back and forth across the room like a bee on cocaine negated their intended calming effect.

Predictably, her sister had had enough. "All right. *That's it.* Get him out of here," Diana hissed.

Salvador, returning from his kitchen with a bowl of boiled water and sterilized towels, gave Gia a nudge. "Maybe it's time," he stage-whispered.

"*Hey,*" Alec protested. "That is not why I—I mean, *we*—chose you to deliver our baby."

"I'm sorry, Alec, but my first duty is to my patient," Salvador said as he set the supplies on the table next to the bed. "And Diana can burn this place down if she's doesn't get her way, so out you go…"

Hiding her amusement, Gia clapped her hand on the vampire's shoulder. "I'm afraid I have to side with your physician on this one. And for future reference, I think we've just established delivery rooms are no place for vampires."

Pushing down on his shoulder, she sent him through the floor, shuttling him outside the cottage. He rose in front of the fire pit, but only up to his waist. She kept the rest of him securely bound to prevent him from running back inside.

Gia approached the window, calling out to him. "My apologies, but Diana needs you to stop driving her up the wall. She is trying to give birth to your child, for the Mother's sake."

She turned back to Salvador with a grin. "Have I told you how convenient I find these dirt floors?"

He laughed, but subsided quickly when Diana shot him a fiery glare. Head down, he checked under the sheet covering her legs. "You are fully dilated. You can start pushing."

Diana set her lips in a mulish line. "I don't think so."

Salvador's head drew back. "Excuse me, what now?" he asked, eyes widening.

Diana was firm. "I've changed my mind. I won't be having any children today."

With an understanding nod, Salvador rose to take her hand. "That is a very common sentiment during delivery, but I'm afraid there's no turning back now."

Sweat beaded on her hairline, Diana stubbornly shook her head. "Nope. Not gonna do it."

Salvador grinned, showing his straight white teeth before he caught Gia's eye and jerked his head significantly in Diana's direction. "I think you should be the one holding the patient's hand," he suggested in a strained voice.

Gia hurried to take over before Di crushed all the bones in Salvador's hand.

"Gia, I think this was a big mistake," Diana whispered as if

Salvador couldn't hear them. "I don't have a maternal bone in my body. This should be you. I really think you should be doing this instead of me. Can we swap? Don't you know a spell for that?"

Reaching for a towel, Gia wiped her sister's damp brow. "That would be black magic. So, no, that's definitely not happening. But you need to stop worrying. You are going to be an amazing mom."

Diana's usual confidence was nowhere in sight. "I know you think you're telling the truth, but you're wrong. I don't know how to do anything motherly. I don't knit or sew, I don't clean, and Mother knows I can't cook."

"So what?" Gia scoffed. "You don't have to do any of those things. You can be the kind of mother who wields a sword and lops off a few heads before dinner. In my opinion, that's the best kind. Let Alec do the cooking, cleaning, and diaper changing. He's more maternal than all of us put together."

"He is, isn't he?" Diana acknowledged with a frown. "But I'm not sure that's enough."

"Maybe it isn't." Gia shrugged.

Diana shot her a disgusted glance before her fine features twisted with another contraction. "Reverse psychology. *Now*? *Really*?"

"What I was going to say is that you and Alec don't have to do this alone. You have a literal *village* eager to help raise this baby. I can name over a dozen people in Telerin who would drop every-thing to babysit or do an aura cleanse—whatever you need. In fact, Nana told me if you don't bring the baby by in the first few months, she's going to stop making me tamales, so put that on your calendar now."

Resting her hip on the bed, she gave Diana a squeeze. "Then there's T'Kaieri. The Elders are working around the clock on a new baptism ceremony. Apparently, none of the existing ones are special enough for your child. Serin says they've been purifying the temple every day for weeks now."

She leaned over to kiss her sister's forehead. "And don't forget this baby has three bad-ass aunties who will do whatever is necessary to help and guide her. And I don't mean just the fun parts like teaching her how to ride the air currents or wield a mace. I mean the little things, too, like…"

She looked at Salvador, prompting him to help her out with a suggestion by waving her fingers.

"Like helping with potty training or when the baby gets croup," he supplied, checking under the blanket one more time before giving Gia a thumbs-up.

"Okay, that last one is medical, so I'll let you handle it," she admitted, wrinkling her nose.

"I can help with the first one, too." He laughed. "My patients tend to come back for advice on that, so consider me an expert." Salvador sighed, cocking his head as his expression turned rueful. "The things I brag about around you all come back to haunt me later…"

Gia giggled while Diana grunted. "*Fine*. All right. If I *have* to do this."

"Good," Salvador said. "Now, when you feel the next contraction, I want you to push."

Gritting her teeth, Diana didn't answer, but she didn't need to. A wooden picture frame on the dresser burst into flame, which said everything they needed to know. Gia smothered it before it became an issue.

The delivery was fairly quick after her sister began to cooperate. At least the first one was. Diana gave birth to a beautiful little girl, but no sooner had Salvador cleaned and swaddled her than a second head appeared.

Figuring one child was enough to keep Alec occupied, Gia released him, ushering him inside. "Uh, surprise?" she said, handing over his daughter before resuming her station next to Diana.

Bewildered, he cuddled the baby close. "What's happening?"

"Alec, I love you, but please shut up," Diana hissed, her face redder than Gia had ever seen it.

Holding Diana's hand connected them more closely. It was obvious to Gia's sense the second babe was a male, but he appeared to share his mother's stubbornness. It took another hour and every bit of Salvador's skills to coax him into the world.

"How did we not know it was twins?" Salvador appeared as confused as Gia was as he cleaned the baby boy.

"Well, the girl is what we thought," she told the new parents. The gleam of Elemental magic in the sleepy girl's eyes was unmistakable. Gia didn't know if she would be a Fire like her mother, but the newborn girl *had* inherited one of the four elements. That much was clear.

With a nod from Diana, Gia took the boy from Salvador, holding him close for a detailed assessment.

"Well, I guess that explains that," she said, gazing down at the baby boy. He blinked, then gave her a gummy toothless grin. "We didn't know about the second babe for good reason. No heartbeat."

"But vampires aren't born," Alec muttered, studying the boy's bright blue and pupil-less eyes with trepidation. "Neither are Elementals for that matter."

"Oh, this little guy isn't a vampire," Gia said, laying the child next to his sister. "For one, he's warm-blooded."

"Then what is he?" Diana whispered, eyeing her surprise second baby. She held the twins, one in each arm, then stared at Gia with wide eyes. "What are *they*?"

Gia crossed her arms, studying the next generation for a moment before smiling. "Something old... and something new."

The End

Check out my other books written as Lucy Leroux! The steamy second installment of the hilarious Shifter's Claim Series is available now.

Dmitri, a werewolf and thief-for-hire, finds his true mate under the worst possible circumstances—at 35,000 feet.

Available Now

ABOUT THE AUTHOR

L.B. Gilbert is another name for USA Today Bestselling Author Lucy Leroux.

L.B. spent years getting degrees from the most prestigious universities in America, including a PhD that she is not using at all. She moved to France for work and found love. She's married now and has a polyglot 4 year old. The family moved back to California a few years ago.

She has always enjoyed reading books as far from her reality as possible but eventually the voices in her head told her to write her own. So far the voices are enjoying them. And judging by the awards, a few other people are as well. You can check out the geeky things she likes on Twitter or Facebook.

If you like a little more steam with your Fire, check out the author's award-winning Lucy Leroux titles, FREE to read on Kindle Unlimited

www.elementalauthor.com

or

www.authorlucyleroux.com

facebook.com/elementalsauthor

twitter.com/elementalauthor

instagram.com/elementalauthor

www.ingramcontent.com/pod-product-compliance
Lightning Source LLC
Chambersburg PA
CBHW070435170726
48291CB00002B/521